Return of the Native Son

Return of the Native Son

A Novel by

Ben Walker

Return of the Native Son

ISBN 978-09666145-4-1

This is a work of fiction. All the events and characters are either fictitious or are used fictitiously.

Cover design, book layout & illustration by Rich Allen
www.artzdesign.com

Published in the United States by
Jamin Press
Jacksonville, FL
www.jaminpress.com

Acknowledgments

Thanks again to my friend and colleague Barbara Pinkerton for her inexhaustible patience in pouring over this and other manuscripts and offering her perceptive insights. Also to her husband Bob, who always brings to the work a fresh perspective and useful suggestions.

Other readers include Bob Bliss, a fellow author, and David Dowling, who, as a native of Beaufort, offered invaluable observations about the area that only a native could know.

To

Elizabeth Walker Slifer

My ever-supportive sister and confidante

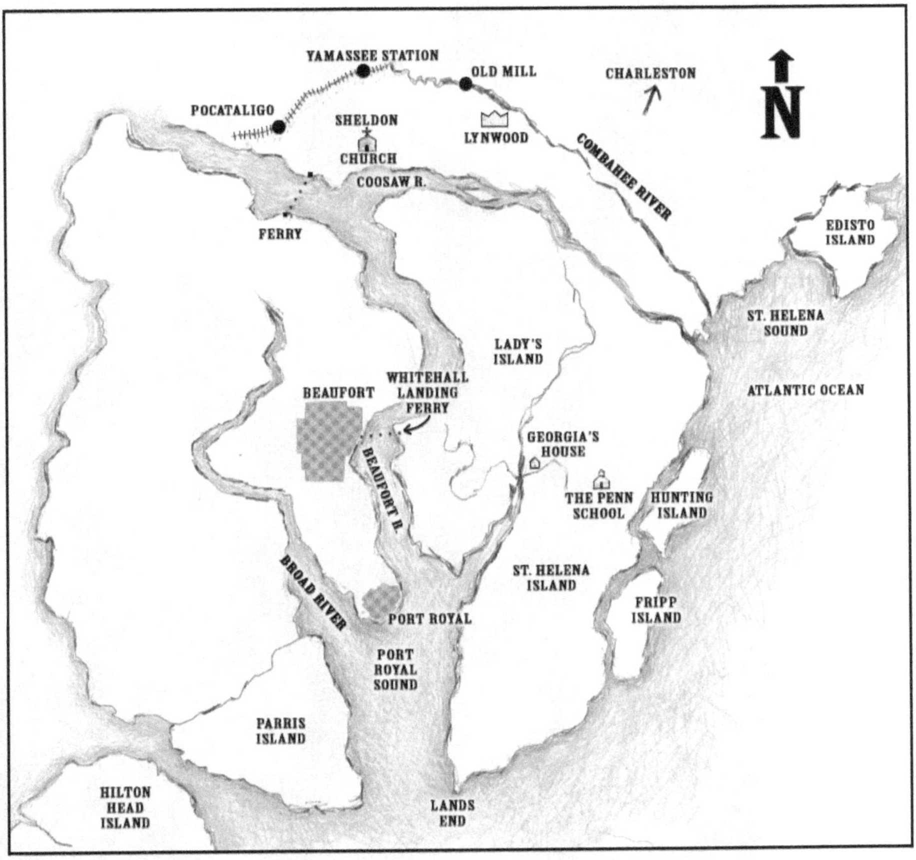
YAMASSEE STATION
OLD MILL
CHARLESTON
N
POCATALIGO
SHELDON
CHURCH
LYNWOOD
COMBAHEE RIVER
COOSAW R.
FERRY
EDISTO
ISLAND
ST. HELENA
SOUND
LADY'S
ISLAND
ATLANTIC OCEAN
WHITEHALL
LANDING
FERRY
BEAUFORT
GEORGIA'S
HOUSE
BEAUFORT R.
THE PENN
SCHOOL
HUNTING
ISLAND
ST. HELENA
ISLAND
BROAD RIVER
PORT ROYAL
FRIPP
ISLAND
PORT
ROYAL
SOUND
PARRIS
ISLAND
HILTON
HEAD
ISLAND
LANDS
END

CHAPTER 1

A tall young man wearing a broad-brimmed beaver hat with a scarlet feather in its band stepped onto the platform at the Yemassee station sixteen miles north of Beaufort, South Carolina. He appeared to be something of a dandy, at least by local standards, not only judging by his colorful headgear, but by the bright yellow cravat tucked into a blue silk waistcoat and matched by yellow patent leather shoes.

A porter stared at him for a few moments before approaching cautiously. It wasn't so much the young man's dress that gave him pause, but the color of his eyes: they were a pale blue. This would not have been unusual but for the hue of his skin, which was tea-colored, or perhaps cafe-au-lait.

The porter reached for the young man's valise, which was of the carpetbagger type that he had seen so much of during Reconstruction. This one, however, was colorful like the man himself, with a rich pattern of flowers and vases. "Take your grip, sir?"

The young man seemed not to notice him at first, as his eyes scanned the scene, which wasn't a pretty one. There were numerous uprooted trees and other debris piled up along the road from the station almost as far as the eye could see. Once having taken it all in, he looked at the porter. "What? Oh...yes. Yes, of course." He noted the array of carriages just off the platform. "I need to get to Beaufort. To St. Helena Island, actually."

The porter picked up the valise and shook his head. "The road's done cleared to Beaufort, but half of St. Helena is still underwater. And the ferry's underwater, too. Might get a skiff over that way. That all your luggage?"

"Yes. That and the portmanteau there. The brown one with the steamer markings on it."

"A lady with you?"

"No, just me."

"You just climb into ol' Tom's buggy and he'll carry you to Beaufort.

Watch your step."

The young man did as he was bidden, still taking in the dismal scene, hardly noticing that 'ol' Tom' was staring at him with the same intense curiosity as the porter.

The carriage was an old-style open phaeton with the driver seated on an elevated bench at the front. A single horse, a bay mare, who had no doubt seen better days, responded reluctantly to the driver's whip and pulled them out onto the thoroughfare, which was deep in mud and rutted with numerous carriage wheels.

"Where you from, Boss?" the driver said after a few minutes on the road.

"Paris," the young man said.

"Paris? Up near Greenville? I got kin there and–"

"No. Not near Greenville. Paris, France."

The driver remained silent for several moments. "You come across the Big Pond?"

"That I did. Le Havre to Charleston. Seven days of pretty rough weather."

"Not as rough as round here, I'll bet. That hurricane just about blowed this county off the map."

"I can see that...were there many casualties?"

"Casualties? Some say a thousand. Some say two thousand. They ain't calculated them all yet. Some bodies still floatin' round Port Royal Sound, I reckon."

They remained silent for several minutes, each lost in his own thoughts.

"Your people make it through all right?" the young man said.

"Me and my wife live in town. Couple of ships sittin' on Bay Street, lookin' like beached whales. We'uns live eight blocks north, pretty high and dry. Lost nigh ever' tree and half the roof, but we be all right, I reckon. Got plenty of work to do, though."

"You have children?"

"Chillun? Oh, yeah. They be growed, though. My boy work at the lumber yard in Bluffton. He got plenty of work now on account of Mr. LeRoux. They hardly got they feathers ruffled."

"Lynwood? The plantation?"

"That's it. Say, how come you know about Lynwood? And how come you don't talk like a Frenchman?"

The young man chuckled. "I'm not a Frenchman. I've just been living in France for the past few years. I was actually born here. On St. Helena."

The driver pulled on the reins and turned around. "I had a feeling you was one of us. How you get all the way to Paris, France?"

The young man chuckled. "It's a long story. Say, what's going on up ahead?"

The driver turned to face the road. "Look like a carriage done lost a wheel and run off the road. Look like ol' Riley's rig. Got a lady with him."

"Let's see if we can help."

They approached the stricken carriage, where Riley had just retrieved the wheel from a ditch and was cleaning the mud off as it rested against the fender. The young lady, not dressed for such a venture, stood nearby studying the situation with the air of an engineering student. "Perhaps a hairpin would do it," she said.

Riley shook his head. "Ain't no hairpin in the world hold this big ol' wheel to that axle. Need somethin' stronger."

"Riley!" Tom called out. "What you got yo' self into? The lady ain't hurt, is she?"

Riley continued to stare at the wheel and the axle, as if he hadn't heard his friend. But the lady looked up.

"I'm not hurt at all," she said, "but we have a problem here." It was now clear to the young man in Tom's carriage that the young lady was very attractive: high cheekbones, a fine straight nose, blue eyes that sparkled, and blond hair pulled back into a bun beneath a straw hat with a blue ribbon trailing from the crown.

The young man stepped out of his carriage and approached, removing his hat as he did so. "Antonio Jones, Jr., at your service, Miss."

The young lady stared at him for a moment rather quizzically, then broke into a broad smile. "Jacqueline LeRoux. I don't have a middle name, unless it's Benson, which is my mother's maiden name."

"Benson," young Mr. Jones said thoughtfully, putting his forefinger to his chin. "I've heard the name. And certainly everyone around here knows the name of LeRoux. You're heading for Lynwood?"

"I am," Miss LeRoux said. "Or was–until this carriage wheel went careening off into the ditch. You seem to be familiar with the area. Are you from Beaufort?"

"St. Helena. I was born and bred there."

"St. Helena? Oh, I see. Well, Mr. Jones, I appreciate your stopping to help, but I don't see what you can–"

"I need a cotter pin," Riley suddenly called out, as if he hadn't been listening to this conversation. "Tom! You got one in your buggy? This one's done sheared off like a busted matchstick."

"Sho' do," Tom said. He reached beneath the driver's seat of his carriage and pulled out a long, flat box. "That all you need?"

"That'll do 'er," Riley said.

Once the cotter pin was produced, Antonio removed his jacket and he and Tom lifted up the back end of the carriage while Riley mounted the wheel on its axle and inserted the cotter pin.

"Pliers," Riley said. "We need pliers."

"Right c'here," Tom said, producing a pair from his pocket. "You think I didn't know that?"

"There's a heap of things you don't know," Riley said.

"If you so smart, why don't you carry an extra cotter pin in yo' tool box?"

As this banter continued for a while, young Tony turned his attention again to Miss LeRoux. "I understand Lynwood was spared the worst of the storm."

"Oh, I hope so. The telegraph lines are still down, so I don't know what to think."

"Where are you coming from?" Tony said.

"London. I've been living with my aunt there for the past year."

"London? Funny, though I've spent the last three years in Europe, I've never visited London."

Miss LeRoux's eyes brightened. "It's a wonderful place–so much to do, so much excitement in the air. Where were you in Europe?"

"Paris."

"Well, that's no sleepy borough, either. What did you do there?"

"Paint."

"Paint? You're an artist?"

"Of sorts."

"Miss LeRoux," Riley said, "we'd best be gettin' on–the sun goin' down soon and the Sheldon Road be half washed out."

Miss LeRoux reluctantly acknowledged Riley's plea and moved towards the carriage. "Yes, I'd better be going. Thank you for your assistance, Mr. Jones. I hope we meet again. I'd be most interested in hearing of your adventures in Paris."

Tony took her hand and assisted her into the carriage. "There isn't that much adventure in sitting in a studio all day and splashing paint onto a canvas."

Miss LeRoux laughed as she sat back in the carriage. "You're being modest. I can't imagine that you were confined to your studio for the whole of three years. And even if you were, I would think creating a work of art would be a great adventure in itself."

"One must experience life to create great art."

"I couldn't agree more. You see–you've just admitted to having adventures outside of the studio. Au revoir, Monsieur Jones!"

As Riley snapped his whip and the horses began moving, Tony remained in the road staring after this unexpected apparition. Indeed, she seemed to have stepped out of a dream, hidden from view by the mist that still enshrouded the area. He chuckled, though, at the irony of her feeble attempt to speak French, considering her surname. "Oh-rah-vwarh,' she had said. Like a school girl taking her first lesson. Oh, but what a beauty! Why had he never encountered her while growing up in Beaufort? His face fell. Actually, he had hardly ever set foot in Beaufort, and she had probably never set foot on St. Helena. He was a black man, after all.

"You coming, Mr. Jones?" Tom said. He was in his driver's seat, his whip poised in the air.

Tony continued to stare after the carriage until it became as small as a toy in the distance. "I'm coming, Tom."

CHAPTER 2

The ferry at the Broad River between the mainland and Port Royal Island was back in operation. The crossing was uneventful and there seemed to be little damage at the north end of the island with the exception of uprooted trees. But as they approached the town of Beaufort the extent of the devastation became clear. Houses with missing roofs, some with entire walls ripped from their frames as if they were cracker boxes torn open by a hungry giant, telegraph poles lodged against trees, piles of smoking debris every block or so.

The streets were crowded with wagons hauling trash, fresh water (from where?), lumber, medical supplies (Clara Barton herself was said to be directing the relief effort), and a diverse array of foodstuffs, mostly in cans or boxes. As they approached Bay Street, they saw the masts of sailing vessels and the smoke stacks of steam packets so close to the commercial buildings that they seemed to erupt through the roofs. It had been more than a week since the hurricane passed through, and the town was still a beehive of frenzied activity.

"Reckon you'd better lay up tonight in town and see if you can hire a flatboat to Lady's Island in the morning," Tom said. They were now at the wharf, but many pilings were missing or lying on the shore, the water having receded, leaving tons of debris in its wake.

"I can't wait till morning," Tony said. "I have to find out if my parents are still alive."

Tom sighed. "Cain't even get a dingy out of here this afternoon. Not till the tide come back in, and then you got to have a long pole to poke through all the trash. That ain't gonna be cleaned up till after they take care of the peoples on dry land."

Tony scanned the scene from the wharf south, to the bend in the river below Beaufort. "Maybe I can find someone with a boat in Port Royal–from there directly across the sound to St. Helena."

Tom rubbed his chin. "Might do that. Port Royal hit hard, too, though. I got a uncle down that way got a little rowboat–maybe he could take you."

"I'll make it worth his while. And yours, too."

Tom turned the carriage onto Bay Street and clicked his tongue. "Git on there, ol' Blue–we're goin' to see Uncle Lulu."

"Uncle Lulu?"

"That be his Gullah name. It mean 'five,' 'cause he be the fifth child."

"He must have taken some ribbing for it."

"Some. But he good with his fists. After he whup up on a couple of 'em, they leave him alone."

Tony smiled and leaned back in the carriage. "I have a feeling if anybody can get me to St. Helena's Island, it's Uncle Lulu."

Tom laughed and cracked his whip.

Uncle Lulu stood in the yard behind his ramshackle house beneath a copse of oak trees that miraculously survived the storm. He was in his early fifties but looked much older with deep creases in his forehead, a receding hairline, and gray at the temples. He studied the wide expanse of water between Port Royal and St Helena Island. "Tide's coming in. It'll be hard on my back goin' out."

"But easier coming back in." Tony pulled a couple of coins from his change purse. "How about an extra two bits in case you need to purchase some liniment for that back?"

Uncle Lulu stared at the coins for a moment, then returned his gaze to Port Royal Sound. "Ain't got no life belts, neither. Had two, but the storm washed them away with the bait and tackle boxes. We was lucky the boat got stuck between them two pilings holdin' up what's left of the dock."

Tony sighed and pulled two more coins from the purse. "All right. Here's another fifty cents. And if you get me there safely you'll get the same amount for the trip back."

Uncle Lulu looked at the four coins. "You plannin' on coming back to Port Royal once you find your kinfolks?"

"I suppose so. Eventually."

He took the money. "You just let me know. You can stand on the shore there and wave a white flag. I'll come runnin'."

"What if it's dark?"

"Then wave a torch. I can see it from my bedroom winder."

The tariff settled, Uncle Lulu led the way to the rowboat, untied it from its mooring, and they shoved off for St. Helena Island. He seemed to have no back problems and rowed with a strong, steady, rhythm as he faced Tony sitting in the rear of the boat. "Whereabouts your folks live on the island?"

"In a house overlooking Cowan Creek. Near Plantation Oaks Road."

"I know exactly where it at. Up on a bluff."

"Not a very high one. I'm worried that it may have been swept away by the storm."

"Storm surge, they say up to sixteen feet. Even more in some places."

"The bluff there is maybe nine or ten feet. That's the concern."

Uncle Lulu smiled. "I got a feeling your folks is lucky. What they names?"

"Jones. Like me. Antonio and Georgia Jones."

Uncle Lulu suddenly stopped rowing. "But you black like me. Major Jones and his missus is white."

"That's a fact. They adopted me right after the war. I don't know who my real parents were. Slaves, I suppose. But I couldn't have asked for better parents than my adoptive ones."

Uncle Lulu resumed rowing, but now with a big smile on his face. "I know your daddy from the old days. During the war. He headed up the Freedman's Bureau."

"That he did."

"And at the end of the war, he helped me and my missus buy the land we got on the sound. The old massa what owned it before the war was hoppin' mad. Said it was too valuable a parcel for a nigger to have, what with it bein' on the water and all. But your daddy showed him General Sherman's Field Order Number 15 and the deal was done. And I didn't pay nothin' down."

Tony looked over the rising waters at St. Helena, which was looming out of the mist. "That was thirty years ago. You paid it off yet?"

"Shore. Long time ago. Mostly from catchin' crabs and oysters. The storm washed away the oyster beds, though. And don't ask me where the crabs went. They'll be back, though."

Uncle Lulu turned the bow up Cowan's Creek and the rowing seemed to get easier. The tide was with them now, and they made good time over the next mile or so. There were few houses along the creek, most set well back, but the damage to these few was extensive. The ones made of brick fared the best, while the frame houses looked to be piles of splinters, some of it floating in the creek so that Uncle Lulu had to maneuver carefully to avoid a collision.

"I see the house!" Tony shouted.

Uncle Lulu turned his head. "That it on the bluff?"

"That's it! It looks to be intact."

Uncle Lulu resumed rowing. "Better wait till we up to the bluff. Sometimes the water pick the whole house up off its foundation and set it down somewheres else."

"It looks to be in the same spot. Maybe we can tie up at that branch leaning out over the water." Tony was excited now, and stood up in the boat to get a better view.

"Better set down, Mr. Jones. We could get a switchback with this tide before you can say 'Jack Robinson.'"

Tony watched the swirling water as it rushed into coves and tributaries, reversed course and rushed out again. He sat down.

They tied up at the tree and Uncle Lulu heaved Tony's portmanteau onto the bluff. "You want me to take it up to the house?"

"No, I can manage." Tony pulled out his purse and handed him a silver dollar. "Thank you, sir. You're an expert oarsman."

"Been doin' it all my life. Want me to wait till you see about your folks?"

Tony fixed his eyes on the house which was about a hundred yards up from the bluff. "No, that won't be necessary. I'll send up a signal if I need you again."

Uncle Lulu watched as Tony picked up both articles of luggage and trudged up the hill. He lingered for a while to see that Tony could manage, then untied the boat and pushed off into the creek, rowing against the tide.

As Tony approached the house, he was relieved at first to see that there was little visible damage. Like most Lowcountry houses, it sat on brick piers some two to three feet off grade. There were torn shutters hanging loose from the windows, some scattered about the yard with other debris. But the roof seemed to be intact, and the porch was serviceable, though a few planks had popped loose. Apparently, the water had reached the top of the steps at the height of the storm and then receded.

He continued to the steps and set his bags down. Now that the sun was setting, rays of light streaked through the moss-laden trees and cast grotesque shadows over the house. Through a window he could see the glow of a lighted candle in the living room.

He left his bags where they were and scampered up the steps, careful not to trip over any of the loose boards. He started to open the screen door, but then checked himself, remembering that he had been away from home for three years and was not expected. He raised his fist and knocked lightly against the door, which was loose against its hinges.

He heard nothing at first. “Mama? Papa? It’s me, Tony.”

Then he heard a scraping sound, like the movement of heavy furniture across a wood floor. “Papa?”

Footsteps. Light, with a shuffled gait. “Tony?”

It was his mother, or rather the shadowy outline of his mother through the screen door. “Oh, Tony! You’ve come all the way from France!”

“I had to, Mama. Even the Paris papers carried the story. I caught a steamer as soon as I could.”

His mother opened the screen door, which nearly came off its hinges, and he rushed to embrace her. She burst into tears.

“Oh, Tony, Tony! I’m so happy you’ve come, even though it’s a sad time for us.”

“Sad? Well, yes, it is sad–so many people have lost their homes, and...and I’ve heard there were a lot of casualties, but Mama–” He pulled away from her, still grasping her shoulders. “You look fine, just fine, and as beautiful as ever. Where’s Papa?”

Georgia turned away and cast her eyes to the floor.

“Mama? Is he all right? Where is he?”

She started crying again. “In the yard–out near the bluff.”

Tony turned and looked towards the bluff. Seeing nothing but uprooted trees and scattered debris, he turned back to her. “Where? Is he–”

“Dead,” she said. “Dead and buried.”

Tony turned back towards the bluff. “No, it can’t be. Papa? How?”

“Come in and sit down,” she said. “Have you had any supper?”

Tony followed her into the living room. It was as he remembered it, with a large fireplace in the center of the far wall, its massive carved mantelpiece supporting numerous photos and figurines, facing a sofa and a pair of comfortable armchairs. There was the same handmade carpet woven and decorated by local women, a gift in appreciation of his mother’s years of teaching their children at the Penn School.

“I’m not very hungry, Mama. How did it happen?”

She sat down on the sofa. “Didn’t you bring any luggage? Surely you didn’t come with only the shirt on your back.”

“It’s...it’s outside.

“Better go and get it. I think it will rain soon.”

“Mama–”

“Go on! I just need to rest a bit and then I’ll see about fixing some supper.

We're lucky Miss Barton is here. She brought me some tins of beans and okra and even some ham. We'll have a fine meal."

Tony reluctantly complied and returned to the back yard where his portmanteau and valise rested at the foot of the steps. He surveyed both the steps and the porch, as well as the upper story of the house and decided that he would begin the necessary repairs first thing in the morning.

The sun had set, but there was still light shining through the trees to the west. He picked up the bags and started back to the house when he noticed a wooden cross near the crest of the bluff. He put the bags down again and walked the sixty feet or so to the cross, stepping over the trunk of an oak tree that he had once supported a swing. The very rope that had been employed for this purpose so many times was still attached to one of the limbs, now lying limp and useless on the ground.

The cross was crudely made, obviously in haste, and bore the simple legend:

ANTONIO JONES
b. April 16, 1833
d. August 28, 1893

He would have to order a more suitable headstone after the repairs to the house were made. There was a small vase at the base of the cross containing a single red rose. No doubt his mother had placed it there.

Suddenly he was overcome with emotion and dropped to his knees. "Oh, Papa! I never dreamed that when you saw me off in Charleston I'd never see you again! There were so many things I wanted to tell you, and now it's too late...too late."

He remained there on his knees, tears running down his cheeks, his hands folded together as if in prayer for some time; he didn't know how long. Then he remembered that his mother must be waiting for him and rose to his feet.

"Goodbye, Papa."

CHAPTER 3

While unpacking and putting his things away in his bedroom, Tony happened to gaze out of a window and saw the little cross in the yard, partially lit by the remaining rays of the sun. What would his mother do now that Papa was gone? She was still comparatively young, in her mid-forties. Certainly she would continue teaching at the Penn School, but her income would be sharply reduced–she may have had to let go of some of the servants. Come to think of it, where were they? Sally the cook, Peter the gardener, Scratch the stableman? Not that they were ever full time, but there was usually one or two of them around. Did they perish in the storm as well?

As he was perusing one of the books that he used while at the Penn School, he heard his mother call up to him that dinner was ready. He descended the steps and this time lingered for a moment as he stared out of the foyer window at the barn. The gig looked to be intact, but he couldn't see whether there were any horses in their stalls. There were three when he left for Paris: Leto, once a magnificent chestnut mare when his father was a young officer with the Freedmen's Bureau but already older than most horses; Victoria, a gray mare who was employed for a variety of duties, mostly to pull the gig for short trips around the island; and Marmaduke, a sturdy bay gelding who, along with Victoria, pulled his mother's elegant brougham, which she used only for special occasions. What happened to the brougham?

When he entered the dining room, his mother was putting bowls of steaming vegetables on the table.

"Oh, Tony," she said, almost in a festive mood, "won't you light the candles?"

Tony obliged, going to the sideboard to look for matches. He found them in the top drawer and went to the table, where his mother had placed two silver candelabra. It occurred to him that they had been better off than most families on the island. His mother had come from a fairly wealthy family in Georgia before the war, and his father, a New Yorker and Union Army officer, started the First National Bank of Beaufort shortly after the Freedman's Bureau had been dismantled by President Johnson. Yes, they were among the prosperous, even the elite, of Beaufort, not to mention St. Helena.

Georgia then brought out a platter of baked ham, one of the gifts of Miss Barton. "You're the man of the house now, Tony. You can do the carving."

Tony picked up the silver-handled carving knife, one he had rarely seen as a child, usually at Christmas or Thanksgiving, and began slicing the ham into thin strips while his mother seemed to think of something missing. "Oh! The biscuits! They'll be burnt!"

She rushed back into the kitchen and pulled a tray out of the iron stove. Smoke billowed from the oven door. "Oh, I've ruined them!"

"It's all right, Mama," Tony said. "I've been living on hardtack lately. I can do without it."

"This isn't hardtack. They're as light as a feather when they're baked properly. It'll only take a few minutes." She opened a window and closed the kitchen door to prevent any more smoke from entering the dining room. "Open a bottle of your father's wine," she called. "It's in the sideboard."

Tony put down the carving knife and opened the paneled door of the sideboard. There were several bottles of wine there in a rack and he pulled one out. The label read:

Chateau Lafitte
Paulliac
1878

This was a wine he could never have afforded while he was living in Paris. It was his father's favorite. Perhaps it was fitting that he and his mother should drink it in commemoration of his...well, his life. He would have approved.

His mother returned and saw the label as he was removing the cork. "Oh...do you think we should open that one?"

"Can you think of any tribute that Papa would like better?"

"Well..." Georgia seemed to struggle within herself for a moment and then broke into a nervous smile. "I suppose you're right. He would like that."

"Sit down, Mama. We'll have a fine dinner."

Once seated, Georgia folded her hands and closed her eyes. "Would you like to say the blessing?"

Tony's eyes were still open and fixed on his mother. "The blessing? I'm afraid I don't know any."

She opened her eyes. "Of course you do. You learned them growing up."

"I don't recall Papa ever saying a blessing."

Georgia sighed. "He wasn't the religious sort, that's true. I suppose I was the one who always said it. Don't they say blessings in France? Perhaps you can say one in French."

Tony stared at her for a moment. "Maybe I can improvise." He closed his eyes and bowed his head as Georgia followed suit. "Mon Dieu, merci beaucoup pour vos cadeaux, surtout ce repas et le vin rouge bien aimé de Papa. Amen!"

Georgia raised her head and opened her eyes. She smiled. "I caught the part about the wine and Papa. If only your grandmother were still alive–she would be so proud of your speaking French!"

Tony transferred a slice of ham from the platter to her plate. "Grandma Rhodes was my inspiration to go to France in the first place. She was my first tutor in French."

"Yes, she was a Francophile. I'm only sorry I didn't get the education that she did."

"You were my real teacher. Incidentally, how is Miss Towne?"

"Older now–she must be nearly seventy–but as energetic and committed to the children's education as ever."

"She escaped the ravages of the storm then?"

"Yes. Oh, there was some flooding on the Seaside Road, but I understand the damage was hardly as much as we had at our end of the island. And she sent her man around to all of the stricken homes with coal for their stoves and eggs from her hen house."

"A stern but compassionate woman."

"Yes." Georgia turned her eyes down again to her plate. "Yes, she is."

They ate in silence for several minutes.

"Mama–tell me. How did he die?"

Georgia looked up from her plate, first at Tony, then away towards the yard. "Doing what he always did–helping those in need. Word came that a shrimp boat had run aground at Land's End. He rushed out there to help. When he got there, the boat was foundering on a sand bar and the waves were breaking the vessel up. Two or three of the men managed to get ashore on the lifeline, hand over hand. Then the rope snapped. Your father dove into the water, found the end of the rope, and swam to the boat where one of the crew members secured the line. Then he helped the remaining crew members grab onto the rope until they made it ashore. Then–" she looked down at her plate again and seemed unable to continue.

"The rope snapped again?" Tony said.

She looked up and brushed away a tear. "Yes. The terrible irony of it is that he was a strong swimmer. But the current, the waves, were even stronger." She paused for a moment to collect herself. "They found his body washed up on Cat Island three days after the storm. Less than a half a mile from here."

"I'm sorry, Mama. I'm sorry you had to see him like that."

"Oh, I didn't see the body. The men who brought him up to the house had already put him in a coffin and nailed the lid shut. I was thankful for that."

They sat in silence for a few moments, neither eating, Tony simply staring at his mother, whose face was again cast downward.

Then she looked up. "What will you do now, Tony? I don't suppose there's much for you here in Beaufort–"

"There's not much for me in Paris, either, I'm afraid. I was barely able to pay my rent in the garret I occupied on the Left Bank."

"But you had shows–"

"Yes, I had a couple of shows. I even won a prize at one of them. But the paintings didn't sell. At first a half a dozen galleries carried them, then two, then one. The art market in Paris is fickle, it seems. Or maybe I just don't have the talent."

"Of course you have the talent! Why, your father brought home a copy of the *New York Herald* not six months ago with a review saying that you were one of the most promising young painters in Paris!"

Tony smiled. "I have stacks of good reviews in my garret. Right next to the paintings I had to take back from the galleries. No, Mama, it's too precarious a living. I think I have to do something else."

Georgia looked again towards the bluff. "Perhaps you could find a position at your father's bank. It's all in disarray now, with the upheaval caused by the storm and your father's–your father's absence. They'll need plenty of help."

Tony toyed with the remnants of food on his plate, then put his knife down and picked up his glass. "Perhaps. In the meantime, there's plenty of work to do around here. What happened to the brougham?"

"Oh–fortunately, I had it sent into Beaufort for repairs before the storm hit. I suppose it's safe in the blacksmith's shop. But I don't know."

"I'll go into Beaufort as soon as I fix a few things here and see. You haven't touched your wine, Mama. It's marvelous–and it'll help you sleep."

Georgia looked for a moment at the nearly full glass of wine in front of her, then picked it up and took a sip. "Yes, it *is* marvelous. Your father paid a pretty penny to have it shipped from New York. There's more of it in the root cellar–that is, if it didn't float away in the storm."

Tony laughed. "I'll see about it tomorrow." He raised his glass. "Here's to Papa–and to all who have been touched by his generosity and encouraged by his example."

Georgia smiled and raised her glass. "Not the least of whom was you. To Papa."

And they both drank.

CHAPTER 4

After Tony had made repairs to the house and the stables–with the help of Scratch the stableman–he saddled up Leto and headed for Beaufort. Leto was old but still serviceable, and had lost none of her proud bearing, though her once bright chestnut coat was now faded and shot through with gray.

Crossing the creek that divided St. Helena from Lady's Island was a bit problematic, as the little wooden bridge had washed away in the storm and the water came up to Leto's belly in some places. Nevertheless, they crossed without incident and headed for the ferry landing, which Scratch said was operating again.

Along the way it became evident that Lady's Island had been hit harder than St. Helena. Hundreds of trees lay flat, some blocking the road, and the remaining trees were littered with debris, even rooftops. Islanders were everywhere clearing the wreckage, assisted by a detachment of U.S. Marines from Parris Island.

There was a large crowd of people at the landing, waiting for the ferry to return from Beaufort. Tony recognized several of them. He was wearing ordinary work clothes as opposed to his attire upon arriving just a few days before. This was just as well, as he didn't want to stand out as some sort of elite aristocrat looking down his nose at the wretched victims of the hurricane.

And many were wretched. Some had been wearing the same clothes for days, caked with mud and torn from removing debris from their property. Most were black, though there were a few whites among them who had remained after the war and reclaimed at least part of their former plantations. The majority of property owners on the two islands, however, were the former slaves of these same masters. They lived together in a curious symbiosis.

"Tony!"

Tony turned to the sound of a familiar voice. It was David Alexander, a former classmate at the Penn School. David, unlike Tony, was as black as coal and had rugged features and a muscular build that sometimes frightened white people. But he was a gentle soul and one of the better students at the school. He was driving a buckboard, apparently intent on picking up some supplies in Beaufort.

Tony dismounted. David jumped down from the buckboard and embraced him.

"How are you, David?" Tony said. "You seemed to have gotten through the storm all right."

David laughed. "I guess you could say that. Flattened my place, though. I'm out at Coffins Point, you know. Me and Lizbeth hunkered down in Miss Towne's barn until it blew over."

"Lizbeth?"

"You remember Lizbeth–the pretty little girl whose pigtails you used to pull in Miss Towne's Rhetoric class."

"That Lizbeth? I never knew that–"

"You're lucky I didn't thrash you right there. But I bided my time until I saw you lost interest and then I moved in." David gave a hearty laugh. "We got married last September. Lizbeth's got a job teaching at the Penn School and I'm making a go at rice farming."

"Well, what do you know–any children?"

"Not yet." David slapped Tony on the back. "I can't do everything all at once, my brother. Give me a little time. Say, the last time I saw you, you were headed to Harvard. Harvard! We all could hardly believe it. You done graduated?"

Tony shrugged his shoulders. "Not exactly. I dropped out my junior year and went to France."

David looked at him quizzically. "Oh, yeah–I heard you were an artist. You were always real good at drawing. How's that worked out?"

Tony sighed. "Not so well, really. That's one reason I'm back in Beaufort."

"Oh–well. It was worth a try, I guess. Paris! Why I bet you you're the only black man in America whose been to Paris!"

Tony chuckled. "Actually, there're quite a few. There're even a couple of black painters there who have been very successful. Just didn't look like I was destined to be one of them."

"Maybe you could take another shot at it when all this mess settles. How's your folks?"

"Mama's fine. I'm afraid Papa didn't make it."

David's jolly expression evaporated. "I'm sorry to hear that, Tony. Your daddy was a good man. He did a lot for this community."

"That he did. That's one reason I'm going into town. I've got to see if they're even aware that he's not coming back to the bank."

David sighed and sat down on the edge of the buckboard. "You know, your daddy helped get me a loan when nobody else would. I'll miss him."

"Me, too."

David seemed not to know what else to say at this point and simply looked down at the ground.

"Here he comes!" Someone shouted. "Here come the ferryman!"

David stood and looked to the landing. He extended his hand to Tony. "Let me know if I can help, Tony. Must have a lot of work to do at your place."

"Probably not as much as you do at yours. Call on me anytime."

"Yeah." David suddenly lunged forward and gave Tony a bone-crushing hug. "Good seein' you, Tony. Better get on, now."

David's buckboard and the other wagons took up so much space on the ferry that Tony had to wait for the ferryman to come back again. Finally, after mollifying Leto with some oats he carried in his coat pocket, the ferryman returned and they mounted the vessel along with a dozen or so horses and mules driven aboard by their masters.

In town, the devastation was still evident, though the streets had been cleared and soldiers were keeping order. After visiting the blacksmith's shop and finding that the brougham was intact, though still in disrepair, he went to one of the Red Cross tents set up in Union Square and waited in line for an hour before he was able to obtain a few sacks of flour and additional tins of mixed vegetables, salted pork, and lard. Much of it seemed to be surplus rations from the days of the Union Army's occupation, but it was welcome nevertheless. Clean drinking water was another popular item, as many cisterns in the area had been contaminated with salt water. Fortunately, Antonio, Sr., had had the foresight to build a water tower on their property that was well away from the creek and served their neighbors as well. It was not damaged in the storm.

The final stop was the First National Bank of Beaufort.

This venue was almost as crowded as the Red Cross tent. It seemed to be a run on the bank. Numerous depositors–only about half were black–were waving their arms and shouting, demanding to see the manager. Finally, the manager did appear and told them that their money was safe, the storm did little damage to the building, and in any case no water had reached the vault, which was above ground and encased in steel and concrete. He even offered a tour of the vault's interior, which several people took him up on, and this seemed to calm everybody down. Still, some depositors chose to withdraw their money in spite of being reassured that it was safer in the vault than in their homes.

Tony waited until this tumult died down and introduced himself to the manager, who was fairly new to the bank. He was, in fact, a white man named Hedrick Ferguson.

"Antonio's son?" he said. "I thought you were in France."

"Indeed I was," Tony said, taking his measure of the man. He was rather stout, about average height, and seemed to be of indeterminate middle age. Balding, with gray at the temples, he peered at Tony over the steel rims of his glasses. "But I returned as soon as I got word of the storm."

"Ah, well, why don't you step into my office, or rather your father's office since–"

"My father's dead," Tony said.

Mr. Ferguson looked surprised, then patted Tony on the back of the head. "My dear boy–I'm so sorry. We've been in disarray since the storm hit, as you can see, and we missed your father's steady hand. His very presence seemed to have a calming influence on people. Well...please step into the office–we have much to discuss."

Tony was familiar with the office–in fact, he was familiar with nearly every nook and cranny of the bank, including the vault, as he had worked there for two summers before going off to Harvard. There was his father's rather impressive oak desk, with its carved cabriole legs and its inlaid brass bordering the green baize covering the top. It, like most of the other furnishings, had been purchased from the Freedmen's Bureau when it shut down in '76. Other items included a gilt-edged portrait of General, and later President, Grant; two rather worn armchairs upholstered in a needlepoint fabric depicting scenes from classical antiquity; and bookcases containing his father's favorite works of literature, philosophy, and science. It resembled more of a scholar's study than a bank president's office.

Mr. Ferguson asked Tony to sit down in one of the armchairs and then seated himself behind the desk. He folded his hands together and leaned forward in a grave manner. "We knew, of course, that St. Helena and Lady's Island were hardest hit by the storm, and all communication was cut off until today. I, for one, feared the worst, as your father never failed to show up for work, even in the most extreme circumstances. How...how did it happen?"

"Drowning," Tony said. "Trying to save some shrimpers stranded on a sand bar at Land's End."

Mr. Ferguson's grim visage slowly expanded into a broad smile.

"Ah! Just like him." He crossed himself. "God bless his soul!"

Tony wasn't entirely convinced that Mr. Ferguson regretted the passing of his father. It seemed to portend a promotion for him.

"Now," Mr. Ferguson said, returning to his grave countenance. "What can I do for you, Tony?"

Tony, who had been slouching slightly in his chair while reminiscing over the familiar portraits and furniture, sat up straight. "I'm not quite sure, Mr. Ferguson. It seems that my father's death has created somewhat of a void here at the bank–perhaps some reorganization will be necessary."

Mr. Ferguson's eyebrows arched high above the rims of his glasses. "Oh? In what way?"

"Well, between my mother and me, we own a majority of the bank's shares."

"I'm aware of that."

"Well–I know something of the bank's operations, having worked here a couple of summers before I went off to college."

"I'm aware of that, too. Your father informed me of your brief tenure here and the other employees spoke highly of you. You were a quick study, they tell me."

"I appreciate that, Mr. Ferguson. But the point is, we need to name a successor to my father."

Mr. Ferguson leaned back in his chair, his eyes intensely focused on Tony. "Do you have any suggestions?"

Tony could feel the tension in the air. He hadn't intended to confront, much less challenge, his father's second-in-command when he walked in the front door. "No, I don't really. Not at the moment. But I think we should set up a meeting with the other officers, yourself, me, and perhaps my mother."

Mr. Ferguson again leaned forward and folded his hands on the green baize. He seemed somewhat relieved. "I think that's an excellent idea. What do you say..." He consulted his calendar. "Next Tuesday at ten o'clock. That'll give you and your mother time to sort things out on the Island and to arrange for the transit. Your mother is well?"

"As well as can be expected. My father's death was a terrible blow to her."

Mr. Ferguson stood, as did Tony. "No doubt. Poor woman." He extended his hand across the desk. "It's been a pleasure to meet you, Tony. Give my condolences to your mother."

Tony accepted the hand proffered to him, though he was somewhat annoyed that Mr. Ferguson felt it necessary to demonstrate the strength of his grip.

Once out into the lobby, he saw that the crowd had diminished and that only a handful of depositors were standing in orderly lines at the two teller windows. He nodded to the tellers, who he knew well, but didn't wish to interrupt them while they dealt with the customers, and so turned to leave by the front door.

As he approached the door he saw the image of an elegantly dressed young woman through the frosted glass panes and opened the door for her.

It was Jacqueline LeRoux.

CHAPTER 5

As Tony stood on the ferry deck adjusting the hood on Leto's head–she was always fearful of large expanses of water–he ruminated over his encounter with Jacqueline LeRoux. She had a draft on an English bank with her that the Bank of Beaufort either would not or could not cash. He escorted her to Mr. Ferguson's office, and though the telegraph lines were still down, Mr. Ferguson agreed to advance her half of the money until the lines were restored and he could verify that the funds were available. He was reluctant at first, knowing little or nothing about the LeRoux family, but Tony had vouched for her.

She was a beautiful woman. Of that there was no doubt. Physically, they could not be more opposite. She, blue-eyed with blond hair, fair-skinned, and from a wealthy family with a long pedigree of prominent South Carolina ancestors; he, an abandoned black baby adopted by white parents out of the kindness of their hearts–not to mention their abolitionist sympathies during the war. True, he was very light-skinned and blue-eyed himself. There was always some speculation that he was the son of a white planter and a black slave. He would probably never know for sure.

No, it would never work. Even the relatively progressive attitudes of most Beaufortonians did not go so far as to approve of mixed-race couples. This was not Paris, where such unions were looked upon as delightful curiosities, especially among the artists of the Left Bank.

When he arrived at the house, Scratch was up on the roof replacing shingles. As he put Leto into the barn and replenished her trough with oats, he reflected on Scratch's background. They were about the same age, and both had been adopted. Scratch, however, had been adopted by a black couple who were illiterate, former plantation slaves. Though they owned their own property now thanks to the Freedmen's Bureau, they had struggled to make a go of cotton farming. Often cheated by the factors in Charleston because they could not read the contracts, they barely managed to get by, and Scratch, a talented carpenter, hired himself out to the other islanders, both white and black.

Tony carried the sacks of flour along with the tins of food into the house. His mother was in the pantry taking inventory of what goods they had. She turned to look as Tony entered the kitchen and deposited the tins on the kitchen table.

"Oh–wonderful! What's in them? And flour! You got some flour–now I can bake some bread and some pies as well."

Tony picked up the tins one by one. "Mixed vegetables. Corned beef. Pork. Even diced pineapple. Don't ask me where that came from."

Georgia laughed and went to the table. She gave Tony a kiss on the cheek and picked up one of the tins. "And tomatoes!" She read the label aloud. "U.S. Army Field Ration–packed November 16th, 1864. Oh, my goodness! Can they still be edible?"

Tony chuckled. "We'll find out. There's more in the barn. I'll get them."

Tony went to the barn, where he found Scratch gathering some lumber and nails. "Scratch, you haven't told me about your family. Did everyone make it through the storm all right?"

Scratch paused for a moment. He shook his head. "Most did. Ellie drowned, like your dad."

"Sorry to hear that, Scratch. Ellie was your sister?"

"Yeah. She maybe six, seven. Don't rightly remember. The youngest. Too weak to swim against the flood waters. Mama nearly lost her mind when we brought her to the house. She still ain't right in the head yet."

"Again, I'm sorry. What about the others?"

"Lulu, Sally, Mike, Jasper, Oola–they all make it through, though Oola got some kind of ring worm now. She scratch it till her skin bleed. But Miss Towne come to see her yesterday and put on some liniment. She be all right, I reckon."

Tony sighed. "It's been tough for everyone. I got some foodstuffs in town. You need some?"

Scratch eyed one of the sacks that Tony had slung over Leo's rump. "You got any cornmeal?"

"Got a whole sackful. Here, it's yours."

Scratch grinned and eagerly took the sack of cornmeal. Then Tony gathered up the remaining goods and returned to the house.

As he helped his mother stock the shelves in the pantry, he could only think of Jacqueline LeRoux.

"What do you know of the LeRoux's, Mama?"

Georgia stopped for a moment and looked at Tony quizzically. "About as much as you do, I suppose. Or maybe a little more. Why?"

"Because I met Jacqueline LeRoux on my way in from the train station. She's a very pretty girl."

Georgia continued with her work. "Yes, I understand that she is. I've never met her myself."

"You know, she's been in London for the past year or so. With her aunt Lucinda. Did you know her?"

"Well, yes, I'm acquainted with Lucinda. But it's been a long time since I've seen her. She went off to London years ago–shortly after you were born. She had some falling out with Edwina, Jacqueline's mother, it seems."

"What kind of falling out?"

Georgia placed another tin on the shelf and went back into the kitchen. "Why are you so curious about this..this Jacqueline? She may be pretty, but–"

Tony followed her into the kitchen. "But what?"

"But the LeRoux–actually, they're Bensons. Edwina married Mansfield LeRoux, who was an old college friend of Edward Benson, her brother. Edward was not a very nice man."

"He wasn't? What wasn't nice about him?"

Georgia went to the sink and washed her hands in the basin. "It's very complicated, Tony. Suffice it to say that he defended slavery before the war and was unrepentant about it afterwards."

"And he was allowed to keep his property?"

"Yes. Your father, as head of the local Freedmen's Bureau managed to sell off at least part of it to the former slaves, but when President Johnson took office after the war, he nearly undid everything that Mr. Lincoln tried to accomplish."

"So Mr. Benson went right back to being a slave driver?"

"More or less. His former slaves signed labor contracts with him, or became tenant farmers."

"What happened to him?"

"He was murdered by one of his tenants."

Tony's eyes grew large. "Murdered? Mama, how come you never told me all this before?"

Georgia put her hands on Tony's shoulders. "Because there was no reason to. The Bensons, or now the LeRoux, have nothing to do with you. They're a troubled family, that's all. You'd best forget about this Jacqueline girl."

"She asked me to call her Jackie."

"Oh? When did she do that? The moment you met her?"

"No. this morning. She came into the bank to cash a bank draft. I helped her with it. By the way, we need to meet with Mr. Ferguson next Tuesday to determine the future of the bank."

Georgia stared into Tony's eyes for a moment as if to reprimand him for some childish indiscretion. Then she went back into the pantry. "I'll be happy to meet with Mr. Ferguson. Did he say anything about the other directors?"

"No. I suppose they'll be notified. Mama, what is it that you've got against the LeRoux?"

Georgia reappeared in the door of the pantry. "Nothing. Nothing at all. It's just that I think that this Jackie girl isn't right for you."

"Right for me? Did I say anything about courting her? I just said she was pretty."

"And I know what that means. You're my son, Tony. Don't you think I know what that little glint in your eye means? Don't get entangled with this girl. It can only come to a bad end."

Tony pouted like the school boy that he had been only a few years before. "You're jumping to conclusions, Mama. I was just curious about the family."

"Well, now your curiosity has been satisfied. And speaking of young ladies, whatever happened to that young lady in Paris you wrote me about? She came from an aristocratic family, you said."

Tony slumped into one of the kitchen chairs. "Yes...well, she decided that she was too aristocratic to consort with a starving artist. Especially a black one."

"She was prejudiced."

"Of course. Oh, she put on a show about being enlightened and progressive and all that, but when we went to dine with her parents, she tried to pass me off as a charity case in need of patronage. I didn't see her again."

"Weren't there others?"

Tony smiled as he thought of 'the others.' "Yes, there were others. Mostly artists' models. Completely free of prejudice. Also completely free of learning and common sense."

Georgia suppressed a smile as she returned to her work. "Perhaps you ought to look around Beaufort for a girl who graduated from the Penn School, like you."

"Well, yes, there was Violet..."

"Violet? Oh, yes, I remember Violet–you were crazy about her."

"Not exactly 'crazy.' I liked her, though. Perhaps I'll go see her folks and find out how to get in touch with her." He rose from his chair. "In the meantime, I think I'll see if I can help Scratch with the roof repairs."

"Good idea. Ask him to join us for dinner."

Tony went into the back yard where he could hear Scratch pounding some nails into the wooden shingles he had fashioned in his workshop. A long ladder rested against the eaves of the house. "Need some help, Scratch?"

Scratch stopped pounding the nails and looked down at Tony. "I reckon I could use another stack of shingles."

"Coming right up." Tony went to the barn to retrieve the shingles.

CHAPTER 6

Lynwood was left remarkably untouched by the storm, or rather the main house was. Many of the out buildings, especially the former slave cabins, now occupied by tenants and sharecroppers, did not fare so well.

Jackie, as she liked to be called, discovered this fact on her tour of the property on horseback. The cabins nearest the Combahee River were the most affected. Two or three were completely swept away by the tidal surge. Others were severely damaged, and the occupants were busy repairing them with what materials they had.

Jackie stopped at one of these and inquired of the patriarch of the family in what way she might be helpful. The patriarch was named Sanko, a lean, sinewy man with long arms and huge hands. What little hair he had left on his head was speckled with gray, except at the temples, where it was entirely gray. He leaned on the handle of a rake with which he had apparently been removing debris, while two young men straddled a joist to which they were in the process of attaching a rafter.

"Well, well," Sanko said with a broad smile, "if it ain't Miss Jackie! We thought you was galavantin' with them kings and queens over in England. So you come back to see us."

"Yes, Sanko–but only for a visit. I've found a career for myself in London."

"A career? A career doin' what?"

"Acting. Aunt Lucy introduced me to her friends in the theater there and, well, one thing led to another."

"Well, I'll be a 'possum's uncle! Then you a big star now."

Jackie laughed. "Not yet. Just small parts so far, but you never know."

"That's right. You never know. Why, that Queen Victoria might come see you and then you off and runnin'!"

Jackie laughed again. "Perhaps. But Sanko, I've come to see how everyone's fared in the storm. Your cabin looks like a cannon ball hit it. Was anyone hurt?"

Sanko looked up at the young men on the roof. "Hey, what you boys lookin' at? Get along with them joists. Mr. Sun smilin' now, but Ol' Man Thunder be back tomorrow. I ain't gonna spend another night soakin' wet and catchin' my death. Get on now!"

The boys went back to work and resumed pounding nails into the joists.

Sanko turned back to Jackie with a gentle smile. "I got to get after them boys ever' minute. They'd play hoops and skittles all day if'n I didn't."

"Where are Mattie and the girls?" Jackie said.

"They be down to the river washin' clothes. Ever'thing shot through with mud and phosphate."

"Phosphate?"

"Yeah. That come up from the ol' mill where Major Jones discovered it at the end of the war. He turned it over to we'uns so we could make some money, but it never worked out too good. The storm done give it the final blow, I reckon."

Jackie now made the connection between Major Jones and Tony. She had heard the Jones name a few times growing up and knew that Major Jones had something to do with the Freedmen's Bureau, but her parents never spoke of him.

"Can I do anything to help?" she said.

Sanko knitted his brows, looked down at the ground for a few moments as if in deep thought, and looked up again. "I reckon we could use some cornmeal and sugar. Some coffee might be nice, too, if your folks got any they ain't drinkin' they selves."

"I'll see what I can do. It's good to see you, Sanko. Say hello to Mattie and the girls for me."

"I'll do that, Miss Jackie. Sho' good to see you, too."

Jackie pulled on the reins of her horse and continued on her tour of the property. At each cabin she came upon, it was much the same story. The brick structures fared the best, of course, while the ones of logs or lumber resembled piles of match sticks. The Negroes were busily repairing them, and they all were in need of foodstuffs of one kind or another. Coffee was the most prized item.

When she got back to the main house, she found her mother, Edwina, in the breakfast room overlooking the river, sipping on a cup of tea.

"Won't you have some tea with me, Jacqueline?" her mother said. "And have some of these cakes–they're delicious!"

Jackie wondered at the fact that her mother, unlike everyone else in the family, always insisted on calling her 'Jacqueline.' It was her formal upbringing, she supposed. "Thank you, Mother, but I had a hearty breakfast with Papa this morning before you were up."

"Suit yourself. But surely you will have some of this wonderful tea you brought all the way from England. Why, we haven't had any *real* tea for ages!"

Jackie removed her riding habit and sat down in a chair opposite her mother. She pulled off her boots. "I suppose a cup would do me good. Mother–the Negroes are rather desperate for food and supplies. Didn't Papa send something out for them after the storm?"

"My dear, we hardly have enough for ourselves. In fact, your father went into town today to see if he could procure some fresh meat–the storm washed away the smoke house, you know, and drowned quite a few of our animals."

"Fresh meat?" Jackie said. A maid suddenly appeared and poured some steaming water into her cup. "Thank you, Hanna. I would think that there would be little fresh meat available in Beaufort, either."

Hanna, a girl of about seventeen, retreated into the kitchen. Once she was out of earshot, Edwina turned again to her daughter. "One can procure just about anything when one has money, dear. I'm sure your father will find a willing vendor."

Jackie put a teaspoon of sugar into her cup and stirred it. "I hope he'll procure enough to supply the Negroes, too. They're on the brink of starvation."

Edwina smiled. "Oh, they're very resourceful. And you know that they don't need as much as we do to sustain themselves."

Jackie took a sip of her tea and put the cup down. "I would think they need more. After all, they do all the hard labor around here."

Her mother shook her head. "They're made for such labor. I wouldn't worry about them. Now, Jacqueline, you must tell me about Aunt Lucinda. Is she well?"

Jackie sighed. "Quite well. And as energetic as ever. She's directing a production of *Twelfth Night* in the West End at the moment. I was cast as Olivia, but of course I had to leave as soon as I heard about the storm."

Edwina shook her head. "Oh, my dear, that was completely unnecessary, as you can see. We're doing perfectly well in spite of the storm. Of course we're delighted to see you, but I'm sorry you had to give up such a wonderful role."

Jackie's eyes went to the windows, where she could see men replanting shrubs and trees in the garden.

"It seems to me that not everyone is doing so perfectly well."

Edwina's eyes followed hers to the men in the garden. "Don't concern yourself with the Negroes, Jacqueline. They're accustomed to hardship. I suppose that Lucinda has been indoctrinating you with her peculiar brand of idealism while you've been in London. Lucinda was always the dreamy one, given to flights of fancy and sentimentality. The theater is the perfect place for her."

Jackie's eyes returned to her mother's, touched with a flash of resentment. "So the theater must also be the perfect place for me as well, I suppose? Given to 'flights of fancy and sentimentality.'"

"Oh, Jacqueline, save your theatrics for the theater. The Negroes are better off than ever since the war, many of them farming their own little plots and supplementing their income with fishing and hunting. They'll never starve. And of course we employ many of them who aren't so resourceful here at the house. What else could they do?"

At that moment, Hanna re-entered with a second tray of cakes.

"Tell Miss Jacqueline," Edwina said, "what you did before you came to work for us."

Hannah stood stock still for a moment, unsure of what was expected of her. "Well, I went to the Penn School on St. Helena Island, Miss."

"And did you find employment after you graduated from the vaunted Penn School?" Edwina said.

Hanna's eyes darted towards Jackie, who was listening with rapt attention. "Yes, ma'am."

"And where was that?" Edwina said.

"The textile mill in Greenville," Hanna said.

"And were you happy there?"

"No, ma'am."

"Why not?"

"Well, you know..."

"But Miss Jacqueline doesn't. You can speak freely, Hanna."

"Yes, ma'am. Well, the days were long–from seven in the morning till nine at night and only a half a day on Sunday."

"And?"

"And the foreman cracked our knuckles with a stick if we didn't keep up. Miss Towne never did that."

"And?"

"And the ones he liked, he took them into his office and–"

"Yes, go on."

"He did indecent things to them."

"So you came back to Beaufort."

"Yes, ma'am."

"And are you happy here?"

"Oh, yes, ma'am."

"You have your own room, don't you?"

"Yes, ma'am."

"And you don't have to lift anything heavier than a tea kettle. Is that right?"

"Yes, ma'am."

"And your work is done after supper."

"Yes, ma'am."

Edwina turned to her daughter. "You see, Jacqueline? They're so much better off here, with light work and comfortable accommodations and no one molests them." She turned back to Hanna. "Isn't that right, Hanna?"

"Yes, ma'am."

"You may go now."

"Thank you, ma'am."

When Hanna had gone, Edwina turned again to Jackie. "You see, Jacqueline, when one probes a little deeper into things, one often comes to a completely different conclusion than one might after only a superficial examination."

"You should have been an attorney, Mother."

Edwina smiled. "I might very well have been if those jackanapes in the state house would only allow women to enter their august temples of the law. It's like a secret society that does its best to keep its rituals hidden from the eyes of our fair sex. Those of ability should be allowed to pursue their dreams without regard to–"

"Race, creed, color, or sex?" Jackie said.

Edwina's nostrils flared as if she had gotten wind of a disagreeable odor. "I wouldn't go so far as to include all of those categories, Jacqueline. That's your Aunt Lucinda's influence again. But I would think that all well-born white women should certainly be considered."

Jackie finished her cup of tea and stood. "I think I'll have a nap before dinner, Mother. I'm not as used to riding as I once was. Have Hanna knock on my door at half-past one, will you?"

"Of course, dear."

Jackie started for the door.

"Oh, Jacqueline," Edwina said, "you won't pursue this line of inquiry with your father at the dinner table, will you? You and I enjoy our little debates on contentious issues, but they absolutely distress your father."

"You know I never trouble Papa for anything unless it's something I really want, Mother."

As Jackie left the room, Edwina turned her gaze back to the garden. "That's what I'm afraid of."

CHAPTER 7

During the interim between Tony's first visit to the bank and the Tuesday meeting, the brougham had been repaired. This elegant conveyance had an interesting history, having been custom-built for his mother by a benefactor of the Penn School shortly after the war. Why a 'benefactor' of the school should single out a particular teacher for such an extravagant gift, Tony couldn't fathom. When he asked his mother about it, she simply said that the benefactor was 'highly eccentric' and generous with his money. This explanation never quite satisfied his curiosity, but he chose not to pursue the matter.

Scratch secured the harnesses for Victoria and Marmaduke, while Leto remained in the barn. These two horses seemed to come alive when they were hitched up to the brougham, as if it were a point of pride to be given the privilege of pulling it.

The Whitehall ferry was now fully operational, and the municipal dock had been restored. The largest of the marooned ships, however, were still teetering precariously along the waterfront, listing to one side or the other, many of them picked clean by looters and scavengers.

Mr. Ferguson welcomed them in the lobby and ushered them into the conference room. A number of customers waited in line at the teller cages, but all was orderly and calm compared to the chaos of the previous week.

The other directors were already there. The most distinguished of them was Mr. Robert Smalls, who had famously escaped from slavery during the war by commandeering a Confederate warship and delivering it to the Union Navy just off Charleston Harbor. He had also been elected both to the South Carolina Legislature and the U.S. Congress during Reconstruction, but had been forced out of office on bogus corruption charges after Union troops left the state in 1877. He was now Collector of Customs at the Port of Beaufort, and deeply involved in civic, as well as business affairs.

Mr. Smalls was the only African-American director on the board. The others, besides Georgia, were all white men, either former Union Army officers like Tony's father, or local businessmen, also supporters of the Union cause. The First National Bank of Beaufort had been founded as a successor to the Freedmen's Bank, which was shut down in 1874. Originally intended to serve the freedmen exclusively, it reached out to the white community as well during the eighties and greatly increased the number of its depositors. It had been doing quite well until the hurricane hit, and though many depositors, both black and white, had withdrawn their money, the bank was still solvent and hopeful that most would return.

Georgia, as the major stockholder and temporary successor to her husband as chairman of the board, called the meeting to order. "Gentlemen, first I want to thank you all for your kind words and condolences for the loss of my husband, Antonio, Sr. It has not been easy these past two weeks for any of us, and I offer my own condolences to those of you who have lost both loved ones and property during this catastrophe. However, we must move on and do our part to rebuild Beaufort and, especially, to assist those in the community who have lost everything.

"Now to the first order of business–who is to succeed my husband as the president of the First National Bank of Beaufort?"

Mr. Cooper, who was the owner of a clothing store called the Emporium, spoke first. "I think we should ask Mr. Ferguson to leave the room since he's a potential candidate and not a board member."

Everyone looked to the door, where Mr. Ferguson had been standing expectantly, but now flushed with embarrassment. "Yes, of course. I have work to do."

Once Mr. Ferguson had left the room, Captain Westerfield, who had been both a fellow officer and partner with Antonio, Sr. in their phosphate mining venture after the war, spoke. "I think that Mr. Ferguson would be a logical choice since he has proven himself as a competent manager, but I think the bank needs some fresh blood, someone younger with innovative ideas."

"I agree with Captain Westerfield," said Mr. Christensen in his heavily accented English, "that we need someone with fresh ideas. But we also need someone who presents an image of maturity and sound judgment. Someone of distinction like Dr. Hazel of Parris Island."

"Dr. Hazel," Mr. Cooper said, "is no longer with us. He drowned during the storm."

There was a silence out of respect for Dr. Hazel for several moments.

"It seems to me," Mr. Smalls said, "that we're getting farther and farther away from the original conception of the bank. It was founded to help the freedmen, many of whom are still struggling, especially since the all-white legislature has essentially disfranchised most blacks with these so-called Jim Crow laws."

There was some nodding of heads and muttering of agreement at this statement.

Mr. Smalls continued. "We need someone like the late Major Jones, who was committed to the rights of the freedmen, and who was part black himself, though he didn't look it."

Tony looked at his mother with astonishment.

She looked away and turned to Mr. Smalls. "That's true, Mr. Smalls," she said. "Antonio was one-eighth Negro. His mother was one-quarter and an escaped slave, but he always passed for white. This was widely known in the first years after the war but now is nearly forgotten–especially on the part of the younger generation. But I think it's beside the point. The question is–who will be our next president?"

Several names were submitted, and the slate of candidates was narrowed down to three: Tony, Mr. Ferguson, and Georgia. Georgia, however, quickly withdrew her name, citing her continued commitment to her teaching duties at the Penn School. That left Tony and Mr. Ferguson. The vote was four to one, with only Mr. Christensen voting for Mr. Ferguson.

Tony, who, like Mr. Ferguson, had been asked to leave the room during the voting, was now invited back in to applause all around. He was handed the gavel and stood at the head of the table where his mother had been sitting, but who was now sitting in the chair that he had recently vacated, beaming with pride. Tony was not sure what was expected of him. While standing out in the lobby and having caught the eye of Mr. Ferguson, he considered withdrawing his name from consideration, but he didn't like the idea of Mr. Ferguson winning the position by default. At the same time, considering Mr. Ferguson's experience in the business, he assumed that he would prevail. Now there seemed to be no turning back.

Tony rapped the gavel on the table. "I would like to thank you all for your confidence in me. It is a great honor. However, you must know that I have not been trained as a banker, but as an artist. And though I am familiar with the operations of the bank, I have not had time to examine the books or the bank's current policies. Therefore, I ask for your patience while I bring myself up to speed and can recommend a plan for the bank's future.

I suggest that we meet again one week from today at this same time." He looked around the table and, seeing heads nod, rapped the gavel again on the table. "All right, then. Next Tuesday at ten o'clock. Thank you, gentlemen."

His mother threw her arms around him. "Oh, Tony, I'm so proud of you. And don't worry about your lack of experience. Mr. Smalls made a very convincing case for you, and the vote was nearly unanimous."

'Nearly unanimous.' Tony could guess who the one dissenting vote was. Mr. Christensen, however, was a gracious man, and extended his hand in congratulations.

Out in the lobby, at the entrance to the president's office, stood Mr. Ferguson. There was no concealing the disappointment on his face as the board members stood around Tony shaking his hand with broad smiles on their faces. Tony noticed this and walked over to Ferguson.

"I know you're disappointed, Mr. Ferguson," Tony said."

Mr. Ferguson seemed speechless and stood staring for a moment as if he were a feral animal on a railroad trestle blinded by the headlight of a speeding train. "Yes, Mr. Jones, of course. I want to be of assistance."

It was no longer 'Tony,' but 'Mr. Jones.' Tony did not correct him.

After a short meeting, Tony emerged shaking Mr. Ferguson's hand and then asked that the staff be called into the office. Mr. Ferguson made the announcement to them that 'Mr. Jones' was now the bank's president and Tony made a short speech recapitulating what he told the board of directors.

At last he joined his mother, who was waiting outside in the brougham. They sat together as Scratch drove the vehicle to the ferry with Georgia's hand in his, still beaming with the pride of a mother whose son has succeeded early in life to the highest pinnacle.

But Tony was troubled. Not that a great responsibility had suddenly been thrust upon him, but at Mr. Smalls' comment prior to the voting. "Why was I never told that Papa was one-eighth Negro?"

Georgia's cheery countenance turned to one of grave concern. She withdrew her hand and gazed out of the window of the brougham as they crossed the river to Lady's Island. "It didn't seem important. Your father always passed for white and everyone treated him as white. I didn't know myself until he told me and by that time I was in love with him."

"What about grandmama? Didn't she object?"

"Yes, at first. It was a struggle for her, being born in Georgia and raised as a genteel Southern lady. But your grandfather, Zimri, was from Connecticut, and was quite open-minded about such things. She finally accepted it."

They traveled in silence for a few miles once they reached the island. Tony turned this new intelligence over and over again in his mind. "And that's why you both decided to adopt a little black boy? Why didn't you just have a child of your own? He would have been one-sixteenth and would have passed for white just like Papa."

"Well..." Georgia said, "I couldn't have children. And there you were, an abandoned orphan, of whom there were so many on the island, and we felt it our duty to take you in. It just seemed right." She smiled and took his hand in hers again. "And we never regretted it, Tony. You've made us both proud and we love you so much." She gave him a kiss on the cheek.

Tony smiled and clasped her hand. He noted that she spoke of his father as if he were still alive. But more questions lingered in his mind as they approached the house.

CHAPTER 8

Several weeks passed and once again the town of Beaufort seemed to be a bustling community. New buildings went up, telegraph lines were restored, and grounded ships were refloated and refitted. The Penn School reopened and St. Helena's dikes were rebuilt and strengthened, though many of the rice fields were so inundated with salt water that they had to be abandoned.

Lynwood was operating much as it had before the storm. Her parents well and the house in order, Jackie prepared to return to London to pursue her acting career. Something, though, made her hesitate. She had run into Tony Jones again while shopping in Beaufort and he had asked her advice about a gift for his mother. Such a charming and interesting man! If only there were something to hold her in Beaufort for a while, perhaps somehow...but no, it was impossible. Her mother would be horrified at the idea of her consorting with a black man, however diluted his blood and bright his prospects. Imagine! Only twenty-four years old and already a bank president!

These thoughts raced through her mind one bright and sunny morning as she sat in the breakfast room–the most popular room in the house, with its floor-to-ceiling windows facing the Combahee River–sipping on a cup of tea. Her mother was already in the garden directing another planting project, and her father had retired to the library where he was working on a book–a history of South Carolina. She smiled at this thought; he was constantly writing letters to state legislators, congressmen, even the president. Nothing ever seemed to come of it, but now he felt sufficiently informed to write an entire history of the state! He was a dear man, she thought, but quite opinionated and rather quixotic in his efforts to restore the Old South. Ah, well, he was a doting and affectionate father.

She heard the door bell ring–it amused her to hear the system of bells in the house connected to a chain at the front door. In London, nearly all the door bells were activated electrically by pressing a button. She wondered who it might be.

A few minutes later her father appeared at the door of the breakfast room accompanied by a tall, broad-shouldered gentleman of about his own age. He was rather handsome, she thought, with long silver hair combed back over his ears and curls at the back just above his shoulders. He was dressed in hunting clothes with riding boots to his knees, a tweed jacket and an ascot. He seemed vaguely familiar.

"Jackie," her father said, "you remember Mr. Coleman, don't you? You sat upon his knee when you were a little girl."

Now she remembered. He had brown hair then, and muttonchop whiskers. The whiskers were gone and he had gained a little weight, though he was still athletic-looking.

"Let's not be so formal, Mansfield," Mr. Coleman said with a hearty laugh. "Jackie's a grown woman now. You must call me Rav."

Jackie stood and 'Rav' opened his long arms like a great bird and approached her. She instinctively tensed her shoulders and brought her elbows into her sides, afraid he might hurt her.

Rav enveloped her and lifted her off her feet. "My, what a beautiful woman you've turned out to be! Where have you been hiding her, Mansfield?" He put her down and she breathed a sigh of relief.

"We sent her off to London," her father said, "precisely to keep her away from lecherous old gentlemen like yourself."

"Lecherous? You do me a disservice, Mansfield. 'Old,' I'll confess. But 'lecherous'? Certainly not! I've always been a perfect gentleman."

"Ha!" Mansfield said. "You haven't forgotten those days at the Citadel when you used to smuggle ladies of the town into our dorm room, have you?"

"Ladies of the town?" Rav said with mock indignation. "Why, you know perfectly well that those were some of the most respectable young ladies of Charleston society. In fact, I married one of them."

Her father laughed. "That's a fact. How is Marian, by the way? It's been ages since–"

"I'm afraid I neglected to bring you up to date in our correspondence, old chum–Marian died of a fever two years ago."

"Oh," Mansfield said. "I'm sorry, Rav. I didn't–"

"It's all right, Mansfield. I've quite gotten over it. One has to move on, you know." Rav turned to Jackie and brought her hand to his lips. "With so much feminine beauty in this world, there's no sense in grieving forever." He winked at her. "Welcome home, Jackie. It's wonderful to see you again."

"Thank you, Mr. Coleman–"

"Rav."

"Yes...Rav. I'm so sorry for your loss. What brought you to Lynwood?"

Rav let go of her hand. "Partly to see if I could be of any assistance to your family after that ruinous hurricane. And partly to join your father in a bit of hunting. The season is on, you know, and well, it seems as if old Lynwood is puttering along just as it did before the war."

Her father chuckled. "Not quite. We were lucky with the storm. A labor shortage is our biggest problem these days."

Rav's cheery bonhomie evaporated for the first time since his arrival, "Labor...yes, we have the same problem in Charleston. The niggers no longer want to work and we can't make them. I've proposed a bill in the legislature–"

"Why don't I give you a tour of the property, Rav?" Mansfield said. "You can get your bearings again and perhaps make a few suggestions as to how we can improve things. Not that I'll take your advice, of course, but I'm always open to suggestions."

Rav laughed heartily. "Not that you ever took my advice! But maybe during the ride I can bend you to my will. Which way to the stables? Or did they blow away in the storm?"

"Still perfectly intact," Mansfield said. "But why don't we have a brandy in the library first? There're a number of things that we need to catch up on."

Rav turned to Jackie and again brought her hand to his lips. "And I trust that Jackie will join us for dinner after our perambulation of this vast estate?"

"Certainly she will," her father said. "Won't you, Jackie?"

"Yes," Jackie said. "Of course."

After the two men had left, Jackie sat down again at the breakfast table and gazed out the window. Ravenel Coleman was one of the most powerful and influential men in the state. She had been little aware of his activities when she was a child and he had visited the house only a few times. But now she recalled reading of his election to the state legislature shortly before she left for London. The article said that he had become very rich after the war as a cotton broker in Charleston. Like her father, he was of the old school, desperately trying to bring back the glorious days of the antebellum

South. Also like her father, he looked down upon the Negroes as an inferior species, fit only for menial labor.

She thought of Tony. Handsome, though in a softer way then Ravenel. Also bright, talented, and refined in a way that the Ravenel Coleman's of the world scarcely could comprehend.

As she turned these thoughts over in her mind, Hanna came into the room.

"Another cup of tea, Miss Jackie?"

Jackie, distracted from her reverie, looked at Hanna. "Hanna–"

"Yes, Miss?"

"Do you have any...plans for the future?"

"Why, I...well, yes, Miss Jackie. Why do you ask?"

"Just curious, that's all. If I'm not being too nosy, what sort of plans?"

Hanna seemed apprehensive, and looked furtively about the room, then through the window where she saw that Mrs. LeRoux continued to oversee the planting. "Well, I'm hoping to get a scholarship to Howard University in Washington. Miss Towne is helping me with my application."

"Howard University?"

"Yes, ma'am. Howard is–"

"I know about Howard University, Hanna. I think that's marvelous! I hope you get accepted."

"Thank you, ma'am. Did you want some more tea?"

"No, no thank you, Hanna. That will be all."

Hanna curtsied and left the room.

Jackie remained and went to a bench seat, where she sat down on the cushion and gazed out into the garden. She saw that her mother had disappeared, probably to get out of the hot sun. The gardeners, however, remained and were busily planting shrubs and a variety of small trees. It was such a lovely setting. In London, her aunt Lucinda's flat was comfortable enough, and in a fashionable neighborhood, but the tiny garden behind the building was hardly larger than a chicken coop. Aunt Lucy often spoke of Lynwood and, as Jackie understood it, shared a half interest in the estate. There had been some complicated legal business when her uncle Edward died, and apparently that was how things played out. As the only child, she assumed that she would inherit her parents' half of the estate. But then how would it be divided?

Well, her mother was quite active and healthy, and inheritance was a distant prospect. She shouldn't be thinking of such things.

She absently picked up a copy of *The New South,* a Beaufort newspaper, lying on the bench. There were several articles about the hurricane and its aftermath, along with news of the relief efforts, including an interview with Miss Clara Barton. She skimmed these and turned to the arts and entertainment page. Here, she found a short article of interest:

The Beaufort Players to Present
The Second Mrs. Tanquery

> Mr. Arthur Wing Pinero's smash hit play in London is coming to Beaufort! The Beaufort Players, newly installed in the old Bannister House on Craven Street, will hold auditions on Saturday from 10-12pm, and from 2-5pm. Both amateur and professional actors are encouraged to attend.

Jackie smiled. Mr. Pinero's new play! Why, she had seen the play on opening night in London in May. Of course it was a rather silly play, about 'fallen women' and all that, but she had rather liked it, and the part of Ellean, the daughter, was a plum role.

She put the paper down on the bench and brought her knees up to her chin the way she used to when she was a little girl, gazing out of this same window.

Suppose she got the part...it would mean that she would remain in Beaufort for at least another six weeks...and perhaps Tony Jones would come and see the play and...then what?

She extended her legs and rose from the bench, pulling herself up to her full height, which was five-foot seven. Rather tall for a woman. Tony was a shade over six feet, she would guess.

She gazed down at the newspaper, picked it up, folded it, and with a mischievous smile, left the room.

CHAPTER 9

Miss Towne persuaded Georgia to remove the remains of her husband to the Brick Church across the street from the Penn School.

"He belongs to all of us," she said.

Tony concurred, especially as he found it somewhat depressing to rise in the morning, gaze out of his bedroom window, and start the day contemplating his father's shallow grave.

He was properly buried in the cemetery adjacent to the church, with an impressive limestone monument that read:

Major Antonio Junius Jones
b. 1833 - d. 1893
In Loving Memory of His Service to the
Freedmen of St. Helena Island

After the ceremony, which concluded with the choir's lively rendition of "Swing Low, Sweet Chariot," Tony was besieged by several luminaries who attended the service, including Robert Smalls.

"I hope you will consider running for the state legislature, Tony," Smalls said, placing his hat on his head and giving it a tap. "I've been effectively disqualified by the Democrats, but you've got a chance. Beaufort County is perhaps the only county in the state that has a majority of Republican voters,"

"I have very little interest in politics, Mr. Smalls," Tony said. He noted that his mother was in deep conversation with Miss Towne. "I have my hands full as it is with the bank."

"Pretty soon the bank will be running itself," Smalls said. "You've already nearly doubled the number of depositors, and your farm loan program is bringing in new customers every day. Surely Mr. Ferguson can handle the day-to-day operations without your supervision."

"I still have much to learn, Mr. Smalls, and if I have any free time in the coming months, I'd like to do some painting."

Mr. Smalls laughed and shook his head. "Painting? Now, I know you're talented in that area, Tony. But the blacks of South Carolina are losing their rights under the domination of the Democrats in Columbia. If they keep on with their shenanigans, it may be against the law for black folks to even paint a picture, unless it's of Wade Hampton!"

Tony didn't know much about Wade Hampton except that he was a former governor of South Carolina and was no friend of the black man.

Miss Towne spoke to him as he and Mr. Smalls approached.

"We shall miss him," she said to Tony. She clasped his hand in both of hers. "He did so much for the freedmen and now it seems you've assumed his burden."

Tony hadn't planned on assuming anyone's burden, but it seemed that Mr. Smalls, Miss Towne, and even his mother expected him to. He enjoyed helping the freedmen with loans to purchase seed, equipment and even land, but plunging into politics was almost anathema to his soul. His soul! It belonged to the world of art, not politics. As soon as the bank was once again on a firm financial footing, he intended to return to Paris. Maybe he didn't have the talent to be a great painter like Mr. Sargent or Mr. Whistler, but then did they never question their talent when they were young?

This reverie was broken by a middle-aged black man who introduced himself as 'Primus.' It seemed an odd name, even by Gullah standards, but he had heard it many times both at home and while attending the Penn School.

"Mr. Jones," Primus said, doffing his cap, "I know your daddy from the time I was a boy like you at the Penn School till I went off to work for Mr. Benson at Lynwood. You may not know this, but he save the life of Roadie Mack."

Tony had never heard of Roadie Mack and turned to his mother.

Georgia smiled. "That's right, Tony. Your father leaped into the lake behind the school after a rowboat that he and Primus were in capsized."

Primus nodded in agreement. "He done sunk to the bottom like a rock. I was hanging on to the gunnel treadin' water when your daddy and Mr. Smalls come along and your daddy pulled off his boots and dove down to the bottom where Roadie Mack was settin' like a blowed-up toad."

Mr. Smalls laughed. "That he did, Primus. Then he brought him up, tossed him into the boat–he was a little fellow–and we pumped the water out of him."

"He was a good man, your daddy was," Primus said, fingering his cap, "and I'm sure sorry to see him go. Well...that's all I wanted to say." He lingered for a moment, staring at Tony intently. "You know, I can see you got your daddy's strong jawline, his fine nose, even the way he put his finger to his chin when he busy studying something." He put his cap back on his head and nodded to Georgia, then Mr. Smalls. "Well, I better get back to Lynwood–Mr. LeRoux don't like me being away so long."

After he had gone, Tony turned to his mother. She seemed to be avoiding his gaze.

"Primus always had a fanciful imagination," she said. "I would consider it a great compliment, Tony. Your father's influence was so strong that you even took on some of his mannerisms."

"I suppose so." He helped her into the carriage and sat next to her. Her skin smelled like lilacs. It was a perfume, actually a cologne, that she often wore when she and his father dressed for one of the rare social events they attended when he was a boy.

Lilacs. Or was it not even the cologne, but the flowers that his father pinned to her dress on such occasions?

CHAPTER 10

To no one's surprise, Jackie got the part. Not only was she the only actress with professional experience, but she was the right age and had the elocution that the director was looking for. This was an English play, after all.

It also didn't hurt that she was by far the prettiest of those who auditioned. Mr. Oliver, the director, made little effort to conceal his preference.

"You are just the sort of girl that every father would wish his daughter to be, and that every swain would desire to be his wife," he said.

Jackie, of course, was very flattered, but was wary of Mr. Oliver's motives. He was rumored to have been married three times and had come to Beaufort to escape alimony payments in New Jersey. She would have to be on her guard.

Her mother was delighted.

"That means you'll be with us for at least another six weeks," she said as they ate supper in the cavernous dining room. "And I do hope you'll stay permanently. A year in London has done much to broaden your horizons, of course, but one needs to settle down and find a husband before it's too late." She winked at Mansfield at the other end of the long dining table, so far away that her failing eyesight could hardly make out the color of his tie. "When I returned from my Grand Tour, I was a few years older than you and already considered to be at the brink of my dotage. Your father, fortunately, always had a preference for older women."

Mansfield pushed aside the candelabra in front of him so he could see his wife. "You were only twenty-four, my sweet."

"In those days that was considered to be nearly over the hill for a single woman. I made my debut in Charleston at sixteen."

"But Mother," Jackie said, "things have changed since then. Some girls are waiting until they're twenty-one before even considering marriage. Look at Aunt Lucy–she's never married."

Edwina seemed to turn up her nose at the food on her plate. "Your Aunt Lucinda is an exception. And a bit of an odd duck if you ask me. She was always contrary in everything she did. She's my dear sister, of course, but I wouldn't advise you to follow her example."

Jackie smiled and poked at some peas on her plate. "She's got a beau."

"Of course she does," her mother said. "Hanna, this beef is underdone–take it back to the kitchen."

"Yes, ma'am." Hanna was in the process of pouring wine into Mansfield's glass. She put the bottle down on the sideboard, retrieved Edwina's plate, and disappeared into the kitchen.

"As I was saying," Edwina said, "Of course Lucinda has a beau. She always has a beau–a continuous string of them. How is this one any different?"

"He's a furniture maker."

Edwina looked up. "He's a what?"

"A furniture maker." Jackie smiled. She loved to stick pins in her mother's balloon of conventional notions. "He makes all kinds of furniture."

"You mean he's a manufacturer?"

"I guess you could say that. But he doesn't use machines–only old-fashioned tools, like they've used in Britain for centuries."

Hanna returned with Edwina's plate and set it down before her. She poked at it with her knife and, satisfied that it was done enough, dismissed her. "So this is a hobby of his?"

"Oh, no," Jackie said. "He's deadly earnest. It's all part of the Arts and Crafts movement in England. He believes that machines have dehumanized the worker and that craftsmanship has all but disappeared. It's a revival of sorts."

Edwina cut into her beef, lifted a small morsel to her mouth, chewed, swallowed, and chased it down with a sip of wine. "It sounds as if Lucinda has finally succeeded in ferreting out every crackpot in England. I thought she had reached the limit of extremes when she took up with that sword-swallower in Kensington."

"He wasn't a sword-swallower. He was a juggler. And quite good at it, too."

Her mother sighed. "At least the sword-swallower presented the possibility of mortally wounding himself. You know I had my doubts about sending you to live with your aunt, Jacqueline. But after all, she is your aunt and I did so want you to have something on the order of the Grand Tour, like

I had. Did you do nothing but sit in your aunt's parlor and observe the parade of charlatans and lunatics?"

"I did go on a tour of the Continent shortly after I arrived in London. Rome, Venice, Athens, and parts of Germany. But I got bored with all the museums and gondola rides and crumbling ruins, so I returned to London where Aunt Lucy encouraged me to audition for one of her plays."

"Yes, well, that is one thing Lucinda is good at. And it seems that you have a talent for it as well. But it's no pursuit for a respectable young woman like yourself to more than dabble at."

"Isn't Aunt Lucinda respectable?"

"Barely. Like me, she came from a good family. But she has insisted ever since we were children on running in the opposite direction every time a sensible opportunity presented itself. I do hope that you won't follow her into that kind of life. Besides, she has a tidy income from her half ownership in Lynwood. You may be an old woman before you inherit our half–that is, your father's and mine's–of the estate. In the meantime you need a more secure income than you're likely to find in the theater."

Jackie looked down at her plate. "You mean that I must marry a prosperous merchant"–she looked up and smiled–"or a banker, perhaps."

Her mother put down her knife and fork and patted her lips with a napkin. "Yes. Something along those lines. Mansfield, don't we know some young man of eligible age? What about Ravenel Coleman's boy? He's quite nice-looking, I'm told, though I haven't seen him since he was a child."

Mansfield signaled Hanna who had just returned to the dining room, and indicated that he could do with another glass of wine. "Yes, he is a handsome lad, and he's already managing one of his father's plantations on Edisto Island."

"Do you hear that, Jacqueline," her mother said. "Handsome, rich–and only a short boat ride away. Perhaps your father could arrange a tête-à-tête."

Jackie looked down again at her plate and said nothing.

Her mother stared at her for a moment. "We don't want to push you, my dear. But perhaps we could invite young–what's his name, Mansfield?"

"Octavius."

"Octavius? Surely people don't go around calling him 'Octavius,' do they?"

"He goes by Tavi," Mansfield said.

"Oh, I see–Ravi and Tavi," Edwina said. "That's rather charming. Well, let's do invite him. Jacqueline, dear, you've hardly touched your supper. Would you like some lemon meringue pie? Louise baked it just this afternoon."

"No thank you, Mother. I'm rather tired. The audition was exhausting." She stood and put her napkin down. "If you'll excuse me, I think I'll go to my room and read for a little while before turning in."

After she had gone, Edwina addressed her husband. "Perhaps I broached the subject too quickly, Mansfield. The poor girl must have some time to readjust to country life after being dazzled by the carnival world of her aunt in London. Hanna–take a piece of that pie up to her after she's had a chance to undress and settle into her nightclothes. She'll be hungry by then."

"Yes, ma'am." Hanna collected the plates and returned to the kitchen.

CHAPTER 11

Tony was not optimistic that the old mill on the Combahee River could be salvaged. At least not to the extent that it could again mine enough phosphate to provide a living for the half a dozen or so freedmen who now owned the property.

Nevertheless, he agreed to ride out and take a look at it. Jessie Sams, one of the principles of the Beaufort Phosphate Mining Company, accompanied him.

"Ain't much left of the dock," Sams said, as they approached the mill. "But the mill is like a fortress–tabby walls two-foot thick. A little water on the floor is all."

They dismounted from their horses and walked around the 'yard,' which was a sea of mud and debris left behind by the receding waters of the storm surge. There were planks torn loose from the dock, broken furniture, oil cans, buckets, burlap sacks, and an uncountable number of loose pages, presumably from the company ledger. Tony picked up one of these pages in the vain hope that it would reveal something of the company's financial condition before the storm hit, but only a few numbers were decipherable in the smeared ink. "You say that the company was operating at a profit at the time of the hurricane?"

"That's right, Mr. Jones." Sams seemed a bit nervous.

"Can you remember the numbers?"

"Well..." Sams rubbed his chin. He was a large man with a broad back, accustomed to heavy labor from early childhood. Since Emancipation, however, he had been a businessman and his girth had increased accordingly. "I reckon we had a profit of thirty-five thousand dollars for the first six months of the year."

Tony's eyebrows arched. "As much as that? What happened to it?"

Sams wiped his brow with a handkerchief. It was hot and humid, even though it was well into October. "Most of it went to back wages for the diggers and crushers. It be hard work, you know that. The rest went to new equipment and machinery. But that's tied up on the docks in Savannah. They say it'll be six more weeks before they repair the boats so they can ship 'em."

Tony dropped the wet ledger page in the mud. "So all you need is that new equipment and you are in business again?"

Sams followed Tony around the side of the mill to where all that remained of the dock were pilings jutting up out of the water. "That's about the size of it. In the meantime, we got to repair this dock, pull that crane out of the water along with them pulleys and cables, shore up the rails that carry the dolly and...well, you can pretty much see what's got to be done. And we got to pay the workers."

Tony stood on a plank that was still attached to two pilings and peered into the water. "What about the phosphate? I've heard that most of it washed away, down river."

"That's just the loose stuff. There's still plenty beneath the river bed."

They went around to the front door of the mill, or the landward side, and Tony tested the heavy oak door. It was stuck.

"Here," Sams said. "I'll get her open. Just some mud backed up behind it." He put his shoulder to the door and pushed it open.

There was enough light in the main room that they didn't need a lantern. The light streamed in through two barred windows about twenty feet off the floor.

They stepped inside and Tony looked around. Debris strewn around, much like in the yard, but the walls, as Sams said, were sturdy and undamaged. There was a curious piece of furniture that caught Tony's eye on the far wall. It was a wooden plank jutting out from the wall and secured by chains at either end, like a bunk bed that folds down on a ship.

"What's that for? Naps?"

Sams laughed heartily. "Old man Benson used to lock up his slaves here before the war. The ones that give him trouble. Maybe he didn't want 'em to catch cold sleeping on the floor, so's they could go back to work when they done they time."

Tony walked over to the plank and tested its stability. Assured of this, he sat down on it. He looked around the room again, then up at the window high above his head. "Looks like somebody cut through those bars. You think maybe one of those slaves escaped?"

Sams chuckled. "They all kinds of stories. I like the one about Miss Rinaldi."

"Miss Rinaldi? That's a funny name for a slave."

"That weren't her real name. They say she escaped twice–once with the blessings of Mr. Benson's daddy, and once from this place, when Mr. Benson done caught her again. But she was too smart for him."

Tony smiled. "Seems she was. What happened to her?"

"They say she made it all the way to New York and became an actress."

"You don't say." Tony brushed some of the dirt from the plank. "That's quite a story. What's this?" He looked down at one corner of the plank and saw several lines of text carved into it. "A message? A call for help, maybe?"

"Message?" Sams stepped closer to look. "Just some whittlin', I reckon."

Tony took a penknife from his vest pocket and scraped the grime out of the gouges in the wood. "It's...it's like a poem."

"A poem?"

Tony finished scraping with the penknife and squinted at the words. He read them aloud:

Here lies in chains poor Cora Rinaldi
Who rose from slave to queen with
astonishing ease
But now shares her cold porridge
with Baldy
Who, as a rodent, is partial to cheese.

Both men laughed.

"That was her, all right," Sams said. "Lawdy! What a woman she must have been!"

Tony folded up his penknife and put it back into his vest pocket. "And with a sense of humor, too." He stood. "I'll tell you what, Jessie. I have a feeling that your phosphate business is doomed, but what about transforming this place into a saw mill?"

"A saw mill?"

"Sure. You've got a hundred acres or so, maybe eighty of it with good hardwoods. I noticed some pine, too, on the way in. The market's good for cut lumber now, and the equipment you'll need is far less expensive than phosphate machinery."

"What about them crates sittin' on the dock in Savannah?"

"Cancel the order."

"I cain't do that, Mr. Jones. I already paid them a thousand dollars, and–"

"That's just a deposit. You can tell them that the delay is intolerable. In fact, that should be in the contract. And they'll have to return your deposit."

"What if they don't?"

"Then it'll be a small fraction of what you'll have to spend on the saw mill equipment. It'll be worth it."

Sams rubbed his massive chin again. "I don't know, Mr. Jones–"

Tony clapped him on the shoulder. "Trust me, Jessie. If you take delivery on that phosphate machinery, you'll be bankrupt in another six months. Start cutting and sawing lumber and you and your partners will be rich by next summer."

"I don't know nothing about the lumber business."

"You learned the phosphate business, didn't you? That's got to be more complicated."

"Well, I dunno..."

"Think about it, Jessie. Talk to your partners about it. In the meantime, I've got to get back for another appointment."

The two men lingered in the yard for a few minutes, where Jessie asked Tony some more questions about the lumber business. Of course, Tony knew even less than Jessie did, but he knew the phosphate business, in South Carolina at least, was unlikely to be resuscitated. Lumber, though! Why, half the city of Beaufort was in the process of being rebuilt, not to mention all the towns along the coast from Savannah to Charleston.

After Jessie had gone, Tony remained for a few moments to examine the mill. What a curious tale of that escaped slave! It suddenly made him proud to be a member of the African race, a feeling he hadn't had since he returned to Beaufort.

He gazed downstream to the next visible structure on this side of the river, and realized it was the family seat of the old Benson plantation. Now it was the home of the LeRoux.

He decided to take the long route back to Beaufort, the one that passed by Lynwood.

CHAPTER 12

Jackie sat uncomfortably on the wicker swing as it moved gently back and forth on the veranda.

There was a light breeze coming up from the river and there was no reason that she should have been uncomfortable–other than the fact that Octavius Coleman was sitting beside her and seemed to have forgotten how to speak.

She tried to help him. "Tavi–may I call you Tavi?"

"Oh...well...of course," Tavi said.

"Good. You may call me Jackie."

Tavi looked askance at her without moving his head. "Yes. All right–Jackie."

"Tavi, you must tell me what things are like on Edisto Island."

Tavi tugged at his starched collar as if that had been the only impediment to forcing the words out. "There's not much to tell, really. Lots of darkies to keep in line, but the overseers are pretty good at that. I spend most of my time in the office trying to balance the books."

"I see. Well, you can't spend all of your time balancing books. What do you do in the evenings for entertainment?"

"Entertainment? Oh, I read mostly. Not much else to do."

"What do you read?"

Suddenly Tavi became animated. "History. And an occasional novel, but mostly history."

"What sort of history?" Jackie's questions were becoming automatic, as if they issued from a gramophone.

"Military history." Tavi shifted his position slightly so that for the first time since they sat down, he was nearly facing her. "Did you know that the Chinese were the first to discover gunpowder?"

"Gunpowder? No. No, I didn't know that."

"Well, it's true. They were fiendishly clever. And they even used it to launch rockets against their enemies."

"Did they? That was clever of them, wasn't it?"

"Oh, yes. They were far ahead of their times. Or our times, I should say. While they were bombarding castles with rockets, our ancestors were still flinging rocks at each other."

Jackie struggled to appear interested. "That's quite amazing. But tell me, Tavi, there must be something more to do on Edisto Island than reading books about military history."

Tavi turned his knees back to their original position. "I'm afraid that I'm boring you."

"Oh, not at all! It's just that–well, I'm not terribly interested in military history, and I'm...I suppose I'm curious about your island. I've never been there."

Tavi brightened. "Would you like to go? You know, there's actually lots to do. I forgot to mention that I usually go for a ride on the beach before supper. Sometimes Father comes down from Charleston and brings a lady friend with him. Perhaps you'd like to join us. It would be great fun!"

Jackie was about to say that she enjoyed riding and would love to splash through the surf on a spirited horse, something she seldom had the opportunity to do in Beaufort, but she decided she didn't want to encourage Tavi. "I'm afraid I'm not a very good rider. I might break my neck trying to keep up."

"Nonsense! You're an expert horsewoman." This was the voice of her mother, who seemed to feel that from her listening post behind the curtains in the parlor that things weren't going as planned. "Jackie's just being modest, Tavi. Why, she's broken wild horses on Hunting Island! Why don't you children come inside and have some ice cream? The sun's going down and the no see'ums will be out soon."

Tavi had quickly risen from the swing as soon as Edwina appeared, and Jackie was relieved that she had been saved from any further discourses into military history.

"That would be delightful, Mrs. LeRoux," Tavi said.

Jackie stood and folded her hands in front of her. "That's an excellent idea, Mother. Perhaps Father can join us."

"Oh, he's retired to the library, as usual," Edwina said. "But he'll join us for supper. And he suggested that you and Tavi might enjoy a game of billiards afterwards."

"Billiards?" Tavi said. "I used to play with Father in Charleston whenever he was in town. I'd like to order a table for the house on Edisto."

Edwina winked at him in a conspicuous way. "You'd need to get back into practice Tavi, dear, if you expect to beat Jacqueline. Her father absolutely refused to play with her anymore after losing six consecutive games to her when she was twelve."

Jackie blushed and glanced at Tavi. "Mother, that's not true. Father gave up after only three games. And he'd had a bit too much to drink that night."

"Three, six," Edwina said, opening the French doors to the parlor. "What does it matter? Come along, children–Louise has made some peach cobbler to go with the ice cream. Just make sure that you save room for supper. Goodness! I shouldn't be encouraging you to eat your desert first."

After supper Edwina and Mansfield discreetly excused themselves to pursue their respective pastimes in the library (Mansfield to compile his history of the LeRoux family and Edwina to do her needlework), Jackie and Tavi found themselves in the billiard room with little to say to each other. Tavi, however, somewhat emboldened by the wine he had drunk at supper, made an effort to break the ice.

"I wonder at your courage in traveling alone about the continent of Europe," he said, chalking his cue.

Jackie waited until he took his shot. "I wasn't alone the whole time. I had letters of introduction to acquaintances of my aunt in every city I visited."

Tavi missed his attempt to put a ball in the side pocket. "Your aunt must be quite famous in Europe."

Jackie took aim at the seven ball and saw it drop gently into a corner pocket. "Not exactly famous. But she is well known in theatrical circles." She watched the cue ball ricochet from the rail and settle behind the nine ball. She dropped the nine in the same corner pocket and chalked her cue before setting up for the next shot.

Tavi leaned on his cue thoughtfully "I suspect you must have had some quite exciting adventures."

"Actually, it became rather tiresome after a while." Jackie banked the cue ball off of the side rail and saw it nudge the five into the pocket on the opposite side. "Of course I enjoyed the operas and plays in the evenings, but the sightseeing in the daytime became such a bore. Eight ball in the corner pocket." She sank the ball and chalked her cue. "Are you keen on another game?"

Tavi, still leaning on his cue, blinked as if he had just awakened from a dream. "Oh–my word. You've just won, haven't you? Certainly, we'll play another. I'll be sure to concentrate this time."

Tavi's efforts at concentration were to no avail, and he lost the next two games.

"Another?" Jackie said, pertly.

Tavi stared stupidly at the table, which contained all of his balls in addition to the cue ball, but none of Jackie's. "Well, I don't much see the point. You just ran the table again."

Jackie felt somewhat embarrassed. She hadn't meant to humble her opponent, especially since he was her guest. "Oh–well, I do get lucky sometimes. Perhaps you'd rather do something else."

Tavi considered this offer. "Why don't we stroll in the garden? It's a nice night out."

"All right."

They came downstairs and passed by the library where the door was open and Edwina noted their passing with a smile of approval. Emerging through the French doors onto the terrace, they both looked up at the stars, which were particularly bright on this clear night.

"Do you go in for astronomy?" Tavi asked.

"Only insofar as the stars make a pretty tableau," Jackie said. "I suppose I'm more interested in the aesthetics of it than the scientific aspect."

"Well, yes, I see what you mean. It is beautiful, isn't it?"

"Yes. And the same everywhere. Do you want to sit down?"

"Ah, no," Tavi said. "Why don't we stroll out to the dock instead? I think your family's yacht is quite magnificent."

"The *Southern Pride?* That was my Uncle Edward's doing. It was a Yankee gunboat during the war that sank in the Coosaw River, I'm told. He refloated it and converted it into a luxury yacht. I'm afraid it's little used, though. My mother thinks she'll get too much sun and it'll ruin her complexion."

They walked down the grand staircase to the terrace and strolled through the garden to the dock. Torches illuminated the footpath and continued onto the dock. The *Southern Pride* was secured at the end, while Tavi's little runabout was tied up just behind it.

Jackie took him on a tour of the yacht and then they sat in a couple of deck chairs on the stern.

"Your uncle did a magnificent job of refurbishing the gunboat," Tavi said. "Was he in the war?"

"Oh, yes," Jackie said. "Nearly all of the men of that generation were. Uncle Edward, though, had a particularly hard time of it."

"Did he? What happened to him?"

Jackie sighed. She didn't really want the conversation to go in this direction, though she was glad Tavi had loosened up enough to be somewhat more sociable. "He was in a Union prisoner-of-war camp in Maryland, I think it was. At the end of the war he returned to Lynwood, but much of it had been sold off to the freedmen and he spent the next several years trying to get it back."

"That was a tragedy, wasn't it?" Tavi's tone rose almost to the level of anger. "It wasn't fair–the Yankees stole my father's property, too, but like your uncle, he managed to get most of it back. Thank heaven for President Johnson! He put an end to that sort of thievery, and President Hayes, even though he was a Yankee, cleared the way for people like my father to regain control of the legislature. It seems that things are back on track again."

Jackie was a bit startled by this outburst. She wasn't sure what she had said to provoke it.

"What happened to him?" Tavi said.

"Who?"

"Your uncle."

"Oh..." Jackie was reluctant to answer this question for fear of setting Tavi off onto another rant. "He was...murdered."

Tavi turned to her in astonishment. "Murdered? By whom?"

"By one of his sharecroppers."

Tavi's eyes bulged out of their sockets like vitreous globes emerging from a steaming cauldron. "A black man?"

"Yes."

"Why, I hope they strung him up from the nearest tree!"

"I'm afraid not." Jackie now found herself taking a perverse pleasure in having roused Tavi from his torpid demeanor. "There was a trial and the black man–Francis was his name–was acquitted."

Tavi suddenly leapt up from his chair. "Acquitted!" He began pacing around in a circle. Then he stopped and stared into Jackie's eyes in a way that he had been afraid to before. "How could a white jury acquit a black man of murdering his master?"

"I don't think it was an all-white jury. Anyway, it was a military court. They found that Francis acted in self-defense."

"Self-defense? Impossible! Thank God Reconstruction is over! Now we can keep those savages in their proper place. I'd put mine in cages at night if the law would allow it."

"Mr. Coleman–is you all right?" Jackie and Tavi both turned to the sound of the voice coming from the launch. In the moonlight they could see a round black face with the gleaming whites of his eyes peering out of the door to the cabin.

"Oh–it's you, Akiti." Tavi composed himself and sat down again in the deck chair. "Yes, it's all right. Miss LeRoux and I–we were just play acting. Where's Ibrahimi?"

"He be sound asleep, Mr. Coleman. You want anything?"

"No, no. It's all right, Akiti. Go back to sleep."

"Yes, suh. You just call out if you need anything."

Akiti retreated to the cabin and closed the tambour hatch behind him.

Jackie stared at the hatch for a moment. "Akiti? Ibrahimi?"

Tavi sighed. "Many of the darkies on Edisto still have their African names. Just goes to show you that I was right about their still being savages."

Jackie tried to suppress a smile. "Aren't you afraid they'll murder you on the way back to the island?"

"Akiti and Ibrahimi? No, no. They're civilized enough. Loyal servants. I never worry about them."

Tavi seemed to fall back into his phlegmatic humor and again found it difficult to initiate conversation.

After a few minutes of utter silence, Jackie put her hand to her mouth and yawned.

"Oh," Tavi said. "Am I keeping you up?"

"Well, I do have a busy day tomorrow. Mother said you were staying the night. Perhaps we'd better make our way back to the house." She stood.

Tavi stood as well. "I'm afraid I've got a busy day tomorrow, too. I'd better wake the boys and head back to Edisto. I've had a delightful evening. May I see you again?"

"Well...of course. You're always welcome at Lynwood–as is your father."

"My father? Of course–I sometimes forget that he and your father were school mates before the war." Another awkward pause ensued, during which Tavi seemed to be trying to force words out of his mouth.

"Yes?" Jackie said, dreading the inevitable.

"Would you...would you mind if I kissed you?"

"That's very sweet of you, Tavi." She turned her cheek towards him.

Tavi hesitated, then planted a kiss on her cheek.

"That was very nice, Tavi," Jackie said. "Are you sure you won't stay the night? My parents were expecting you to."

"Well, no, as I was saying, there's much to be done at the plantation tomorrow. Besides I didn't bring a proper change of clothes with me. You will explain to your parents won't you?"

"Of course."

"I–I suppose I should escort you back to the house."

"Oh, don't bother. The path is well-lit."

"It is, isn't it?" Tavi turned his head towards the launch. "Akiti! Ibrahimi! Wake up! We're returning to the island."

Jackie folded her hands and watched as Tavi climbed into the stern of the boat and Akiti once again appeared in the hatchway. Then Ibrahimi emerged and leapt onto the dock to loosen the lines.

She waved as the boat pulled away from the dock while Tavi stood in the stern with a nervous grin on his face and waved back.

CHAPTER 13

Georgia walked into the dining room after a particularly trying day at the Penn School only to find Tony sitting on a stool with a paint brush in one hand and a palette in the other. He was wearing a white smock and seemed to have gotten more paint on it than on...the wall.

"Tony!" she said. "What are you doing to the wall?"

Tony did not turn around at her voice, but remained intent on his work. "I am brightening up this rather dark and cheerless dining room. It will appear larger as well."

Georgia, breathless, sat down on one of the dining room chairs and stared at the wall. "Why it looks like an entry to a lovely garden. As if one could step right through it!"

"Exactly," Tony said. "It's called 'trompe l'oeil.' It's quite popular in Paris these days, though the technique has been around for ages. I earned enough at it to pay for my passage home."

Georgia watched him paint for a while. "This is what you really want, isn't it?"

"I suppose it is. I like the work at the bank, but numbers and ledgers have no soul, no life of their own. A painting, even something as pedestrian as this, almost breathes. It connects us to the natural world–and to ourselves."

"That's a beautiful way of putting it." Georgia leaned back in her chair and slowly exhaled. "I can feel myself drawn into your imaginary garden. Tony..."

"Yes?"

"Must you go back to Paris to paint? Can't you do that right here? After all, Paris is full of artists and they're all painting the same thing. That new tower they have–"

"The Eiffel Tower."

"Yes, that one. The cafe scenes, the Luxembourg Gardens, the Arc de

Triompe, and...each other. Why, there's so much natural beauty here and no one's painting it."

Tony put down his brush and stood up from his stool to examine his work. "That's true, I suppose. And it occurs to me now that the garden I've created here is a corner of the Luxembourg that I used to frequent." He sighed and turned to her. "Not very original, is it?"

"Oh, I think it's lovely! I've never been to the Luxembourg Gardens and neither has just about anyone else around here. How would we know?"

Tony looked at his handiwork again. "I think I'll eliminate the statuary at the 'entrance' to the garden."

"Don't you dare! It's perfect just as it is!"

Tony smiled. "All right. If you think it's perfect, it's perfect. What's for supper?"

"Anything you like. But I'll need a hot bath first. The children were particularly boisterous today."

Tony went over to his mother and kissed her on the cheek. "Why don't you do that–and take your time. I'll cook dinner tonight."

"You? Since when did you learn to cook?"

"Since I attended cooking classes in Paris. I was advised by one of my colleagues that it was a good way to meet women."

"And did you?"

"Did I what?"

"Meet women."

Tony laughed. "A few. That's where I met Marie."

"Marie?"

"The one who asked me to dinner with her parents."

"Oh. Well, I don't intend to inquire into your personal life while you were there. Now for that hot bath. Every muscle aches!"

After Georgia had her bath, she tried to help in the kitchen, but Tony would not allow it except to ask where certain items were. So Georgia sat in the living room reading, occasionally raising her head when an unfamiliar smell reached her nostrils. Oregano, basil? Where was Tony getting all these spices?

Finally, they sat down to supper.

"Bouillabaise à la Jones!" Tony said. "Oh, I forgot to light the candles." He got up, found some matches and lit the candles

"It smells wonderful," Georgia said, putting her nose close to her plate and savoring the aromas.

"Where did you get the saffron?"

Tony poured some wine. "Mr. Cooper's store. He seems to have everything. A very resourceful man. Bon appétit!"

They ate in silence for several minutes.

"By the way, Tony," Georgia said, "did you ever find out what's happened to Violet?"

"Violet? Oh, yes. I saw her mother at the Emporium. She says Violet has moved to Orangeburg."

"Orangeburg? That's not so far away. Perhaps you could–"

Tony took a swallow of his wine and put his glass down. "Mama, it's no use you match-making. I'll have to find a girl through my own devices."

"I don't mean to interfere, Tony–I know a mother can't push her son into a relationship he doesn't want. I just think that Violet is such a nice girl."

Tony laughed. "And just right for me. Let's see–she's black like me, she's smart, she's well-educated, and she's pretty. I must admit she has nearly all the qualities I'm looking for. Except one."

"Which one is that?"

"I don't have any requirements in regard to race."

Georgia frowned. "I never said you had to marry a girl who was black."

"No, but you implied it. Mama, I hardly knew any black girls in Paris. The French are color-blind."

"You said that one girl snubbed you because you were black."

"That's not what I said. She didn't snub me because I was black. I snubbed her because she patronized me in front of her parents."

"Still, I'm sure that racism was at the bottom of it."

Tony stared at her for a few moments. "Mama–you're more race-conscious than I am."

Georgia sighed and looked down at her plate. "I can't help it, Tony. You've been insulated from racism here on St. Helena and even in Paris. But I grew up in the days of slavery and I saw the struggles your father had even though he passed for white. And things are getting worse now that the Democrats have succeeded in passing these so-called Jim Crow laws. I don't want you to get hurt."

Tony considered this. "What if I did marry a white girl? Beaufort is different than the rest of the South. It's different from Boston, for that matter."

"Perhaps. But we don't have the Federal army here anymore to protect us."

"No, but we do have the sheriff who is an ally of Mr. Smalls, and Mr. Smalls himself who wields a great deal of influence over the community's leaders."

Georgia looked skeptical. "They can only do so much to protect us. And Mr. Smalls is not so young anymore. Or influential."

"Well...I'll take my chances."

Georgia finished her wine and set the glass down. "Tony..."

"Yes, Mama?"

"I hope you're not thinking of that Benson girl again."

"Benson girl? You mean Jackie–she's a LeRoux."

"Benson, LeRoux–it's the same family. It could never work."

Tony put his utensils down on his plate with a clatter. "There you go again–assuming I'm all in love with Jackie LeRoux. Mama, I've hardly spoken to the girl more than once or twice. And what if I did ask her to dinner some day? Would that be so earth-shaking?"

"No, not earth-shaking. I suppose you must be civil to her."

Tony laughed. "You speak as if our families have been at feud with one another for centuries. What have the LeRoux, or the Bensons, ever done to us?"

Georgia pushed her plate away. "It's not so much what they've done to us, as what we've done to them."

"What we've done to them? Mama, you've never told me the whole story. Just that Edward Benson was a unrepenant slave-owner. What did we do to them?"

"Well...it's not that we–or I–did anything to them. But Edwina and her husband think that I was responsible for her brother's death."

Tony stared at her as if she were a sphinx. "Mama–I'm not Sherlock Holmes. You've been dropping clues about the Bensons and the LeRoux ever since I returned from Paris. Can't you just tell me the whole story?"

Georgia stood and began collecting the plates. "That was a wonderful meal, Tony. I have some strawberry tarts in the pantry. Why don't we have those for dessert?"

"Mama–*were* you responsible for Edward Benson's death? What happened?"

Georgia started for the kitchen. "Why don't you go to your father's study and pour us each a glass of sherry? I'll join you there."

Tony watched as his mother disappeared into the kitchen. Then he rose from the table and went to the sideboard.

As he poured the sherry, Georgia called from the kitchen. "Tony..."

"Yes, Mama?"

"Who is Sherlock Holmes?"

CHAPTER 14

It was a bright and sunny morning, a bit of fall chill in the air, and Tony walked from the Whitehall landing to the Beaufort Inn for breakfast. This was becoming a ritual, as his mother was always in a rush to get to the Penn School in the morning and had no time for a leisurely breakfast. And Tony liked a leisurely breakfast. After all, he was a banker now, and the bank didn't open until nine o'clock.

He felt that his mother's story about Edward Benson was rather anticlimactic. She only felt responsible because Benson provoked his father into a duel out of jealousy over her, and then proceeded to get himself shot by one of his tenants after his father fired his pistol into the air. The most surprising thing was that his father had once fought a duel!

He sat by a bay window that looked onto Craven Street where he could watch the traffic, both pedestrian and vehicular.

He opened the pages of *The New South* as he waited for his breakfast and perused the news, which was mainly local. He would have to remember to stop by the Emporium after work and pick up a copy of *The New York Herald* for national and international news.

Mr. Smalls seemed to be as active as ever in local politics. Though no longer a congressman or state legislator, he was the de facto leader of the Republican Party in Beaufort and was gathering delegates for the upcoming Constitutional Convention in Columbia. It seemed that the old constitution of '68 was anathema to the now-ruling Democratic Party and the new constitution urged by Governor Tillman would be designed to remove as many blacks from the voting rolls as possible.

One step forward, one step backward. Beaufort seemed to be moving ahead while the rest of the state was determined to move in the opposite direction. Would he, as a bank president, be denied the right to vote if the new constitution were approved?

As Carrie, the waitress, set his Spanish omelet down before him, he put the paper aside.

"Thank you, Carrie. What do you think of this talk about a new constitution?"

Carrie, who was a dark-skinned woman of about his mother's age, frowned. "I don't think there's any good that can come of it, Mr. Jones. Ever since Governor Hampton came into office, we colored folks have been losing one right after another. I was up in Charleston recently visiting my daughter and we got turned out of a restaurant because we were black. In the old days, right after the war, we could go anywhere we wanted."

"Hmm. Are you married, Carrie?"

"Yes, sir."

"And did your husband vote in the last election?"

"No, sir."

"Why not?"

"He flunked the literacy test. And he can read and write as well as you or me."

Tony examined Carrie more closely. She was rather pretty, though a bit overweight, and had long braided hair pulled back into a knot. He wondered at her elocution. "Where did you learn to read and write, Carrie?"

"Oh–the Penn School. I only got through eighth grade, but Miss Towne made sure we knew our letters by that time."

Tony chuckled. "I know she did. I was one of her students, too."

"I would have graduated, but my family needed me to help in the fields."

"Well, you certainly took advantage of your opportunities. What does your husband do?"

"He's got a blacksmith shop over on Carteret. But he says smithies are a relic of the past. He's thinking of opening a repair shop for bicycles and motorcars."

Tony laughed. "Well, I'd advise him to hold off on that a bit. There're still plenty of horses that need to be shod, and carriages to be repaired. I don't think I've seen a single motorcar since I've been in Beaufort."

"Oh, there're two or three rich folks that have them. But he won't give up on the smithy right away. Can I get you anything else, Mr. Jones?"

"Another cup of coffee perhaps."

"I'll be right back."

Tony cut into his omelet, took a bite, and opened the pages of *The New South* again. He skimmed a couple of articles about Beaufort's rapid recovery from the hurricane and then turned to the entertainment page–a habit he developed in Paris, while reading *Le Figaro*, but there was little here that could be described as 'entertainment,' much less 'the Arts.' However, there was an announcement that caught his eye:

The Second Mrs. Tanqueray will have its Beaufort premiere Friday evening at 8pm at The Beaufort Players' new home on Craven Street. The cast is as follows:

Paula Tanqueray–Kate Williamson
Aubrey Tanqueray–Eliot Nichols
Ellean Tanqueray–Jacqueline LeRoux

He read no further. So Jacqueline LeRoux was to appear on the stage Friday night! He had been wondering how he might approach her ever since that day she walked into the bank to cash her check. He could not call on her at Lynwood, obviously. Nor could he approach her in the street; even the more enlightened denizens of Beaufort would likely construe this as an impertinence, if not an assault. But a play was open to all! He had never been a stage-door Johnny, but it was a perfect ruse. He would be an ardent admirer–which in fact he was.

He folded up the paper and put it under his arm as he rose from the table. He paused to watch a motorcar pass by at nearly fifteen miles per hour. No doubt there would soon be signs posted all around Beaufort limiting the speed of these contraptions to five miles per hour or so. Progress!

CHAPTER 15

The Bannister House was once owned by a Revolutionary War hero named Colonel Nathaniel Bannister, who served as an adjutant under George Washington. He was rewarded for his service with a grant of land on Lady's Island that stretched from The Beaufort River on the south end of the island to the Coosaw on the north. He was said to have owned more than a thousand slaves.

Though the plantation on Lady's Island was broken up over the years and devolved to his numerous progeny and their children, the elegant town house remained the domicile of the scions of the family until the 'Big Shoot' of 1861, when the Union Navy entered Port Royal Sound and the slave owners abandoned their town homes as well as their plantations and their slaves.

When the Beaufort Players signed an agreement to stage plays there for the fall and winter seasons, they did so with the understanding that there would be no permanent alterations to the structure of the dwelling.

Thus, the stage was the home's spacious parlor, and the actors' dressing room was the Bannisters' dining room.

Jacqueline LeRoux sat before a large, gilt, rococo mirror that had lost some of its silver backing over the past two centuries. There was much she liked about the house, but it wasn't well-suited for theatrical performances. Other actors stood behind her, craning their necks to see if their cravats were straight, their make-up adequate, or their false beards groomed. She worried that the fact that she was the only blond in the cast, male or female, that she would appear to be upstaging the other actors. It seemed to her that her gleaming hair was like a beacon from a light house in a befogged harbor.

"Absolutely beautiful, Miss LeRoux. You'll have all the men panting with their tongues hanging out." It was Mr. Oliver standing behind her and addressing her reflection in the mirror.

"I certainly hope not, Mr. Oliver," she said "Mrs. Williamson is the focus of the plot. I should be a supporting character, not a distraction."

"Men come to the theater to see beautiful women, Miss LeRoux. Not matronly types."

She turned around and looked at him, then at Mrs. Williamson, who was adjusting the hem of her dress. She seemed not to have heard Mr. Oliver's comment. "Mrs. Williamson is hardly a 'matronly type.' She's only thirty-seven."

Mr. Oliver shrugged. "The script says twenty-seven. But she's been married twice already. And is rather plump. 'Matronly' is a fair description."

Jackie turned back to the mirror and adjusted a barrette in her hair. "You're the director."

"Yes," Mr. Oliver said. He bent down and kissed her on the neck. Jackie started. "And I know a thing or two about casting. Curtain in five minutes, everyone! Places!"

Jackie looked around to see if anyone had been watching when Mr. Oliver kissed her on the neck. They had. The actor playing Aubrey Tanqueray quickly turned away, and Mrs. Williamson did as well. She blushed with embarrassment.

Her character, Ellean, did not appear until the second act. As the other actors rushed into the parlor to take their places behind the curtain (they were all men in this scene) Jackie tiptoed through the butler's pantry to get a peek at the audience. She was aghast at the crowded room, with an equal number of men and women seated in the chairs but mostly men standing at the back, some on the spiraling staircase leading up to the second floor. From that vantage point they could actually look down on the actors and, she presumed, into her décolletage.

"They're all here to see you, Jacqueline, dear."

Jackie turned to see Kate Williamson, the 'matronly' actress playing Mrs. Tanqueray, looking over her shoulder.

"I hardly think so, Kate," Jackie said, again surveying the crowd. "Your're the star, after all."

"'I'm not naive, dear," Kate said. "I'm supposed to be over-the-hill, and that's why Mr. Oliver cast me. You should have heard the comments that I heard at the Tillman's the other night."

"The Tillman's?"

"Yes. The governor. In Columbia. His wife is a terrible social climber, but she throws marvelous parties!"

Jackie continued to peer at the audience.

"Oh, look," Kate said. "There's Ravenel Coleman–he was there. You should have heard his rapturous praise of your virtues! I think he's brought half the eligible men in Columbia with him."

"And he's brought his son, too."

"His son?" Kate said. "I don't think his son was there. Which one is he?"

Jackie pointed him out.

"Oh," Kate said. "He's not nearly as tall as his father. I can hardly see him...oh, yes. There's a likeness. But he's not as handsome as his father, either."

Jackie had to agree with Kate on that score. Tavi seemed to be absolutely shrinking behind his father, who was a commanding figure in any crowd. And she was somewhat afraid of Rav, though she felt she shouldn't be.

As the lights dimmed and the curtain went up, her eyes ascended the staircase and she suddenly saw Tony, whose skin looked to be the same color as the others in the darkening shadows. But the footlights reflected softly off of his fine features so that he bore a resemblance to some of the Greek statues that she saw in Athens. An Alexander, an Adonis!

"I'd better get back to the dining room," Kate said. "I go on at the end of this scene."

After Kate left, Jackie continued to observe Tony. He had a quiet dignity about him, a reserve that concealed a complex personality. How absurd it was of her parents to bar him from their door simply because of the color–the shading–of his skin! And Tavi–to whom blacks were savage beasts fit only to toil by day and be caged at night to suppress their violent impulses.

"Miss LeRoux!" It was Mr. Oliver. "I've been looking for you all over the house. What have you done with that sprig of gorse?"

"That what?"

"The gorse. It has to be attached to your dress so that when Aubrey–"

"I know the line, Mr. Oliver. I don't need to walk about with a bouquet of moss pinned to my dress. I'll put it on before my cue."

"It's not moss–it's gorse. At least that's the way you should think of it."

"Shh!" a member of the audience said.

Jackie backed away from the door to the parlor and whispered. "I know gorse from moss, Mr. Oliver. Don't worry about it." She brushed by him and passed through the pantry to the dining room to wait for her cue.

The performance went smoothly, though many cast members struggled with their British accents, often lapsing into colloquial American pronunciations one minute then over compensating with an exaggerated Oxbridge accent the next. Only Jackie's accent seemed authentic and she moved around the stage with an ease that suggested she had always been at home in such an environment, as indeed she had–not only with her year-long tenure in London, but growing up at Lynwood where her mother, Edwina, insisted upon aping the manners and elocution of the British upper classes.

Although hers was a supporting role, she had the last, dramatic (some would say melodramatic) lines in the play:

But I know I helped to kill her.
If only I had been merciful!

whereupon she falls to the floor in a swoon. This nearly brought the house down with the men, especially, cheering and clapping loudly.

After taking her bows with the rest of the cast, she retreated to the dining room and sat before the mirror. Before she could remove the pins from her hair, she saw several men crowded at the door with bouquets of flowers in their hands. The one in the front was Ravenel Coleman; behind him was Tavi, and behind Tavi was Tony. There were still others behind them.

Ravenel stepped into the room. "You were absolutely magnificent, Jacqueline!"

Jackie glanced at Kate, who sat only a few feet away, looking somewhat disgruntled. After all, she had the leading role. "Thank you, Rav, but don't you think Mrs. Williamson was even more magnificent?"

Ravenel glanced at Mrs. Williamson, "Well, yes, of course. I mean that you were equally magnificent." He laughed rather awkwardly. "Kate and I are old friends, aren't we, Kate? But as a newcomer, Jackie, you've taken Beaufort by storm." He extended the bouquet to her as she turned around to face him. "I think one of these camellias would look lovely in your hair, not that you need any adornments to enhance your beauty."

Jackie accepted the camellias and put them in a vase on the table. "Thank you, Rav, but I've had enough vegetation attached to my person this evening. Perhaps I'll take up your suggestion in the morning when the sun will show it to its best advantage. Hello, Tavi."

Tavi was still obscured somewhat by his father's large frame. "Hello, Miss LeRoux. As father said, you were quite magnificent." He thrust a bouquet of lilies in her direction. "These came straight from Edisto. They seem to thrive in the sea air."

Jackie accepted the lilies as well and looked about for another vase. Finding none, she turned to Mrs. Williamson. "Perhaps there's another vase in the parlor."

"I'll see," Mrs. Williamson said. She went to the parlor, brushing by Tony in the process, who was standing with a bouquet of his own in his hands.

"Oh, Tony!" I didn't see you there. Goodness! We'll be awash in flowers. What kind are those?"

Tony stepped forward and offered the flowers. "They're roses. Painted roses."

"Painted?" Jackie accepted them and examined them carefully. "Why, they're lovely! I don't think I've ever seen painted roses before. What a clever idea!"

"It's become a rage in Paris lately," Tony said. "Do you like them?"

"Like them? I *love* them! So creative, so beautiful!"

Ravenel and Tavi looked at each other with obvious displeasure at this interloper.

Jackie noticed their discomfiture. "Oh, do sit down–all of you. But only for a minute or two–I have to change."

Ravenel regarded Tony again with a jaundiced eye and then addressed Jackie. "Tavi and I were hoping you would join us for a bit of supper after you've changed." He forced a laugh. "All those petticoats must be difficult to navigate through doorways."

"Yes, they *are* awkward. And hot. I'd be delighted to join you–and Tony, why don't you join us as well?"

Ravenel and Tavi looked at Tony, who suddenly seemed bereft of speech.

Jackie smiled at the tableau of three suitors staring at each other in impotent silence. "Why don't I meet you at the Beaufort Inn? You could all have a whiskey in the bar while you wait."

The three men continued to stare at each other for several moments. Finally, Ravenel spoke:

"Why not? Perhaps Mr..."

"Jones," Tony said.

"Mr. Jones. Perhaps Mr. Jones can bring us up to date on the state of the economy in Beaufort County." He laughed at this facetious suggestion.

"I'd say the economy here is fairly thriving since the storm passed through," Tony said. "We've made a record number of loans this month."

"Loans?" Ravenel said.

"Mr. Jones is the president of the Beaufort National Bank," Jackie said. "He should know."

Ravenel looked dumbfounded, as did Tavi.

"Well," Ravenel said, "then you're a good man to know. I have some agricultural concerns in this part of the state."

"I'm always receptive to the planters' needs," Tony said. "I'll be glad to talk about it, Mr.–"

"Coleman." Ravenel shook Tony's hand. "And this is my son, Octavius. He needs a new cotton gin at our Edisto plantation, he tells me. They're outrageously expensive these days."

Tony extended his hand to Tavi, who stared at it dumbly.

"Shake the man's hand, Tavi," Ravenel said.

"What? Oh, yes, of course. I was distracted there for a moment by–by those extraordinary flowers you brought for Miss LeRoux. Tell me, did you actually paint them yourself?"

"I did," Tony said.

"It must be a devilishly difficult process."

"It just requires some patience."

The three men looked at each other again mutely.

"Go on!" Jackie said, as if shooing away children. "I'll be there shortly." She looked at Mrs. Williamson. "Perhaps Kate would like to join us."

"Oh," Ravenel said. "Yes, Kate, why don't you? And where's that rascal of a husband of yours?"

"Home with the grippe."

"The grippe? What a shame. Then he missed your performance. I'm sure he'd want you to celebrate."

Kate smiled coyly. "Well, if you're buying..."

After the men and Mrs. Williamson had left, Jackie sat admiring Tony's painted flowers and wondered how she might find a way to take him aside at the Beaufort Inn and plan their escape from the others.

CHAPTER 16

Ravenel Coleman sat at the head of the table and seemed to consider himself the master of ceremonies. Mrs. Williamson sat on one side of him and Tavi on the other. And it seemed to Tony that Ravenel's attentions to Mrs. Williamson were a little more than innocent flirtations.

"Well, Kate," Ravenel said with a grin, "I think you did a wonderful job of portraying the fallen woman. You've had some practice, it seems."

Rather than showing offense, Mrs. Williamson answered pertly:

"Not as much as you, you old reprobate. Why isn't there such a thing as a fallen man? You've stumbled more than once, I believe."

Ravenel laughed loudly. "I've stumbled in the grass, I've stumbled in the fields, I've stumbled on steamships and I've stumbled in carriages. But I've always conducted myself as a perfect gentleman." It was clear that he was already a bit tipsy.

"Ha!" Mrs. Williamson said. "Gentlemen don't impugn the reputation of ladies by winks and innuendos, Rav. What will these young people think? You must apologize."

Rav took Mrs. Williamson's hand, brought it to his lips, and kissed it. "I apologize, Kate. It was only a jest."

Mrs. Williamson smiled and seemed to accept this apology as Jackie entered the room.

Ravenel, spotting her, abruptly dropped Mrs. Williamson's hand and stood. "Ah! The beauteous Miss LeRoux. Absolutely charming, Jacqueline. The absence of petticoats makes you look five pounds lighter."

"Then I looked fat on the stage," Jackie said.

"No, no, no! You misinterpret my meaning, dear girl. You were the picture of virginal beauty on the stage and you are simply stunning now. Sit down, sit down! Tavi, move over for Miss LeRoux. Waiter! A glass of wine for the lady and drinks all around!" He pulled out the chair that Tavi had just vacated and Jackie took her seat.

The rest of the dinner went tolerably well, with Ravenel whispering risqué remarks to Mrs. Williamson, and her giggling in response. Occasionally he would look past her to Jackie and make some reference to her beauty and the high character of her parents. Jackie merely nodded with a polite stoniness and looked away, usually at Tony, to whom she allowed herself a discreet smile.

Tony smiled back and wondered how he could separate her from Ravenel. Meanwhile, Tavi took advantage of his father's preoccupation with Mrs. Williamson by regaling Jackie with the transcendent nature of life on Edisto Island.

Suddenly the sound of stringed instruments was heard emanating from the main salon. Tony put his napkin down and stood from his chair. "Would you care to dance, Miss LeRoux?"

Ravenel looked up from his tête-à-tête with Mrs. Williamson, first at Tony, then at Jackie, then back to Tony again. "Now just a minute, Jones!" He rose from his chair

Mrs. Williamson pushed him down again. "Ravi, dear, don't be a boor. What's the harm?"

Ravenel seemed dumbfounded for a moment, then settled back into his chair. "Save the next one for me, Jackie."

"Certainly," Jackie said. She grasped Tony's hand and they passed through the doors to the salon.

The orchestra started off with a Viennese waltz and Tony and Jackie were able to converse while dancing.

"What connection does Coleman have to your family?" Tony said.

"He's just a friend of my father's," Jackie said. "They went to the Citadel together before the war."

"Seems that the war is not over for him."

Jackie sighed. "I'm afraid it's not over for my father, either. Their generation is hopelessly mired in the past."

"It's not just their generation–Tavi seems to have both feet in it as well."

Jackie laughed. "I can attest to that."

The music stopped. Ravenel Coleman emerged from the dining room with Mrs. Williamson's arm in his and Tavi trailing behind. He took a long, censorious look at Jackie and Tony, then turned back to Mrs. Williamson as the orchestra struck up another tune. Tavi stood by looking forlorn as his father danced away with Mrs. Williamson to a lively polka.

"Poor Tavi," Jackie said. "He looks marooned."

"Maybe you should dance with him."

"I will–if he has the nerve to ask me."

"Not likely. I'll go over and speak to him. He just needs a little encouragement."

Jackie found Tony's offer both amusing and gallant. He feels sorry for the poor man! She saw Tony say a few words to Tavi and then sit down in a chair against the wall.

Tavi seemed frozen to the spot for a few moments, then approached her. "Would you, uh, care to dance, Miss LeRoux?"

"I'd be delighted, Tavi. And you must stop calling me 'Miss LeRoux.'"

"Oh–sorry. 'Jacqueline.'"

"'Jackie.'"

"Right."

Tavi turned out not to be a bad dancer. At the end of the tune, however, he again seemed at a loss for words.

"That was very nice, Tavi," she said. "You're a wonderful dancer. Where did you learn?"

"Oh, in Charleston. Father sent me to a sort of gentlemen's school. Dancing, fencing, things like that."

"It must have been great fun."

"Sometimes."

Coleman came over to them with Mrs. Williamson in tow. "Where's Mr. Jones?"

"Oh," Jackie said, "He's over there–no, he's gone. To get some refreshments, I suppose."

"Well, while he's getting refreshed," Coleman said, "I'll take the next dance, if you please."

"Oh–of course."

"Tavi," Coleman said, "you will have the honor of dancing with Mrs. Williamson. Be careful with her–she's of a delicate constitution."

Mrs. Williamson laughed. "I'm not sure who's the more delicate, Tavi–you or me. But let's try it, shall we?"

Tavi looked searchingly to his father, then to Mrs. Williamson. "All right."

The music began again and Tavi and Mrs Williamson spun away.

Coleman took Jackie in his arms and stared deeply into her eyes. "You know, your father would be furious if he heard that you were dancing with a Negro."

"I suppose he would," Jackie said, looking around the room for Tony.

"But it's none of his business."

"None of his business? Of course it's his business–he's your father. If I found out that Tavi was cavorting with a black girl in public, why I'd take a horse whip to him."

"I'm sure you would. You're hurting me, Rav."

"What? Oh, I'm sorry." He relaxed his grip, which had been squeezing her waist. "I'm a little upset over this situation. I know young girls are rebellious, and I like that. But there are limits."

She suddenly stopped dancing and faced him. "There are limits to my patience, too, Rav. I don't enjoy dancing with a man who treats me like a child."

Coleman seemed stunned. "I don't think of you as a child, Jackie. Not anymore. But as your father's best friend, I feel that–"

"Excuse me." She released herself and went in search of Tony.

She looked in the dining room, then the bar, and even the cloak room. He seemed to have vanished. She did not want to return to the salon, so she wandered out onto the veranda that faced the square. Seated on an upholstered settee was a man whose features were obscured by the shadows cast by the gallery above. The moonlight, however, illuminated his blue-and-gray striped trousers and yellow patent-leather shoes. It was Tony.

She went and sat down beside him. "The square is a lovely sight at night," she said.

"It is," Tony said. "Some city council members have suggested that the name be changed."

"Changed? To what?"

"I don't know. Perhaps to Confederate Square."

"Oh, that's ridiculous." She folded her hands in her lap. "It's been Union Square for as long as I can remember. People should accept the fact that we're one country now."

"With justice for all?"

"Yes."

They sat in the shadows for a while without speaking. Jackie felt as if she knew what Tony was thinking. She looked at his hands. They were finely shaped, the fingers were long, the nails carefully manicured. She reached for the nearest one and took it in hers.

He turned to look at her. "It will never work, Jackie."

She looked not at him, but at his hand, turning it over as if examining a fine leather glove. "You're right. These are the hands of an artist, not a banker."

"That's not what I meant."

She looked at him. "What *did* you mean?"

Tony sighed. "Us. It's clear what we're both thinking."

She laughed. "Are you so sure that you know what *I'm* thinking?"

"Very sure."

She smiled. Then she leaned forward and kissed him.

He received this unexpected favor passively at first, somewhat startled at her boldness. But as her lips lingered on his, he became more bold himself. She seemed to melt into his arms.

"Jackie?" It was Coleman, who had just stepped out onto the veranda.

She turned to the sound of his voice. Tony pulled away, hoping the shadows would make him invisible.

"I've been looking for you everywhere," Coleman said. He stepped towards them, now in the light of the street lamps from the square. "What are you and Mr. Jones–It's late. I'll drive you home."

"Primus is waiting for me at the Bannister House," Jackie said. "I'll be perfectly safe."

"Then I'll walk you back to your carriage. I feel responsible–"

"Mr. Jones has offered to walk with me."

"Mr. Jones? Your father would not approve–"

"Thank you for your advice, Rav. I'm sure Father will thank you, too."

Coleman started to speak, thought better of it, and went back inside.

Jackie turned to Tony. "You were saying something about something never working. What was that?"

Tony looked down at his feet. "My shoes–they don't really go with my trousers, do they?"

CHAPTER 17

Jackie slept late the next day and after a bath, went down to breakfast.

Her mother was deeply absorbed in a copy of *The Beaufort Gazette*, a rival newspaper of *The New South*. When Jackie entered the room, she looked up and smiled from ear to ear.

"You seem to be an overnight sensation, Jacqueline," she said. "I regret your father and I missed the performance."

"It couldn't be helped, I suppose. Is Father feeling better?"

"Much better. He even got down some chicken broth this morning. It seems to be some sort of island fever he caught from one of the Negroes. He's been working with them down by the river, you know."

Jackie sat down and her mother slid the newspaper across the table. Jackie picked it up and began reading.

"Was Tavi there?" Edwina said.

"Yes. And his father, too."

"Ravenel is such a rake, you know. But Tavi is a very nice boy. Did you get a chance to talk to him?"

"To whom?"

"Tavi. Whom else were we speaking of?"

"Oh, yes. We had a late supper after the play at the Beaufort Inn."

Edwina leaned froward expectantly. "Just the two of you?"

"Um, no. Rav was there, too. And Mrs. Williamson. And a host of others."

Edwina leaned back in her chair and gazed out the window. "Not much of an opportunity for romance, then."

Jackie finished the article and put the paper down. "The reviewer was unfair."

"What?"

Jackie picked the paper up again. "The person who wrote this review. 'Mrs. Williamson, though competent, was rather on in years for the part of Mrs. Tanqueray.'"

Her mother chuckled. "Well, that's quite accurate. She claims to be thirty-seven, but I have it on authority that she's at least forty-two. She's an old flame of Ravenel's, you know."

"No, I didn't know."

"It was absolutely scandalous. Both were married at the time and John Williamson challenged Rav to a duel."

"No!"

"Yes. They even appointed a time and place, but John didn't make an appearance. As I understand it, from then on he accepted the situation and Ravi and Kate carried on as before."

"Rav's a bully," Jackie said. "And now it seems that he's an adulterer, too."

"I wouldn't be too hard on him. He's your father's best friend and, besides, the standards for men are quite different than they are for women."

"Well, they shouldn't be. What if Father were to carry on like that□with a married woman of your acquaintance?"

"Whether she was an acquaintance or not, I'd scratch her eyes out for leading him into it."

"And Father?"

"I would certainly be careful to preserve his eyesight, but I'd box his ears until they didn't stop ringing for a week.'

Jackie looked out of the window. The skies were quickly turning gray. "Where's Hanna ? I'm starving."

Edwina rose from the table. "I'll send her in, but don't stuff yourself. Dinner will be at precisely two o'clock. And I think your father will be well enough by then to join us."

After breakfast, Jackie wandered out into the garden, stooping to admire the flowers that seemed to flourish no matter the time of year. Roses, chrysanthemums, peonies, geraniums–her mother certainly seemed to have a green thumb. Or perhaps the gardeners did, her mother always barking out instructions to them to plant these here, those there...it seemed curious to her that her parents ever got together, they were so different. Her father reminded her of Tavi–rather meek and gentle except when his dander was up about something. With Tavi it was 'those savage beasts,' with her father it was 'those damned Yankees'...Her mother seemed to be from another planet altogether–kind and loving in her own way, but encapsulated in a sort of ether of propriety. The two of them even slept in separate bedrooms and had done so for as long as she could remember. How did they ever conceive a child?

She sat on a bench for a while and gazed out over the river. The *Southern Pride* had been tied up at the dock for years without anyone using it, though her father employed a small crew to maintain it and to take it down to Port Royal Sound once or twice a month to make sure the engine was still working and the hull was free of leaks.

She thought of Tony. He seemed so surprised the night before when she kissed him. In fact, she surprised herself. Was she being too forward? Well, she couldn't help it. It just happened. She remembered kissing a boy in Charleston like that when she was at boarding school. She had a crush on him and after a dance at his military school, they took a carriage ride along the Battery. The carriage driver stopped to point out Fort Sumter and while he was expounding upon its colorful history, she kissed the boy. He was as startled as Tony was at the Inn, but unlike Tony, he began pawing at her like an animal and she nearly jumped out of the carriage. Later, he apologized, saying something about 'the sacred honor of Southern womanhood,' and 'the equally sacred honor of the Corps,' and numerous other 'honors' that she couldn't recall at the moment. Her 'crush' ended right there.

She rose from the bench and walked down the gravel path to the dock. This boat, or yacht, or gunboat, or whatever it should properly be called, was a favorite hiding place for her when she was a child. There were hatches, ladders, ropes, lifeboats, storage lockers–every device or secret compartment that a child could desire for climbing or exploring. And once in a while, she would stow away when the crew took the vessel out for its routine maintenance cruise.

But there had been no other children to play with except for her cousins when they came to visit, which was seldom. Of course there were the children of the servants, but her mother discouraged this after the age of six or seven.

She ascended the gangplank and walked up to the bow, which was pointed upriver. Leaning on the railing, she could see the old mill that used to be a phosphate mine until the storm washed away the apparatus for digging the stuff out of the river, and before that a mill for grinding rice.

"Miss Jackie?"

This voice gave her a start, but she recognized it instantly and turned around to the familiar face of Louis, the chief steward of the yacht.

"Hello, Louis," she said. "Where have you been? I haven't seen you since I got back from London."

"I've been out to Lady's Island helping my kinfolk. Their house just about washed away in the storm. I've been helping pour some footings and rebuild the foundation."

"Oh, it must have been awful! Did your relatives all survive the storm?"

Louis lowered his eyes. He was nearly sixty now and looked even older, with gray hair at his temples and crow's feet around his eyes. "My grandbaby didn't make it. Washed away with all the floor boards and shutters and furniture and what not..still ain't found him."

"I'm so sorry, Louis. We were so lucky here."

"Yes, ma'am. 'Cept for the surge along the river banks, we mostly 'scaped the worst of it."

"What about the *Southern Pride*? It seems to be perfectly intact."

"Yes, ma'am. Oh, we done some repairs to the wheelhouse and had to pump out the engine room. But we ain't got no salt water up here and that was a blessing."

"Salt water? Didn't that come up the river?"

"Yes, ma'am, but then it surged right on back downstream to St. Helena Sound. The *Pride* just got a bath, that's all."

Jackie laughed. "And it probably needed it after sitting idle for so long. Tell me, Louis, do you still take the yacht out for a cruise now and then?"

"Oh, yes, ma'am. Ever' Thursday. Got to keep it hummin'."

"But nobody ever uses it. It's a shame."

"'Tis. Your mama don't like the sun 'cause it burns her skin, and your daddy ain't much of a sailor–he's a huntin' man. But now that you're here, maybe you'd like to ask some of your friends out. I'd sure like to see some young people on the deck enjoying the view and the sea air."

"A cruise? We could go anytime?"

"Sho'. Anytime you like."

After Louis excused himself to supervise some work being done below deck, Jackie wandered back to the stern and sat in one of the chairs. She gazed downriver, but saw mostly trees and fields on either side of the banks, as the river at this point had many twists and turns until it flowed into the Coosaw, then St. Helena Sound.

What if she invited Tony to accompany her on a cruise? Her parents wouldn't ever have to know about it. She could arrange to meet him at the Whitehall pier in Beaufort. What a wonderful idea!

She mulled this thought over in her mind as she closed her eyes and turned her face up to the sun, which peeked out from the gathering clouds. Unlike her mother, she loved the outdoors. Riding, sailing, even tennis.

She had played in London when weather permitted and had gotten quite good at it.

She frowned as another thought intruded into her reverie. People would surely see Tony board the *Southern Pride* and they would know the yacht. There would be talk, and it would get back to her parents...what if they rendezvoused at night? No...Louis would not venture to take the boat out at night and risk grounding it...maybe some other landing...

And with these thoughts swimming in her head, she fell asleep.

CHAPTER 18

The Second Mrs. Tanqueray ran for six nights and eight performances, which was its intended run. Shortly before the last performance, a theatrical entrepreneur from Savannah approached Mr. Oliver and convinced him that the play would do well in that city, but that there would have to be some changes in the cast. Mrs. Williamson would not do, he said, since she was too old for the part of Mrs. Tanqueray. Captain Ardale, Ellean's supposed lover, was lacking in 'stage presence.' There were others. Jackie, however, was pronounced 'magnificent' for the part of Ellean, and the impresario insisted that she remain.

A contract was drawn up, and the production moved to Savannah for a six-week engagement. During the play's tenure in Beaufort, Tony attended every single performance. Each night he would observe some new gesture, or some nuance of speech that had not been present in previous performances. Jackie seemed to be refining her role, and her craft, though she claimed that the character of Ellean was 'thin,' and that she was growing bored with the part. She wasn't sure that she wanted to move to Savannah for six weeks and stay in some dreary hotel for the duration, nor did she want to be separated from Tony for that long.

One night, after the performance, she and Tony met at the Whitehall landing and took the ferry across the river to Lady's Island, where Tony liked to dine at a quiet country inn called The Retreat. This was an antebellum mansion that belonged to a slave owner on the island prior to the war, and was sold to a group of freedmen during the early days of Reconstruction. It was nestled in a grove of trees on high ground and thus escaped the ravages of the storm.

They sat in a corner booth away from the other diners, most of whom were black. Tony knew the proprietor well, as they had both attended the

Penn School at about the same time. It was not unusual to see mixed-race couples at The Retreat, but Jackie's blond hair and fair skin contrasted sharply with that of most of the patrons, and 'Badu,' as he was called, was known for his discretion and respect for his customers' privacy.

"How did he get the name 'Badu?'" Jackie said, after the proprietor had exchanged greetings with Tony and taken their order.

"'Badu' is an African name that means 'the tenth son,'" Tony said with a smile. "And that's what he is–the tenth male child of a family of fourteen."

"Goodness!" Jackie said. "So many children. How did they manage it?"

"Badu tells me that his parents lined the children up each morning and assigned them specific tasks for the day–the oldest might go into the fields with his parents, the next might be assigned to clean out the barn, the next would go into town for supplies, and so on."

"And Badu was the tenth–what was his assignment?"

"Badu was sent to school. There were no chores left by the time they got to him."

They both laughed.

"So Badu was the only one who received an education?" she said.

"No. When his folks found out how useful he could be as a interpreter and–"

"An interpreter?"

"Yes. Gullah to English and English to Gullah."

"All right. And?"

"And that he was especially useful in reading contracts written up by cotton brokers, they started sending *all* of the kids to school who could be spared from the fields."

Jackie shook her head. "Amazing. Your people are so resourceful, so resilient!"

Tony frowned. "My people?"

"Oh, Tony, I didn't mean–"

"I know what you meant. You're patronizing me."

"You're being overly sensitive. I only meant–"

"Besides, my people are white."

Jackie stared uncomprehendingly at him for a moment. "What do you mean?"

"I mean my parents are white. My adopted parents, that is."

"Oh. I didn't know you were adopted. I thought your father–"

"My father–as my mother recently informed me–was actually one-eighth Negro. But he always passed for white. That was how he became an officer in the Union Army."

"Oh." Jackie was at a loss as to what to say at this point. Badu suddenly appeared with two glasses and a bottle of champagne.

"Champagne?" Tony said.

"On the house," Badu said. "It isn't often that we get a bank president in here." He glanced at Jackie. "And his beautiful lady friend."

Tony smiled and glanced at Jackie, who blushed slightly.

Badu uncorked the bottle and poured out the champagne. "Your supper will be ready in about ten minutes. Quail takes a little longer than fish or beef."

After Badu left, Tony raised his glass. "To your continued success in the thespian arts."

Jackie raised her glass. "And to us."

They sipped their champagne. Tony put his glass down and seemed to study the tablecloth.

"You seem to be in a bad mood," she said.

He looked up. "I am a bit."

"Why?"

"Because you're going away to Savannah for six weeks."

She smiled. "I have an idea."

"What idea?"

"What do you think of going on a cruise?"

"A cruise?"

"Yes. You know we have that yacht–the *Southern Pride*–that just sits at the end of the dock and nobody uses it."

"Yes, I saw it once when I was inspecting the old mill upriver from Lynwood. Does it still run?"

"Of course. Father keeps it in top condition."

"Why doesn't he ever use it?"

"Because–it doesn't matter. The fact is, that it's just sitting there waiting for someone to enjoy it."

"Just the two of us? Out sailing around on a hundred-foot yacht? Sounds like a waste of time and money. Besides, I wouldn't know how to operate such a vessel. I'd need a crew."

"There *is* a crew. Waiting all the time for someone to use it. That's the point."

Badu arrived with their dinners and set them down. "Can I get you anything else, folks?"

"We're fine, Badu," Tony said. "It looks delicious."

"Well," Jackie said, after Badu had left. "What do you think?"

Tony cut into his quail. "I don't really have time for it, Jackie. Besides, your parents would never stand for it."

"They don't have to know about it."

Tony refilled their glasses. "How could they not know about it? A hundred-foot yacht disappears from their dock and doesn't return for a several hours? And how would you smuggle me aboard?"

"I wouldn't have to smuggle you aboard. And it wouldn't be for several hours–it would be for several weeks. Six weeks, actually."

"Six weeks? What are you talking about?"

"Could we have another bottle of champagne? This is delicious."

Tony looked at her curiously for a moment, then signaled Badu. "All right, Jackie. Spit it out–what is this scheme you've cooked up?"

Jackie giggled. "It's simple. I'll be in Savannah at the theater there for six weeks. It's too much of a commute every day by carriage, and the railroad bridges are still washed out between here and Savannah. The *Southern Pride* is the perfect solution!"

Badu arrived with the second bottle of champagne and popped the cork. They complimented him on the meal and he retired again to the kitchen.

"All right," Tony said. "So your parents approve of this scheme. It makes sense, except for the expense, of course"

"They don't care about the expense. They just want me to be comfortable–and safe."

"Safe? So there you are on a yacht in the Savannah harbor, with a crew of–forgive me–horny sailors, and you're safe?"

Jackie laughed. "What a funny word–'horny.' Well, I'd be safe there with you and Louis."

"Louis?"

"He's the steward. And the four young men in the crew are his sons."

Tony took another swallow of the champagne as he considered this proposal. "I can't take off from the bank for six weeks."

"You could come back to Beaufort every Monday and see that things are running smoothly. There are no performances on Monday."

"How? By sea? We turn the boat around and–"

"By stage. There're two each day between Savannah and Beaufort."

Tony put his glass down. "And where am I to sleep?"

"Anywhere you like. There're six state rooms."

Tony drummed his fingers on the white tablecloth. "I can't stay the entire six weeks. But I could come to visit for a few days at a time."

"You could come and go as you please."

"I could do some painting."

"Of course you could. You would have the whole panorama of the harbor as your subject."

"Hmm. Or maybe I could set up an easel in the square."

"The possibilities are endless!"

Jackie's ejaculation was so loud that Tony looked around to see several of the patrons staring at them.

"Jackie–"

"Yes, my dearest?"

"I think we've had enough to drink."

CHAPTER 19

Jackie's parents, though sceptical at first, approved of her plan to live on the *Southern Pride* during her stay in Savannah. The fact that Louis and his sons would be aboard assured them that she would be safe. Mansfield, however, insisted that at least two of Louis' sons escort her to and from the theater each night.

"There are brigands and ruffians that lurk about the waterfront," he said. "I'll tell Louis to arm his boys with pistols and clubs."

"Oh, don't be so dramatic, Mansfield," his wife said. "I hear that the town fathers there have transformed the waterfront into a tourist mecca. It's as safe as downtown Beaufort. Safer, even."

Mansfield stood in the midst of the garden watching Edwina plant tulip bulbs. He was dressed for hunting with Ravenel Coleman, who was expected at any moment. "It's also a mecca for cutthroats and pick pockets. Don't you think they know that tourists have fat wallets?"

Edwina sighed as she dug another hole. She wore pads on her knees and hiked her dress up to her thighs, which weren't what they used to be in the old days. In fact, as Mansfield could not fail to notice, they were slack and shot through with varicose veins.

"You sound more like an old woman everyday, Mansfield. Why, when I was Jacqueline's age, I used to walk about the waterfront at all hours of the day and night without a thought of 'lurking brigands and ruffians,' as you so colorfully put it."

"That was in Beaufort. Savannah's a big city. Anyway, she'll be safe with Louis and the boys."

"I certainly expect so. Where's Ravenel?"

"I don't know. It's not like him to be late. The quail have all returned to their roosts by now. We'll be reduced to shooting rats down by the river."

Mansfield's ears pricked up. "I hear a carriage in the drive. That must be him." He walked back to the house and entered through the breakfast room, at which point he heard the bells at the front door. A servant opened the door and he saw Ravenel standing at the threshold with a crutch under one arm.

"Rav, old boy," Mansfield said. "What happened to you?"

"Damned motorcar," Ravenel said. Eddie, his valet, stood next to him supporting the other arm. "This one had a horn as loud as a ship's. Terrified my horse and down I went."

Mansfield laughed and slapped him on the shoulder.

"Ow!" Coleman said.

"Oh–sorry, old man. Eddie, take that crutch and put it in the library. We'll use it for firewood. There's a real gentleman's walking stick in the umbrella stand there. Bring it along."

"Eddie retrieved the crutch from a hospital, which happened to be across the street. Damned uncomfortable. Chafes the armpit."

"A good brandy will make it better."

After Coleman was comfortably settled into an armchair with a glass of brandy in his hand, he did indeed seem to feel much better. "The day's hunting is shot, I'm afraid."

"No matter," Mansfield said. "We'll rise early tomorrow. What have you been up to lately?"

Coleman took a sip of his brandy. "The usual. Looking after my properties and attending the legislature when I have the time. I'm happy to say that we've just about cleaned the niggers out, except for the handful you have here in Beaufort."

"They've always had a strong foothold here," Mansfield said. He swirled the brandy around in his glass and stared into it. "It was the Yankee occupation, you know. Sold off half the land to them. Lucky for Edwina and me that her brother got most of it back for us."

Coleman furrowed his brow. "Her brother? Oh, yes–Edward. A good man. The damnedest thing was, one of his own niggers shot him. And got clean away with it! That could only happen in Beaufort."

Mansfield sighed. "I'm afraid so. But things are improving. Like you said, we're the last bastion of niggerdom in South Carolina, but they're only a few still eligible for the legislature. That Smalls fellow, for example, who caused so much trouble for us, is now merely Collector of the Port." He laughed. "A sinecure. And quite a step down from congressman and state senator."

Coleman frowned. "He still has a great deal of influence–here and around the state. I understand he'll be going to the '95 convention."

"But can he succeed in getting his amendments and proposals approved?"

"Not likely. But he can raise a stink. And all the Yankee papers will make a martyr out of him when he's voted down."

Mansfield chuckled. "What do we care about the Yankee papers? Boston, New York–they might as well be in another country. And now that the Federal troops are gone, we'll do what we damn well please."

Coleman smiled and raised his glass. "Hear, hear!"

They both drank.

Mansfield turned his attention to Eddie, who had been standing by the fireplace all this time holding the crutch upright as if it were a spear. "Eddie–I thought I told you to toss that crutch into the fire."

"Hold on, Mansfield," Coleman said. "I might need it."

"Nonsense. You'll be staying with us until your shoulder–"

"It's my knee."

"Your knee, then. We'll take care of you. In the meantime, that walking stick will be all the support you need."

"All right. Eddie, do as the man says."

Eddie tossed the crutch into the fire, which had been dying out.

"They're some more logs in the woodshed, Eddie," Mansfield said. "Why don't you fetch an armload for us?"

Eddie nodded and went out one of the French doors to the back lawn.

"Sometimes I think Eddie must be deaf," Mansfield said.

Coleman chuckled. "He just pretends to be. My wife used to say it was his way of assuring us that he could be trusted with the family secrets."

"A valuable asset in a servant, to be sure." Mansfield stared thoughtfully into the fire. "Rav–"

"Hmm?"

"I've been thinking of your boy lately."

"Which one?"

"Octavius."

"Tavi? What about him?"

"He seems sweet on Jacqueline."

Coleman frowned and swirled the brandy around in his glass. "I've noticed that myself."

"They'd make a splendid match, it seems to me."

"Well, I suppose. But I fear that Jackie's too high-spirited for him. She needs a man who can put her in her place–gently, of course."

"Of course."

Eddie returned with an armload of firewood and deposited it in the bin next to the fireplace. The crutch had been nearly consumed by the flames and he began laying the logs across the andirons.

"I was just thinking," Mansfield said.

"Yes?"

"Perhaps Tavi would like to go down to Savannah and visit Jackie."

"Savannah? What's she doing in Savannah?"

"Haven't you heard? That play's she in–*Mrs. Tanzler* something–"

"*The Second Mrs. Tanqueray.*"

"Right. They've moved the production to Savannah and I've sent her down there on the *Southern Pride* with Louis and his boys."

"On the *Southern Pride*? Why can't she stay in a hotel?"

"Oh, she's worried about security, doesn't want to be alone and all that. She'll be perfectly safe on the boat. Tavi could go down and stay with her for a while. In a separate stateroom, of course."

"Of course."

"More brandy?"

"Please." Coleman brooded over this information. "I don't think Tavi can get away."

"Why not?"

"Well...he's ordered a cotton gin and while he's waiting, the cotton's piling up in his storehouse. When it comes, he'll have to work like the dickens to deliver on his contract. Maybe I could go in his stead."

"You?" Mansfield poured some more brandy into Coleman's glass. "I'm sure you'd be welcome, but that rather defeats the purpose, doesn't it?"

"Not at all. I could put in a good word for Tavi. You know, puff the goods, so to speak. And when he's fulfilled his contract, he could go down there and the primrose path would be all prepared for him."

Mansfield sat back down in his chair and stared at the fire, which was roaring again. "I suppose that might work. When do you think Tavi will be done with the cotton?"

"Oh, I should say in about two weeks."

"She'll be down there for six."

"Then it's settled. I'll pay her a visit next week. My knee should be mended by then."

"Excellent! I'll send her a telegram to that effect. The lines have all been restored, you know. She'll be delighted to see you."

"Who will?" Edwina appeared in the door to the parlor.

"Jackie, of course," Mansfield said without getting up, though Coleman stood in spite of his injury.

"Hello, Ravenel." Edwina was still wearing her sun hat and in the process of removing her gardening gloves.

"How are you, Edwina?"

"Well, thank you. You're speaking of visiting Jacqueline in Savannah, I take it. You have business down that way?"

"Well..."

"He's going down to do some spade work, dearest," Mansfield said.

"Spade work? Sit down, Ravenel. You look like you're having trouble standing."

"He had a little accident," Mansfield said. "With some rest and relaxation with us for a few days, he'll be as good as new."

"Of course. Stay as long as you like, Rav. But what's all this about 'spade work'?"

Coleman grinned, sat down, and looked at Mansfield.

"He's going to put in a few good words for Tavi," Mansfield said. "And then we'll send Tavi down after he's finished up his business at Edisto."

Edwina smiled broadly. "Why, that's an excellent idea. You two devils have been hatching this scheme for some time, I take it."

Mansfield laughed. "Only just now–it came into our heads like a thunderbolt."

"Well, I must admit that the two of you are proving yourselves to be better matchmakers than I. That's ordinarily womens's work, you know. Are you going hunting, or are you going to remain here and drink yourselves into a stupor before dinner?"

"The hunting's off for today. But we'll set the brandy aside while Eddie helps Rav get settled in. I think I'll go down to the river and shoot a few rats. Primus tells me they're getting into some of the cabins down there."

"Very well," Edwina said. "That'll give me time for a bath. I do hope you'll have a speedy recovery, Ravenel. Don't hesitate to call on any of the servants to assist you."

"Much obliged, Edwina."

"Dinner will be at the usual time." She disappeared again into the parlor.

CHAPTER 20

The *Southern Pride* was, in spite of Tony's characterization, not a one hundred-foot yacht, but merely eighty-two feet in length. Build as a gunboat, it had a shallow draft and easily navigated the inland waters that meandered between the coastal islands that separate Beaufort from Savannah.

Tony alighted from the hired carriage and handed the driver a fifty-cent piece.

"Carry your grip aboard the ship, Captain?" The driver said, stuffing the coin into his pocket. He was a tall, lean Negro who sported a top hat of the type worn by planters and politicians a generation ago.

"I can manage it," Tony said.

"Suit yourself, Captain," the driver said. He climbed onto the forward seat of the carriage and drove away.

Tony examined the *Southern Pride* now at close quarters. It was truly an elegant vessel, with a gleaming white hull, shiny brass hardware, and teakwood decks. A single smoke stack erupted from a structure just behind the wheelhouse. There was a young Negro on the bow, apparently splicing a line. Another of about the same age was at the stern, polishing a railing. Still another was atop the wheelhouse, making some sort of repair.

Tony stood for a moment with his grip in his hand wondering whether there was some protocol for going aboard. Should he simply march up the gangplank unannounced?

The answer to this question came quickly. An older man, dressed in a white tunic adorned with brass buttons and a pair of navy blue slacks with a red stripe down each side, stepped out of the wheelhouse and scampered down a stairway to the gangplank.

"Mr. Jones?"

"The same," Tony said.

"I'm Louis, the steward of this vessel. Sherman! Take Mr. Jones' luggage and show him to his stateroom."

The young man at the bow immediately dropped the line he was splicing and sprang to obey.

Tony stepped onto the gangplank and met Louis at the top.

"Welcome aboard, Mr. Jones," Louis said, taking the grip from him and handing it to the young man called Sherman. "We've been expecting you. This all you have?"

"That's it," Tony said. "Is Miss LeRoux aboard?"

"She's at the theater," Louis said. "They rehearsin' this time of day. But she be along presently."

Sherman escorted Tony through a door that opened into the main salon. This was a spacious room furnished like the living room of a large house. There were oriental carpets on the floor, richly upholstered armchairs, brass spittoons, even a fireplace.

He followed Sherman down a passageway until he stopped and opened a door. Tony stepped inside.

"This be the Jeff Davis room," Sherman said with a flourish of his arm.

"Jeff Davis?"

"Yes, sir. He be the–"

"I know who he was, Sherman. And don't tell me: you were named after–"

"William Tecumseh Sherman. He give fits to Mr. Davis."

Tony laughed. "I guess it helps to have a sense of humor around here."

"Yes, sir. It do help." Sherman put the grip down on the luggage rack and went to a porthole to draw back the curtain.

Tony followed him and peered out. There was a panoramic view of the harbor, with a mix of steam and sailing ships, and towards the city, a number of ancient-looking buildings, some fronting on the river, some on squares spaced at intervals between tree-lined streets.

"Can I get you anything, Mr. Jones?"

Tony turned around and took a good look at Sherman. He was rather short, but powerfully built, like a stevedore. He wore a sort of generic sailor suit, more along the lines of the British navy than the American, all white except for a blue flap at the back and the same color at the turned- up cuffs. His straw hat had a red ribbon around the crown with the letters "S. S. Southern Pride" sewn into it. His complexion was rather on the light side, like his own.

"Louis is your father, I take it."

Sherman grinned. "Can't deny it. Though some say I was the one in the woodpile. Mama and Daddy both be black as ebony. Uli, Champ, and Frederick all look like them more than me."

"Okay, I get 'Champ' and 'Frederick,' but where did "Uli' come from?"

"Ulysses S. Grant, of course."

"Of course. I should have guessed it."

Sherman continued to stand in the doorway with his hands folded behind his back. "That be all, Mr. Jones?"

"Yes...Oh." Tony reached into his jacket, pulled out his billfold, and produced a two dollar bill. "This is for the duration, Sherman. At least until my next visit."

Sherman took the bill and put it into his pocket. "Much obliged, Mr. Jones. Make yourself at home."

Tony unpacked his valise, which contained only the minimum in the way of shirts and toiletries, put them away in the drawers that were built into the cabinetry, loosened his tie, and flopped down on the bed. Or was it a bunk? Whatever it was called, it was spacious and comfortable.

In moments he was asleep.

Sometime later–Tony couldn't say how long he'd been asleep–there was a knock on the door.

"Come in."

The door opened and Jackie appeared. "Oh–are you asleep?"

"I was. I dozed off, I guess." He sat up. "How did your rehearsal go?"

Jackie came inside and sat on the bed beside him. "All right. It's become routine now. How was the stage ride?"

"I came by train. The bridges are repaired now. Much faster–and more comfortable."

"What did you tell the people at the bank?"

"I'm not accountable to anyone at the bank, but I told Mr. Ferguson that I was thinking of opening a branch down here. And I am."

"Really?"

Tony smiled. "Why not? Savannah's much bigger than Beaufort, and an international port. There's much money to be made here."

Jackie smiled. "So you've become an entrepreneur. And here I've gone through all this trouble to set you up as an artist."

"'Set me up' as an artist? What do you mean?"

"I mean that I've visited a few art galleries here and told them about you. Some even said that they'd heard of you. They would be interested in looking at your paintings. In fact, *I* would be interested in looking at your paintings."

Tony stood and went to a mirror to straighten his tie. "Most of them are in storage in Paris. I don't really have anything to show them."

"You will soon. I've bought you some paints and an easel."

Tony turned around. "Really? Where are they?"

She rose and put her arms around his shoulders and gave him a kiss. Then she adjusted his tie.

"Up on the deck. In a locker. Come, I'll show you."

She started for the door, but he pulled her back and gave her a long, lingering kiss.

There was a knock on the door and they quickly disengaged.

"Yes?" Jackie said.

"It's Louis, Miss Jackie. Sorry to disturb you, but I've got a telegram for you."

"A telegram? Slip it under the door, please."

"Yes, ma'am."

Jackie went over and picked it up. "It must be Father needing assurance that I'm all right." She opened the envelope and read. "Oh, no!"

"What is it?"

She handed him the telegram. "See for yourself."

Tony read aloud: "Rav arriving Tuesday on the ten o'clock train. Stop. Please extend the usual LeRoux hospitality. Stop. Reviews here highly favorable. Stop. Affectionately, Father."

He looked at Jackie, who was now sitting on the sofa opposite the bed. "Coleman?"

"Do you know any other 'Rav's'?"

"No." He sat down beside her. "Tuesday. That's tomorrow."

"Last I heard."

Tony handed the telegram back to her. "What do we do?"

"What *can* we do? He'll be here tomorrow afternoon and–"

"I'll have to go to a hotel."

"Oh, Tony! He's set out to ruin us! I wonder if he knows–"

"I don't see how. Only Mr. Ferguson and a couple of bank employees know I'm down here. And they think I'm exploring business opportunities."

"Then why would he be coming?"

"To see you, of course. He's determined to marry you."

"*Marry* me? He's twice my age!"

"Or more. But his intentions are obvious. And he considers me his principal rival. Or possibly number two."

"Who's number one?"

"Tavi."

Jackie laughed, then reverted to her previous state of alarm. "You know, you may be right. He may be preparing the way for Tavi, who's too shy to do it for himself."

"Possibly. But I still think that he's set on having you for himself."

Jackie folded her arms across her chest. "Well, he hasn't a ghost of a chance. I can tell you that."

"No?" Tony said. "He's very rich."

"I don't care if he's as rich as Croesus. He disgusts me."

"Disgusts you? Really? Most women seem to find him charming. And handsome."

"Well, he's very distinguished-looking, I'll say that for him. And he can be charming when he chooses to be. But he's an arrogant, self-absorbed bully."

"Just the qualities that every woman wants."

Jackie punched him in the shoulder. "No, that's *not* what every woman wants. A least not this woman. Why are you arguing his case?"

"I don't know." Tony looked around the cabin. There was a framed photograph on the night table that contained Jackie as a child, her mother and father, and another woman he didn't recognize. "Somehow I don't fit into this picture."

Jackie followed his line of sight. "My Aunt Lucinda didn't fit into it either. That's why she went to London. Lots of families have members who don't fit into their little insular world of what's expected of them. They adjust. Or if not, the black sheep can go elsewhere and start life anew."

Tony turned to her. "I'm used to being the black sheep. But you–could you get used to it?"

Jackie threw her arms around him. "Oh, Tony–I not only could get used to it, I'd go anywhere with you and endure any hardship. Can't you see that?"

"I'm not sure I do. You're only twenty-two, Jackie. And you're not used to 'hardships.' I have very little money, though I could sell my shares in the bank and we could live on that for a while. Then what would we do?"

Jackie smiled broadly. "Are you asking me to marry you?"

Tony laughed.

"Why are you laughing?"

"Because you are a totally impractical girl. And perhaps that's what I like about you."

"Oh, Tony–" She kissed him.

His hands began to wander, but she brushed them aside. "We're not engaged yet."

Tony laughed. "No, we're not. Is that a pre-requisite?"

"It is where I grew up."

"I grew up not fifteen miles from where you grew up. I don't remember any such strictures."

"St. Helena's different. It's full of libertines."

Tony leaned back on an overstuffed pillow with his hands behind his head. "Libertines? I never met any on St. Helena. Seems to me all the libertines live on plantations like Lynwood."

She leaned back on the pillow with her head next to his. "That's not true. Well, partially true. Aunt Lucinda is a libertine–at least Mother and Father think so."

"And is she?"

Jackie thought for a moment. "Yes."

Tony laughed. "See? I was right."

"But she's so sweet. And so honest."

"I'd like to meet this Aunt Lucinda of yours. Does she ever come to visit?"

"She hasn't set foot on Lynwood in twenty years."

"Then maybe we'll have to go visit her."

Jackie sat up. "Oh, Tony! That would be wonderful! I'm sure the two of you would get along."

Tony sighed. "But first we have to decide what to do about Mr. Coleman."

Jackie put her head down again. "What can we do? I suppose you'll have to go to a hotel like you said and I'll have to entertain him until he decides to leave."

"Hmm. I don't like the idea of you being alone on the boat with him."

"I won't be alone–Louis and his sons will be here."

"That gives me an idea." He sat up.

"What idea?"

"I could stay on the boat."

"And what–hide in a closet?"

"No–I could disguise myself as one of the crew. One of Louis' sons. Or some sailor they picked up on the docks because they were shorthanded."

"Are you crazy? He'd recognize you instantly!"

"Why? He only saw me that night after the play. He probably couldn't pick me out of a crowd of Negroes at fifty paces."

Jackie stared at him. "You really *are* crazy. What if he does recognize you?"

"Then he'll storm off the boat and return to Beaufort, or Charleston, or wherever he's from. What else can he do?"

"He can go straight to my parents, that's what. And Father will instruct Louis to turn the boat around and return to Lynwood where I'll be locked in my room until I'm an old maid."

Tony sighed and leaned back on the pillow. "It *is* a crazy idea. Forget I mentioned it."

Jackie stared at the photograph on the night table for a moment. "What if you wore a mustache? Like the one that Father had when that photograph was taken?"

Tony looked at the photograph. "That *does* change a man's appearance. And with the sailor's outfit, he'd look right through me."

Jackie laughed and traced her finger along his upper lip. "A little pencil mustache, not a big one. That's all it would take. I'll bring you one from the theater. There're boxes full of them."

"And you could give me some pointers about acting."

"I won't have to. You've got a natural talent for it."

"Me? I've never acted in my life."

She laid her head against his shoulder. "Oh, no? You've been doing a pretty good job of imitating a bank president."

Tony chuckled. "You're right. It's a daily masquerade that I go through."

"Then don't worry–you'll be perfect."

CHAPTER 21

The crew's accommodations on the *Southern Pride* were spartan and a bit cramped, but not uncomfortable. Tony's return voyage from Paris to Charleston was equally spartan, though a bit more spacious, as he was obliged to travel second class.

His bunk mate was Sherman, who slept on the bottom. Louis and his boys were of course briefed on the subterfuge, and even seemed to relish it.

"You ever splice a rope?" Sherman said the next morning. He was dressing before the mirror, which was just large enough to reflect his head and neck.

"Can't say as I have," Tony said. He sat on the edge of the upper bunk surveying his new quarters.

"I can show you. You sure look different with that mustache."

"It's supposed to make me look different. But I'll try to keep my distance from Mr. Coleman all the same."

Sherman laughed and adjusted his cap. "Miss LeRoux say she gonna teach you how to act. But we colored folks been acting all our lives."

Tony chuckled. "I'm just as colored as you are."

"But you don't look it. Oh, you 'bout the same shade as me, but the way you dress and talk, you seem more white than colored."

"I'm afraid I can't help it. But maybe you can tutor me on how to conduct myself."

"Tutor?"

"Uh...'coach' is perhaps a better word."

Sherman turned to face him. "Let's start right there. We don't use no big words like 'tutor,' even if we know them. The white folks got to think they smarter than we."

"I'll remember that."

The ship's bell rang three times.

"Breakfast," Sherman said. "Come on. Frederick will show you some real fine Gullah cookin'."

After breakfast, which among other things, included chitterlings and fried eggs smothered in ketchup, Tony followed Sherman to the bow where he was initiated into the art of splicing rope.

Jackie played her part by ignoring him as she went about her morning ritual, which involved a brisk walk around the deck followed by settling into a chaise on the stern beneath a sun hat and either reading a mystery novel or reciting her lines to no one in particular.

After splicing lines together for the next two hours, Tony looked up to the sound of carriage wheels rattling up to the gangplank. Even from that distance, it was clear that the visitor was Ravenel Coleman.

The first to step out of the carriage was a black man Tony had not seen before. He was dressed in a kind of livery, short green jacket with a yellow border at the lapels, much like the uniforms that doormen at elegant hotels wear, only without the top hats. He looked to be about thirty-five and moved nimbly to the luggage rack behind the seats and retrieved a rather large steamer trunk. Was Coleman planning to stay for a month?

Jackie also saw the carriage drive up and went to the gangplank to receive him. Tony watched as Coleman embraced her and she offered her cheek, whereupon he gave her a polite buss.

"I hope you had a pleasant journey," Jackie said.

"Pleasant enough," Coleman said, "aside from the delay at Pocotaligo–seems that a group of squatters had pulled up the ties for firewood. Or maybe for the lumber, I don't know. Anyway, we had to wait while a crew from Beaufort came out and repaired it."

"Oh, what a nuisance!" Jackie said. "Well...Louis here will show you to your stateroom. Is that all your luggage?"

"I usually travel with more, but I don't want to impose myself on you for more than a week or so. I understand there's a steeple chase this Saturday, so I had Eddie pack my riding clothes."

"You intend to enter it?"

"No, no. I just like to dress the part, you know. Makes it more amusing. I trust you'll accompany me."

"Well, I don't know" Jackie said. "There's a matinee Saturday–"

"Drat! I didn't think of that. Well, maybe we could go in the morning and at least catch the first race."

"We'll see."

Louis then led the way to the stateroom followed by Coleman and Eddie with the steamer trunk over his shoulder.

"Look like he here to stay for a while," Sherman said. He squatted beside Tony on the bow, coiling some rope.

"Looks like it," Tony said. "Do you know his man there?"

"That's Eddie. He come out to Lynwood with Mr. Coleman from time to time to go huntin.' Don't talk much."

"That's part of his job, I guess."

Sherman laughed. "And he know it well. Rumor is that Mr. Coleman got mistresses all the way from Charleston to Havana. But Eddie's lips is sealed."

"A real ladies' man."

"That what they say." Sherman looked down at the rope in Tony's hand. "Ain't you tired of splicin' rope? You got enough line there to tie us up to the lighthouse at Tybee Island."

Tony looked down. "I guess you're right. What else can I do?"

"There's always something to do around here. Come on–I'll show you where we got to scrape the railing at the stern so we can re-varnish it."

"Not exactly skilled labor, is it?"

"Nope. Just elbow grease, and plenty of it." He stood up and led the way to the stern.

Tony went to work scraping the railing, all the time watching the door to the aft cabin to see if either Coleman or Jackie might emerge. Finally, they did, with Jackie appearing first, followed by Coleman. Jackie acknowledged Tony's presence with a wink and sat down in one of the chairs. Coleman remained standing for a few moments and surveyed the harbor.

"A magnificent view you have, Jackie!" he said. "Ships loading cotton, barges plying the river with coal from Newcastle, molasses from Cuba, hemp from Jamaica."

"You seem to have overlooked the natural beauty of the marshes and the sea birds, Rav. Do you always see things in commercial terms?"

Coleman sat down in one of the chairs. "There's beauty in commerce, too, Jackie. Goods moving from one place to another, longshoremen and stevedores employed who would otherwise turn to crime and mayhem in the streets, planters and manufacturers growing rich and advancing civilization in the process. There's beauty in that, don't you think?"

"I suppose you're right," she said. "I tend to see things as the Romantic poets see them. The lush tapestry of nature, unspoiled by the hand of Man."

Coleman chuckled. "That lush tapestry was a jungle before the hand of Man tamed it. No, no, Jackie. I appreciate natural beauty as much as anyone. But I appreciate progress even more."

"Do you? Progress in all things?"

"Certainly."

"Progress in–race relations, for example?"

"Race relations?" Coleman wrinkled his brow. "What do you mean?"

"I mean just that. Don't you think that these new laws separating the races is a throwback to antebellum days? If so, what did the war accomplish?"

"Well first of all, the antebellum days weren't so bad as that. Secondly, you're right–the war didn't accomplish much. The Yankees simply invaded the South, laid waste to it, and returned to the North as if nothing had changed. Well, in a way, that's true. The slaves are free, but they're right back in the fields doing what they've always done and the only thing they can do. Except for some of the smarter ones like Eddie, and–" he glanced at Tony, who seemed to be intent on his scraping– "and Louis and his boys who know how to run a ship. But we're going to build a New South, Jackie, and it's going to be an economic powerhouse like nothing the world has ever seen. Why, with these new cotton gins and steam engines and–telephones! Do you know that soon you'll be able to call someone in New York or London and talk to them just as you and I are talking to each other right now? That's progress!"

Jackie remained silent for several moments. "Still, some things remain the same that need to change, and some things change that need to stay the same. Don't you agree?"

"Now you're talking in riddles. I'm more interested in seeing your performance tonight. I understand that you've taken Savannah by storm."

Jackie laughed. "I think that most Savannahans are doing the things you were just talking about–rebuilding the city and plunging into this new world of motorcars and telephones. But we *are* filling the theater seats."

"Of course you are." Coleman seemed to struggle with himself. "Jackie–I'd like to ask you a personal question if I may."

Jackie glanced at him out of the corner of her eye. "Personal?"

"Yes. Tell me if I'm stepping out of line, but do you and Tavi–I mean do you see Tavi as a friend, or–"

"I *do* see Tavi as a friend. Nothing more."

Coleman seemed relieved. "Just as I thought. He's a good boy, Tavi, but still has a lot of growing up to do."

"My sentiments exactly."

"Good! Well...what's on the agenda for this afternoon? I mean, I thought we'd go to dinner first, then–"

"Frederick is preparing dinner for us right here on the boat. You'll have the rest of the afternoon to do as you wish–perhaps you'd like to take a nap."

"Um...yes, that sounds like a good idea. I could use the rest after that abominable journey on the train. Then to the theater, and after that a fine supper at my favorite eatery in Savannah. How does that sound?"

"Perfect!"

Coleman rose from his chair and grinned from ear to ear. "I have a feeling that this is going to be a rewarding evening. For both of us." Then he took Jackie's hand and kissed it. "I'll go below and dress for dinner."

"Why, Rav–you're positively Continental."

"Continental? Well, just Southern. The Europeans have nothing on us Southerners when it comes to manners. Dinner's at–"

"Two."

"Right. Until two, Jackie, dear."

After Rav disappeared into the cabin, Jackie whispered to Tony:

"I don't think he recognized you."

"Of course not. I told you he'd look right through me. I don't think I even need the mustache."

"I think it's cute. Don't touch it."

"Just for insurance. Besides, if I took it off now, he'd notice the difference."

"Oh, Tony!"

"What?"

"I don't know if I can bear to spend the whole evening with him. What will you do?"

Tony went back to his scraping. "I suppose I'll stay on the boat. Once I finish my chores, I can do some reading."

"Why don't you do some painting instead?"

"Painting?"

"Sure. I'll show you where the storage locker is." She stood up, ready to lead the way.

"No–just tell me where it is–Coleman musn't see us together. I'm a deck hand, remember?"

"Oh–of course."

"And don't wink at me–Coleman's not blind."

Jackie giggled. "But you're so cute in your sailor suit."

Tony sighed. "I know I'm irresistible, but try to restrain yourself. You know what will happen if Coleman finds us out."

"Maybe you could come to the performance tonight and take a seat in the balcony. I'll give you a ticket and–"

"Don't be ridiculous! Listen–he's coming back."

Jackie quickly resumed her position and Tony went back to his scraping.

"Jackie, dear!" Coleman stood in the door to the cabin.

"Yes, Rav?"

"Do I need to dress for dinner?"

"Not at all. Very casual. We'll eat right here on the deck."

"Right." He disappeared again into the cabin.

CHAPTER 22

Tony finished scraping the stern railing shortly after dinner, during which time he was tormented by Coleman's endearing platitudes offered up to Jackie. Eventually he could stand this no more and moved up to the bow.

Around four o'clock, Coleman suggested they get started early so that they could have a carriage ride around the city. By this time Tony had scraped every railing in sight and was ready to start varnishing, but Louis told him that Uli and Champ had already been assigned that job, and besides, they could do it more quickly.

"But I'm a painter," he protested.

"Ain't the same thing," Louis said with a genial smile. "Varnish got to go on thick, and you got to keep it off the deck. The deck take linseed oil."

"Hmm. Any objection if I set up an easel at the stern?"

"'Long as you don't spill no paint on the deck. And keep out the way."

"I think I can manage."

Tony put up his scraper and went to the storage locker with the key Jackie had given him. By this time she and Coleman had pulled out of the parking area adjacent to the dock.

He set up his easel at the stern where Uli was beginning to varnish the railing. Champ was assigned to the bow.

Uli was unlike his brothers in that he had been a merchant seaman and had seen the world. They chatted as Tony surveyed the waterfront, looking for a suitable subject.

"Why did you return to Beaufort, Uli?" Tony asked. "It must have been an exciting life out on the high seas, stopping in exotic ports like Bali, Tahiti, Hong Kong..."

"Almost too exciting at times," Uli said. He looked to be about thirty or so, with dark skin, a powerful build like Sherman, only taller, and a nasty-looking scar in the shape of a crescent beneath his left eye. "I was lucky to get out of some of them ports alive."

"Are sailors all that violent?"

"Only when they in port and get drunk. Mix in a couple of island women and you got trouble."

Tony chuckled and squeezed out some cobalt blue onto his palette and mixed it with some green. "Women are trouble, aren't they?"

"Mostly. But blokes will scuffle whether they be women around or not. Just the nature of the beast, I guess."

Tony had intended to paint one of the square-riggers anchored offshore, a type of vessel that was fast becoming extinct, but now he took a particular interest in Uli. "How did you get that scar under your cheek, Uli?"

"Bottle. Bloke in Singapore come after me 'cause he say I making eyes at his woman. Turned out she wasn't his woman a'tall and I wasn't making eyes at her–she was making eyes at me."

"What was he? An American?"

"No–Fijian. They got a nasty temper."

Uli seemed uninterested in conversation after this and focused on his varnishing. He worked quickly, expertly painting around the hardware and, as Louis predicted, without spilling a drop on the deck.

Tony squeezed some red and yellow onto his palette, mixed them, and dissatisfied with the result, looked in his paint box for some black. Finding a tube, he mixed it with the red and yellow. This combination seemed to match the hue of Uli's skin.

They both worked quietly for the next hour or so, with Uli eventually moving up to the bow. By late afternoon, with the sun going down Tony had his portrait–Uli varnishing the railing, an intensity in his eye, an air of dignity in the pride he took in his work.

As Tony packed up his paints and cleaned his hands with turpentine, Uli returned and looked at the portrait.

"That don't look like me."

"Well," Tony said, "it's not meant to look *exactly* like you. It's more of a suggestion of you–and others like you."

"Others like me? What others?"

"Other sailors. Men who have seen the world, been scarred and beaten up by it, but nevertheless have survived and emerged all the stronger and wiser for it."

Uli continued to stare at the painting for a few moments and then broke into a big smile. He slapped Tony on the shoulder, almost knocking him down. "You got it right! That's me all right. Them brushstrokes are kinda–I mean they kinda bold, you know what I mean? Like big pieces of me you picked up off the floor after a fight and patched me together again. I mean it look like me and it don't look like me at the same time."

"I think you've got the idea," Tony said.

Tony had supper with Louis and his sons in the galley where Uli set up the painting for all to see. The others had much the same initial reaction that Uli had, staring at it with some wonder. But after Uli explained how they should not expect to see a realistic representation but instead look at it as a kind of shared experience, the others smiled, laughed, slapped their knees, and hooted.

"I couldn't have explained it better myself, Uli," Tony said. "The painting's yours if you like it."

Uli beamed. "Shore, I like it. I'll put it up over Sherman's bunk so he'll have to look at it every morning when he wake up."

Everyone laughed, including Sherman.

Later, Tony retired to his quarters and read for a while. He fell asleep and didn't stir until he heard iron-rimmed wheels crunching against gravel. He sat up and looked through a porthole where he saw Coleman assisting Jackie as she alighted from the carriage. He seemed a bit unsteady, as if he had had too much to drink.

Jackie hurried up the gangplank.

"Jackie!" Coleman shouted. "What's the hurry? Wait for me, dammit!"

But Jackie was already aboard and didn't answer. Coleman stumbled up the gangplank, looked first to the bow, then to the stern, as if baffled at Jackie's disappearance. Then Louis appeared.

"May I assist you, Mr. Coleman?" Louis said.

"No you may not, dammit! I don't need any assistance. Where did that girl go?"

"I believe she's already retired to her cabin, sir. She must be exhausted. Can I get you anything?"

Coleman stood at the top of the gangplank and seemed confused. "No...I mean, yes. Bring me a bottle of brandy. I'll take it in the main salon. Or– never mind that. Bring it to my room."

"Yes, sir."

Coleman disappeared from Tony's sight and Tony leapt out of bed, waking Sherman.

"Where you goin'?" Sherman said.

"Out for some fresh air."

"Bring some back with you," Sherman said, and immediately fell asleep again.

Tony carefully closed the cabin door behind him and went out on deck. By the position of the moon, he guessed it was about two a.m. Louis was nowhere to be seen.

He made his way to the aft stateroom, careful not to touch the railings, which were still not dry, and stopped at the first lighted porthole. He looked in and saw Coleman sitting in an armchair, his head on his chest, dozing off. He continued to the next stateroom and peered into one of its two portholes. Jackie was undressing for bed.

He hesitated for a moment, thinking that he should go back to his cabin and look for an opportunity tomorrow to take Jackie aside and find out what happened. Then he looked in again and saw that Jackie had removed all but a corset with the laces untied and hanging loosely from her bodice. He tapped on the porthole glass.

Startled, she instinctively pulled a petticoat to her breast. Then she recognized him and signaled him to come around to the passageway leading to her stateroom.

By the time he stepped into the stateroom, she had put on a dressing gown.

"You should close your curtains when preparing for bed," he said.

"It's so late–I didn't think of it." She went to the portholes and closed the curtains.

Tony sat down on the bed. "What happened?"

She sat down beside him. "He was fine until after the performance and we went to supper. We ate at the Planter's Club where everybody knew him and he was determined to show me off."

"Well...why wouldn't he?"

"But he started buying everybody drinks and stood up and demanded that they toast to my beauty and success as an actress."

Tony chuckled. "I think I might have joined them."

"But Tony–he was so crude and obnoxious. When my entrée arrived he took one look and sent it back to the kitchen."

"What was wrong with it?"

"Nothing. He just wanted to show off his influence. Said my steak was overdone. It wasn't."

"Is that all?"

"No. On the way home in the carriage, he tried to kiss me."

Tony sighed and looked at their reflection in the mirror over the dresser.

"That doesn't surprise me. What did you do?"

She glared at him. "What do you think I did? I pushed him away."

"And he gave up?"

"No. He was persistent. He was too drunk to reason with."

"Okay. So what now?"

Jackie looked at the reflection in the mirror. "I don't know. He'll be here for a week. I don't think I can stand it."

"He'll probably apologize tomorrow."

"But then he'll want to go to tomorrow night's performance and it'll happen all over again."

"Put him off."

"How?" She laid her head against his shoulder. "Oh, Tony, I don't know what to do. If I'm rude to him, my parents will never forgive me. If I'm nice, it will only encourage him."

"Tell him...tell him you're engaged."

She raised her head. "Engaged? To whom?"

"To...an actor. An actor in London."

"Oh, Tony–that will never work. He'll only tell my parents and they'll want to know who this actor is."

"Tell him it's a secret engagement. Insist that he not reveal it to your parents."

"Why would it be secret?"

Tony cast about for an answer to this question. "Because your fiancé is ...a Jew."

Jackie burst out laughing. "A Jew! I might as well tell them I'm engaged to you."

Tony looked at her. The sash holding her gown together had loosened and her breasts were partially exposed. "You're going to have to tell them that eventually, anyway. You might as well break down their resistance a little first by telling them you intend to marry a Jew."

She smiled and put her arms around him. "That's a very roundabout way of asking me to marry you."

"Well...I guess that's what I'm saying, isn't it?"

"Yes. And the answer is yes." She leaned forward and kissed him.

Tony kissed her back for a moment, then paused. "You know you're half-naked, don't you?"

"I'm dressed for bed."

"And we're engaged."

"Don't think you can take liberties."

"What else am I to think?"

She laughed and leaned back on the bed. "I'll need some assurance that you're sincere."

Tony looked around the room. "I have it."

She sat up. "What?"

He rose from the bed and went to a tray on the dresser. He picked something up on it and returned.

"What is it?" she said.

"A napkin ring. Sterling silver."

Jackie took the ring from him and placed it on her finger. She removed it. "It's too big."

"You can wear it only in bed. It's a secret engagement, remember?"

Jackie laughed and put the ring back on her finger. "All right. Now what?"

"We'll think of something."

CHAPTER 23

Tony's prediction that Coleman would apologize the next day for his boorish behavior the night before was borne out.

"I don't normally drink to excess," he said to Jackie while they were having breakfast on the rear deck. "It was just ...well, the excitement of your performance."

"I'm not even the star." She dug into half a grapefruit with a spoon made for that purpose. "Mrs. Seterus is."

"Seterus? Is that her name? I hardly noticed her presence. I think Mrs. Williamson did a better job in Beaufort. Why didn't they keep her?"

"Mr. Oliver was overruled. Are you coming tonight?"

"Of course. But this time we'll have supper at that new French restaurant."

"Not tonight Rav. It keeps me up too late. I think I'll just have a snack from the galley when we get back. Frederick makes wonderful pastries!"

"Oh? Well, if you prefer..."

Jackie assured him that she did prefer, and excused herself, saying that she needed to memorize, some new lines in the script.

Coleman remained on the deck, gazing out over the harbor with a wistful expression on his face. No, he wasn't the charmer he once was–he was getting paunchy and drank too much. But Dammit! Jackie was a great beauty and he had to have her. What good was great wealth if one couldn't obtain what one wanted with it?

He resolved to be more patient, to bide his time. He would be a perfect gentleman for the rest of his visit and...a gift! Of course. He had forgotten all about a gift for her, other than the flowers after her performance...but what could he buy her that she didn't already have? Edwina and Mansfield had spoiled her rotten, giving in to her every desire. That was part of the problem right there. She was a spoiled child. Well, he just might spoil her some more...but what? A motorcar? That was an idea, but she didn't seem to care for such things. Besides, the roads in Beaufort were so bad as to be impassable, especially after a hard rain. A horse? She had her pick at Lynwood. What else?

"Will there be anything else, Mr. Coleman?"

He looked up and saw one of Louis' boys–Sherman, he thought his name was. "Oh, no, that's all, Sherman–it is Sherman, isn't it?"

"That's right, sir."

"How in tarnation did you get a name like that?"

"It come from General Sherman, General William Tecumseh–"

"I know who he was, Sherman. Your daddy named you after him just to poke his finger in the eye of the Confederacy."

"I don't know about that, sir."

"No, of course you don't. Well, at any rate, it's not your fault. Mind if I call you 'Willie' instead?"

"Suits me, Mr. Coleman."

"Good." He stood up from the table. "I feel better already, Willie. Think I'll go for a walk."

"Yes, sir."

Up at the bow, Tony was trying to make himself useful. Uli had finished varnishing the railing all around, and now was the time for the linseed oil. Compared to varnishing, this was easy. Just pour it onto the deck and rub it in evenly with a cloth. Spilling the stuff was part of the process.

"You'll get that linseed oil all in your clothes, Mr. Jones."

Tony looked up to see Louis standing over him. He had just opened a can of the oil and was ready to apply it to the deck. "So what? The clothes can be washed."

"But it get into your skin, too. Miss Jackie like to shoot me if you come round her with the stink of linseed oil on your hands, even your hair. Better leave it to my boys."

Tony was beginning to feel absolutely pampered. What had Jackie been telling Louis, anyway? "She can smell the stink of oil paints on my clothes, too. What's the difference?"

Louis smiled his usual genial, condescending smile. "She seem to like that stink better."

Tony sighed and resigned himself to his fate of a pampered Lord Fauntleroy–at least as long as he was on the *Southern Pride*. He put the lid back on the linseed oil and stood. "Okay, what if I go back to my real job of painting pictures?"

"Why don't you paint one of Miss Jackie?"

"I just might do that. Is she still aboard?"

"She is."

"What about Mr. Coleman? I can't do it with him around."

"I just seen him walk down to the dock. Look like he headed for the Cotton Exchange."

"How long you think he'll be?"

"Can't tell, exactly. Maybe an hour. Maybe two or three. Cotton's his business, you know."

"True. Well, I doubt if I can get Miss Jackie to sit for me that long, but maybe I can set up my easel and just paint whatever comes to mind."

Tony went to the storage locker, extracted the paints and brushes, and set up his easel on the rear deck as before. The sun was bright and rising over the stern so that it shone into his eyes. He adjusted the easel, but still, the sun was too bright. He went to his stateroom, which he hadn't slept in since Coleman arrived, rummaged through the dresser drawers, and found a pair of dark-tinted spectacles. He donned these and returned to the deck.

He sat in his chair, eyes protected from the sun, paint brush in hand, and stared into the clear blue sky.

"Well?"

He turned to the sound of the voice. It was Jackie, in her boating outfit, a floppy-brimmed straw hat on her head. "Well, what?"

"Aren't you going to paint something?"

"I can't think of a subject."

"Can't think of a subject? Why, look at the panorama here–ships, buoys, the docks, stevedores, the Savannah skyline–pick one!"

Tony sniffed. "Postcard subjects. I want something more interesting, more particular, more personal, more–" He looked at her. "Why don't you sit down on the chaise? No, better yet, sit on the railing. It should be dry by now."

"The railing? I might fall off."

"It's only about four or five feet to the water. Can you swim?"

"Of course. But I don't know if I have time to pose for you."

"I work fast."

Jackie looked around, scanning the waterfront. "Where's Rav?"

"Louis said he went to the Cotton Exchange. Sit down."

"Well...all right." She stepped cautiously onto the lower metal support of the railing. "It's slippery."

"Then just lean against it. Your arms out to each side, hands on the railing."

"Like this?"

"Perfect. Don't move."

Tony went to work with his brush.

"You look like a painter I once saw in Hyde Park. He was wearing dark glasses just like that."

"Any idea who he was?"

"No. He was very short. I think something was wrong with his legs."

"Sounds like Toulouse-Lautrec."

"Who?"

"A very good French painter. Liked to paint whores at the Moulin-Rouge."

"Oh."

Tony, as promised, worked quickly.

"Tony–"

"Yes?"

"Did you paint...those ladies, too?"

Tony laughed. "I painted ladies in my studio. I don't know whether they were whores or not."

"That's such a harsh word. Father always referred to them as 'women of ill repute.'"

"A euphemism. It hardly sounds more flattering."

"No, I guess not. The poor things–I feel sorry for them."

Tony did not comment further on this subject, and continued to paint. After a while, Uli appeared with a box of tools in his hand. He stared at the painting in progress.

"That's different than the one of me," Uli said.

"It should be," Tony said. "It's of a beautiful woman, not a brawling sailor."

"You've done a portrait of Uli?" she said. "Oh, let me see it!"

"Stay still. Uli will show it to you later."

Uli remained for a few minutes watching Tony work, then moved on to complete his task of repairing a winch on the bow.

After an hour or so, Tony put down his brush and leaned back in his chair. "It's done. I think."

"Let me see." Jackie came around and stood next to him. "It's ...it's different."

"You don't like it?"

"I didn't say that."

"It takes a while to shed one's notions about representative art. Photographs have taken over realism. Painters are left to experiment with color and subjective reality."

"I *do* like the colors–so bright and vibrant!"

"But is it you?" Tony said, with a furrowed brow. "That's the question."

"The *real* question is, does the lady like it?"

They both turned to the sound of Coleman's voice, who had approached them without a sound.

"Oh, Rav," Jackie said, a bit disconcerted. "What do you think?"

"I think it's rather strange," Rav said, squinting in the sunlight. "But it seems to capture your charm if not your beauty, which after all, may be impossible."

By this time, Louis had appeared and was also studying the painting.

"Who is this man?" Coleman said, indicating Tony. "Since when do sailors neglect their duties to loll about on deck painting pictures?"

"This is Pierre, Mr. Coleman," Louis said. "He come from the Islands. We needed another hand."

Coleman looked at Louis, then Tony again. "The Islands? What islands?"

"The Caribbean," Louis said. "Isn't that right, Pierre?"

"Oui," Tony said. "Port-au-Prince," which he pronounced in the French manner, 'Porto-Prawns.'

"Well...it seems he has some talent for painting," Coleman said. "Jackie–do you like it?"

"I think it's marvelous!"

"Then it's yours," Coleman said. "How much do you want for it, Pierre?"

Tony glanced at the painting, then returned his darkened eyes back to Coleman. "Five hundred doh-lar, Monsieur."

"Five hundred dollars!" Coleman's eyes bulged from their sockets. "Are you out of your mind? Why, your salary here on the boat can't be but, but–"

"Six dollars a week," Louis said.

"Right," Coleman said. "So how can you justify–"

"That is zee price, Monsieur," Tony said. "How you Americans say–'take eet, or leeve eet.'"

Coleman grumbled something unintelligible, then looked at Jackie. "All right. It's highway robbery, but I'll pay it. Will you accept a bank draft?"

"Certainement, Monsieur."

"Then it's done. I'll get my check book."

They watched as Coleman went to his stateroom.

"Where will you hang it, Jackie?" Tony said.

"I don't know. I suppose somewhere at Lynwood. Mother and Father will have a say in it."

"If you hang it at Lynwood, I'll never get a chance to see it."

"Why don't you hang it here on the *Southern Pride*," Louis said. "Right there in the main salon?"

"That's an excellent idea, Louis!" Jackie said. "But we'll still have to get Father's permission. And we'll need a frame."

"I'm sure Rav will take you shopping for one," Tony said with a grin. "What's a few more dollars to him?"

CHAPTER 24

Coleman left Savannah at the end of the week, but not before extracting a promise from Jackie to visit him at his home in Charleston over the Christmas holidays. Jackie was reluctant, but the gift of the painting, combined with Coleman's exemplary behavior after that first night, made her feel that it would be rude to decline the invitation.

Shortly after Jackie's return to Lynwood, Primus carried the portrait that Tony had painted into the parlor, set it up on a table, and uncovered it.

"That's the ugliest thing I ever saw," Mansfield said. He stood before the painting with his briarwood pipe in hand, and peered at it with an expression that might be said to be halfway between befuddlement and disgust. "It looks like some lunatic in an insane asylum did it."

"Tosh, Mansfield," Edwina said. "You know nothing of modern art. It's meant to convey a mood, an inner spirit of the subject. Isn't that right, Jacqueline?"

"That's what I've been told," Jackie said. She stood before the painting with her hands folded in front of her. "The artist, they say, was trained in Paris."

"Paris?" Mansfield said. "The sink of iniquity. Degenerate art, degenerate morals, corruption in the church, corruption in the government. I hope you weren't exposed to any of that when you were there."

"Of course she was exposed to it," Edwina said. "One could hardly help it. But of course her superior breeding and good taste insulated her from its worst excesses. I must say, Jacqueline dear, that this new style of painting takes some getting used to. Do you think it captures your inner beauty? For surely it does little for your more obvious charms."

"Oh, I can't agree, mother," Jackie said. "I think it does both. The artist seemed to look into the depths of my soul."

"Indeed? Who is this extraordinary artist?"

"They say he came from the Islands. A French Creole."

"Creole?" Mansfield said. "Does that mean he's a Negro?"

"Partly. His mother was white, as I understand it."

"Hmpf," Mansfield grumbled. "Mongrelization of the races. No wonder his painting is so, so–"

"Abstract?" Edwina said.

"*Dis*tracted, I was going to say. Like the mind of a madman." Mansfield tapped the ashes out of the bowl of his pipe into an ashtray. He filled it again with tobacco and lit it. "But if you like it, Jackie, you're certainly welcome to hang it in your room. Just don't hang it here, or anywhere else that visitors can see it."

"You're being too harsh, dear," Edwina said. "After all, it was a very thoughtful gift from Ravenel. What if he should visit again and not see it? He'd be very offended."

"I suppose he bought it for her because she expressed an interest in it." He sighed and puffed on his pipe. "All right, Jackie, hang it anywhere you like. Maybe Edwina's right–I'm just too old-fashioned in my tastes."

What about the *Southern Pride*?" Jackie said. "That way nobody has to see it but me and Ravenel when he visits."

"Excellent idea!" Mansfield said. "Primus, take the thing out to the boat and hang it in the main salon. Speaking of Rav, did he behave himself while he was in Savannah? He had a couple of lady friends there in the old days."

"He was a perfect gentleman," Jackie said, biting her lip. "By the way, he invited me to Charleston over Christmas."

"Charleston? At his house?

"It will be like a house party, he says."

"Will Tavi be there?" Edwina said.

"I suppose so," Jackie said. "And numerous other relatives."

Edwina winked at Mansfield. "Sounds like a gala event, doesn't it, Mansfield?"

"Yes," Mansfield said, sitting down in a chair and puffing on his pipe. "Rav knows how to throw a party. Perhaps his other sons will be there as well."

"Other sons?" Jackie said. "How many does he have?"

"Three, four," Mansfield said. "I've lost count."

"Perhaps I'd better accompany you, dear." Edwina took a seat next to her husband and picked up her knitting basket. "We don't want you staying alone in a house full of men."

"Good idea, Winnie," Mansfield said. "She'll need a chaperone."

Jackie found this to be agreeable, though the only other time she had traveled to Charleston with her mother was when she went off to finishing school. At that time, she found her presence to be suffocating, even embarrassing, but under these circumstances, she welcomed the extra line of defense.

She followed Primus out to the *Southern Pride*, and with the help of Uli and Sherman, they hung the painting in a prominent place in the main salon.

CHAPTER 25

Tony had been using the gig for transportation lately because it was light and easily maneuverable over the rough roads of St. Helena. It also fit neatly onto the ferry, which was packed with carriages and buckboards as construction on the island accelerated.

He pulled into the drive at his mother's house one afternoon after a long day at the bank and saw an unfamiliar carriage parked in front of the door. Scratch came running out of the barn to take charge of Victoria, who was wet and hungry after standing in the rain outside the bank for most of the day. The sun was out now, but it was difficult to locate it in the haze that lingered over the landscape.

"Dry her off, Scratch," he said. "And give her a full bucket of oats. Who's the visitor?"

"That be Mr. Cooper," Scratch said, unbuckling Victoria's harness. "Come in just before you did."

"Mr. Cooper from the Emporium?"

"I reckon."

Tony stepped down from the gig and walked to the front door, examining Mr. Cooper's phaeton as he did so. A typical conveyance, he thought, except for the plush red leather seats and rather elegant landau hood with shiny hardware. Mr. Cooper was known to be somewhat of a dandy, as befitted the owner of the Emporium, a purveyor of fine clothes and accessories from around the world. His mother often shopped there. Maybe she was ordering some dresses.

He knocked the mud off his boots at the edge of the steps and approached the door. He could hear the voice of Mr. Cooper as he reached for the latch.

"I just wanted you to know that I will always be available to assist you in any way that I can, Mrs. Jones. You only have to–"

"Oh, do call me Georgia, Mr. Cooper. After all these years–"

"And please call me Hiram."

"Hiram."

Tony knocked lightly on the door as he entered. "Hello, Mama–am I intruding?"

Georgia stood up. "Of course not, Tony. Mr. Cooper–Hiram–and I were just chatting."

Tony stepped into the parlor, where Mr. Cooper was now standing as well. He extended his hand. "How are you, Mr. Cooper?"

Mr. Cooper accepted his handshake and made no attempt to correct Tony's more formal mode of address. "Fine, Tony. I understand you are performing wonders at the bank."

Tony chuckled. "Hardly wonders. Unless you consider foreclosing on planters a 'wonder.'"

Mr. Cooper laughed. "Certainly no profitable enterprise can carry underperforming loans for long without drawing the line somewhere. Tell me, is it the freedmen who are so delinquent?"

Tony resented the implication. "No more than their former masters. About the same."

Mr. Cooper seemed to be aware of his faux pas. "Well...yes, of course. I would expect it would be." He looked first at Tony for a moment, then to Georgia. "I suppose I should be going."

"Oh, Mr. Cooper–" Georgia said. "I mean Hiram–won't you stay for supper?"

"That's very kind of you, Georgia, but I must be going. The store stays open till nine tonight, you know."

"Oh, yes, it's Friday, isn't it? Well, I'm so pleased that you could make the time to visit us. I know how busy you are."

"Yes, well..." Mr. Cooper awkwardly made his way to the door, where he took down his hat from the hall tree. "Like I said, Georgia–don't hesitate to call on me if I can be of assistance. Anytime. Goodbye."

"Goodbye, Hiram."

Mr. Cooper quickly made his exit and the clatter of his heels could be heard as he descended the steps.

Tony turned to his mother, who smiled rather sheepishly, he thought. "What was that all about?"

"He was just being thoughtful. His wife died last year of a fever and–Oh! Look at these flowers, Tony. Aren't they beautiful?"

Tony looked to the side table beneath the window. There was a large ceramic vase in the center of it stuffed with a variety of flowers–lilies, begonias, peonies, sunflowers…"He's come to court you!"

Georgia blushed. "Oh, Tony, he's just a lonely widower looking for some companionship. He and his wife had no children, you know."

"No, I didn't know." Tony removed his coat and put it on the hall tree. "But I suppose you're right–he must be lonely in that big mansion on Bay Street."

"Poor man–he expected to have a large family, but his wife had two miscarriages. Would you like an apéritif before dinner?"

"I think I'll have a bath first. It's cold and nasty outside."

"I'll boil some water."

"Don't bother. I can heat some up in my room." Tony sighed. "When will gas heating come to St. Helena Island? Why in Paris–"

Georgia laughed. "This isn't Paris, Tony. Or even Savannah. And speaking of Savannah, you haven't said a word about your trip."

"I'll tell you all about it at supper."

As Tony sat soaking in the tub, he wondered what he was going to tell his mother about Savannah. Surely she knew that Jackie was there performing in *The Second Mrs. Tanqueray*–it was in all the local papers. And it wasn't likely she would buy the story he had given Mr. Ferguson about going down there to explore the possibility of opening a branch office. Even Mr. Ferguson knew that the Savannah market was highly competitive and besides, where would the seed money come from?

He continued to brood over this dilemma as he dressed for dinner. When he came downstairs he found his mother setting the table.

"I can do that, Mama," he said.

"All right. And you might put some wine glasses out, too." She went back into the kitchen.

Tony finished setting the table, went to the sideboard, and pulled out some glasses along with a a bottle of wine. As his mother returned with a platter of roast fowl, he poured the wine.

"Chicken?" he said.

"Duck. Scratch went hunting this morning and bagged six of them out by Cowan Creek. He's left two for us."

"Very generous of him. I haven't had duck for a very long time."

They sat down to dinner and Georgia said grace. Tony carved the duck, served them both and sat down.

After a few minutes of silence, Georgia patted her mouth with a napkin.

"Well?"

Tony looked up. "Well, what?"

"How was your trip to Savannah?"

"Routine. Not much to report."

They continued eating for a minute or two.

"Did you see that LeRoux girl in the play?"

"I did. She was very good. Just as she was here."

"And did you see her afterwards?"

Tony put his knife and fork down with a clatter. "Mama–I know you don't like the LeRoux. But I like Jackie and she likes me."

"It's not that I don't like them–it's that I'm afraid you'll get hurt if you pursue this girl."

"Hurt? Why should I get hurt?"

"It should be obvious, Tony. The LeRoux are not among the more enlightened families in the Beaufort area."

Tony took a sip of his wine. "You mean that they don't approve of black people overstepping their bounds."

"Something like that."

"Well, I can vouch for one member of the family who *is* enlightened. And that's Jackie."

Georgia said nothing in response and seemed to concentrate on her food. Another minute of silence passed.

"The duck is delicious," Tony said.

"Tony..."

"Yes?"

"I have something to tell you."

Tony wiped his mouth with his napkin, regarding his mother with a curious stare. "What?"

Georgia took a deep breath. "There are things that your father and I felt were best kept from you when you were young. We planned to tell you–"

"Tell me what?"

"I'm coming to it–don't rush me."

"Is it as shocking as all that?"

"Yes."

Now Tony's curiosity turned to alarm. "What is it, Mama?"

"Your father and I were not married when you were born. In fact, we were never properly married."

Tony poured some wine into Georgia's glass, then into his own. "I always wondered why there were no wedding photographs. I used to see them at my friends' houses growing up. So why did you not make it legal?"

"There were complications–complications beyond our control."

"What complications?"

"Oh, Tony–don't make this any more difficult. I've put it off for twenty-five years..."

"Mama–I know it's hard for you, but it shouldn't be. I always knew I was illegitimate–or at least I assumed I was. What difference does it make whether you and Papa were married when you adopted me?"

"That's the thing–you weren't adopted."

"I wasn't?"

"No. You are my natural child."

Tony stared at her for a moment, at first incredulous, then a big smile came to his lips. "Mama–that's wonderful! Then we're all of the same flesh and blood. You and Papa and–"

"I was married at the time."

Tony, who had risen with the intention of going to her and giving her a warm embrace, sat down again. "Married? But I thought you said–"

"I was married to Edward Benson."

Tony pushed his plate aside. "Mama–I don't understand any of this. If you were married to Edward Benson when I was born, then *he* must have been my father. But if he was–"

"I told you–Antonio was your father."

"Then you had an affair with Papa. Now I'm beginning to understand. But if you were married to Edward Benson at the time, then you became his widow after he died. And Lynwood would have been yours!"

"It *was* mine. But I gave it to Edwina and Lucinda for certain considerations."

"You *gave* Lynwood to them? For what considerations?"

"Never mind. Let's just say that it benefited the children at the Penn School. The point is that the Bensons–now LeRoux–and the Jones' have not spoken to each other in nearly thirty years. Edwina and Mansfield would never accept you as a suitor to their daughter–much less as a husband–even if you were white. Which you are, as a matter of fact. Fifteen-sixteenths, to be precise."

Tony could hardly digest this avalanche of revelations. It was the stuff of fiction. Or rather melodrama. *The Second Mrs Tanqueray* was a tale of conventional morality by comparison.

"Mama," he said, "I know this has been hard for you–but I'm not in the least upset. In fact, I'm delighted to find out that you and Papa are my real parents. You don't know how often I wondered, even agonized over, the identity of some black couple who were too poor or too indifferent to raise me as their own. Now I know. And I am forever grateful to you for telling me the truth."

Georgia wiped a tear from her eyes with her napkin. "I love you, Tony–and I would have loved you just as much if you had been adopted."

Tony rose from his chair and went to his mother. He gave her a kiss on the cheek. "And I would still have loved you. But this is so much better!"

The tears now began to flow freely down Georgia's cheeks and she tried vainly to wipe them away with the napkin. "Now that you know the truth, what do you intend to do about–that girl?"

"Do? I don't think it changes anything. I love Jackie, she loves me, and we intend to get married."

"Oh, Tony! You've missed the whole point. I've revealed this to you to make you see that it's impossible."

"Why? So the LeRoux don't accept it. Jackie and I both know that. We'll simply elope. The only thing that could have wrecked our relationship is if Edward Benson had been my father instead of Papa. Then we would have been cousins!"

"Cousins often marry. That would not have been an obstacle. But how could you ever overcome the bigotry of the LeRoux? It doesn't matter to them that you have only a fraction of Negro blood in your veins. They see only that you have the physical characteristics of a black man."

"They haven't seen me at all yet." Tony went to his chair and picked up his plate. Then he came back to Georgia's and offered to take hers. "Finished?"

"Yes. Thank you."

Tony headed to the kitchen.

"Tony–" she said.

"Yes?"

"I'm sorry. I don't really know the LeRoux anymore. I may be jumping to conclusions."

Tony let out a sigh. "There's nothing to apologize for. You're probably right. Besides, I'm thinking of taking Jackie to Paris with me. Even though there's some racial prejudice there, it isn't institutionalized as it is here. And people like Ravenel Coleman are determined to see that it remains an institution."

"Ravenel Coleman? The state senator?"

"The same. And he's not only a close friend of the LeRoux, he's just as determined to make Jackie his wife as I am."

"His wife? He...he must be twice her age."

"Easily. And he's very rich."

"What does Jackie have to say about him?"

"She despises him."

"Well, then. You have no competition."

"I'm not so sure. He's showering her with gifts. And it wouldn't be the first time that a woman marries for money rather than love."

Georgia stared at her glass for a moment, then reached for it and brought it to her lips. "No–it wouldn't be the first time."

CHAPTER 26

Jackie grew increasingly apprehensive as the Christmas holidays approached. She would have preferred to spend this time with Tony, but she had promised Ravenel that she would come, and besides, there seemed to be no way to celebrate with Tony without some subterfuge that would be of a far more complex design than the assignation in Savannah.

The dreaded day finally arrived and Jackie found herself sitting in a dining car with her mother as the train approached Charleston. Her father was laid up with the gout at Lynwood and would have come if not for that.

"I think this is going to be such fun," Edwina said, as she deposited nearly a full tablespoon of sugar into her tea. "Don't you, Jacqueline, dear?" She stirred the tea as Jackie stared out the window.

"Hmm? Oh, yes, Mother. I'm sure it will be a gala event. I understand that Rav spares no expense on such occasions."

"I daresay not. He was always throwing lavish parties, even as a young man. And I'm sure there will be many eligible young bachelors there vying for your attention."

"Yes. Surely."

Edwina blew across the surface of her tea and took a tentative sip. "Gracious! They do bring the water to a high boil on these trains nowadays. Better let yours cool for a while."

"Yes. I will."

"You seem distracted, dear. In fact, you've seemed to be in a world of your own since you came back from Savannah. Is it something about Tavi?" Edwina smiled slyly. "I think you know what I mean. Ravenel, though charming, was never too subtle in dropping hints. I suspect he revealed to you Tavi's intentions."

"Mother! You sent Rav down there to flog for Tavi, didn't you?"

"Flog? I don't know what you mean by 'flog.'"

"It's an English expression, I suppose. To press Tavi's suit. Wasn't that the reason?"

"No, no, no! Rav went down on business as I understand it. But I always thought that he saw it as an opportunity to 'press Tavi's suit,' as you put it. Haven't you the slightest interest in the boy?"

Jackie looked down into her tea. "Yes. The slightest."

"That's no way to talk about a fine young man who–"

"I didn't say he wasn't a fine young man. I just meant that I have no romantic feelings towards him."

"No? Why not? He's good-looking, he's rich, he's–"

"Mother–one has little control over one's attraction to the opposite sex. It has nothing to do with Tavi's qualities as a person. I just don't find him particularly attractive, that's all."

Edwina took a sip of her tea and put the cup back onto its saucer. "Well, if you want to know a secret, I didn't find your father particularly attractive when we first met, either. But I could see that he had all of the qualities that I could want in a husband–honesty, loyalty, an agreeable disposition–"

"And was he rich?"

"He was well enough off. That was actually not high on my list of requirements."

Jackie smiled. "So you looked at the loftier virtues of his character first."

"Yes. You might say that. But it didn't hurt that he brought a considerable amount of–how should I say it–breeding to the relationship. His family lost a fortune in the panic of '37, but the name of LeRoux opened doors throughout the state. Still does."

Jackie knew little of her father's life prior to the war and even less about his family. She knew only that he graduated from the Citadel with Ravened Coleman, and that they served in the same regiment in the Confederate Army.

"Oh!" Edwina exclaimed suddenly. "There's the Ashley–we shall be in Charleston presently."

They took a hackney cab from the train station across the Ashley and into downtown Charleston. Both Jackie and her mother had been educated at Mademoiselle Gaillard's lycée on Pinckney Street and Edwina directed the cab driver to pass by the revered institution.

"I hardly remember a word of my French," Edwina said, as they watched some of the girls loitering about the entrance, looking like sisters in their plain black dresses and starched white collars, clutching their books to their chests. She waved. "Bonjour, mademoiselles, bonjour!"

The startled girls looked up and after a moment of puzzlement, waved back. "Bonjour, Mesdames."

"Speak to them, Jacqueline," Edwina said. "I've exhausted my repertoire."

"Oh–all right." Jackie leaned out of the cab window. "Aimez-vous votre école, mademoiselles?"

The girls looked at each other and laughed. "Mais oui, madame! C'est très amusant!" A bell rang and they scampered into the building.

As the cab continued down Meeting Street, Jackie wondered at the fact that the girls addressed her as a married woman. Did she already look so old as that?

"Goodness!" Edwina said. "I've never seen so many motorcars in one place in my life! There must be a dozen of them."

"We've passed only three by my count," Jackie said, amused at her mother's alarm. "Or rather, they've passed us."

"Well, I think they're a nuisance. And unsafe. You won't catch me riding in one."

At last they pulled up to the Coleman mansion, which dwarfed the houses around it.

"Can this be it?" Jackie said, wide-eyed at the impressive facade and the sheer size of the house. Towering Corinthian columns ringed the entire structure, supporting a slate roof surmounted by a cupola resembling a lighthouse. Shaded by the roof was a broad veranda that also seemed to encircle the house. Though the grounds were partially obscured by an ivy-covered brick wall surmounted by wrought-iron spikes, Jackie could see the tops of manicured trees spaced at regular intervals.

"It makes Lynwood look like a country cottage by comparison, doesn't it?" Edwina said. "Rav's father used to have parties here before the war. We girls at the lycée would stand there at the gate peering in, wondering at the grandness of it all before being shooed away by a porter. Of course we were too naive to know what shenanigans were going on inside, but our imaginations ran to romance in those days rather than to debauchery."

"Debauchery?" Jackie said.

"Only rumors. Who knows? Pull around to the front door, driver. I see that we're not the first to arrive."

Indeed, there were a number of carriages parked in the drive, along with two of the motorcars that had passed them earlier.

A doorman in livery rushed down the steps to greet them and assisted them out of the cab. As they ascended the brick steps to the veranda, Jackie could better see the gardens that fanned out from the walkway. Though it was December, the poinsettias were in bloom, as were the azaleas, with red, white and pink flowers. She supposed the small, neatly trimmed trees were pomegranates, but it was hard to tell this time of year, as they were not in bloom. In the center of the walkway, stone dolphins spouted gently arcing streams of water from a fountain encircled by boxwood.

Two porters had been summoned by the doorman to carry their luggage, which was voluminous considering they were there for only a one week stay.

"Edwina! Jackie! Welcome." Ravenel appeared at the massive front door which exceeded that of Lynwood's in height. He was dressed in a hunting outfit, with a black coat, bright red vest, and white trousers. He held a tumbler in his right hand with a sprig of mint floating on the surface of the beverage, which Jackie assumed to be bourbon. He gave Edwina a buss on the cheek, then Jackie. "Rupert will show you to your room upstairs. It's the presidential suite. If you need anything, the upstairs maid will fetch it for you. Her name is Loretta."

"You've started with the libations rather early, haven't you, Rav?" Edwina said with a wry smile. "We may have to put you to bed before supper."

"Nonsense, Edwina," Coleman said with a hearty laugh. "This is the Christmas season. We Charlestonians start getting in shape for it soon after Lent. You'll have to come downstairs once you're settled and join the rest of the guests for mint juleps."

"Jackie might be interested in a tour of the house and gardens first," Edwina said. They were standing in the cavernous foyer by this time. "This is her first visit, you know."

"Of course, of course," Coleman said. "I'll lead the tour myself. Jackie, you look absolutely stunning."

Thank you, Rav," Jackie said. "But the journey has made us tired and a bit frazzled. You'll forgive us if we take a little time to freshen up."

"Of course. Rupert, make sure the ladies are comfortable. Where's Eddie? The rascal is hiding from me. I need another drink."

Rupert led the way up the spiral staircase to the second floor, followed by the two porters carrying their luggage. Jackie admired the portraits along the way, wondering what role they played in Rav's family. Farmers, soldiers, planters. Was there an aide-de-camp to General Washington here? An ambassador to France? Perhaps. But there was one thing they all had in common–ownership of slaves. This was simply a fact of life in South

Carolina, something that the offspring of slave owners like herself took for granted. But now she was beginning to look at the past through Tony's eyes. What were his ancestors like?

"Isn't this a magnificent room, Jacqueline? Where is that maid Ravenel was talking about? We need her to help us unpack."

"Loretta is her name," Jackie said, taking in the sumptuous elegance of the room and its furnishings. "I suppose we'll have to sleep in the same bed."

"Of course we will–there's ample room for the two of us. The only question is, can you put up with my snoring?"

Jackie laughed. "I didn't know you snored."

"Only when I sleep on my back."

"I'll remember to give you a nudge."

Loretta appeared and introduced herself. She was a woman of about forty, light-skinned and rather pretty, with her black hair teased into spit curls that framed her round face. After showing them the tiled bathroom and how to adjust the steam heat which warmed the tile floor as well as the room, she began hanging dresses in the armoire.

"How long have you worked for Mr. Coleman, Loretta?" Jackie asked.

"Oh," Loretta said. "Ever since I was a girl. Mr. Coleman brought me here from Edisto Island when I was just thirteen."

"Edisto? The plantation?"

"Yes, ma'am."

"Did you attend school there?"

"No, ma'am." Loretta folded some linen and put it in a drawer. "I had to help in the fields. There wasn't any time for book-learning."

"But...you seem educated."

Loretta smiled. "Mr. Coleman taught me how to read and write."

"Don't bother the girl with a lot of questions about her personal life, Jacqueline," Edwina said. "That's rather rude. Here, Loretta, help me with this clasp–I can't reach it."

Jackie followed her mother's advice and refrained from asking Loretta any more questions. The conversation piqued her curiosity, though. Did Rav rescue her from the hard labor at Edisto out of the kindness of his heart? Or was it that she was pretty and he wanted her for...other purposes? Well, he taught her to read and write–he must have seen something in her besides a pretty face.

After unpacking, Loretta reminded them that dinner was at three, and showed them the electric buzzer system for calling her and other servants if they needed anything. Then she excused herself.

"It's a shame," Edwina said, lying down on the bed.

"What's a shame?"

"Educating these servants beyond their capacity to make use of it. It only makes them dissatisfied with their lot in life."

Jackie lay down beside her. "Yes, it must be frustrating. That's one thing, Mother, that I think we can agree on."

But her mother did not reply–she was already fast asleep.

CHAPTER 27

Coleman began his tour of the property with the gardens, which he explained had been laid out by a famous French landscaper who had once been the head gardener at Versailles.

"It's not so grand as Versailles," Coleman said with a laugh. "But you can see the influence."

Indeed, Jackie could see the influence, having visited Versailles during her year abroad. The shrubs and trees were laid out in geometrical patterns, with brick walkways radiating from each grouping. Fountains were often at the center, with various animals and sea creatures spouting forth water in a gentle, almost soundless arc.

"It must be even more magnificent in the spring, when everything is in bloom," she said.

"It is glorious," Coleman said. "I hope you'll pay us another visit at that time."

"Well...we'll see."

"Where's Tavi?" Edwina said. "It's a bit chilly out here–shouldn't we go in?"

"Tavi's entertaining some of his friends in the tower," Coleman said. "You should have worn a shawl, Edwina. I'l send for one."

"No, no," Edwina said. "I've seen all this before. I'll just go in and meet you there later."

"Suit yourself."

They both watched for a moment as Edwina walked briskly to the house.

"She's getting to be a bit irritable in her old age," Jackie said.

Coleman laughed. "Oh, she's not so old as that. In fact, she's younger than I am."

"Well," Jackie said. "I didn't mean that, exactly. She just seems more irritable than she used to be. Physically, I mean. Too cold one minute, too hot the next."

Coleman smiled. "Well, she is about that age, you know. Come–I'll show you the greenhouse. You'll get a preview of what the gardens will look like in the spring."

Coleman led her to the greenhouse, where the temperature and the humidity were significantly higher, and flowers bloomed in a riot of colors. He took a pair of shears and cut off a rose, which he presented to Jackie. "This is a Rose du Roi à Fleurs Pourpres. A hybrid created by our friend, Louis Lelieur."

"Oh, it's lovely, Rav! And your French is perfect!"

Coleman chuckled. "I only know enough to pronounce the names of flowers and items on a menu. I think we can find a pin in the house to attach it to your dress."

"Oh–I have one." She pulled a pin from her hair.

"Here–allow me," he said, taking the pin and attaching the flower to her bodice, just above her breast. "There."

She looked down at it. "Oh, it's–"

Coleman leaned forward and kissed her.

"Oh, Rav–please don't–"

"Beauty often overwhelms me, Jackie. Especially your beauty."

She pulled away from him. "I'm very flattered, Rav. But I don't feel right about this."

"Why not? It's the most natural thing in the world. And my intentions are honorable, Jackie. I intend to make you my wife."

"Your wife! You're old enough to be my father!"

"I'm actually older than your father. But I'm far more vigorous–and richer. Have you considered what it would be like to live in this house? This is the center of Charleston's social life. And when I'm elected governor–"

"I'd like to go back to the house now, Rav. Please don't make a scene."

"A scene? I have no intention of making a scene. I only ask that you think about it."

"Yes...I'll think about it."

As they made their way back to the house, Jackie reflected on her relationship to this man, who she at various stages of her life considered to be avuncular, dashing, rude, even loathsome, and now the charming gentleman her mother always insisted he was. She also marveled at his capacity for alcohol, which seemed not to affect him until late in the evening, at which time he reverted to the boorish behavior he displayed in

Savannah.

The main parlor was crowded with guests. Coleman introduced her to several luminaries of Charleston society, nearly all of whom commented on her beauty. One or two had seen her performance in either Beaufort or Savannah.

While Coleman went off looking for Eddie to bring her a mint julep, Tavi came down the stairs with several of his friends following behind. He affected not to see her, and began conversing with an elderly woman who seemed startled at his imposition. Jackie was amused at his shyness, as she saw it, and left alone for a moment, gazed around the room. It seemed to her more like a museum than a parlor, with velvet-patterned wallpaper and paintings hung from the wainscoting to the ceiling, which was nearly twenty feet high. The furniture was from another period–Regency, she thought, with an occasional Oriental knick-knack, and busts of presumably important people atop pedestals at regular intervals along the walls. The carpet beneath her feet was Persian, she would guess, with a deep blue field and populated with variegated symbols and stylized animals. This room alone, she estimated, was worth the entire dwelling at Lynwood, whose furnishings were tasteful, but not extravagant.

"Hello, Jackie."

She raised her eyes to see Tavi standing before her, along with one or two of his friends behind him looking eagerly over his shoulder. "Oh–hello, Tavi. I was just admiring your father's good taste."

Tavi's eyes quickly swept around the room, then returned to hers. "Yes, Father does know a lot about fine things. But it was Mother who really decorated the house."

"Oh–I'm so sorry I never had the chance to meet her. She must have been an extraordinary woman."

"Yes, yes she was." Tavi was suddenly punched from behind. "All right, Bert. Um, Jackie–allow me to present my friend, Bert Jaeger. One of my college chums."

Bert stepped forward and extended his hand to Jackie. "Charmed, I'm sure, Miss LeRoux. I saw your performance in Savannah."

"Did you?" she said. "And what were you doing there?"

"Business, of course. Buying and selling. That's what everyone's doing, isn't it?"

"Well...in a sense, I guess we all are."

Tavi started to introduce his second friend, the one standing behind Bert, when his father arrived with a mint julep in each hand.

"Here you are, Jackie," Coleman said. "You know I do believe Eddie's going deaf. I had to nearly shout in his ear to get his attention."

Tavi chuckled in his quiet, low-key way. "I believe he's trying to avoid you, Father. He thinks you drink too much."

"If he thinks that, he's wrong," Coleman said. "And if he persists in thinking that, he'll soon be looking for another job."

Tavi didn't laugh at this comment, and neither did Bert, or their friend Hollis. Rather they all looked to his father to gauge his response. After a moment, Coleman laughed. "Eddie can think anything he likes, as long as he keeps his mouth shut about my drinking or anything else. He knows me better than you do, Tavi."

Tavi looked hurt at this comment. "Yes–I suppose he does. He's known you longer, at any rate."

"Dinner is served!"

Everyone turned to the sound of Rupert's baritone voice. He stood at the door to the dining room, and confident that everyone in the parlor had heard, stepped aside.

The dining table sat twenty-four, and Coleman took his usual place at the head of it. Crystal chandeliers hung at each end, electrified with dozens of incandescent bulbs, while brass sconces along the walls illuminated numerous paintings. A huge gilt mirror rested over the mantelpiece, which was festooned with laurels of holly. Though the house enjoyed steam heating throughout, a yule log burned in the fireplace.

Place names directed the guests to their seats, and Jackie found herself sitting on Coleman's right, while her mother sat on his left. Tavi sat at the opposite end of the table, flanked by his college friends.

After welcoming the guests and wishing them a merry Christmas, Coleman bowed his head and offered a prayer. Then he raised his glass in a toast to the South and its rising like a phoenix from the ashes of the 'Late Unpleasantness,' which drew chuckles from Tavi's end of the table.

"That was not meant as a joke," he said, which produced a respectful silence among Tavi and his friends. But a smile quickly returned to his lips and he sat down. "Be merry!"

Jackie felt a bit unsettled by Coleman's toast. "If the 'Late Unpleasantness' isn't a joke, what did you mean by it?"

Coleman furrowed his brow. "I meant that the South doesn't even recognize the legitimacy of the war. To do so would be to validate the North's claim that we had no right to secede."

"I thought that had been settled."

"Nothing's been settled but the extinction of slavery. That's the law now, North and South. But our way of life will continue." He nodded towards a servant who promptly filled his glass with champagne. "As you can see."

Jackie glanced at the servant, who was a young black man about Tony's age. Their eyes met for a moment, and the servant quickly looked away. "Yes. I do see. Things will remain the same–at least for you and your family."

Coleman smiled. "And your family as well."

"'What did you say, Rav?" Edwina said. She leaned towards him. "I can't hear you with all this chatter."

Coleman turned to her. "I said, your family and mine are in the same boat."

"Boat? Do you mean the *Southern Pride*?"

Coleman chuckled and winked at Jackie. "I do believe you've become hard of hearing, Edwina. But you've got the gist of it. Our families have always been close and by staying close, we'll all prosper."

Edwina smiled at this and raised her glass. Coleman responded by clinking his against hers and turned to Jackie, whose glass remained on the table.

"Jackie?" he said.

She stared at her glass for a moment and then lifted it.

Coleman clinked his against hers. "To the LeRoux and the Colemans. May they ever be united in peace and in war!"

Coleman's voice boomed out so loudly that the other guests suddenly fell silent and looked to see what such a toast was about. After an awkward moment or two, Tavi stood and raised his glass. "To the LeRoux and Coleman's! May they ever be united!"

"Hear! Hear!" repeated the others, still puzzled as to the purpose of the toast.

Jackie stared into her glass, feeling as if she had somehow been violated.

After dinner, she excused herself as the other guests assembled on the south lawn to watch Tavi and his friends play badminton. She was asked to join, but complained of a headache and retired to her room. Her mother accompanied her.

"It must be all that alcohol," Edwina said. "I think that Rav drinks entirely too much, though it doesn't seem to affect him. The rest of us either have to race to catch up, or abstain altogether. How do you feel, dear?"

"Just tired, Mother." Jackie lay on the bed and closed her eyes. "I don't really have a headache."

"Well, that's a relief. I don't blame you for making an excuse. But you know, I"m not tired at all. I think I'll go downstairs and watch the badminton."

"Do. And tell Tavi I regret not being able to join in. He seemed hurt when I said I wouldn't be watching."

"Tavi's very sensitive–a rare quality in a man. Such men tend to make excellent husbands. Why, look at your father–"

But Jackie appeared to be already asleep, and Edwina, not wishing to disturb her, quietly left the room and closed the door behind her.

CHAPTER 28

Mansfield LeRoux was not the sort of man to enjoy solitude. Though he was a student of history and possessed an impressive collection of books, he saw himself more as a country gentleman than a scholar. In fact, he spent less time in his library than he did hunting. His reading usually consisted of an hour or so after supper, accompanied by several glasses of sherry. Then he dozed off.

Without Edwina to wake him and guide him upstairs to bed, he often fell asleep in his armchair and didn't awake until Primus looked in on him and shook him gently by the shoulder. He would wake up, look to the armchair opposite his expecting to see Edwina, and seeing that she was not there, called for Jackie. Being reminded that both were in Charleston visiting the Colemans, he would ejaculate an "Oh, damn! That's right," and doze off again.

On the third day of Edwina's and Jackie's absence, however, Primus presented a telegram to Mansfield as he was having breakfast in the sun room.

"What's this?" he said, looking at the envelope set before him. "Something from Edwina?"

"No, sir," Primus said. "The man at the telegraph office said it came from New York."

"New York? I don't know anybody in New York except a couple of scalawags we ran out of town in '76. New York, you say?"

"Yes, sir."

"All right." Mansfield picked up the envelope and opened it. He began reading:

In New York on business. Stop.

Arriving by train on 23rd. Stop.
Reindeer on strike. Stop.
S. Claus

"What the devil is this? A joke?" He read it over a second time. "'S. Claus.' Who can it be?"

Primus cleared his throat. "The man at the telegraph office say it paid for by a Miz Benson."

Mansfield looked at Primus as if he had conspired with the sender. "Benson? Then it's Lucinda?"

"It seem so."

Mansfield shook his head and put the telegram down. "Just like Lucinda. Everything's a joke to her. But what 'business' can she have in New York? And now, after twenty years–or is it thirty?–she comes back to Lynwood. What can she want?"

Primus said nothing.

"All right then. We'll have to put her up in her old room. Tell Hanna to give it a thorough cleaning. No one's slept in it for years."

"Yes, sir." Primus started to go.

"Just a minute. I want you to send a telegram to Edwina in Charleston. She won't want to have Lucinda moving in and taking over the house in her absence."

"No, sir."

Mansfield dictated the telegram. When Primus left, he mulled over the occasion for this visit. Was Lucinda going to exercise her rights to Lynwood? This was something that he and Edwina had feared for years...Lucinda would demand that her half of the estate be sold and thus break up the property...parts of it had already been sold off to the freedmen during Reconstruction...soon it would be reduced to a mere few hundred acres or so...

On the other hand, she may simply want to make a surprise visit and celebrate Christmas with her family. But why now, after all these years?... Jacqueline...of course! How could he be so dense? Lucinda's coming not only to claim Lynwood, but Jacqueline, too!

This thought so agitated Mansfield that he leapt up from his chair, heedless of his gout until he felt a sharp pain in his big toe. "Damn!" He sat back down, removed his shoe, and massaged the toe. "Ah...I'd as soon cut the damn thing off...but it comes and goes..." Indeed it soon went away, momentarily at least, and he put the shoe back on. He tested the toe gingerly, took a few steps, and assured that the pain was at least manageable, stepped out onto the terrace. Strolling–even hobbling–about the lawn was his way of blowing off steam and working things out in his head.

That Rhodes woman had bewitched Edward in every way. First she married him for his money, then got herself pregnant by that Jones fellow. When the child turned out to have negroid characteristics, the whole household became a veritable Bedlam. Edwina was beside herself. He himself had considered going after Jones with pistol and ball–never mind a duel. He would have shot him on sight. But the Rhodes woman worked out the agreement with Edwina and Lucinda. She gave up any claim to Lynwood and just walked away. Amazing! Of course she got some sort of compensation–he couldn't remember what, exactly.

But that Jones fellow! He was the devil incarnate. He not only got the Rhodes woman pregnant, but Lucinda, too! He should have shot the scoundrel anyway.

By this time, Mansfield had wandered out to the dock where the *Southern Pride* was tied up. He stood before it for a few moments trying to assess its role in the whole affair. Edwina had actually encouraged Edward to take Miss Rhodes on an excursion to impress her and finally to propose to her. He and Edwina had discreetly excused themselves to their stateroom while Edward regaled his intended with champagne and tales of his exploits during the war in order to induce her to marry him. And she did–knowing all the time that she was pregnant by another man! No, no, it wasn't Jones that was the Devil, it was Miss Rhodes! She was the Siren of the Seas, enticing sailors to their doom!

He walked up the gangplank, where he saw Sherman and Uli leaning over the starboard side pulling on some lines. They were fishing. When they became aware of Mansfield's presence, they immediately dropped their lines in the water and stood at attention like sailors surprised at an unannounced inspection.

He ignored them and walked up to the bow, where he paused at the railing.

"Welcome aboard, sir. Can I get you anything?"

He turned around to see Louis, looking immaculate in his uniform, smiling at him.

"Oh, hello, Louis. I must say, you and your boys keep this old tub sparkling like a diamond. Don't you get bored with nothing to do but polish the brass and paint everything else?"

Louis laughed. "Oh, there's always something to do, Mr. LeRoux. Me and the boys just wish you and Miz LeRoux would take the old girl out now and then."

Mansfield turned away and put his hands on the railing. "I'd like to, Louis, but Mrs. LeRoux is afraid of sunburn, afraid of storms, afraid of drowning, afraid of nearly everything, actually–except gardens and dinner parties. Why is it, do you think, Louis, that women are afraid of the great outdoors? Of Nature?"

"Well, Miss Jackie ain't afraid of them things. She love the salt air, the ebb and flow of the tide, all the little sea creatures–and she don't mind a little sunburn now and then, either."

Mansfield chuckled. "No, no. She doesn't. It's a wonder she's so different from her mother. More like...more like her Aunt Lucinda."

"That's a fact."

"Damn!" Mansfield took off his shoe and rubbed his toe. "The gout's acting up again. I need to sit down."

"Why don't you settle into a chair in the salon?" Louis offered his arm. "I'll bring you something to drink."

"Good idea." Mansfield put the shoe under his left arm, took Louis' arm with his right, and hobbled along as his trusted steward led the way. "Make it a brandy. Doctor's orders."

Once settled into a comfortable chair in the salon, Mansfield put the shoe down on the carpet and looked around the room as Louis went to the bar to fetch the brandy. "Yes, you and the boys keep the old tub in tip-top shape, Louis. I've got to hand it to you. I–what's that?"

Louis returned with the brandy on a tray. "What's what, Mr. LeRoux?"

Mansfield took the brandy in his hand. "*That*. That painting, if it can be called that."

Louis looked at Tony's portrait of Jackie, which hung over the mantelpiece at the far end of the room. "That's the picture of Miss Jackie that Mr. Coleman purchased for her down in Savannah."

Mansfield squinted at the object in question. "Oh, yes–now I remember. Must be getting old.Dammit! Can you put something under my foot there, Louis? It's killing me."

Louis retrieved an ottoman from another chair and slipped it under Mansfield's foot.

"Ah! That's better," Mansfield said. He took a sip of his brandy. "Louis..."

"Yes, sir?"

"You've been with us for a long time."

"Yes, sir."

"Even before Edwina and I were married."

"Yes, sir."

"You were here when Jacqueline was born."

"That I was."

"And when...when that Rhodes woman gave birth to...to her child."

"Yes, sir."

"You probably know more of the family's secrets than I do."

"Oh, I wouldn't say that, Mr. LeRoux."

"You're just being your usual discreet self. I know you do."

Louis said nothing.

Mansfield downed the remainder of his brandy. "I think I'll have another."

"Yes, sir." Louis took the empty glass and went to the bar.

Mansfield stared at the painting until Louis returned with a fresh glass. "Sit down, Louis."

"Sir?"

"I said sit down. Nobody can see us in here. I want to talk to you–man to man."

Louis looked confused for a moment, looked to the portholes of the salon, and seeing no signs of his sons bustling about, sat down in a chair next to his employer.

"That's better," Mansfield said. "Hurts my neck to be looking up at you all the time."

Louis remained silent.

"Louis...you were here...at the house, I mean...when that, that child of the Rhodes woman was born."

"Yes, sir."

"And you saw that it was not Mr. Benson's child, but the child of that Jones fellow, the major."

"Well, sir, I don't know–"

"You don't have to say it outright. You knew. Everyone knew. It was obvious. But that's beside the point. The fact is, you were also present a few months later when Jacqueline was born."

"Yes, sir."

"That's what I want to talk to you about." Mansfield continued to stare at the painting as if it harbored a great secret. "You know that Jacqueline is not my wife's child."

Louis said nothing.

"All right, all right. I know you were sworn to secrecy, as we all were. But what I want to know is...if Major Jones was the father, as we all suspected, then why the devil does Jackie look the way she does? I mean with blond hair, blue eyes, and fair skin–like Edwina? That's how we pulled off this masquerade and have been able to do it for more than twenty years. She looks like Edwina's child, not Lucinda's. And certainly not Major Jones'."

Louis shrugged. "I couldn't say, Mr. LeRoux."

Mansfield looked directly at Louis, as if to penetrate his inscrutable mask. "No, I guess you couldn't. But it's a devil of a mystery to me. And now Lucinda's coming to claim her child. If she does, I don't know what we'd do. Edwina couldn't have children, you know."

Louis looked placidly at his employer and again said nothing.

Mansfield sipped his brandy. "Well...that's all I wanted to say, Louis. You must have some duties to tend to."

Louis stood. "Yes, sir. I'd better see that the boys ain't slackin' off. And Frederick's cookin' up some gumbo. You want to eat here, Mr. LeRoux?"

"What? Oh, no. I'll take dinner at the house. That is, if I can get there under my own power. Is there a cane around here somewhere? I didn't need one when I left the house."

"Yes, sir. I'll bring you one."

Mansfield remained in his chair sipping his brandy and staring at the painting while Louis retrieved the cane.

"Here you are, sir. I'll help you to your feet."

"No, that's all right. I'll stay and finish my brandy, then I think I'll be able to stand with the help of the cane. You better go see about the stew Frederick's cooking up."

"Yes, sir. Just holler if you need me."

Mansfield studied the painting as if it contained the solution to his dilemma. "You know," he said to himself, "her eyes are crossed. When Jacqueline was little, her eyes were crossed for a while. Edwina and I worried about it, took her to the doctor, and he said not to worry, her eyes would straighten themselves out in time. And they did. Curious, isn't it? How could the painter have known that?"

CHAPTER 29

Since returning from Savannah, Tony put his paint brushes away and replaced them with his briefcase and bowler hat.

The Saturday before Christmas–the big day was, awkwardly this year, on a Monday–he sat in his office discussing delinquent loans with Mr. Ferguson. They went down the list, marking those that would receive an extension with a check mark and those to be foreclosed upon with an 'x.' Fortunately, there were fewer 'x's than checks, far fewer in fact, and both men felt confident that the bank could absorb any losses as a result of the foreclosures.

Just as Mr. Ferguson was leaving his office, Mr. Hartsfield, a teller, appeared at the door with an attractive middle-aged woman standing just behind him. She was a brunette–actually, her hair was as black as his–and smartly dressed. She wore an elaborate felt touring hat bedecked with flowers and feathers, a blue silk dress with leg o' mutton sleeves, and a tiger-striped cravat snug against a high collar. She also carried an umbrella, though the sky was clear and cloudless.

"Sorry to disturb you, Mr. Jones," Hartsfield said, "but this lady has a bank draft she'd like to cash, and it's on a foreign bank."

Tony stood up from his desk. "A foreign bank? That shouldn't be a problem, Mrs.–"

"*Miss*," the lady said, almost defiantly. "Miss Lucinda Benson."

Tony was stunned for a moment, then came out from behind his desk. "It's a pleasure to meet you, Miss Benson. I've heard a great deal about you. Won't you sit down?"

Mr. Hartsfield quietly slipped away and Lucinda stepped forward. "I don't know what you've heard, Mr. Jones–oh, my goodness! You're not... Antonio's son?" Tony smiled. "I *am* the son of Antonio Jones, Miss Benson.

Welcome home."

Lucinda stood transfixed for a moment as if confronted with a specter. Then she smiled broadly.

"You're just as handsome as your father, only–"

"Only a bit darker?"

"Well, yes, of course. But the features are the same." She looked around for a place to put her parasol.

"I'll take that, Miss Benson." Tony took the parasol and hung it on the hall tree next to the door.

Lucinda sat in an armchair opposite the desk. "You must call me Lucinda."

Tony went behind his desk and sat down. "Lucinda. Well, yes...it will take some getting used to. I know that you were a close friend of my father's. In fact, I remember him telling me that you once directed him in a production of *Othello*."

"Did he? Then you know–everything."

Tony's eyebrows rose. "Everything?"

Lucinda seemed flustered, confused. "I mean everything about the play. Antonio was a wonderful actor. It was an amateur production, but he had some professional experience before the war and such a stage presence! If it hadn't been for his duties with the Freedmen's Bureau, why he might have returned to New York and had a successful career as an actor. Have you any interest in acting, Mr. Jones?"

"None, I'm afraid. And please call me Tony."

"Tony." Lucinda smiled. "Charming. 'Antonio' is so...so..." She waved her hand with a flourish. "...*theatrical*, isn't it?"

"I suppose so, though everyone seemed comfortable using it. I was called Tony simply to distinguish us. I mean in the way of–"

"But you were saying, Tony, that you have no interest in acting? I could see you as–"

"Actually, my avocation is painting. But of course your niece has created quite a sensation around here with her prodigious talent."

"Has she? Well...I'm happy to hear it. She got some highly favorable reviews in London, you know. Have you met her?"

Tony fiddled idly with the pen on his desk. "Yes. I attended her performance here in Beaufort. One of several stage-door Johnnies, I'm afraid."

Lucinda laughed in her peculiar way, as if she were having trouble breathing. "The same thing happened in London. Rather a lot of competition, no?"

Tony was becoming more and more uncomfortable. He wasn't sure how Lucinda might react to a possible liason between himself and Jackie. "I didn't really see it that way. I simply admired her performance and thought I should express my appreciation."

Lucinda turned her head aside and gave him a sly look. "Yes, of course you did."

Tony cleared his throat. "Now, Miss–Lucinda–I understand you have a bank draft you wish to cash."

Lucinda maintained eye contact for a moment, then opened her purse. "That's correct." She pulled out a piece of paper and slid it across the desk. "It's on my London bank."

Tony looked at the check. "Child & Company. A very reputable institution. And the exchange rate is rather favorable at the moment." He initialed the check.

"Lovely. You know, I have to do some last minute Christmas shopping for my niece and Edwina and her husband. Is the Emporium still in business?"

"Indeed it is. Mr. Cooper is the proprietor now."

"Cooper? That sounds familiar. Well–" She stood up. "It's such a delight to meet you at last, Tony."

Tony stood. "It's been a pleasure for me as well, Lucinda." He handed her the bank draft. "Take this to Mr. Hartsfield at the first window. He'll be happy to assist you."

Lucinda put the draft in her purse and retrieved her parasol from the hall tree. She paused at the door. "Oh, Tony–you must come and visit us at Lynwood over the holidays. I'm sure my niece would be delighted to see you."

"Well...yes, that would be very nice. Are you sure Mr. And Mrs. LeRoux wouldn't mind?"

"Mind? Of course not. Why, you're practically one of the family."

"Me? One of the family?"

Lucinda gave him one of her sly looks. "Didn't your mother tell you that you were born at Lynwood?"

Tony stared blankly at her for a moment. "Born there? No. No, she didn't."

"Well, it's true. I was present as well. You were such a beautiful baby!"

Tony managed a half-hearted smile. "That's comforting to know."

"Come see us Christmas Day for dinner," Lucinda said. "It will be like a family reunion. Ta, ta!" She twirled her parasol with a flourish and disappeared into the lobby.

Tony stood before his desk like a statue. What more would he learn about his birth, his parentage? Had his mother told him the truth? If so, she had left out a few things.

He went behind his desk, sat down and spun his fountain pen around a few times on the blotter. How could he go out to Lynwood on Christmas Day? His mother would be apoplectic at the idea. And speaking of apoplexy, how would Mr. and Mrs. LeRoux react when they saw him making his way jauntily up the stairs to their front door? A black man coming to court their daughter!

No, no, this could never work. Lucinda must be joking. He pulled his watch out of his vest pocket and looked at it. Two o'clock. Not much left today for him to do at the bank.

He stood, looked around the office at its elaborate trappings, and wondered what he was doing here at all. What business did he have being a bank president? He put his watch back in his pocket and went to the hall tree, where he picked up his bowler and put it on his head.

By the time he got on the ferry and crossed over to St. Helena, his mother would be home from the Penn School.

CHAPTER 30

As the weather was unusually warm for this time of year, Tony and Georgia had a light lunch on the veranda facing Cowan Creek.

"You're very quiet today," Georgia said. "Is something on your mind?"

Tony pushed his plate aside and wiped his mouth with his napkin. "Lucinda Benson came into the bank today."

"Oh." Georgia put down her lemonade. "Where did she come from?"

"London. By way of New York. She had some very interesting things to say."

"Really?" She stood up to collect the plates. "Are you finished?"

"Yes. That was a good sandwich. We should have them more often. Saves time."

Georgia said nothing but took the plates into the kitchen and returned with a pitcher. "More lemonade?"

"Sure."

Georgia poured them both some lemonade and sat down. "What brought her back to Beaufort after all these years?"

Tony stared out over the bluff at nothing in particular. "I don't know. Ostensibly to visit her sister's family for Christmas. She invited me to join them for dinner."

Georgia remained silent.

Tony turned to her. "Well?"

"Well, what?"

"Do you have any objection?"

"None whatsoever. You're a grown man now. You may accept whatever invitations you wish."

Tony sighed and looked out over the bluff. "I thought you might like to go with me."

"What!"

"Why not? Lucinda said I was practically one of the family. And if I am, you are, too."

Georgia put her lemonade down and leaned back in her chair, a rocker. She closed her eyes. "What did she tell you?"

"Nothing of great interest. Just that I was born at Lynwood."

Georgia remained silent, her eyes still closed.

"Is that true?"

She opened her eyes "Yes, it's true."

"Then you and Papa had–intimate relations–while you were living with Benson?"

"No. We did not."

"No?"

"No."

Tony threw his napkin down on the table. "Mama–you're not being very helpful, dribbling out this information–this critical information about the circumstances of my birth one drop at a time. Can't you tell me the whole story?"

Georgia sighed. "I think I *have* told you the whole story. I didn't think it was necessary to tell you exactly where you were born. What does it matter?"

Tony stood and shoved his hands into his pockets. "It matters a great deal. All this time I've been thinking that you were an adulteress. Now you tell me you weren't, but what am I to think? You were married to Edward Benson, you gave birth to me at his house, but you assure me that Papa was my biological father. Weren't you both adulterers?"

"No. I was pregnant with you before I married Edward Benson."

Tony could no longer restrain himself. "You married Benson knowing you were pregnant by another man?"

Tears began flowing from Georgia's eyes and she tried vainly to stop them with her napkin. "Oh, Tony, why are you making all this so hard for me? You don't know what things were like just after the war. I was just nineteen and in my first year at the Penn School–I was afraid I'd lose my job and be disgraced if I had a child out of wedlock."

"So you thought that by marrying Benson–a man you didn't love–you'd solve the problem."

"Yes."

Tony sat down again. "And so I was born at Lynwood with everyone thinking that I was Edward Benson's son until...I made my debut in the world."

"Yes." Georgia dried her tears and composed herself.

Tony looked at her and smiled. She managed to smile back, feebly. He burst out laughing. "What a sight I must have been! What a scandal! Distinguished Southern gentleman and his lily-white wife give birth to a black baby! I can hear the roars, the screams of shame and outrage ringing throughout the house. It must have been pandemonium!"

Georgia managed something resembling a laugh, but her lips trembled.

"Where was Papa all this time?"

"He was at the Beaufort Inn. That's where he was living."

"The Beaufort Inn? He didn't own a house?"

"No. He had been living at General Saxton's house on Bay Street, but then the general was transferred to Washington, so he had no other place to live."

"The Beaufort Inn, eh? So that's where I was conceived?"

"No. Oh, Tony–this is useless! A child can't know every last detail of the circumstances of his birth. You already know more than I know about my own parents' courtship. Can't you leave it alone?"

Tony sighed and rocked back in his chair. "I guess you're right. I didn't mean to upset you so, Mama. It's just that...all of this confusion about... about who I am..."

"You're my son. And the son of your father–Antonio Jones. And that's the truth."

"I guess that should be enough. And I'm grateful, Mama. Grateful for all that you and Papa have done for me." He reached over, took her hand, and kissed it.

"Do you still want to go out to Lynwood on Christmas Day?"

"I don't know. It might upset Jackie."

Georgia leaned back in her rocker. "I haven't met the girl, but from what I've heard, she's nothing like her mother."

"And I haven't met her mother, but from what I've heard, she's nothing like her daughter."

They both laughed.

After a moment or two, Georgia said:

"If you don't go, I think it would be nice if you stayed here and got to know Hi."

"Hi?"

"For Hiram. Hiram Cooper. I've asked him to join us for Christmas dinner."

"Mama–are you serious about this man?"

"Oh, I wouldn't say serious–he's just a very nice man who says all the things a woman likes to hear. He reminds me a bit of your father, actually–only a little gentler, perhaps even more refined."

"I guess Papa was a little rough around the edges–the army must have done that to him. What did Mr. Cooper–Hi–do during the war?"

"He was a haberdasher in Boston, involved in the abolitionist movement. He came down here after the war to work for Mr. Forbes, the founder of The Emporium. And now he's the owner."

Tony considered this. "I wonder if...I wonder if both of you might like to go out to Lynwood with me."

"Me? Edwina wouldn't allow me in the front door. Besides, Lucinda invited only you–and you may not get past the front door, either."

"I'm going to have to meet the woman some time. It might as well be sooner rather than later."

Georgia seized his hand and patted it. "Later, Tony. Later. I want you here with us. I promise you, you'll find Hi far more receptive. Do you know he's been singing your praises as president of the bank?"

Tony chuckled. "To whom? To you, of course. He wants to get on your good side."

"Well...a woman does love flattery–especially when it's directed towards her children."

"All right, Mama. I'll stay here. It's Christmas, after all."

CHAPTER 31

Lucinda arrived at Lynwood just a few hours before Edwina and Jackie arrived from Charleston.

Primus pulled up to the front steps and got down from his perch to assist the ladies from the carriage.

"How does she look, Primus?" Edwina said.

"As pretty as ever," Primus said. "The years ain't hardly touched her."

"Hmph," Edwina said. "Is that a fair assessment, Jacqueline?"

"I wouldn't know, Mother. I didn't know her when she was young."

"Of course you didn't. It was a stupid question. Well, I suppose we'll have to get on with it. Lucinda's timing has always been very poor–or very clever, depending on how you look at it. She's succeeded in cutting short our visit with Ravenel. I had so hoped–"

"It's just as well, Mother. All the tours and games at Rav's townhouse were becoming quite tiresome. It's a relief, really. And I'm so excited about seeing Aunt Lucy–you should patch up your differences, with her."

"Oh, you're exaggerating our differences. She just has a habit of needling me at every opportunity. Or at least she used to. We're both older now. Perhaps she's grown out of it."

Jackie said nothing in response to this, and they ascended the steps. Just as they reached the top, the door opened and Lucinda appeared.

"At last you've come!" she said.

Edwina gave her sister a rather frosty smile, followed by an obligatory hug. "Yes, Lucinda–we have come. I must say you're looking well. Where's my husband?"

In the library," Lucinda said. "The poor thing has had an attack of the gout."

"We knew that, Lucinda. Well–I take it you're all settled?"

"Yes, of course. I've got my old room. Jacqueline, darling, give your auntie a hug."

Jacqueline obliged her. "What prompted you to visit us over Christmas, Aunt Lucy? And why didn't you bring Nigel?"

"Nigel?" Edwina said, her nostrils flaring as if she had gotten wind of some foul odor.

"Nigel Bingham," Jackie said cheerily. "Aunt Lucy's beau."

"My *ex*-beau," Lucinda said. "Nigel's gone back to Yorkshire to join a commune. His friends considered set construction to be pandering to the bourgeois class. He's making furniture for factory workers now."

"Oh," Jackie said. "I'm so sorry, Aunt Lucy. I thought he was such a nice man."

"Actually, he was rather stupid," Lucinda said. "And he didn't believe that women should have the right to vote."

"By that definition," Edwina said, "your brother-in-law is rather stupid, too."

Lucinda grinned. "Mansfield was never the progressive type, was he, Edwina? That's why you married him."

"Don't start, Lucinda," Edwina said. "You've just arrived and already you've managed to insult both me and my husband."

"Insult?" Lucinda said. "You're too sensitive, Edwina. I'm just stating the facts. But speaking of Mansfield, why don't we look in to see how he's doing?"

Sherman appeared and assisted Primus in carrying the ladies' luggage upstairs, while the three women entered the library. They found Mansfield sitting in his favorite wing chair with his leg propped up on a leather ottoman. He seemed to be engrossed in a book.

"We are here, Mansfield," Edwina said. "What is it that you're reading?"

Mansfield looked up. "Oh–so you are. How was the trip?"

"Beastly, as usual," Edwina said. "Isn't that the English expression, Lucinda?"

"'Bollocks' is more up to date, actually." Lucinda winked at Jackie.

"'Bollocks'?" Edwina said. "Isn't that a nautical term?"

"It is if you consider that sailors use it a lot," Lucinda said.

"Well, be that as it may," Edwina said, "The train had to stop three times for the porters to clear cows off the track."

"They were nosing about for bollocks, no doubt," Lucinda said, again winking at Jackie, who managed to suppress a smile.

"What's all this barnyard talk, Lucinda?" Mansfield said. "I thought you were immersed in Shakespeare and Byron and all of those other lofty English poets."

"Shakespeare is rather bawdy at times, Mansfield," Lucinda said, "and Lord Byron actually lived the life Shakespeare only wrote about. What's that you're reading?"

"I've already asked him that," Edwina said, "and he's refused to answer me."

Mansfield turned the cover of the book over. "*The Life of Jefferson Davis.* A great man, you know."

Lucinda rolled her eyes. "A great scoundrel, if you ask me. Didn't he abscond with all the Confederate gold at the end of the war?"

"He did not abscond with it," Mansfield said indignantly. "He safeguarded it with the idea of using it to mount another attack on the Yankees. And if he had–"

"Please don't go on about the war again, Mansfield," Edwina said. "I shall have to pack my ears with cotton if you do."

Mansfield opened his book again and mumbled something unintelligible.

Jackie, ever the peace-maker, looked at her mother, then her aunt. "Why don't we leave Father to his reading while we retire to the breakfast room? The sun is out and I'm famished!"

"Good idea, Jacqueline," Edwina said. "I could use a bit of sustenance myself. The food on the train was absolutely inedible. Coming, Lucinda?"

"I've eaten," Lucinda said. "You two go on. I think I'll stay here with Mansfield and do a little reading myself. And maybe Primus will bring us a brandy or two, eh, Mansfield?"

"Best idea you've had all day, Lucinda." Mansfield reached for a bell cord. I'll ring for the rascal–time he earned his keep."

CHAPTER 32

Christmas Day turned out to be much cooler than the previous two weeks, which invigorated the denizens of the Lowcountry and put them in the seasonal spirit. Temperatures were in the thirties until noon and didn't rise above the low forties the rest of the day.

Mr. Cooper arrived in his phaeton at precisely noon wearing a stylish overcoat, an article of clothing rarely seen south of Baltimore.

Tony wore a red plaid vest, gray trousers, and his patent yellow shoes, which he wore rarely on the premise that they were unbefitting of a bank president.

Georgia, for her part, fell somewhere in between these extremes, and greeted Mr. Cooper at the door dressed in a blue velvet dress and a silk blouse with a ruff collar of fine lace. She had in fact purchased these items at the Emporium some years earlier.

"Oh, Hi–that's such a smart coat!" she said, as she closed the door behind him.

"Just came in from Boston," Cooper said. "Wait till you see the lining." He unbuttoned the coat, which extended below the knees,and opened it for her to see.

"Oh, my," Georgia said. "Silk?"

"The finest. Well, I can't wear it in the house, can I? Where should I–"

"I'll take it," she said. "I wouldn't want it to get all crumpled up on the hall tree. It requires a hanger."

Cooper removed the coat. "It's not that delicate. You could throw it over a chair and it would be fine. Where's Tony?"

"In the kitchen. Cooking." She hung the coat in the hall closet.

"Cooking? Isn't that your job?"

"Tony's a better cook than I am. Those years in Paris, you know."

"Well...he's a man of many talents. Here–I've brought you something." He extracted a small package from his vest pocket. "You can open it now, if you wish."

Georgia looked curiously at the package, which was really just a box with a red ribbon tied around it. There was a tiny envelope beneath the ribbon. She took it and opened the envelope. "To my dearest Georgia–Merry Christmas. Your Hiram."

"Oh, Hi–I hope it's not too expensive."

Cooper chuckled. "I always get a discount. Besides, nothing can be too expensive for you."

Georgia pursed her lips in a way that suggested such a compliment was excessive, but then eagerly removed the ribbon and opened the box. "Oh, Hi...it's beautiful!"

Tony emerged from the kitchen, wearing a white apron and drying his hands on it. "What is it, Mama?"

"It's a...bracelet." She looked up at Cooper. "Isn't it?"

"It is indeed," Cooper said. "But more than that–it's a wrist watch."

"Oh," Georgia said, taking the item out of the box. "I've heard of wrist watches, but I don't think I've ever seen one. Are those real diamonds?"

"They are. I purchased it at the Paris Exposition a few years ago. Many think of it as jewelry, but it's practical, too."

"They're quite common in Paris these days," Tony said. "All the fashionable women wear them."

"Well..." Georgia said, admiring the piece and then placing it on her wrist. "It sparkles so! I think it must be too expensive to wear day-to-day. Perhaps to a fancy ball."

"I insist that you wear it day-to-day," Cooper said. "That's what it's for. Here, let me show you how the clasp works." He took hold of the two ends of the bracelet and joined them together. "There!"

Georgia held her wrist up to better view it. "What a pretty thing! But Hi, I don't think I should wear it to school. It would be too distracting to the children, and besides, Miss Towne would consider it to be...to be..."

"Too showy?" Tony said. "What about the brougham?"

"That's for special occasions," Georgia said. "And besides, the children love to ride in it. But this–"

"You don't like it?" Cooper said.

"Oh, no! I didn't mean that. I love it!"

"Then you should wear it," Cooper said.

"Well...I will." Georgia went to the hall mirror, where she held it before the mirror and examined it from every angle. "It is lovely. I suppose in between gala balls we'll have to keep it at the bank."

Cooper laughed. "It's probably just as safe right here. You'll have to start locking your doors, though."

Georgia came back to the middle of the room and gave Cooper a kiss on the cheek. "Thank you so much, Hi. Now I've got something for you."

"Hold on!" Tony said. "We've got to have dinner first. Or at least hors d'oeuvres. We'll open the rest of the presents later. Why don't you open that bottle of wine on the sideboard, Hi, while I see about the duck. The hors d'oeuvres are on the table." He went back to the kitchen while Hi stood for a moment admiring the watch and its wearer.

"Georgia, I–"

"Yes, Hi?"

"I think you look as beautiful as I've ever seen you."

Georgia blushed. "Diamonds make any woman more beautiful. Do you know I've never owned one?"

"Now you own a dozen. Didn't Antonio give you a ring when you were married?"

Georgia lowered her eyes. "No. He couldn't really afford one on his army pay. Even when we were better off, I don't think it even crossed his mind."

"Well...I suppose he had...other things to think about."

"Yes. He was always very busy...Oh! Let's open the wine. Tony says that it needs time to breathe."

"Yes...of course." Cooper went to the sideboard and picked up one of several bottles resting there. "My God! Chateau Lafitte! And here I thought you and Tony were living like monks!"

Georgia laughed. "That was the one department where Antonio was extravagant. He loved that wine. There's a whole cellar full of it."

"Well, I suppose we'll have to drink it up." He cut the foil and inserted the corkscrew. "How long does Tony say it has to breathe?"

"I don't know. An hour, I think."

"An hour? I don't think I can wait that long."

"I'll go ask him."

In the kitchen, Georgia noted that Tony had already opened a bottle and was sipping from a glass as he tended to the cooking.

"Here," he said. "Take this bottle to the dining room and we'll let the other one breathe. It's delicious in any case."

"Be careful you don't get tipsy before we even eat," she said.

"Me, tipsy? Don't be silly–I never get tipsy."

Georgia returned to the dining room with the open bottle and Cooper poured each of them a glass. They sat on the sofa in the living room, where Tony had built a fire earlier. It was beginning to fade, so Cooper threw another log on and jabbed at it with the poker.

Tony joined them after a few minutes and replenished his glass. He sat down in an armchair near the fire.

"There was a young lady in the shop yesterday asking about you," Cooper said.

"Oh? What did she look like?"

"A pretty young colored girl," Cooper said. He had one arm draped over the back of the sofa behind Georgia's head and a glass in his free hand. "She said you attended the Penn School together. I can't remember the name–Violet, I think."

"Violet? Violet Heyward?"

"That's it. She said she was home for the holidays."

"Oh, Tony!" Georgia said. "You should go and see her. It's too late to ask her to dinner, but–"

"I'll drop in on her after Christmas," Tony said, without enthusiasm. "She's a good girl. Smart, too."

"Yes," Cooper said. "I could tell she was well-educated. I think she said she was teaching at that new school for coloreds in Orangeburg."

Tony's mouth turned down at Cooper's use of the word 'coloreds.' "Yes, I've heard. I suppose that's the only place they would give her a job."

"Oh, Tony," Georgia said. "I'm sure she could have gotten a job at the Penn School. Miss Towne would have been delighted to have her. But a college professor! That was a better opportunity."

"Yes," Tony said. "Of the two, I suppose she made the right choice."

"Of course she did," Georgia said.

There was a long silence as the three of them stared into the crackling fire.

"More wine?" Tony said. "I think the second bottle has had enough air now." He went to the sideboard and opened a third bottle before returning to the living room.

At dinner, Tony sat at the head of the table while regaling Georgia and Hiram with tales of his days in Paris. Cooper was no stranger to the city, having made several buying trips there over the past decade.

Georgia felt a bit left out of this discussion, as she had never ventured farther north than Charleston or south of Savannah. And she was a little concerned at Tony's drinking, which seemed to reveal a coarser side of his personality that she had never seen before.

"Now this girl," Tony said, pouring himself still another glass, "fancied herself an artist, but the truth of the matter was that she was a ragamuffin I picked up in the gutter at Pigale. And when I brought her back to the studio–"

"Tony!"Georgia said. "Do we have to hear about your more sordid adventures in Paris?"

Tony held his glass in mid-air and looked surprised. "Sordid? Who said anything about sordid? I was about to tell you about this girl's peculiar habits. She–"

"I think your mother would rather hear about art galleries, the theater, the–" Cooper began, but Tony cut him off.

"The theater!" he said. "Now there's a topic for genteel conversation, especially in Paris. In some of the shows the dancers appear topless and–"

"Tony!" Georgia threw her napkin down on the table and rose from her chair. "We have a guest who doesn't appreciate such allusions to–"

"It's all right, Georgia," Cooper said. "I've seen some of those same shows–the Parisian think nothing of it."

"Well, I think something of it and that is that it's not a proper subject for discussion at the dinner table–especially on Christmas Day. Excuse me, gentlemen–I'll leave you to your ribald stories and start cleaning up in the kitchen."

"Mama–" Tony threw his napkin down as well. "I'm sorry if I offended you. We'll help you."

"No, no, don't bother. You and Hiram continue your discussion. Three in the kitchen is a crowd. Why don't you start opening the presents?"

Tony and Cooper were left staring at each other while Georgia disappeared into the kitchen.

"That was an excellent meal, Tony," Cooper said, twirling his glass on its stem. "Obviously you learned a few things in Paris besides how to pick up show girls."

"Simone wasn't a show girl–she was a model." Tony said.

"Yes...of course. Well, speaking of art, have you done any painting while in Beaufort? I suppose with all your duties at the bank–"

Tony gestured to the far wall with his glass. "That's it. What do you think?"

Cooper turned to look at the trompe l'oeil. "You did that? Why, I think that's marvelous. It looks so real–I'd almost thought it was a door to the garden."

"It's all the rage these days in Paris. Requires little imagination. Anyone can do it."

"Well, I know I couldn't do it. I wonder if you might do something like it at my place. I need something to liven up the old manse. I'd pay you, of course."

"I'll do it for nothing, Hi. After all, you're a major depositor and shareholder. Shall we retire to the living room as Mama suggested? Bring the bottle."

By this time, Cooper was getting a little tipsy himself, and he picked up the bottle as he followed Tony into the living room.

By the time Georgia finished up in the kitchen and appeared in the living room, Tony and Cooper were talking and joking like old friends. But when they saw Georgia, they suddenly became silent.

"Am I interrupting, gentlemen?" she said.

"Of course not," Cooper said. He stood, while Tony remained seated. "Why don't you have a seat here on the sofa while Tony hands out the presents?"

Georgia sat down without comment.

Tony got up from his chair and went to the tree, which was one he had cut down in the nearby woods. It was really a small pine since there were no firs on the island, but it passed for a Christmas tree. He and Georgia had decorated it the night before with the balls of yarn and cloth dolls that had been in her family for generations.

"To Mama," Tony said, extracting a gift from beneath the tree. "From Tony."

Georgia's cheery countenance returned as Tony handed her the gift. It was a large package, obviously containing some article of clothing. She unwrapped the box and extracted a long, silk robe embroidered with flowers, bees, and tiny birds.

"Oh, Tony," she said. "This is lovely. And just what I need. The old one is threadbare and falling apart."

Tony grinned. "I noticed. And Hi helped me pick it out."

"Did he?" She glanced at Cooper. "Well, thank you both."

"Speaking of Paris," Cooper said. "That's where it came from."

"Well," Georgia said with a slight grimace. "They do make some fine things. I have to say that."

This traditional exchange of gifts seemed to have a dampening effect on the high spirits of both Tony and Cooper, and gave them a respite from their drinking. On the other hand, now Georgia became a bit tipsy. She sat closer to Cooper, and as Tony could not fail to notice, put her hand on his knee.

This induced Tony to refill his glass, but not Cooper's, who held his out, but to no avail.

"Well," Tony said after tipping his glass up, "I guess that just about does it. I think I'll go for a ride."

"A ride?" Georgia said. "To where?"

"I don't know. Anywhere. I need to work some of this alcohol off. A little exercise will help."

"I think that's a good idea," Georgia said. She put her own glass down on the coffee table. "Maybe Hi and I will go for a walk."

"Do that," Tony said. "And don't wait up for me. I may be gone for a while." He then went to the hall tree, put on his coat and gloves, and left the house.

Georgia and Cooper looked at each other.

"Did I say something wrong?" Cooper said.

"No, no. Of course not. Like he said, he's just had a little too much to drink. He's not used to it. The ride will do him good."

Once outside Tony went to the barn and saddled up Leto. He led her out to the drive and started to put his foot in the stirrup, when he had a second thought. This second thought was to retrieve two more bottles from the root cellar, whose door he carefully opened and closed so as not to make any noise. Then he put the bottles into his saddle bag, mounted Leto and trotted off down the driveway.

CHAPTER 33

Christmas dinner at Lynwood was a sedate affair, with Lucinda uncharacteristically subdued and on her best behavior. Jackie found this to be surprising and was even a little bit disappointed, as she had been looking forward to some of Lucinda's irreverent remarks and the inevitable clash with her mother.

Instead, Mansfield seemed to dominate the dinner conversation, taking the opportunity as master carver to expound upon the current state of affairs in South Carolina, and especially the impending Constitutional Convention in Columbia.

"The Yankees imposed a whole set of nonsensical rules on us in '68," he said, "and the nigras turned the convention into a circus. Ravenel was there. He told me–"

"Mansfield, dear," Edwina said, "the servants will hear you."

"They may hear me all they like, dear, and in fact, they had better get used to white people taking control of their affairs, as we did in the old days. They'll be a damn sight better off for it, too."

"Fortunately," Edwina said, "only Louise and Hanna are here today to suffer your harangues and fulminations about the inevitable decline of civilization. The rest of the servants are off celebrating Christmas with their families. Poor Hanna has no family left after the storm, and Louise□"

She was interrupted by the crescendo of bells ringing at the front door.

"Now who can that be at the dinner hour?" Edwina said. "Hanna!"

"I don't think she can hear you, mother," Jackie said. "She's in the kitchen with Louise."

"But surely she heard the bells," Edwina said.

"Who didn't?" Lucinda said, putting down her knife and fork. "Those bells would rouse a hibernating bear. Fortunately this bear is stuffed with enough food to last the rest of the winter. Louise is a marvelous cook."

"That she is," Edwina said. "Perhaps Hanna has–"

As if on cue, Hanna appeared at the dining room door. "There's a colored man at the door, Mrs. LeRoux. I told him to go around to the servants' entrance, but he refused."

"Refused?" Edwina said, incredulous.

"What have I been telling you?" Mansfield said. "The nigras–except our own, of course–have been getting more insolent and brazen every year."

"He says he's an invited guest," Hanna said.

"Invited?" Edwina said. "Send him away, Hanna. But be careful–he may be dangerous."

As Hanna started to leave the room, Lucinda called her back. "Show him in, Hanna. *I* invited him."

Edwina turned to Lucinda as if stung by a bee. "*You* invited him?"

Lucinda smiled like a cat who's just devoured a canary. "It's Antonio's son–he's all grown up now and the president of a bank. And quite handsome, too!"

Edwina was aghast. "Lucinda–you cannot, you would not–"

"We should let bygones be bygones," Lucinda said. "It's been twenty years. And Tony, as they call him, is quite respectable. A leader in the community."

Mansfield was nearly speechless–but not quite. "Do not let that man in here, Hanna. He's the son of a whore."

"Mansfield!" Edwina said. "Control your tongue. He did not choose his parents or the circumstances of his birth. Nor did any of us. However foolish Lucinda was in inviting him to our house–and on Christmas Day!–nevertheless he is, as he says, an invited guest. Hanna–show him in."

Jackie turned to her aunt. "What did you mean by 'let bygones be bygones' Aunt Lucy?" And then to her mother: "And how do you know, Mother, about the circumstances of his birth?"

Edwina glanced first at Mansfield, then at Lucinda–who was still grinning–then rested her gaze on Jackie. "It's very complicated, Jacqueline, dear. Suffice it to say that young Mr. Jones was born out of wedlock."

"What difference does it make? Jackie said. "Lots of babies were born out of wedlock during the war."

"This was after the war, dear. And Mr. Jones' mother–"

But Edwina was interrupted by the appearance of Mr Jones himself.

Tony stood in the door of the dining room with Hanna just behind him looking very anxious. He was still wearing his overcoat, with his hands in its pockets, and a wide grin on his face.

"Merry Christmas, folks," he said.

"Mr. Jones," Edwina said frostily. "I understand my sister has invited you to dinner. Unfortunately, there must have been some confusion as to the time, because as you can see, we have nearly finished."

"That's all right, Mrs. LeRoux" Tony said. "I've already eaten myself. But I thought we might have a chat."

"A chat? What about?"

"Oh, things in general, I suppose. Do you mind if I take off my coat?"

"Hanna–take Mr. Jones' coat."

Hanna obeyed, and helped Tony with his coat. But before she could take it away, he stopped her and reached into the pockets. He extracted the two bottles of wine he had brought with him from St. Helena.

"Voilà!" he said. "I thought I at least might contribute something."

"Wine?" Edwina said. "We have plenty of wine, Mr. Jones. It's completely unnecessary to–"

"Chateau Lafitte, '76. A particularly good year. I thought you might enjoy it."

"Lafitte?" Mansfield sat up in his chair and strained to see. "That's damn difficult to find these days. At any price. Where did you get it?"

"It was a particular favorite of my father's. He ordered it by the case from Delmonico's in New York."

"My word," Mansfield said. "I had no idea he was such a connoisseur."

"Put Mr. Jones' coat in the hall closet, Hanna," Edwina said. "And when you return, you may open the wine. Have a seat, Mr. Jones–I see you have become acquainted with my sister."

Tony nodded towards Lucinda. "Indeed I have. Lucinda–"

"I'm so glad you took me up on my invitation, Tony."

Edwina turned to Lucinda. "Tony?"

"That's what I'm called, Mrs. LeRoux. To distinguish me from my father, Antonio."

"Yes, of course. And have you met my daughter Jacqueline?"

"Yes, ma'am. We met at the bank shortly after she arrived in Beaufort. She needed to cash a bank draft–just as her aunt did more recently."

"Well," Edwina said, "it seems that your bank is quite the place for meeting young ladies–and not so young ladies." She shot a supercilious glance towards Lucinda.

"It happens on occasion," Tony said. "Nearly everyone comes into the bank at one time or another. Where shall I sit?'"

"Anywhere you like, Mr. Jones." Edwina said. "Just put the wine down on the sideboard and Hanna will take care of it."

Tony complied and sat down in an empty chair between Lucinda and Jackie. He grinned at both. And both grinned back.

Hanna returned and went to the sideboard to open the wine.

"Oh, Hanna–" Tony said. "You need to decant the wine. So it can breathe a little."

"Why, you are a connoisseur of fine wine, it seems, Mr. Jones," Edwina said.

"Just a practical measure," Tony said. "To realize the full potential of the wine."

They all sat in silence for a minute or two while Hanna cleared the table and returned to the kitchen.

Nearly everyone stared at Tony as if he were some exotic animal that had wandered into the house from the nearby woods. Nearly everyone but Mansfield, that is. He stared at the bottles on the sideboard.

"How long do we have to let it air?" he said.

"Oh, ten, fifteen minutes," Tony said. "An hour would be optimum, but who can wait that long? Even my father–"

"How is your father, Tony?" Edwina said. "The last we saw of him he was slaving away–if you will pardon the expression–at the phosphate mine up by the old mill."

"He drowned, Mrs. LeRoux. During the hurricane."

"Oh, I'm sorry," Edwina said. "It must have been a great tragedy."

"It was–especially for my mother."

"To be sure."

Again the room fell silent, a silence that was only broken by Hanna returning from the kitchen with a tray full of dessert plates. She distributed the plates quickly and asked Tony about the wine.

"Another five minutes, Hanna," Tony said. Hanna returned to the kitchen.

If Tony seemed unusually sober after his performance at his mother's house, it was probably the exercise he got from the ride out to Lynwood, which required an hour and two ferry crossings.

"Delicious," he said, after eating a spoonful of chocolate pudding. "You must allow Louise–your cook–to give me the recipe."

"Recipe?" Edwina said. "You're a chef as well as a wine connoisseur, Mr. Jones?"

"Tony's a wonderful cook!" Jackie said. She caught herself, too late.

"Is he?" Edwina said, casting a stern look at her. "How would you know that?"

"Well..." Jackie said, gathering her thoughts. "The night of the premiere of *The Second Mrs. Tanqueray*–Tony–Mr. Jones–dined with us at the Beaufort Inn. He and the chef had a lively discussion about French cuisine."

"I see," Edwina said. "So you are acquainted with many things French, Mr. Jones. Just how did you acquire such refined tastes?"

"I spent three years in Paris, Mrs. LeRoux."

"Did you? And just what did you do there?"

"All this talk about food and wine is making me thirsty," Mansfield said. "Isn't that wine about ready now?"

Edwina picked up her little bell and rang it. "I can see that your mouth has been watering ever since Mr. Jones arrived, Mansfield. It won't be long now."

Hanna returned and poured the wine into each of their glasses.

Mansfield swirled the wine around in his glass and plunged his nose into the bowl. His eyebrows arched. He took a long sip. "My God! That's the best thing I ever put into my mouth! Do you have any more of this remarkable beverage, Mr. Jones?"

Tony chuckled. "As I said–we have cases of it at home. I'll bring you a few bottles."

After they finished their dessert and Hanna cleared away their plates, Mansfield wiped his lips with his napkin and looked to the two bottles on the sideboard. One was empty and the other full. "I don't suppose you'd care to retire to the billiard room, Mr. Jones, and shoot a game or two? Perhaps we could take that other bottle with us."

Tony smiled and looked at the bottle. "Certainly, Mr. LeRoux. It belongs to you. But I can't say that I'm much of a billiard player."

"Quite all right, quite all right," Mansfield said. "I'll give you a few pointers. In fact, Jacqueline can give you better advice than I can. Would you care to join us, Jackie?"

"I'd be delighted," Jackie said. She smiled with satisfaction to see her father warming to Tony.

"Well, we can't all play billiards," Edwina said. "And I know Lucinda has little talent in that area. Perhaps we'll retire to the library while you three go to the billiard room."

Thus agreed, the men, along with Jackie, rose and departed through the door to the foyer, while Edwina and Lucinda left through another door that led to the library. Mansfield picked up the second bottle and brought it along.

Once in the library, Edwina carefully closed the door after looking first down the hallway in one direction, then the other, as if expecting spies to be lurking in the dark corners. Then she sat down in Mansfield's favorite wing chair and indicated the armchair opposite it. Lucinda sat down in it and folded her hands in her lap as if she were a child who was about to be scolded for some bit of mischief.

"Now, Lucinda," Edwina said in her magisterial way, "why have you come?"

"Why? To see my family, of course. How can you ask such a question, Edwina?"

"It seems a perfectly reasonable question to me, considering the fact that you've neglected the family for the past twenty years, especially your daughter."

Lucinda's eyes flashed with indignation. "You accuse me of neglect when it was you who insisted that I consent to your scheme?"

"There was no other alternative."

"Of course there was. I could have taken her with me to London and raised her there as her widowed mother."

"Widowed? That would have been your story? Surely you would have been found out."

"How? No one knew me there."

"Jacqueline herself would have asked questions. She's a clever girl, you know."

Lucinda sighed and looked at the portrait of their grandfather, Edward Benson, Sr., over the mantelpiece. "It doesn't matter now. What matters is that I want to cash out."

"Cash out?"

"I'll sell you and Mansfield my half of Lynwood. I'm not greedy–I'll agree to any reasonable price. Lynwood will be yours lock, stock and barrel, and you will enjoy all of the income, not just half." She looked around the room. "From what I"ve seen so far, Lynwood is prospering. In another twenty years, it will be worth far more than it is now. You'll get the better end of the bargain."

"And Jacqueline?"

"Jackie can do as she wishes. I'd love to see her return to London. We became quite close while she was there."

Edwina seemed to consider this. "And do you intend to tell her?"

"Tell her what?"

"Why, that you are her biological mother, of course. Don't play coy with me, Lucinda. I know your ways."

"What ways?" Lucinda laughed. "You've always suspected me of diabolical stratagems and subterfuges, Edwina. I assure you, it's all in your imagination."

Edwina sniffed. "You intend to use this information as a bargaining chip. It's quite clear."

"Bargaining chip? Edwina you give me more credit for cleverness than I deserve. It never crossed my mind."

Edwina turned away from her and gazed out the window. The sun was beginning to set and amber rays of light illuminated the gardens. "Mansfield, of course, will handle the negotiations. He's a fool in some ways but he's a good businessman. And we know a lawyer in town–"

"Choose any lawyer you wish. As I said, I'll agree to anything within reason."

Edwina reached for the cord convenient to her chair and pulled it. "I think I'd like a glass of sherry. Would you care to join me?"

Lucinda grinned. "Why not? Tony's delicious wine has already worn off. We'll have our own private little celebration."

Hanna appeared and Edwina instructed her to pour them each a glass of sherry. Then she left the room.

"No use clinking glasses at this point," Edwina said. "The deal is not done. And though I'll leave most of the details to Mansfield–I'm sure he'll agree–I must insist on one condition."

"What condition?"

"That you never, ever, reveal to Jacqueline that you are her mother. She belongs to me now. I have done all the work of raising her. And besides, I think she'd be devastated to find out the truth."

Lucinda sipped from her crystal glass. "I think you underestimate Jackie, Edwina. She's made of much sterner stuff than you think."

"Promise me, Lucinda."

"No promises. Not in that regard."

"Then promise me this."

"What?"

"That you will never disclose to her the fact that Antonio Jones was her father."

Lucinda emitted an uncharacteristic guffaw, nearly spilling her sherry. "You do amuse me, Edwina. As the good Bard said, 'you are most assured of what you are most ignorant of.'"

Edwina raised an eyebrow. "Am I?"

"You are. Rest assured that I will never reveal to Jackie that she has any biological connection to Antonio Jones whatsoever."

"That's a promise? Will you put it in writing?"

"Certainly."

Edwina studied her sister's enigmatic expression for a moment, then reached for the decanter. "Another glass of sherry?"

Tony bent over the rail of the billiard table and took careful aim at the eight ball opposite a side pocket. He curled his forefinger around the cue, thinking this kind of grip would ensure a smooth stroke. He missed. The ball caromed off of the side rail and came to rest just inches in front of a corner pocket.

"Corner pocket," Jackie said, and hardly even looking, put the ball in the pocket.

Mansfield chuckled. "I told you, Mr. Jones. Jackie's an expert."

Tony stared at the pocket for a moment and chalked his cue. "Is there something wrong with my technique?"

"It's just a matter of experience" Jackie said. "I grew up playing the game. Why don't you and Papa play?"

Mansfield and Tony played three games, with Mansfield winning all three.

Tony put his cue back in the rack. "I'm afraid this isn't my game."

"Well," Mansfield said, taking a swallow of the wine, "you may not know much about billiards, my boy, but you do know your wine. Do you suppose I could purchase a few bottles from you?"

"No charge, Mr. LeRoux–just let me know how many you want and I'll deliver them to you myself."

"Well, ah–Tony. That's very generous of you, but I wouldn't feel right taking even say, half a case from you without compensating you in some way." He scratched behind his ear with his cue stick. "I have it! Ravenel's coming to hunt with me next month. Why don't you join us?"

"I'm afraid I'm not much of a hunter, either, Mr. LeRoux." Tony exchanged glances with Jackie.

"Nonsense!" Mansfield said. "There's no special skill required to shoot a wild boar."

"Boar?"

"Sure. It's great fun. Do you know how to shoot a gun?"

"Well...I did do a little bird hunting with my father on St. Helena. But that was years ago."

"Then you're familiar with firearms." Mansfield took another swallow from his glass. "That's all you need to know. What do you say?"

"Well," Tony said, casting another glance at Jackie, who was shaking her head. "I'll have to check my calendar, Mr. LeRoux. What day did you have in mind?"

"January. I forget the exact date. I'll look it up in the library when we go downstairs. Drat! My gout's acting up again. Now where did I put my cane?"

"Here it is, Papa," Jackie said. "Do you need some help getting down the stairs?"

"No, no–I'm not that old yet. It's just this damn gout. Comes and goes." He took the cane and hobbled over to the door. "Why don't you show Mr. Jones some of the finer points of the game? If he can shoot a straight cue, he can shoot a charging boar. Might help him to steady his nerves."

After Mansfield limped out of the room, Jackie turned sharply to Tony. "What in the world were you thinking? Boar hunting? With Ravenel Coleman?"

Tony shrugged. "I could hardly turn down your father's invitation. And besides, he would think I was weak, a pampered aesthete."

"I like aesthetes, pampered or not. And I like you–just the way you are. Oh, Tony, don't fall into this 'good ol' boy' trap. My father's a sweet man when he's at home with his family or entertaining guests. But when he and Rav are out hunting they can be quite coarse and even reckless."

"You think I've led a sheltered life?" Tony turned his cue up and sighted along its length with one eye closed. "I grew up on St. Helena hunting and fishing and catching crabs just like all the other boys. I can take care of myself in the woods."

"You just told my father you weren't much of a hunter."

"Well...that's true. I'm more of a fisherman, but I know how to handle a gun."

Jackie folded her arms across her chest and leaned against the table. "That's all beside the point. The point is that Rav sees you as a rival and once he gets you out into the woods–"

Tony laughed. "You think he'll shoot me?"

"I wouldn't put it past him."

Tony looked at her soberly for a moment, then smiled. "I'll keep an eye on him. Now that I've taken your advice concerning dangerous predators, how about some advice on how to handle this stick of wood in my hand? I visited the pool halls in Boston a few times and I never saw anyone shoot like you do."

She stared at him for a moment, her arms still crossed in defiance, then took the cue from him and laid it on the table. "All right. Watch carefully."

"I'm watching."

"First, don't wrap your forefinger around the cue–it will deflect the shaft. Second, don't watch the cue ball–watch the target ball and pick out the spot–and only spot–that will propel the ball to the desired hole. Like this–nine ball in the corner pocket."

She drew the cue stick back, sent it forward with a smooth, gentle motion, and watched the nine ball drop into the pocket. "And don't hit the ball hard–you always want to leave yourself with an easy second shot."

Tony stood watching her as she continued to sink six more balls, all from different angles, the last two off the rail.

She handed him the cue stick. "Now you try it. Keep in mind–"

He put the cue stick aside and kissed her.

Jackie allowed this for a moment and then pulled away. "Let's at least close the door."

Tony went to the door and closed it. When he returned, she was sitting on the edge of the pool table, smiling at him. Her legs were apart, the way a man would sit, the skirt just covering her knees. She wore no petticoats on this occasion, only a chemise beneath the pleated fabric.

"You look as if you're wearing a Scottish kilt," he said.

"It's comfortable around the house. No chafing."

"We wouldn't want you to chafe, would we?"

"No."

Tony kissed her and as he did so, she leaned back on the table, sending several billiard balls flying. A clatter arose as they hit the floor and bounced to all corners of the room.

Below stairs in the library, Mansfield looked up from his reading. "What's that?"

Edwina looked up momentarily, then went back to her knitting. "I suppose the children are tiring of billiards. They really should be outdoors in this beautiful weather. Don't you think we should build a tennis court on the lawn? It would be ever so much healthier. And we could keep an eye on them that way."

"I suppose so. Though I hardly think Jackie needs watching."

"Perhaps not. But Mr. Jones may. He's a man, after all."

"Then maybe we should tell them."

"Tell them what?"

"That they're related. Half brother and sister."

"Then we would also have to tell them that we are not in fact Jacqueline's parents. Are you prepared for that?"

Mansfield sighed and reached for the ever-present decanter of brandy that rested on the table next to him. "No, of course not. But the question is: can we keep them from finding out?"

"Lucinda is the only one who can reveal that information–aside from ourselves, of course. And she has sworn herself to secrecy."

Mansfield poured some brandy into his glass. "Has she? And what makes you think she'll honor that pledge?"

"Money."

"Money?"

"I'll explain it to you in due course. There're still some details to be ironed out."

Mansfield stared at his wife with a mixture of curiosity and alarm. Then he swallowed a draught of his brandy.

CHAPTER 34

Hiram Cooper's house, or 'manse' a he called it, sat on Bay Street only a few blocks west of downtown Beaufort. It had once belonged to Rufus Saxton, the Union general who was a hero of Harper's Ferry during the war, and the assistant commissioner of the Freedmen's Bureau for South Carolina during Reconstruction. Saxton later sold the house to J.B. Thornton, a cotton broker from Boston, and Cooper in turn bought it from Thornton.

All of this was unknown to Tony as he stood before the house one Saturday afternoon equipped with his paint box and brushes. He intended to fulfill his promise to Cooper to adorn a room in the house with a trompe l'oeil similar to the one he created at his mother's house.

It was indeed an impressive residence. Two and a half stories, counting the dormers, with a neo-classical Greek pediment at the roof line. Nevertheless, it was unpretentious in the sense that it was of whitewashed clapboard and green shutters, a shade of dark green that was very common throughout Beaufort. There were verandas at both the first and second floors, with the first floor elevated nearly six feet above the ground floor, also common construction in the Lowcountry. Surrounding the entire property at the street level was a wrought iron fence with spiked capitals, breached by stone pillars at the entrance to a brick walkway. Fruit trees bordered the walkway, though their branches were bare this time of year.

He opened the gate and proceeded up the walkway, wondering at the fact that Cooper lived in this large house by himself. He thought of his garret in Paris, a fifth floor walk-up with no heat. It was brutally cold this time of year in that garret, and he usually slept in his clothes, often with an overcoat buttoned up to his neck.

What a contrast! Still, he had neighbors then, young, struggling artists and writers like himself, and he was never lonely.

He mounted the steps and noted the rocking chairs on the veranda as he approached the door. A much more friendly and receptive home than the intimidating façade of Lynwood. After twisting the key to the bell, which produced a low-pitched jingle like those on bicycles, the door opened and a middle-aged black woman appeared, dressed in a uniform of black taffeta and white lace. She was plump, with a round, kindly face that readily broke into a broad smile.

"You must be Mr. Jones, the painter," she said. "Mr. Cooper is expecting you."

Tony nodded and followed her into the foyer. He suddenly felt like a tradesman and wondered if the maid knew he was in fact a bank president.

The maid disappeared and Tony looked at the framed photographs on the wall. Some were of the house, one of a very pretty young woman with blond hair who Tony supposed was Cooper's deceased wife, and two or three of familiar scenes in Europe. He recognized the Louvre in Paris, St. Peter's in Rome, and what appeared to be a castle in Spain. All showed Cooper standing in the foreground with his arm around the blond, though she appeared to be considerably older in these and somewhat heavier.

"Tony! Welcome to the old manse."

It was Cooper, impeccably dressed as usual, but sporting an ascot rather than the cravat he usually wore for work. He clapped Tony on the shoulder. "Let me show you the room. It's formally the library, but I call it my retreat. You'll see that the French doors open onto the garden to the back lawn, so I get plenty of light and a pretty view. But I'm interested in something different than what you did for your mother."

Tony entered the library and saw that it was quite large, richly paneled, and furnished with plush oriental carpets and leather armchairs. Book shelves covered two of the walls from floor to ceiling, while a third was hung with old world paintings–Tony recognized the center one as a Renoir–and the fourth was the largest with the French doors oddly set at one end rather than in the middle. This wall contained a few paintings, but of lesser quality and distinction than the ones adjacent to it.

"You can see my dilemma," Cooper said. "This large space is fine for displaying my paintings, but actually there is plenty of space in the other rooms for them and I don't want the place to start looking like a museum. Do you know what I mean? I'd like something more original, perhaps even serendipitous, to adorn that wall. Something that would surprise me every time I look up from my reading."

Tony chuckled. "That's what a trompe l'loeil is all about. You want it to cover the whole wall?"

"Not necessarily. I'll leave it up to you. Perhaps we could hang a curtain there and when I have guests, I could pull on the cord and 'Voilà!'–a stimulating tableau would appear."

"Stimulating? Do you mean like nudes gamboling in an enchanted forest? Something like your Renoir there?"

"Nudes?" Cooper stared at the wall for a moment as if trying to visualize the scene described by Tony. Then he looked at the Renoir, which was of a nude woman with small breasts and large hips lying provocatively on a velvet divan eating grapes from a compost. "Well perhaps. But nudes gamboling on such a large space–I don't want to be offensive. The enchanted forest idea, though, I like that."

Tony looked at the wall. "How about fantastic animals? Unicorns, narwhals, mythical beasts with the bodies of lions and men but the heads of eagles and crocodiles?"

"Hmm." Cooper rubbed his chin. "Too Egyptian. I don't want to frighten my guests–or the servants. You know how they go in for voodoo and all that."

"Voodoo? Your maid who answered the door doesn't strike me as the type to go in for voodoo."

"No, no–Vivian is quite level-headed. But some of the others..."

"All right," Tony said. "Mythical creatures are out. What about a second French door? That would balance the room."

"Yes, that's an idea." Cooper laughed. "It would even be amusing to see some of my guests mistake the faux door for the real one. But..." He frowned. "They might get hurt."

"We wouldn't want that."

"No." Cooper threw up his hands. "Well, Tony–I think you've got the gist of it. I'll leave the details to you. After all, you're the artist and I have confidence in your good taste."

Tony studied the wall for a few moments. "If you don't like it, I can always paint over it and start again."

"Of course," Cooper said with a smile. "But I'm sure that won't be necessary. Just keep in mind that your mother will have to live with it."

"Live with it? You're getting married?"

Cooper flushed and looked a bit sheepish. "If she consents."

Tony began unpacking his paint box, which he had put on a reading table. "I have a feeling she will. I'll have to take down those paintings."

"I'll get Kena to help you."

"Kena?"

"My gardener and all-around handy man. These Gullah names are curious aren't they? I'm told it has something to do with the white splotches on his skin." Cooper chuckled. "It startles people sometimes, so I keep him out of sight when we have guests."

"Untidy of him to have splotchy skin."

Cooper seemed unsure whether Tony was mocking him. "Well...yes. I'll leave you to your work. I've got to look in at the store. We've made some new hires recently."

After Cooper left the room Tony studied the wall for a time and began taking out his brushes and paints. He decided that Cooper had rather conventional tastes and that 'an enchanted forest' meant to Cooper fairies and nymphs–demurely clothed, of course–gamboling among the trees and perhaps drinking from a spring while birds looked on and sang forth their mating calls.

As he was arranging his materials a black man–or rather mostly black man–entered the room. He immediately perceived that this must be Kena. His appearance was somewhat startling, as Cooper said, with splotches on his face that at first looked like burns, but on closer examination revealed no scarring, only smooth pink skin.

"Mr. Cooper say you need some help with them paintings," Kena said.

That's right, Kena," Tony said. "I'll need a drop cloth, too."

"An ol' bed sheet do?"

"Sure. But let's get the paintings down first. Is there a place to put them?"

"I reckon in the attic till Mr. Cooper figure out where he want them."

"We'll need a ladder, too."

"Got one in the carriage house out back."

Once Kena retrieved the ladder, the paintings came down quickly and together they carried them upstairs to the attic. This was another very large room that contained beds, steamer trunks, lamps, sofas, busts, books, even a bicycle. It seemed enough to furnish another house.

"It seems that Mr. Cooper collects things," Tony said.

Kena laughed. "Most of these things was already here when he bought the house from Mr. Thornton. Some come from the Emporium□things he can't sell, I reckon."

"How long have you been working here, Kena?"

"Oh, since I was a boy. My daddy, Willie, used to work in the yard for General Saxton when he owned it."

"General Saxton? My father used to work for General Saxton."

Kena's eyes brightened. "That so? What his name?"

"He went by Antonio."

Kena rubbed his chin. "No...don't recall that name. He a gardener?"

"Um, not exactly. He was in the army. Kind of an assistant to the general."

"Oh–he like a butler."

Tony wondered at the assumptions even blacks made on account of skin color. "Something like that."

"Well, I'd best be gettin' them bed sheets for you to catch the paint with. Maybe my sister got some old ones she don't need."

"Your sister?"

"Vivian. She the maid that let you in. We don't look nothin' alike." Kena laughed uneasily. "Fact is, nobody look like me."

"You must have had a white mother."

"No, that ain't it. Mama was as black as coal. A doctor say it was mutation, I think he called it. A mutation in my skin. Cain't do nothin' about it."

"You must have gotten teased a lot as a child."

"Reckon so. Well, I'd best get them sheets."

Tony worked quickly, as he usually did, and covered the wall with the pastoral scene he had envisioned. He couldn't resist inserting a turtle crawling out of the spring with a tiny winged fairy riding on its back. He was touching up this figure when Cooper returned around five o'clock.

"Splendid!" Cooper had entered the room silently while Tony had his back to him. "It's like a dream, a vision!"

Tony stood up from his crouched position and faced him. "You like it then?"

"Like it? I love it! It looks like you could just step right into it and get lost. Joyfully lost!"

"Not too fantastic? Or too risqué?"

"No, no, not at all. Don't change a thing. I could sit and look at it for hours." Cooper took his own cue and sat down in one of the leather armchairs. "I think Georgia will love it, too. Tony, you've outdone yourself."

Tony stood back a little to examine his work. "I'll need to come back tomorrow and touch up a few things. The mouth on that nymph and the shell of the turtle–"

"What turtle?"

"The one at the bottom right there, emerging from the spring."

"Oh–why, that's charming. Didn't notice it before." Cooper stood up from the chair. "Tony, I wonder that you're wasting your time at the bank–

you've got so much talent."

"I wonder at it myself sometimes." Tony went to the table and put his brush in a jar of spirits. Then he wiped his hands with a cloth.

Cooper continued to stare at the painting. "I'd like to show it off to some friends. Why don't you bring your mother with you when you come back tomorrow? She can do some shopping while you finish up and then we'll have supper. Did you know that Mr. Smalls is one of my neighbors?"

"No, I didn't know that. Is he a collector?"

"I don't know–I've never been to his house. But I think he might become one once he sees this." Cooper sighed and crossed his arms over his chest, still staring at the wall. "You know, people walk right by my framed paintings without stopping to look. I have a Renoir! A Rembrandt! But they never say anything about them. I'd be willing to wager, though, that they won't be so blasé when they see this. Why, it beckons to you! I feel as if I could step right into another world."

"I'm glad you like it, Hi," Tony said. He was suspicious of all this praise. It seemed an ordinary trompe l'oeil to him. He looked over his work again. 'Serendipitous,' though. He felt he had captured that.

When he got home that evening, he relayed Cooper's invitation to his mother, omitting the gushing compliments that Cooper had paid him.

"How did he like the painting?" Georgia said.

"He said it was fine." Tony flopped down onto the sofa. "I still have a little touching up to do."

"Well, I'm sure it's wonderful. Hi has very sophisticated tastes, you know. He's a hard man to please."

"Apparently, he's very pleased with you."

Georgia brought a tray of crackers and cheese into the living room and set them down on the coffee table. "What do you mean?"

Tony popped a cracker into his mouth. "He intends to marry you."

Georgia smiled. "Don't you think I already knew that?"

"Do you intend to accept?"

"He hasn't asked me yet."

"I have a feeling he will soon."

Georgia sat down next to him and patted him on the knee. "Tony, what possible objection could you have to my marrying Hi? He's a perfect gentleman, he's quite well off, he seems to like you–"

"He thinks I ought to resign from the bank and go off and paint somewhere."

"He said that?"

"Not exactly in those words, but that was the gist of it."

"But Tony–isn't that what you really want to do?"

Tony sighed. "I suppose so–but I think he just wants to get rid of me."

"Oh, Tony–that's ridiculous. He just wants you to be happy."

"Mama–"

"Yes?"

"You remember when I went off for a ride on Christmas Day?"

"Of course I do. I thought it was rather abrupt, almost rude. Hi and I–"

"I went to Lynwood."

"You what!"

"I went to Lynwood. Jackie's aunt Lucinda invited me to dinner–remember?"

"Oh, Tony! You couldn't, you didn't–"

"I did. It worked out perfectly well. I met the LeRoux for the first time in my life and they were very gracious."

Georgia pressed both palms to her cheeks and appeared to be in a state of shock. "They...they were 'gracious'? They accepted you as a guest?"

"Completely. I was too late for dinner, of course, but I sat down with them for dessert. We had a very cordial conversation."

"Why...I can't believe it! Edwina actually entertained you at her table?"

Tony chuckled. "She was entertaining, as a matter of fact. A droll sort of woman."

Georgia collected herself and lowered her hands until they rested on her lap. "Did she say anything about me?"

"Nothing that I can recall. She did ask about Papa. Mostly we talked about wine. That reminds me–I promised Mr. LeRoux I'd send him a case."

"You're on such friendly terms with him as that?"

"He even asked me to go hunting with him next month."

"Oh Tony–this is not good."

"Why not? It seems to me that it's about time to smooth over the differences between our two families. Besides, you know how I feel about Jackie."

"I can't believe they'd even consent to a marriage between the two of you. Edwina must be up to something. Does she know that you and Jackie are... are..."

"In love? No, I don't think so. But the ice has been broken. We'll break it to her gently...over time."

Georgia leaned against the back of the sofa and burst out laughing.

Tony started laughing, too, but a little uneasily. "What's so funny?"

"You father would have found this to be very amusing. Or perhaps incredible, as I do. That his son could ever marry a Benson!"

"She's not a Benson–she's a LeRoux."

"Practically the same thing." Georgia sat up and looked Tony in the eye. "Now I don't want to hear any more objections from you about my marrying Hiram Cooper. That is, should he ask me."

Tony's good humor suddenly evaporated. "He'll ask you all right." He got up from the sofa and went to the sideboard. "I think I need a drink. Would you care for one?"

"Make it a whiskey."

Tony fixed a couple of scotch and sodas and returned to the sofa. He handed his mother her glass and sat down. "I think I'll invite Jackie to dinner tomorrow at Hi's place."

"You may be rushing things."

"You thought the same thing about my going over to Lynwood on Christmas Day."

"But this is different–you'll be asking her daughter to dinner. Your intentions will be clear."

"I want my intentions to be clear." Tony took a sip of his drink. "Edwina is going to have to get used to it."

Georgia sighed. "I hope Jackie has one more quality that you haven't mentioned."

"What's that?"

"Courage. She's going to need it."

CHAPTER 35

Courage takes many forms and is inconstant in its expression.

When Jackie returned to Lynwood from church along with her parents and Lucinda, Hanna informed her that a message was waiting for her in the breakfast room. Surprised that anyone would be sending her a message on a Sunday, and equally surprised that Hanna would wait discreetly until the others had dispersed to other rooms before informing her of this missive, she went to the breakfast room and picked up the small envelope that lay on a silver tray. It was unsealed, and she opened it:

Dearest Jackie,

I know this is very short notice, but won't you join my mother and me for dinner at Mr. Cooper's house in Beaufort this afternoon at three o'clock?

Mama is very anxious to meet you and is relieved to hear that I was well-received at Lynwood on Christmas Day.

While we must be discreet, I think we can move ahead now more rapidly.

Tony

She put the card back into the envelope and turned around to see Primus standing behind her. "How did this get here, Primus? Who delivered it?"

"Hanna say that Scratch brung it."

"Scratch?"

"That's Miz Georgia's man on St. Helena."

"There's no time for a reply."

"No, ma'am."

Jackie considered her options. She could ignore the invitation and tell Tony it did not arrive in time. Or, she could comply with the request and lie to her parents about where she was going and why. Or, she could avoid lying to anyone and tell her parents the truth–that she was going to dine with Tony Jones.

This latter option was, of course, the most honest, but also the most perilous. It was one thing for her mother and father to accept Tony as a guest in their house on Christmas Day–especially after her Aunt Lucinda had invited him–but quite another to announce that, in essence, he was courting her and that she was receptive to his overtures. It would throw Lynwood into an uproar.

"Primus, can you drive me into town this afternoon? I mean without my parents knowing the purpose?"

Primus rolled his eyes to the ceiling as he usually did when asked to do something that could cost him his position. "Well, Miss Jackie, I can't rightly, um, misspeak myself...but it seem to me that it be up to you to say why you goin'."

"Well...yes, of course. I'll have to think of something...is the Emporium open on Sunday?"

"Yes, ma'am. Till five o'clock."

"Then I'll do some shopping. And that will be the truth. Afterwards, you can take me to Mr. Cooper's house."

Primus smiled, revealing a row of perfectly white teeth except for one gold incisor. "Yessum. I can do that."

"Primus–"

"Ma'am?"

"How did you know what was in the letter?"

"It was unsealed, Miss Jackie."

"Still, you shouldn't be reading other people's mail, especially–"

"Scratch opened it. Then he told Hanna. And she told me."

"Oh. Well, get the phaeton ready."

"Yes, ma'am."

Although Edwina wondered what Jackie was so eager to buy that it couldn't wait till Monday, she inquired no further and joined Mansfield in the library where she was anxious to resume her needlepoint.

When Primus pulled up in front of the Emporium, Jackie noticed that there was an elegant-looking brougham just ahead of them. "I wonder whose brougham that could belong to?"

"That be Miz Georgia's," Primus said.

"Goodness! How can she afford that on a teacher's salary?"

"Oh, she didn't buy it," Primus said, careful to choose his words. "It was a gift."

"A gift? From whom?"

"Cain't rightly say–a gentleman friend, as I recall."

Jackie stared curiously at the brougham for a few moments. "Wait for me here, Primus–I won't be long."

Primus checked his pocket watch. "You got plenty of time, Miss Jackie. Ain't but two o'clock."

Jackie stepped down from the carriage and entered the store. It seemed to be as busy as any week day and she wondered if she would run into Mrs. Jones, as she had become accustomed to call her. How would she recognize her?

She stopped to examine some lace at one of the counters, which was surrounded by a number of women. A clerk was helping one of them, a pretty middle-aged woman with dark hair wearing an emerald-green cloak with a fur-lined collar. She also carried a muff in one hand, though it wasn't particularly cold outside.

"This is so very fine," the woman said to the clerk. "Where does it come from?"

"Belgium," the clerk said. "It's of the highest quality. Just came in last week."

"I think I'll have a yard of it–no, two. I have a dress that wants a collar. And there'll be enough left over for doilies on the living room furniture."

"Yes, ma'am. Will there be anything else, Mrs. Jones?"

So that was Tony's mother!

Jackie affected an interest in the lace and debated whether or not to introduce herself, but she took a curious pleasure in observing this woman secretly–a woman she wanted to know so much more about. She was so white! Not that she was particularly fair-skinned, not even as much as herself, but the fact that she was Tony's mother was hard to reconcile with the image she had had of her up to this point. Yes, she knew that Tony was adopted, but still, it must have been difficult to bring him up as her own child when others, of both races, would surely stop and stare.

Georgia moved away from the lace table and began inspecting other items, picking up a sweater here or a blouse there, while Jackie slipped along behind her, averting her eyes whenever Georgia glanced her way. She felt a special thrill at this surreptitious activity, as if she were playing a *femme fatale* in a stage play. She wanted to know all about this woman, observing her when she felt unobserved, perhaps to gain some insight into her character.

"May I help you, Miss LeRoux?"

It was the clerk, who had returned without her seeing him. She didn't recall having encountered him before. "Oh, no, I don't think so–I'm just browsing at the moment."

"Very well, Miss LeRoux. Just let me know if I can be of any assistance."

"Yes. I will." The clerk left her side and again approached Georgia, who was now looking over her shoulder.

I feel like such a fool! Jackie thought, not daring to return Georgia's gaze. She'll think I'm an idiot! Or worse, a sneak, a little vixen!

"Excuse me."

Jackie looked up to see Georgia standing three feet in front of her, her muff in one hand and a parasol hooked over the same arm.

"Are you Jacqueline LeRoux?"

"Yes," Jackie said, feeling as if she were being interrogated on a witness stand. "I am Jacqueline LeRoux."

Georgia extended her free hand. "I'm so thrilled to meet you, Jacqueline. Tony has told me so much about you. What a coincidence that we should meet here at the Emporium. Will you be joining us for dinner at Mr. Cooper's house?"

"Yes. That's why I'm here. Oh, Mrs. Jones, I'm so happy we could meet like this–I mean away from the men. Perhaps we can get to know each other a little before–"

"Exactly what I was thinking. Why don't we look around together? I'm afraid I've already exceeded my budget, but they have such pretty things here!"

Jackie agreed and they moved off to another table that contained silk chemises and night gowns.

Jackie bought a scarf for Lucinda and a purse for her mother–she couldn't very well return to Lynwood empty-handed–as the two wandered about the store.

Georgia stopped to look at her wrist watch, a delicate little thing set in a circle of tiny diamonds. "Goodness! Where has the time gone? It's a quarter to three."

They exited the store carrying their packages to find Primus nodding on his perch.

"How are you, Primus?" Georgia said. "I haven't seen you since my husband's funeral."

Primus, jolted awake, tipped his hat. "Afternoon, Miz Georgia. It's always good to see you."

"Jacqueline, why don't you come with me in the brougham and Primus, you can follow us in the phaeton."

"Sho', Miz Georgia. Ain't but four blocks, anyhow."

Jackie got into the brougham with Georgia and the two carriages proceeded west on Bay Street.

"How do you know Primus, Mrs. Jones?" Jackie asked.

"He was one of my pupils." Georgia laughed. "Long ago. And if he hadn't left the Penn School to become a driver for your uncle, he might have gone on to greater heights. He's very intelligent."

"Yes. Yes, he is." Jackie wondered at how much Georgia knew about her family. Her father had called her a 'whore' on Christmas Day when Tony appeared at the invitation of Lucinda. What did he mean? This elegant, charming woman a whore? Why, she was so refined, so gracious, almost a natural aristocrat! Her own mother, who affected the speech and manners of the British aristocracy, was almost coarse, even comical, by comparison.

They drove up to Cooper's house and the drivers got down from their seats to assist the ladies from the brougham.

"You and Scratch can take the carriages around back, Primus," Georgia said. "There's plenty of room there and, besides, we shouldn't be blocking the street."

So she was familiar with Mr. Cooper's house! Maybe that's what her father had meant when he called her a whore. Just because she and Mr. Cooper weren't married...well, her father was very old-fashioned, after all...

The two women ascended the coquina steps to the veranda and Georgia turned the key that sounded the bell. Vivian appeared, greeted them in her warm and effusive way, and they entered the house.

CHAPTER 36

Vivian escorted the ladies into the library where Tony and Mr. Smalls, along with his wife Annie, were admiring Tony's trompe l'oeil.

Cooper entered the room from another door almost simultaneously. "Georgia!" He came over and put his hand on her shoulder. "See what your son has done?" He paused to look at Jackie. "And who is this lovely young lady?"

"Jacqueline LeRoux," Georgia said. "Jackie, this is Mr. Cooper."

"How do you do," Jackie said. She shook his hand, but her eyes went back to the trompe l'oeil. "Oh, Tony–I think it's wonderful! I didn't know you did things like this."

Tony smiled wryly. "In my spare time. Do you know Mr. and Mrs. Smalls?"

Introductions were made all around and the guests again turned their attention to the painting.

"Pastoral," Mr. Smalls said. "I don't know much about art, but I think that's what you call a pastoral scene."

"You're absolutely right, Mr. Smalls," Tony said. "But with an element of fantasy in it."

"You should see the one he did at his mother's house," Cooper said. "You feel as if you could walk right into it and sit down on a garden bench."

After many such compliments as this, Cooper urged everyone into the dining room, where the table was set and Kena was standing next to a credenza on which rested an ice bucket containing several bottles of champagne. He was wearing a white dinner jacket and standing at attention as if on parade.

Jackie couldn't help staring for a moment at Kena's unusual appearance.

Cooper seemed to notice her reaction. "This is my man servant, Kena."

"Oh–how do you do." Jackie had never been formerly introduced to a domestic servant before and wondered at Mr. Cooper's reason for doing so. Nevertheless, she took her seat next to Tony opposite Mr. and Mrs. Smalls.

She had heard much about Mr. Smalls growing up. Everyone in Beaufort knew about his heroic exploits during the war and even though he fought for the Union, he was well-respected by blacks and whites alike. He had been a state senator and a congressman, but there was some scandal, as she recalled, years ago that ended his political career. But she was more interested in his second wife, who had been introduced to her as 'Annie.' She seemed to be considerably younger than Mr. Smalls and was quite attractive.

Once Kena had served the champagne, Mr. Cooper stood and raised his glass.

"I'd like to make a toast before we start," he said. "This little group–the six of us–would not have been able to sit down and dine together as recently as twenty years ago had it not been for the heroic efforts of men like Mr. Smalls. As a native of Boston, I daresay that it would not even have been possible there before the war. To Mr. Smalls, and to the triumph of reason and right!"

"Hear, hear!" Tony said, and raised his glass. The others clapped politely and followed suit. Mr. Cooper sat down.

Mr. Smalls stood up. "I am honored by your toast, Hiram. But I must say that there are still battles to be won. The Democrats have taken over the state house and effectively disenfranchised the black voters of South Carolina, There is a new constitutional convention that has been called for by Governor Tillman. It will be for the purpose of codifying this disenfranchisement into law. My political career is nearing an end. But my hope is that the younger generation of blacks like Mr. Jones here will rise up and meet the challenge that lies before us. To the younger generation, both black and white!"

"Hear, hear!" Cooper said, clapping loudly. Tony, surprised to hear his name invoked by Mr. Smalls, clapped more politely. He exchanged glances with Jackie, who smiled broadly.

They all drank and Kena rushed to replenish their glasses.

After dinner, the guests moved to the parlor, where they drank cordials from tiny crystal glasses.

Mr. Smalls took Tony aside and, always the politician, followed up on his toast in the dining room. "I think you ought to run for the state legislature, Tony."

Tony was taken aback. "Me? But Mr. Smalls, I'm not even really a banker. Once this upcoming audit is completed, I–"

"Your father said the same thing when I put it to him before the storm hit. But he said he was willing to give it a try. Can you do any less?"

Tony stared at him for a moment. "My father had a great deal of experience in public affairs even though he wasn't a politician like yourself."

Smalls laughed. "*I* wasn't a politician like myself until after the war. I was a slave, and illiterate. But events thrust me onto the great stage of history and I felt that I must seize the opportunity–not only for myself, but for my people."

Tony took a sip of his sherry. "You were the right man at the right time, Mr. Smalls. You had a destiny and you fulfilled that destiny. If I have any destiny at all, it's as an artist."

Smalls' lips contracted as if he were sucking on a lemon. Then he put his arm around Tony's shoulder. "I can see you have talent as an artist, Tony. But can you make a living at it? Apparently not or you wouldn't be working at the bank. Besides, the legislature only meets for a few weeks out of the year. You'd have plenty of time to paint the other eight or ten months."

"I can't be an artist part-time, Mr. Smalls. I'm doing that now and it's killing me."

Smalls sighed and withdrew his arm from Tony's shoulder. "You disappoint me, Tony."

"I'm sorry, Mr. Smalls. A man has to stay true to his nature. I can't–"

"Then promise me this–you'll come to our next meeting–the Beaufort Republican Committee-and cast your vote for yourself."

"Myself? What do you mean?"

"I mean toss your hat into the ring to become a delegate for the Constitutional Convention. We've got five good men, including myself. But we need one more. You're educated, articulate–and the son of a man highly respected in the black community. Your participation could make a difference."

Tony said nothing for a moment or two, and looked over at Jackie, who was conversing animatedly with Smalls' wife. "How long did you say this convention will last?"

"A few weeks. Six at the most. It won't take much of your time."

Tony looked again at Jackie who, this time, caught his eye and smiled. "All right. I'll come to your meeting–when is it?"

Smalls clapped him on the shoulder. "Next Tuesday. At my house. Six o'clock. I'll introduce you to some very interesting people."

The party lasted another half-hour, during which time Tony observed his mother engaged in conversation with Jackie, while Cooper seemed to be entertaining Mrs. Smalls.

At last Mr. Smalls announced that he and his wife had an eleven-month-old child to look after, and they took their leave, walking the short distance to their home on Prince Street.

Tony, Jackie, and Georgia said goodbye to Cooper–as well as Vivian and Kena–and went out the back way to the carriage house where Tony had tethered Leto to a hitching rail. It was decided that Leto would be tied to the back of the brougham while Tony rode with his mother, and Jackie would return to Lynwood with Primus.

"She's a very nice girl," Georgia said as they waited for the ferry at Whitehall. "And very pretty, too."

"I wonder, though," Tony said.

"You wonder what?"

"Whether she knows what she's getting into."

Georgia raised an eyebrow. "And what do you think she's getting into?"

"I don't know. Our family, I guess. She seems very naïve, in a way."

"No more than I was when I fell in love with your father."

Tony turned to look at her, stared for a moment and smiled. He seized her hand. "And that worked out, didn't it?"

She smiled back. "It did–with the inevitable bumps, shocks, and shrieks along the way."

"Shrieks?"

"It occasionally came to that. On my part, that is. Your father was unflappable."

"That's what Mr. Smalls said about him–in so many words. He wants me to go to the Constitutional Convention next year."

"Does he? I think you should go. Your father would be proud."

The ferry approached the dock and the ferryman jumped out to secure the lines.

CHAPTER 37

The Reverend Phillip T. Hall sat in his office at the New Sheldon Church only a few miles southwest of Lynwood, his fingers laced together on his desk, his thumbs rotating now in a forward direction, now backwards. Had they been vehicles, surely they would have collided by now.

But they were thumbs. He stopped their erratic motion and stared at them. Was he 'all thumbs,' as the saying goes? Could he have been any clumsier on that night twenty-three years ago? Or more morally weak?

The occasion of this soul-searching was the appearance of the entire LeRoux family at his church on the previous Sunday. Or rather the one member of the family, a Benson, whom he had not seen in those twenty-three years: Lucinda. Why had she returned from London?

He was accustomed to looking out over the pulpit every Sunday, or at least most Sundays, and seeing Edwina, Mansfield, and, of course, Jacqueline, who had blossomed into a beautiful young woman and was a talented actress. He had even attended the premiere of *The Second Mrs. Tanqueray* and observed her from a dark corner of the theater. He slipped out just before the curtain rang down.

There was a knock on the door.

"Come in."

The door opened and a striking middle-aged woman with high cheekbones and copper skin entered carrying several letters.

"The mail has come, Reverend," she said.

"Put it down on my desk, Tama. I'll get to it later."

Tama (she had no other name) cautiously approached the desk as if approaching an oriental potentate, and deposited the mail as instructed. But before she turned to go, she called his attention to one particular letter.

"This one is from the LeRoux. I think it's a check."

"Hmm?" The Reverend said absently. "A check? Oh, yes–they probably forgot to leave something in the collection plate. I'll–"

"I think it's a big check."

The reverend raised his eyebrows and looked down at the envelope. He picked it up. "Tama–have you been holding letters up to the light again?"

"I couldn't help it, Reverend–the stationery is as thin as tissue paper."

"All right. We'll take a look." He opened his desk drawer and removed a letter opener, which he slipped beneath the flap on the back. He looked up to see Tama still standing there, eager with anticipation. "All right, Tama–you'll find out about it, anyway." He slit open the envelope and extracted a check and a short note:

For the fund to rebuild Sheldon Church. A beginning.
E. LeRoux

The check was made out to this fund in the amount of five thousand dollars.

"Five thousand?" The Reverend said. "That's more than a beginning–that's nearly half the cost!"

"Isn't it wonderful?" Tama said.

"Yes, yes, it is. But what fund? We don't even have a fund yet."

"We'll have to open an account just for that purpose."

"Yes, of course. I'll go into Beaufort tomorrow. I remember giving a sermon shortly before Christmas about the need to rebuild the old church, but it was only a suggestion, almost a ritual every year at this time. Mrs. LeRoux seems to have taken me quite seriously."

"I understand that they have sold some of their timberland off to a group of investors."

The Reverend looked up. "What investors?"

"Local people. I've heard that the Beaufort National Bank loaned them the money to get started. The new president is himself a black man, you know."

"Yes, I know. All right, Tama–thank you. You may go now."

"Of course, Reverend." Tama turned to go, but stopped and turned around again just as she reached the door. "At last, Phillip! At last! After all these years of–"

"How many times have I told you not to use my Christian name on these premises? You don't know who might–"

"I'm sorry, Reverend. It's just that–"

"You may go."

Tama hesitated for a moment, her smile turned to a grimace, and left the room.

The Reverend contemplated the check before him. Why now? The LeRoux–or Bensons–have always been filthy rich, and they have received his plea for funds to rebuild the historic church every year with muted indifference. Mansfield LeRoux, that skinflint, sometimes dropped a Confederate bank note into the collection plate–worthless! Did he think it was a joke? But this check...this check was real. Or if it wasn't, he'd find out tomorrow.

He leaned back in his chair and tickled his chin with the bowed edge of the check–something he couldn't do twenty years ago–he'd had a beard then.

It must have something to do with Lucinda's return...but what?

He got up from his chair and went to the window and looked out through the barren trees at the ruins of the old church. What a magnificent structure! Grand columns all around that once supported the roof and a portico on the west side, arched windows nearly twenty feet high that must have once contained exquisite stained-glass, and a triangular pediment, now lost, that crowned the front entrance. Burned twice, once during the Revolutionary War, then again during the Civil War by that scoundrel Sherman. Or so the story goes.

And now he, The Reverend Phillip T. Hall, would restore it to its former glory!

CHAPTER 38

I still think that's a foolish way to spend your money, Edwina." Mansfield leaned on his cane while his wife dug about in the dirt planting perennials. "What's wrong with the *New* Sheldon Church?"

"Everything, that's what's wrong with it." Edwina placed a bulb in the hole she had just made and covered it up with dirt. "The Negroes put it up slap-dash twenty years ago and they didn't have the slightest idea of what they were doing. It's drafty and it leaks whenever it rains."

"Hall could simply have it patched and maybe replace those benches with more comfortable pews. Pews with cushions on them. It would not only save my backside, it would save money, too."

"It's done, Mansfield. Besides, the old church is an architectural marvel. When it's restored, people will come from miles around just to look at it."

"Well..." Mansfield muttered, "it's your money."

"And when this agreement with Lucinda is finalized, it will be your money, too."

"How do you mean?"

Edwina sat up and looked at him. "Don't be a dolt, Mansfield. When Lucinda relinquishes her half of the estate, we will take the deed as husband and wife. We will be one entity."

Mansfield rubbed his chin. "Then won't the property, the income, everything in fact, be mine? I mean since a man's property includes his wife as well?"

"I am not your property, Mansfield. I am an independent woman."

"But you just said–"

"We will be one entity. Mr. Patterson has assured me that the deed can be taken with that understanding as long as it is worded correctly. That old-fashioned notion that a woman is nothing more than a man's chattel once she is married is out of date, even in South Carolina."

"I don't trust this Patterson fellow."

"You don't have to trust him. He's a very smart lawyer and if he expects to receive his fee, he'll see that the transaction holds up in court–if it should ever come to that, which I doubt."

"What if Lucinda reneges?"

"She won't. She can't."

Mansfield sighed. "I suppose you know what you're doing, dearest." He pulled his watch out of his vest pocket and looked at it. "I wonder where Ravenel is? He should have been here by now."

"I don't think you should be hunting with your gout acting up."

"It's not acting up. Just a little stiffness is all. Besides, we do more sitting than walking when we're hunting boar."

"I suppose young Mr. Jones will be arriving soon."

"Not till tomorrow. We'll be up at four o'clock the next morning to wait for the boar to return to their lairs."

"Then he'll be staying overnight?"

"Of course. It would take too long for him to come in from St. Helena."

Edwina threw her trowel down, stood up, and brushed the dirt from her denim apron. "I don't think it's a good idea for him to spend the night."

"Why not? We've got plenty of room."

"Does it occur to you, Mansfield, that he and Jackie might have some secret rendezvous while he's here?"

"Rendezvous? With Jackie? That's absurd!"

"Why? Jackie obviously finds him attractive."

"But...but they're half-brother and sister!"

"I know that, and you know that–but neither of them know that. It's bad enough that he's black, but can you imagine the scandal, the disaster, if they decided to run off together?"

Mansfield scratched his nose. "What should we do?"

"In the long run, find another beau for Jacqueline. In the short run, keep them apart. And if you hadn't invited Mr. Jones–"

"I thought you had your sights on Ravenel's son–Tavi."

"I've tried my best. But she hasn't the slightest interest in him. He's too timid."

"Who else then?"

"What about Rav himself?"

"What!" Mansfield's eyes nearly jumped out of his head. "You can't be serious!"

"I am serious. Rav is one of the richest men in the state. He's rumored to be in the running for governor next year. He's handsome, charming, and despite a few dalliances since his wife died, would make a tolerable husband. And he's absolutely smitten with Jacqueline."

Mansfield followed his wife as she made her way back to the house. "How do you know he's smitten by her?"

"Because, unlike you, I am observant. Especially when it comes to romance."

"But...but he's easily thirty years older than she. He's older than I am!"

"You were classmates."

"He was a year ahead of me. Took me under his wing. I tell you, the Citadel can be hell for a cadet if an upperclassman doesn't protect him."

"Well, it's just a thought. If Jacqueline objects, then it's off. But Im afraid if she doesn't find a husband here, she'll return to London with Lucinda."

"Would that be so bad? Then we wouldn't have to worry about her taking up with this Jones fellow."

Edwina stopped as they approached the door to the breakfast room and turned around to face him. "Don't you realize that if she returns to London we may never see her again? I couldn't bear it!"

Mansfield stared at her for a moment. "We've got to tell her sometime about her parentage. If we don't, Lucinda will. And besides, what better way to prevent her striking up a romance with her own brother!"

"Half brother."

"All right–half brother. What difference does it make? We've got to prevent it, and the sooner she knows, the better."

"And the sooner she knows, the sooner she'll disown us and return to London with Lucinda. Do you think Lucinda can be a better mother to her than I am?"

They both turned to the sound of the breakfast room door opening. It was Hanna.

"Mr. Coleman has arrived," she said.

Mansfield went to the great entrance hall to greet Coleman while Edwina went up the back stairs to freshen up and change out of her gardening clothes. When she came down again, Coleman had already gotten settled in his room and was having a brandy with Mansfield in the library.

Coleman stood as she entered the room. "Ah, Edwina, you're looking as lovely as ever!" He gave her a warm embrace.

"It's hardly been a month since you've seen me, Ravenel," she said. "But one does age, nevertheless."

"Nonsense. You're ageless, timeless! I wonder at how you manage to preserve your beauty."

Edwina knew this was Coleman's customary flattery, but she liked to hear it. "Exercise. I get lots of it in the garden even though it's hard to get things to grow this time of year. And lots of powder."

Coleman laughed. "You don't need the powder. But I must say that your sudden departure from Charleston was disappointing. The party on Christmas Eve was the talk of the town!"

"I'm sure it was, Rav, but it couldn't be helped. Lucinda made an unexpected appearance and I could hardly leave her alone here with Mansfield on Christmas Eve. Actually, we should never have left poor Mansfield alone in the first place."

"No, no. I suppose not. But tell me–where is Jackie? I had hoped–"

"She's giving her Aunt Lucinda a tour of the *Southern Pride*, according to Primus. Not that Lucinda hasn't seen it before, but Jacqueline wanted to show her that peculiar portrait that you purchased for her in Savannah."

"Portrait? Oh, that. I thought it was peculiar, too, but Jackie seemed to like it, so–"

"Why don't you go out to the boat and surprise her? I believe she thought you were coming tomorrow, as I did."

A broad grin came to Coleman's face. He glanced at Mansfield, who was still seated and looking at him with sober interest. "That's an excellent idea. You know, I haven't seen Lucinda in nearly thirty years. Why, she must be–"

"As full of energy and mischief as ever. I'm sure she would be delighted to see you."

Coleman put his glass down and adjusted his tie. He was grinning from ear to ear.

"You can tell the ladies we'll be dining at the usual time–two o'clock."

"Yes, yes. Of course. We won't be late." Coleman then excused himself and left by one of the French doors that opened onto the terrace.

Edwina winked at Mansfield, who only stared back, looking rather perplexed.

CHAPTER 39

Tony arrived at Lynwood late the following afternoon in the gig carrying, aside from his valise, a case of his father's wine. This offering to the head of the family was both his ticket of admission and his tribute for the hand of the patriarch's daughter, though Mansfield didn't know it yet.

He was in fact greeted with cordial restraint by Mansfield, who stood at the top of the steps and watched while Primus carried the wine into the house. Coleman stood in the shadows of the open door staring out at this scene with disbelief. Mansfield had informed him of his invitation to Tony, but he simply could not understand it.

"You've invited a nigger to hunt with us?" he had said to Mansfield at dinner the previous day.

"We've hunted with darkies before," Mansfield said.

"Yes, but they were guides, gun bearers–not our equals."

"Who said he was our equal?" Mansfield said. "He's simply one of the exceptions among the black race. There aren't many of them around. You'll feel differently once you've met him."

"I have met him. And yes, he's an exception. Still, it's a bad precedent."

"Wait till you've tasted some of the wine he's bringing to us. You've never put anything better into your mouth."

Coleman was not persuaded by this.

Jackie, sitting at the dinner table during the conversation, looked down at her plate and had said nothing.

Lucinda smirked.

But now Tony was being escorted into the house by Mansfield while Coleman stood back and stared.

Tony extended his hand. "How are you, Mr. Coleman? I haven't seen you since the night of the play."

Coleman reluctantly extended his hand. "The play? Oh, yes–you were the man with the painted roses."

"You have an excellent memory," Tony said with a smile. He now knew, as he had suspected, that Coleman had no clue that he was the same man as the sailor-artist on the *Southern Pride* in Savannah. "It was a mere token of my appreciation for Miss LeRoux's considerable talent."

"Yes, she is very talented." Coleman looked momentarily at a loss for words. "Ah...when will we get a chance to taste this wonderful wine that Mansfield's been raving about?"

"At supper," Mansfield said. "Let the man get settled first."

After this chore was accomplished, Tony descended the grand staircase and entered the parlor, where the others were assembled having tea.

"Welcome back, Mr. Jones," Edwina said, though she did not stand when he entered the room. "You remember my sister, Lucinda."

"Of course," Tony said.

"And my daughter, Jacqueline."

"How are you, Jacqueline?"

"Very well, Mr. Jones," Jackie said, trying to look as demure and disinterested as possible.

Lucinda laughed. "Oh, come now, Jackie, you were on a first-name basis with Tony at Christmas dinner."

"Christmas dinner?" Coleman said.

"Mr. Jones joined us at the invitation of Lucinda," Edwina said. "It seems that she was well-acquainted with his father years ago."

"I see," Coleman said.

An awkward moment ensued, with eyes darting from one person to the next, until Edwina finally spoke:

"Please sit down, Mr. Jones," she said. "You've met Mr. Coleman, I presume?"

"Yes–we've met."

Tony sat down and Hanna poured him some tea.

"I understand you are rather...inexperienced as a hunter," Coleman said.

"That's a fair assessment," Tony said. "I used to hunt quail and even deer with my father from time to time, but nothing so ferocious as a wild boar."

Coleman chuckled with the superiority of a master speaking to a novice. "They *can* be ferocious, especially when cornered. And of course that's exactly what one has to do–corner them. Did you bring a weapon?"

"No. I'm afraid not. They're a couple at the house but I'm not even sure where they are."

Coleman glanced at Mansfield.

"We have plenty of weapons," Mansfield said. "Tony can take his pick."

"Can I come along?"

Everyone turned to Lucinda.

"I've done some boar hunting in England," she said. "The European variety, you know, are the most ferocious."

"You can't be serious, Lucinda," Mansfield said. "I didn't know they allowed women to hunt wild animals in England. Birds, perhaps, but–"

"One of my beaus–the furniture maker–was an avid hunter," she said. "But he deplored the use of firearms. Said it wasn't sporting. So we used crossbows."

All looked at Lucinda as if she had lost her reason.

Only Jackie seemed unperturbed. "Aunt Lucinda is actually quite a good shot with a crossbow. She bagged a particularly ugly customer the last time she and Nigel went hunting, and we ate roast pork for a month."

The men continued to stare at Lucinda as she only smiled with her usual coyness.

"I've got a cross bow," Mansfield finally said. "But it's a bit rusty for lack of use. And only that one."

"Primus can sand the rust out and apply some oil to it," Lucinda said. "And I'd be happy to show anyone who's interested how to use it. There's still plenty of daylight. We can practice on the lawn."

"This isn't England, Lucinda," Coleman said. "Women's suffrage here doesn't extend to the field."

"Is there a law against it?"

"No, of course not, but–"

"Then if no one's going to go to jail for it, I see no reason why I can't participate. And after all, I am one of the proprietors of Lynwood." She glanced at Edwina. "At least as long as I choose to remain here."

Again the men stared.

"All right, Lucinda," Mansfield said. '"You've made your case. But you'll receive no special consideration."

"I expect none."

"Can I come, too?" Jackie said.

Coleman gasped.

"I'll have to put my foot down where you're concerned, Jackie," Mansfield said. "You don't have the experience that your Aunt does, and besides, we've only got one crossbow, as I said. And as far as I know, you've never fired a gun in your life."

Jackie stared at her father defiantly for a moment, then relented. "That's true. I deplore firearms, just as Nigel did. It's just not sporting."

"There, you see," Mansfield said. "The woods are no place for a young lady. I won't have my only daughter exposed to such dangers, at least not on my own property."

"Well said, Mansfield," Edwina said. "I must say that I'm proud of you. A father has to assert his authority from time to time."

Jackie was about to say something until she caught Tony's eye, who gave her a look not unlike her father's.

After tea the group broke up with Lucinda and the men going to the gun room to inspect the weapons, while Edwina and Jackie went for a stroll in the garden.

The gun room was a decidedly masculine retreat created by Edward Benson's father in the early part of the century. He was an avid hunter who used single-shot flintlock rifles that required cleaning and recharging with a ramrod after each firing. This tended to put hunter and prey on a more equal footing, though the elder Benson did not hesitate to acquire the new percussion instruments developed in the 1840's and 50's. The gun room was, in fact, a sort of museum that traced the history of the development of firearms from Revolutionary times.

"Now this is the ultimate hunting rifle," Mansfield said. He opened a glass-covered case and extracted the weapon. "The Winchester '73 repeater." He demonstrated the lever action. "It can stop a buffalo in its tracks." He laughed. "But of course we don't have any buffalo around here. An enraged hog can be just as dangerous."

"I'll take the shotgun," Coleman said. He reached into another case and extracted a weapon that looked very similar to the Winchester. "Twelve gauge. At close range, it will take the critter's head right off."

"Hardly sporting," sniffed Lucinda. "Where's the crossbow?"

"Oh," Mansfield said. "Hanging on the wall over there." He chuckled. "Like the artifact that it is. Hasn't been touched since your grandfather was alive. He had the same ideas about giving these beasts a sporting chance. As far as I'm concerned, the nasty things have got enough advantage as it is."

Lucinda went over to the ancient device hanging on the wall and carefully took it down. "It *is* full of rust. No matter. The mechanism seems to be intact. Where are the bolts?"

"Bolts?" Mansfield said. "You mean the arrows? I'm not sure. There may not be any left."

Lucinda started opening drawers beneath the glassed-in cases. "Certainly there must be. Edward showed me how to use it when I was still a teenager. There should be a crank, too, for cocking the thing."

Tony stood before the rows of rifles and shotguns while Lucinda searched for the bolts and crank. He had no idea of what to choose.

Mansfield noticed his indecision. "You might want to go with this bolt-action model, Tony." He extracted the rifle from its case and handed it to him. "It's not as fast as the repeater, but there's no chance of jamming, and it takes a larger caliber cartridge if you prefer it. It'll stop an elephant."

Tony examined the rifle. "Reminds me of the old Springfield my father taught me how to use. Yes, I like the feel of it."

"Aha!" Lucinda exclaimed. "Here they are. And the crank, too." She extracted a bolt from the drawer and examined it. It looked like a conventional arrow, but larger in diameter and tipped with a steel head. The 'feathers' at the base end were only rudimentary, and made of paper. "Where's Primus? I'm anxious to shoot it."

Edwina extolled her plan to expand the gardens of Lynwood as she and Jackie walked through the hedges and statuary, now far from the house. "Bougainvillea thrives in this climate, even in winter," she said. "I've planted some at the west side of the house so that it will be one of the first things that visitors will see."

"I think you've done a wonderful job, Mother," Jackie said. She picked an azalea bloom and brought it to her nose. "Everything seems to be blooming early this year."

"It's been a warm winter, which is conducive to early blooming of course. But gardening is not what I wanted to talk to you about, Jacqueline."

Jackie stopped and looked at her. "No? Then what?"

Edwina seemed suddenly discomfited, and indicated a stone bench between two rows of hedges. "Sit down."

They both sat on the bench, Jackie inhaling the fragrance of the azalea. She was prepared for one of Edwina's usual lectures, this time perhaps an admonishment not to pay too close attention to Tony.

"I don't quite know how to begin," Edwina said.

"Well...just begin."

"All right. It's about your Aunt Lucinda."

"What about her?"

"You've been very close to her of late."

"I suppose so. We get along quite well. She's so–"

"She's more to you than an aunt."

"How do you mean?"

"I mean that..." An uncharacteristic tear emerged from the corner of Edwina's eye and she quickly wiped it away with a handkerchief.

"Mother–what is it?"

"Your Aunt Lucinda...is actually your mother."

Jackie stared at her in astonishment. "What? Is this a joke?"

"It is no joke, Jacqueline. You were born out of wedlock to your mother, who is Lucinda."

Jackie remained in a pose of rigid attentiveness.

"I know it's a shock, dear," Edwina said, wiping another tear away. "This is the most difficult thing I've ever had to do. Mansfield and I have perpetuated this charade for more than twenty years, but believe me, we both thought it for the best."

"Father? Then he and Lucinda–"

"No, no, no! Mansfield had nothing to do with it, except as an accomplice to concoct a story we could all live with. And I must say, Lucinda was in total agreement with the plan, though she did object at first."

"The plan? What was the plan?"

Edwina composed herself though she avoided eye contact. "We–that is, Mansfield and I–saw it as a calamity from which the family might never recover. Of course things have changed since then–at least in some quarters of society. Perhaps Lucinda–your mother–was ahead of her time. She initially wanted to take you to London with her, but she had little money and Mansfield and I thought it would be best for you to remain here so that we could raise you as our own."

Jackie placed the flower in her lap and turned her gaze towards the house. Then she turned back to Edwina. "Then if–Mansfield–is not my father, who is?"

"Oh, dear," Edwina said, still unable to look Jackie in the eye. "This is the difficult part. I had hoped–"

"Mother!" Jackie stood up. "I mean–oh, I don't know what to call you now!"

"I am merely your Aunt Edwina, Jacqueline. We're still quite closely related. I do hope you can forgive me."

"Well, of course I forgive you." She bent down and gave Edwina a kiss on the cheek. "We can still be close. How can we not be? You raised me. But you didn't answer my question–who is my father?"

Edwina applied the handkerchief to her eyes again. "That's why I chose to tell you now, Jacqueline. I've already waited too long."

"This is maddening! Tell me who he is!"

Now Edwina looked at her. "Your father is–or was–none other than Antonio Jones."

Jackie stood staring at her in a state of shock that eclipsed her reaction to all the previous revelations. She was speechless. Finally, she sat down and looked at the ground, seeing nothing.

Edwina put her arm around her shoulder. "So you see why I was so reluctant to tell you, and why I could no longer put it off."

"Because...because Tony and I are half brother and sister?" Jackie considered this for a moment, then looked wildly at Edwina. "But Tony is black! Why aren't I black, too!"

"No one knows, exactly. Tony's father–Antonio–appeared to be white. He was a Union Army officer, after all. And, of course, his mother, Georgia, is white. But Antonio's mother was a former slave–one of your grandfather's slaves, in fact. It's all very complicated, but–"

"I knew that. I mean about Tony's father. But Mother–I mean Edwina–Oh! I don't know what to do! Does Tony know?"

Edwina patted Jackie on the shoulder just as she was beginning to burst into tears. "I don't know. Not unless his mother has told him, and judging from his demeanor, I would guess not."

"His demeanor? What do you mean?"

"Don't you see? That's why I couldn't wait any longer–I could see that the two of you were falling in love. And that would truly be a calamity. No amount of social progress can ever justify incest."

"Incest!" Now Jackie buried her face in the palms of her hand. "Oh, no, no, no!"

"I know it's hard, Jacqueline, but we've nipped it in the bud. You'll get over this infatuation-after all, much of it is the novelty of his appearance and his obvious intellectual achievements. But there are other men just as handsome and just as intelligent."

"Like who?" Jackie suddenly stood up and wiped the last of her tears away. "There's no one like Tony. No one in the whole world!"

"Of course you feel like that now, but you'll soon see that there are others–like Ravenel."

"Ravenel!"

"I know he's a good bit older, dear, but that's not unusual these days. Besides, he's quite healthy and vigorous–almost to a fault. And he's very rich–"

"I don't care for his money!"

"You're young. You don't know how important money is. And Ravenel is no country booby–he's well-educated, from one of the best families in South Carolina, and not only that, he'll be running for governor next year."

"I don't care if he's running for president of the United States! He's a bigot and a boor. There–I've said it. I know he's father's–Mansfield's–best friend, but I can't abide the man. He stands for everything that's wrong with the South. And you're not my mother anymore! You can't tell me who I can marry and who I can't!"

And with this outburst she stormed off towards the house.

Edwina stared after her for several seconds and then looked out over her garden. "What have I done?"

CHAPTER 40

Tony was not accustomed to rising before seven a.m. In Paris, he generally made the rounds at cafes on the Left Bank and retired to his garret on the Rue Henri Barbusse after midnight. In Beaufort, he didn't need to be at the bank until nine o'clock.

Awakened in his guest room at four o'clock by Primus, he at first thought the house must be on fire. He sat bolt upright.

"Do the others know? How do we get out?"

"The others are up, Mr. Jones," Primus said. "Miss Benson is waiting for you in the gun room and Mr. LeRoux and Mr. Coleman are outside with the dogs."

Tony looked around the room, which was dark except for the taper that Primus held in front of him. He moved to light the candles in the sconces while Tony threw the covers back. "Why do we need dogs?"

"It's a mite foggy out," Primus said. "The dogs will be useful in locating the boars."

"Yes...well, I guess that makes sense. Where are my boots?"

Tony dressed quickly and after gulping down a cup of coffee that Primus had brought with him, descended the stairs to the gun room.

"I found another crossbow," Lucinda said. "Carefully laid away in a bottom drawer along with a dozen bolts. Not a speck of rust on it. Would you care to use it?"

Tony looked at the two crossbows that Lucinda had laid out on the table along with nearly two dozen bolts neatly aligned beside them. "I don't know. Do you think it's safe?"

Lucinda laughed. "There's nothing safe about hunting boar. But you showed yourself to be a good shot with it at practice yesterday afternoon. Why not try it for real?"

Tony picked up the newly discovered crossbow and tested the weight and feel of it in his hands. "Why not? The worst thing that can happen is that I'll shoot myself in the foot."

Lucinda smiled. "You're a chip off the old block, all right. Strap the quiver to your back. Rav and Mansfield are waiting for us."

Once the bolts were in the quivers and strapped to their backs, Tony and Lucinda made their way through a narrow passageway. They could hear the dogs barking and howling even before they opened the door to the yard where a well-beaten path led to the kennels some fifty yards or so from the house. Sherman and Uli were standing at either side of the gate with torches as Mansfield and Coleman tossed scraps of liver and bacon to the dogs. Rav seemed to take especial delight in holding the meat above his head to see how high the dogs could jump.

"Where have you two been?" Mansfield said. "It'll be light soon."

"Sunup's at five-thirty," Lucinda said. "Plenty of time. Do we really need the dogs?"

"Jump, Pancho, jump!" Ravenel tossed a morsel high into the air and Pancho leaped full-stretch to catch it in his mouth.

"Fog'll be with us till seven or so," Mansfield said. "Where's your rifle, Tony?"

"I thought I'd try my luck with the crossbow," Tony said.

Mansfield looked at the crossbow in his hand and the quiver on his back. "Where did you find that one?"

"It must have been Grandpas's favorite," Lucinda said. "He oiled it and laid it away in a drawer wrapped in cloth."

Mansfield looked askance at Lucinda, then at Tony. "Damn clumsy contraption. By the time you crank the bow back and reload the bolt, you could have fired off two or three rounds with the rifle."

Tony smiled. "Lucinda's a good teacher. I'll take my chances."

Mansfield looked unconvinced. "Then stay close to her. Rav and I will take the stand after the dogs flush the boar out of the swamp. You two can follow their trail to the lair. Then we'll have'em trapped." He turned to Coleman, who was still tossing scraps into the air. "Stop feeding the hounds, Rav! They'll lose their appetite for the hunt."

"Look at Rocky jump!" Coleman said. "He's got Pancho beat by a nose!"

Sherman put a ham hock into his pocket after passing it beneath the noses of Pancho and Rocky. The other dogs were alert to this and jumped and yelped, nearly falling on top of one another as Sherman and Uli led them out of the kennel and onto the trail that led to the river. Tony and Lucinda followed, barely keeping sight of the dogs as they were engulfed by the fog. Rav and Mansfield took a different path that led to the stand that was mounted on higher ground just south of the *Southern Pride*.

"I can hardly see a thing," Tony said. "What happened to Sherman and Uli?"

"Don't worry," Lucinda said. "Just follow the path. It'll be light by the time we get to the watering hole."

"What watering hole?"

"Where the boars drink. They need fresh water like we do. The river is brackish."

Though dubious, Tony plunged ahead with his crossbow in both hands. He could hear the dogs whelping, but they seemed to be far away now. "What do we do when we get there? Start shooting?"

"No. They'll run from the dogs. We'll follow and like Mansfield said, we'll trap them between us and the stand."

"What's to keep Rav and Mansfield from shooting us?"

"By that time there'll be plenty of light. And the fog will be lifting. Besides, they'll be shooting down. Watch that bog there–it's quicksand."

Tony stopped dead in his tracks and looked at the bog. It was green with a kind of slime and seemed to be bubbling like a cauldron.

"Go around it, to the left. There's firm ground there."

Tony obeyed and skirted the treacherous quicksand. "You know these woods, don't you?"

"I was a regular tomboy. And nothing's changed here in twenty years. Not even the hurricane affected this part of the property."

They plunged ahead, crossing a small stream that came up to the tops of their boots. Once on higher ground, they heard a high-pitched squeal. This followed by barking.

"There's Uli!" Lucinda said. "Follow him."

Tony plunged ahead again, followed by Lucinda. She was surprisingly agile for a woman her age, which he supposed to be about forty-five or so. The sun was coming up, though still obscured by the fog. Everything seemed gray.

"Which way?"

"Just follow the sound. There're several trails here–any one will take us to the stand."

Tony could see the various trails now, and took the middle one. After a minute or two, he came to a fork in the trail. He stopped and turned around, but didn't see Lucinda. "Lucinda!" He said this in a half-whisper, half-shout.

"I'm right behind you." She now emerged from the fog, nearly out of breath. "I'm not as fit as I used to be."

"Which way do we go?"

"To the left. Can't you hear their hooves?"

Tony listened. "I can now. Why did the dogs stop barking?"

"They're tired. But they're still running. The boar will slip into one of their tunnels and make their way to the lair, where Rav and Mansfield are waiting for them. The dogs are probably already stopped because those tunnels are full of briars."

"What about us? How do we get through the tunnels?"

"We don't. They're not real tunnels–just passages they've created through the brush. Keep moving!"

Tony made his way through the thicket, his crossbow cocked and loaded. He could see the so-called 'tunnel' that led to the lair, which looked like a coil of barbed-wire and just as treacherous. Thirty yards or so beyond the opening was a huge oak tree, Spanish moss suspended from its branches like a curtain partially concealing what looked like a tree house. This was the 'stand' where Mansfield and Coleman were perched, their rifles ready. Their camouflaged clothing made them almost invisible.

The dogs, who had been quiet for a while, started barking again. The fog was lifting. Tony saw what he thought was the back of a large animal, shifting back and forth as if making a bed for itself. He raised his crossbow and aimed at this brown mass. Suddenly a shot rang out. Tony couldn't tell whose gun it came from, but it had to come from the stand. There was a frenzied squealing, as if a dozen pigs had been jabbed with a sharp stick, followed by a deeper, guttural snorting and grunting.

The boar suddenly shot out of the thick undergrowth and his entire body was visible. Tusks like a handlebar mustache, only thrust forward like horns on a bull.

The dogs went into a frenzy, barking, howling, as if one had been hit. Suddenly, one of them, Pancho, went sailing into the air.

The boar was heading in Tony's direction, blood trailing like a fine red mist in the haze.

Tony pulled the trigger on his crossbow and let the bolt fly to its target. Again, the squealing, followed by angry snorts.

The boar was huge–four or five hundred pounds, bearing down on him. Another shot from the stand rang out, apparently missing its target.

Tony considered throwing the crossbow down and making a run for it. But where would he run?

Suddenly the boar, about twenty feet in front of him now, stopped. It simply stood there, staring at him with eyes like glowing coals.

He cocked the crossbow and pulled a second bolt from the quiver. Another shot rang out from the stand and whether it hit the beast or not, it appeared to have no effect. More grunts and the animal resumed its charge.

Tony, his hands shaking, placed the bolt in its cradle and aimed. By this time, however, the boar was on him. He pulled the trigger just as the animal crashed into him and knocked him flat on his back.

A scream. A man's scream. Coming from the stand.

Tony must have lost consciousness for a few seconds, for the last thing he remembered was the scream and now he was sitting up, looking down at his legs, where rested the head of the boar. One of his ankles was entangled in its tusks. His leg was bleeding.

"Tony! Where are you?"

"Over here!" Tony said.

"Damn your eyes!" Coleman screamed.

"He couldn't help it, Rav," Mansfield said. "The boar was on him before he could aim the damn thing."

"Goddammit! Get this thing out of me!"

Tony extracted his leg from the boar's tusks and examined it.

"It's just a scratch, Tony." Lucinda was now standing over him and looking at the boar. "It looks worse than it is."

Tony looked up at her. She was still carrying her crossbow, which had released its charge. And the charge, the bolt, was sticking out of the boar's neck, just above the shoulder.

She smiled at him. "A close one, no?"

Tony managed a smile back.

"Help me down from here," Coleman said. "My God, my leg!"

By this time, the dogs had surrounded the boar and were snarling and nipping at the body as if it were still alive and might renew its attack at any moment.

Uli and Sherman went to the stand to help Coleman down. Mansfield stood on the ground below surveying the scene.

"Damn," Mansfield said, shaking his head. "The rest of them got away. Where the hell did they go?"

CHAPTER 41

Sherman and Uli cut down a couple of saplings and made a litter for Coleman. They made a litter for the boar and the two sows that he and Mansfield killed, but the larger male was so heavy they had to create a third litter just for him. Poor Pancho was dead as well, and he was heaped onto the litter with the sows. It took two trips to the house, with the surviving dogs yelping and howling over the death of their comrade along the way.

The dressing of the beasts was also left to Sherman and Uli, with their brother Frederick, the chef, supervising.

"My goodness!" Edwina said as she examined the boar. "It's monstrous!"

Mansfield chuckled with delight. "It's from one of the litters that Edward imported from Germany after the war. Easily four hundred pounds. He'll yield about 220 or so in fresh meat."

"Oh, my Lord," Edwina said. "We'll be eating pork for months."

"Don't forget the sows," Mansfield said. "That's another two hundred pounds."

Meanwhile, Coleman was in the house where he was being tended to by the servants along with Lucinda and Jackie.

Tony stood aside, feeling superfluous. "I'm sorry Mr. Coleman, but I couldn't help it. The thing was on top of me before I could even get my finger on the trigger."

"It would have been better if you hadn't gotten your finger on the trigger at all. Look at my leg!"

Tony looked at the leg as Hanna washed the wound and dressed it. The bolt lay on the table in the gun room, where they all crowded around Coleman. The wound was a clean one and had passed nearly all the way through the upper part of Coleman's thigh.

"Missed the bone," Primus said. "I seen much worse than that. Don't even need a doctor."

"Still," Coleman said, "I'd like one to take a look at it. Could be infected, you know."

"Father–" Jackie caught herself, considered the fact that among present company only she and Lucinda knew of her true parentage, and repeated the word. "Father has already sent for a doctor. He may not arrive until tomorrow, though."

"God, I could bleed to death by then!"

Lucinda laughed, and made no attempt to suppress it. "The bleeding's already stopped, Rav. You're just a big baby. Hanna can dress a wound as well as any doctor."

"You can laugh, Lucinda–it's not your leg." Coleman glanced at the crossbows lying on the table. "What a hare-brained idea–hunting with crossbows! I'd rather have my backside filled with buck shot!"

"And lie on your stomach while Primus picked the pellets out one by one? I don't think so."

Coleman simply shrugged his shoulders and grumbled.

After the wound was dressed, Primus and Eddie created an arm sling for him and took him upstairs to his room. Tony retired to his room to clean up before dinner.

Lucinda, too, was ready for a bath, but before she reached the staircase, Jackie took her aside.

"May I speak to you for a moment, Aunt Lucinda?" she said. "In the library."

"Why–of course, Jackie."

Jackie led the way to the library and closed the door behind them.

"What is it, Jackie? Is it about Tony and the crossbow? I suppose I shouldn't have–"

"Yes, it is about Tony. But it has nothing to do with the crossbow or Ravenel."

Lucinda looked behind her as if she had lost something. The sofa was closest. "All right. I'm sitting. Now what's this all about?"

Jackie sat in a wing chair near the sofa, rested her elbows on the arms, and spliced her fingers together much as Edwina was accustomed to doing prior to a lecture. "I had a heart-to-heart talk with Edwina yesterday."

"Did you? And what did Edwina have to say?"

"She said...she said she is not my mother."

"How extraordinary! And did she offer an opinion as to who your mother might be?"

"She did."

"And..."

"Why are you playing games with me–Mother?"

Lucinda laughed. But it was not her usual soundless, breathy laugh. It was nervous and shrill. "Now who's playing games? Is this your idea–or Edwina's–of a practical joke? I was in London–"

"Sometime after Uncle Edward's death. In the meantime, you were in residence at Lynwood. And apparently seeing Tony's father on the sly."

Now Lucinda reverted to her customary, confident laugh. "On the sly? Oh, yes–Edwina seems to think that Antonio Jones was your father."

"Yes. And I do, too."

"Well, then, Jackie, my dear, you are both sadly mistaken." Lucinda, who was never sick, pulled a handkerchief from her hunting jacket and affected to blow her nose. "I must have caught cold in the woods this morning." She laughed again. "Oh, Jackie, dear, Edwina means well, but she has the most fanciful notions! Antonio was not your father."

"No?"

"No."

Jackie sighed with cautious relief. "Then Tony is not my half brother?"

"I should say not. Of that you can be assured."

"Can I? And of the other thing as well?"

"What other thing?"

Jackie sighed again, this time with exasperation. "That 'other' thing is Edwina's belief that you are my mother."

Lucinda looked to the fireplace, which was heaped with ashes from the previous night's fire. "That part is true."

Jackie stared at her, at first with anger, then with a mix of wonder and distress. Finally, she burst into tears. "Oh, Mother–Mother! How could you do this to me! Why? All these years..."

Lucinda got up from the sofa and went to her. She knelt down beside her and put her arm around her shoulders as Jackie buried her face in her hands. "I'm so sorry, Jackie–it wasn't even my idea. Edwina and Mansfield were horrified that I had become pregnant out of wedlock. They were afraid it would shame the family–as I'm sure it would have. But I was young and determined to defy social conventions. It didn't matter to me, but I saw the difficulties that it would create if I remained at Lynwood with you–my baby!"

Jackie lifted her head and looked at the woman who she had always thought was her aunt. "So you abandoned me!"

Lucinda bit her lip. "Yes, I suppose I did. But Jackie, darling, I always loved you. I couldn't stop thinking about you all the time I was in London–not even for a day."

"Then why didn't you send for me? Or at least come to Lynwood for a visit?"

"I did offer to come back to Lynwood. I even got cold feet once I was in London. I wanted to come home and renege on my promise to Edwina and Mansfield. But they wouldn't hear of it. And I joined a theatrical group–before I knew it, I was settled and pursuing my passion. But I always meant to send for you. And finally I did."

Jackie dried her eyes with her handkerchief. "Yes, you did. Twenty years later. I was all grown up by then. And you were merely my eccentric but glamorous aunt educating me about Shakespeare and the ways of Europe!"

Tears flowed freely now from both of them.

"Yes," Lucinda said. "It was a deception. A subterfuge. A charade, if you will. But you must believe me, Jackie dear, I always loved you and I wanted you to stay with me in London. I still do."

Jackie looked at her through her tears. "It's...it's too late for that."

"But why, Jackie dear? Why is it too late? I'm still an unmarried woman and so are you. We could move to a house in the country if you like. A spacious house! With a garden–I'll be selling my interest in Lynwood to Edwina and Mansfield soon and the money will–"

"I don't want to be a single woman for the rest of my life. I want to–"

"What's all this blubbering?" It was Edwina standing in the doorway. "Oh–oh, my! Forgive me for intruding." And she quickly disappeared.

Jackie and Lucinda were left staring at each other, neither sure of what to do next.

After a moment or two of this paralysis, Jackie said:

"We must tell her the truth–the whole truth. She thinks Tony and I are–"

"Leave it to me. But Jackie–any infatuation you have for Tony is just that–an infatuation. I know–I was infatuated with his father, and though he was handsome and dashing, the reality was that I wanted to make a statement."

"A statement? What kind of statement?"

Lucinda stood up from her crouched position. "Goodness! I must be getting old–my bones are creaking."

"What kind of statement, Aunt–Oh, what shall I call you now?"

"For the time being, I think it best to keep calling me Aunt Lucinda. No sense in throwing the whole house into an uproar."

"All right. But you were saying–"

"The statement? Oh, yes. Well, I think a good part of my attraction to Antonio was just the fact that he was black. Actually, he appeared to be white, unlike Tony. But the idea of it! A Southern white woman taking up with a Negro! And so soon after the war! The mere thought of it was intoxicating to me."

Jackie shook her head. "I don't see Tony that way. I'm not interested in making a statement or defying anybody. I just admire and respect him–and love him."

"Love him?" Lucinda smiled. She looked into Jackie's eyes. "You do, don't you? But Jackie dear, even love has its limits–and is often of short duration. Come with me to London and–"

Jackie stood up. "Now I have two mothers telling me who I can marry and who I can't!"

"Marriage? Has it gone that far? Has he asked you?"

"Well...he's implied it."

"Implied it? Oh, Jackie, 'implied' is even more worthless than a formal proposal. Are you aware of the pitfalls that lay in your path? Come with me to London."

Jackie stared at the woman she now knew to be her mother as if to assess her character and trustworthiness. "I'll have to think about it."

"And well you should. Now I'm very tired, Jackie. If you'll excuse me, I'm going to my room to soak in the tub." She gave Jackie a kiss and a hug and headed for the door.

"You forgot something," Jackie said.

Lucinda stopped in the doorway and turned around. "And what is that?"

"You still haven't told me who my father is."

Lucinda smiled, as one does to a child who has asked a naïve question. "I think we've had enough surprises for one day, don't you? Let's save it for our next tête-à-tête." And she continued on her way.

Jackie remained standing for some moments and then sat down again in the armchair facing the fireplace. She chewed her nails.

"How's my little sweetheart?" It was Mansfield who now stood in the door. "You've missed all the excitement!"

She didn't look up. "No, I didn't, Father. There's been plenty of excitement right here."

CHAPTER 42

A silence fell upon the South long ago like a great curtain. This was the silence of interbreeding between whites and blacks. It was never discussed in parlors, nor in places of business, nor even in the marital bed. Politicians never mentioned it, academicians shunned it. The offspring of these unions often existed in the shadows and were rarely acknowledged, least of all by their progenitors.

Such was the case with Tony. Despite the shocking revelation by his mother that he was not an adopted black orphan of unknown parentage but the biological offspring of a white woman and a one-eighth Negro man who was the son of a slave, neither he nor his neighbors, nor his school mates, nor the community at large considered him to be anything but a full-blooded African. His mother, however, harbored a much deeper, darker secret that she was loathe to reveal and that he would remain ignorant of for some time to come.

The curtain, however, was slowly beginning to rise.

At dinner that afternoon, Tony noticed a coolness towards him on the part of Jackie that had only been hinted at after the hunt when they were both hovering over Coleman as Hanna dressed his wound. This hint consisted of a lack of eye contact, but Tony attributed this to a concern for Coleman's injury. At dinner, this lack of eye contact became a profound indifference.

Coleman was already drunk. He had, not surprisingly, exaggerated the seriousness of the wound and used it as an excuse to consume large amounts of whiskey to kill the pain.

"You know, Tony," Coleman said, stabbing a large slab of meat with his fork, "you're not such a bad fellow as all that. At least you had the guts to hold your ground and face down that ferocious beast. I'm not sure many men would have. Not my boy, Tavi. I can tell you that."

"Now, now, Rav," Mansfield said, "you don't know that. Tavi's an experienced hunter."

Coleman cut off a slice of the meat and popped it into his mouth. "That's true. I've hunted with him many times and taught him all I know. But that boy is missing something–spunk. That's what it is. Spunk. He doesn't have it. This pork is delicious!"

"Frederick roasted it for four hours," Edwina said. "And he basted it with that secret sauce of his that even the house cooks aren't privy to."

"And you can thank Lucinda for bagging this one," Mansfield said. "Tipped the scales at 440 pounds."

"Goodness!" Edwina said. "Weren't you terrified, Lucinda?"

Lucinda laughed. "There wasn't time to be terrified. I saw the beast charging Tony and thought only of hitting my mark."

"And she hit it!" Coleman said. "You're a remarkable woman, Lucinda. Why haven't you ever married?"

"Rav!" Edwina said. "What a question. She has her reasons."

Coleman chewed his meat, swallowed and chased it with a swallow of the wine. He stared at Lucinda. "What reasons? You're a damned good-looking woman–" he glanced at Jackie–"maybe not as young and pretty as your niece, but damn good-looking all the same. Why, if I weren't still grieving for my poor, departed–"

"Grieving?" Edwina said. "It's been more than two years, Rav. It's time you started looking elsewhere–but not in Lucinda's direction. She's quite settled in her ways."

Rav stared at Lucinda for a moment, then at Jackie, who averted her eyes. He looked down at his plate. "Yes, it has been more than two years. But I miss Marian. She was a wonderful woman. I only regret that...that..." He seemed unable to continue.

"Well, yes," Edwina said. "It must be hard sometimes. Jackie, you must sing us a song after dinner. We could all use some cheering up."

After dinner, all retired to the music room. It had a very high, domed ceiling made of translucent glass that allowed enough light into the room so that on a clear day artificial lighting was unnecessary. Octagonal in design, there were alcoves within which rested columns surmounted by busts of great composers of the past.

A piano-forte sat in the middle of the room, with a bench for the player. Chairs for listeners formed a semi-circle around the instrument.

Rav, who had quite recovered from his momentary idyll over his deceased wife, was assisted to a chair by Mansfield and his servant, Eddie.

Tony took a chair nearest to the bench, where Jackie took her seat, still avoiding eye contact with him.

Jackie folded her hands in her lap and looked to Rav. "What would you like to hear, Rav? I'm afraid my repertoire is limited mostly to drinking songs."

Coleman laughed. He was still holding a glass of wine in his hand. "Anything you like, Jackie, my dear. But I don't need any encouragement to drink."

"Jackie's being modest," Lucinda said. "She can sing arias from Verdi or songs from Gilbert and Sullivan."

"How about that one from *The Pirates of Penzance*?" Mansfield said. He, too, was holding a glass of wine and was nearly as tipsy as Coleman. "What's it called? 'Pour the sherry,' or something."

Jackie smiled and tested a key. "'Pour, Oh Pour, the Pirate sherry?'"

"That's the one!"

Jackie played a few bars from the overture and began to sing:

Pour, oh pour the pirate sherry,
Fill, oh fill, the pirate glass;
And to make us more than merry,
Let the pirate bumper pass!

This ditty delighted the listeners, especially Coleman, who applauded at the end until his hands were nearly raw.

Tony enjoyed this one as well, and found himself more drawn to Jackie than ever. What a delight it would be to listen to her beautiful voice every morning, every evening!

Jackie sang two more songs from *Penzance* and finished with two more from *La Traviata*: the 'Brindisi,' or drinking song in the first act, and the finale of the same act in which Violetta realizes she is in love with Alfredo.

Though Tony didn't understand a word of Italian, he was moved by this last aria particularly and once again enjoyed eye contact and a smile from Jackie.

Coleman failed to notice this interchange because he had fallen asleep.

After Mansfield had roused him, Primus and Eddie were called in and assisted him to his room upstairs where he was put to bed like a child and again quickly fell asleep.

"The doctor will be here tomorrow," Mansfield said. "Hanna will look in on him from time to time until then."

"Poor dear," Edwina said. "It must be painful."

Mansfield chuckled. "The alcohol's taken care of that. Best pain-killer in the world."

After the recital, family members and guests dispersed to their usual retreats–Mansfield to his library, Edwina to the gardens and Lucinda to the stables to feed and pamper the horses.

Jackie seemed determined to retire to her room when Tony met her at the foot of the stairs.

"I'd like to talk to you," he said.

Jackie cast her eyes about the spacious parlor and seeing no one, brought them back to his. "I'll meet you at the *Pride* in fifteen minutes. But don't let Mother see you–use the south entry to the house and stay along that side of the hedges."

Tony took Jackie's advice and slipped out through the gun room and out the south entry. From that vantage point, he could not see Edwina, or she him, as she was preoccupied with her bower on the north side of the house.

At the *Pride*, he was greeted by Louis, who seemed forever dapper and ready to receive guests.

"Good evening, Mr. Jones," Louis said, awaiting him at the top of the gangplank. "Looking to enjoy the evening breeze?"

"Something like that, Louis. But I think Miss LeRoux and I would like a little privacy."

Louis' expression betrayed no hint of surprise or sense of impropriety. "The salon, then?"

"That'll be fine."

Once settled in the main salon on a sofa facing the fireplace, Tony stared at his own painting above the mantelpiece. "Do you think Miss LeRoux likes my portrait of her?"

Louis looked at the painting. "I think she does. She comes aboard almost every day to look at it. Can I get you a drink?"

Tony contemplated the painting in light of Louis' comment. "I think I'll have a scotch. I don't know what Miss LeRoux wants–if anything."

"She always seems to like a glass of sherry about this time of day. Will she be here presently?"

"I think so."

Louis disappeared into the butler's pantry. A few minutes later Sherman appeared wearing a white waiter's jacket and carrying the drinks on a silver tray. He was grinning from ear to ear.

"What happened to your father?" Tony said.

"He's at the gangplank waiting for Miss Jackie."

"What are you grinning about?" Tony took the scotch from him.

Sherman kept on grinning. "I guess Mr. Coleman found out you can handle a crossbow."

"Well, I didn't handle it too well, apparently. Lucky the bolt didn't pierce a major artery–or worse."

"Yes, sir. That was lucky. He squealed like one of them hogs though, didn't he?"

Tony tried to suppress a smile. "Yes, he did. Don't blame him, though. I might have done the same."

"Done the same what?" It was Jackie, who appeared in the door of the salon, which was held open by Louis. She had changed her clothes and was now wearing a kind of trouser suit, the kind that Tony often saw women wear in Paris when they were bicycling.

Tony stood. "We were just talking about the day's events–and Rav's unfortunate accident."

Jackie came over to the sofa and sat down. She nodded at Sherman, who put her glass down on the coffee table and disappeared. Assured that he could no longer hear, she said: "Some of the servants don't think that it was an accident."

"What?" Tony slowly sat down. "Why would they think that?"

"I overheard Louise and Hanna talking in the kitchen. They think that you deliberately shot Rav to eliminate him as a rival."

Tony burst out laughing. "That's absurd!"

"Of course it is. But now you're a hero to them."

Tony stared at her for a moment. She simply smiled. He looked to the door that Sherman had just passed through. "So that's why Sherman was so pleased with me. Do all of them think that?"

"It seems so." Jackie picked up her glass and took a sip. "Now–what was it you wanted to speak to me about?"

"Us."

"Yes? What about us?"

"You seem to have distanced yourself from me ever since I arrived at Lynwood."

The corners of Jackie's mouth turned down ever so slightly. "I thought it was understood that we needed to be discreet."

"Yes...but you seem to be drifting farther and farther away. Why?"

Jackie gazed at the portrait over the mantelpiece. "I'm not who you think I am."

Tony chuckled. "Who are you, then? An imposter?"

"In a way–yes. All my life I've thought that I was one person and now it turns out I'm another."

"Is this a riddle? What are you talking about, Jackie?"

She took another sip of her sherry. "Maybe you'd better have some more of your scotch."

Tony obliged her. "All right. Now what's this all about?"

"Edwina LeRoux is not my mother."

Tony's eyebrows rose. "Then who is?"

"My 'aunt' Lucinda."

Tony exhaled audibly and leaned against the back of the sofa. He stared at Jackie for a moment, then leaned forward again. "How did you learn of this startling news?"

"Don't laugh. It's true. Lucinda herself told me yesterday afternoon."

"Ah! That accounts for the frosty reception. But who, then, is your father?"

Jackie sighed. "She won't tell me–at least not yet. But Mother thinks–or rather Edwina–that he was none other than Antonio Jones."

Tony was at first bewildered, then laughed, though a bit nervously. "Why in the world would she think that?"

"Because Aunt–that is Lucinda–was secretly trysting with your father while she was living at Lynwood. He was in one of her plays."

"I've heard that. It's quite possible that he–"

"But he didn't–not according to Lucinda."

"Then who was it?"

"I told you–she won't say."

Tony sighed. "Well, at least we're not half brother and sister!" He laughed and looked at Jackie. "Could two people look more unalike than you and me? Even if we *were* brother and sister, no one would believe it."

Jackie managed a laugh. "I have to admit that it had me quite shaken for a while. But Tony–what are we to do?"

"I don't know. Does it really change anything?"

"Of course it does! What if Lucinda's lying? What if she simply doesn't want to admit that she took up with a black man and was made pregnant by him?"

"My father wasn't really black–he looked more like you than–" Tony stopped himself.

"You see? It's still a possibility. Tony, we've got to stop seeing each other, at least until I can find out the truth about all this."

Tony was silent for several moments. "I see your point. But we may never know. We can't beat it out of Lucinda."

"What about *your* mother? She must know!"

"Yes...she might. She knows a great deal more than I ever thought. I'll have to have a little talk with her."

Suddenly Louis appeared at the door to the salon. "Miss Jackie–"

"Yes, Louis–what is it?"

"I thought you'd like to know that your mother is headed this way."

"My mother? You mean Mrs. LeRoux?"

Louis seemed puzzled. "Yes, ma'am–Mrs. LeRoux. She seems to be in a hurry."

"Uh, oh." Jackie looked at Tony. "You've got to hide!"

"Hide? That's silly. Why don't we just–"

"She still thinks she has to protect me. Go with Louis!"

Louis nodded and came into the room. Then he gestured towards the butler's pantry.

Tony hesitated, then put his glass down on the coffee table. He looked longingly at Jackie for a moment as if it were the last time he would see her, then walked quickly to the pantry. Louis closed the door behind him.

CHAPTER 43

As it turned out, Edwina had been unpleasantly surprised by a snake in her garden–a large black snake, harmless but threatening–and wanted Louis to send one of his boys to kill it. Louis obliged and sent Sherman, who found the snake curled up in the watering can that Edwina had dropped in her haste to flee the scene. He dispatched the snake and brought the carcass back to the *Pride* to show to Louis and his brothers. Frederick said it would make a fine stew.

Jackie remained in the salon listening to Edwina's conversation with Louis, who stood at the top of the gangplank while Edwina remained on the dock. Once the coast was clear, Tony emerged from the pantry, gave Jackie a quick kiss, and returned to the house.

Tony was troubled by this whole business–that is, of Lucinda's revelation that she was Jackie's real mother and that she refused to reveal the identity of the father. Could it have been Antonio after all? Perhaps Lucinda was trying to protect his father's good name–and herself. But then his father was dead and Lucinda never seemed to really care what people thought of her. So why the mystery? The only answer seemed to be that the father was someone prominent. What about Coleman? He may have been at Lynwood at the time. But then that would mean that he was courting his own daughter! Coleman was a reprobate but not totally depraved...was he?

The doctor arrived the next morning and declared Coleman a lucky man. He applied iodine to the wound–which made Coleman howl–and changed the bandage. He then sent Coleman on his way back to Charleston with instructions that a servant should change the bandage twice a day and apply iodine each time. Antisepsis was a relatively new idea, but the doctor was a firm believer in it.

Tony went back to his mother's house on St. Helena Island. She said little about his stay at Lynwood though she inquired about Jackie.

"She said that Papa was in one of Lucinda's plays after the war," he said.

Georgia was preparing dinner in the kitchen while Tony set the table. "I thought I told you–your father played Othello."

"But he didn't look black."

"Lucinda applied charcoal or grease paint or something to make him look the part. It was the hit of the season. People talked about it for ages."

"Did you see it?"

Georgia emerged from the kitchen drying her hands with a dish towel. "No–I was pregnant with you." She smiled. "But I heard him declaring his lines one night. He had a beautiful baritone voice, your father."

Tony went to the sideboard to open a bottle of wine. "They must have spent a lot of time together."

"Who?"

"Lucinda and Papa."

Georgia frowned. "More than I would have liked. Why?"

"Jackie thinks that..." He stopped pulling on the cork. "That Papa may have been her father."

Georgia laughed, a little nervously. "Who put that notion into her head?"

"Lucinda. Lucinda finally confessed that she is not Jackie's aunt, but her mother."

Georgia, breathless, sat down at the dining room table. "And she said that Antonio–"

"No, no. She denied that it was Papa. But she refuses to identify the real father."

Georgia sighed with relief. "Then who *is* the father? Does Jackie have any ideas?"

"No. But I thought that you might."

Georgia's eyes darted around the dining room as if she had put something down and forgotten where she put it. "I can't imagine."

"You were at Lynwood at the time, weren't you?"

"At the time? I was giving birth to you. Antonio was living at the Beaufort Inn."

"Was Lucinda there?"

"Yes. Yes, she was. But I was hardly paying any attention to her."

"Who else was there?"

"I dont know...I'll have to think."

Tony set a glass before her and poured some wine into it. "Have a glass of wine while you're thinking. Maybe it will help."

"Yes...thank you," She took a sip of the wine. "Let's see...there was Edward, of course, and his two sisters, Edwina and Lucinda, and Mansfield...and... the servants."

"That's all?" Tony poured himself a glass and sat down. "No one else?"

"Well...I don't think so...Oh, yes–the clergyman. I forget his name. He was there for the christening."

"Just for the christening?"

"Well, he married us–me and Edward, I mean." Her eyes suddenly opened wide. "Actually, he was living there."

"At Lynwood?"

"Yes. He was new to the area and was still looking for a house...'Hall.' That was his name. Phillip Hall."

Tony grinned at her. "The plot thickens."

"Oh, Tony–you don't think that he and Lucinda–"

"Why not? Just because he was a man of the cloth? He was flesh and blood just like Papa. And I understand that Lucinda was quite a beauty in those days."

"She was. And a seductress. She certainly tried to seduce your father. But if I can believe him–"

"Put your mind at rest, Mama. I think we've found the culprit."

Georgia put her hand to her mouth. "Oh, dear! What about Jacqueline? How will this affect her?"

"I don't know. Of course there's no proof yet. But all indications point to the Reverend Hall. He may not still be around."

"I'm afraid he is."

"He is? Where?"

"He's the rector out at the Old Sheldon Church. Or rather the New Sheldon Church. "The old one is a ruin, destroyed during the war except for the walls."

Tony took another sip of his wine and gazed at his trompe l'oeil as if he could see through it to the garden. "Hmm...perhaps I should pay a visit to the Reverend Hall."

"Oh, Tony! Stay away from this! It's not your business."

"Of course it's my business. Jackie and I intend to get married–even if we have to go to Paris to do it. In the meantime, she has a right to know who her father is."

Georgia sighed. "Poor Edwina. I never thought I'd say that but–what's that smell? Smoke! Oh, my gosh–the roast is burning!" She jumped up and ran to the kitchen, where she grabbed a couple of pot holders and pulled the roast out of the oven. Smoke billowed out and poured into the dining room.

"I'll open some windows," Tony said. "This isn't the only house that's gong to need airing out."

CHAPTER 44

The next day was a Sunday and Tony knew that the LeRoux usually attended church, though until his mother informed him, he didn't know it was the one in Sheldon.

He arrived at the New Sheldon Church for the eleven o'clock service aboard Leto, who, in spite of her age, seemed to enjoy the journey except for the ferry crossings. For those two brief transits, Tony, like his father before him, placed a hood over her head to keep her calm.

The LeRoux' landau was conspicuous among the carriages parked in front of the church. Rather elegant, with a retractable hood for inclement weather, it contrasted with the gigs and buckboards that belonged to the freedmen, some of whom owned and farmed land that once belonged to Lynwood. There were also a few white families who lived in the area, some of whom farmed their own land, as well and some who were sharecroppers.

Tony hitched Leto to a rail and entered the front of the church. All the congregants were standing and singing a hymn. He took a position in the rearmost pew, where a strikingly attractive woman with jet-black hair, an Indian perhaps, handed him a hymnal. As he mouthed the words, he saw the LeRoux standing and singing in the droning monotone characteristic of white parishioners, while Jackie, with her beautiful soprano voice, sang out with enthusiasm. Lucinda looked rather bored, and made no attempt to even mouth the words. The black parishioners, too, seemed very subdued compared to their counterparts at the Old Brick Church, who clapped and stamped their feet and bellowed the words out with abandon.

Tony did not emulate these latter, but he was confident he could carry a tune, and began to sing out. Jackie must have recognized his voice, for she suddenly turned around, spotted him, and smiled. He smiled back.

At the conclusion of the hymn, the Reverend Hall called for all to be seated. He then ascended the pulpit.

The Reverend was an impressive man, now in his early fifties, with a full head of blond hair streaked with gray. He wore it long, though not as long as he had as a young army chaplain during the war. He was often teased by his fellow officers as trying a little too hard to emulate General George C. Custer.

He stood a little over six feet and had broad shoulders, chiseled features, a strong chin–in fact he resembled a matinee idol more than a chaplain. It was easy to imagine women–especially a woman like Lucinda Benson–being strongly attracted to him.

"Cohabitation..." the Reverend began, pausing to assess the effect the word would have on the congregation. "Cohabitation," he repeated, "in the days of Jesus was not considered to be a sin."

This statement did, in fact, arouse several drowsy parishioners, including Lucinda. She raised her head, straightened her spine, and folded her gloved hands in her lap. Jackie, too, seemed transfixed. Mansfield, his eyelids heavy, leaned with his elbow against the armrest of the pew.

"Nor was it looked down upon during the Middle Ages in our mother country, England. In fact, it was encouraged."

Hall placed his arms outstretched, on either side of the lectern. "This is not to say that Jesus approved of fornication. No, quite the contrary. Reckless, promiscuous fornication without commitment was condemned as being contrary to God's will. And that, you see, is the key word–commitment. If the man and the woman were not wholly committed to each other with the intention of marrying after a specified period of time–it could be as long as two years, even more–then the church was compelled to conclude that they were living in sin, contrary to the laws of God. But, what, you may say, if one partner is so committed, and the other is not. If the other, in fact, decides to pursue a life of promiscuity and debauchery? And furthermore, you may say, what if in the meantime the woman gives birth to a child? What then?"

Hall surveyed the congregation as if expecting someone to offer an opinion. When no one did, he continued:

"Is it the child's fault? No, of course not. The woman's? Yes, if she abandons her child. But what if she was deserted by the father, which is usually the case? And what if the woman having little or no means of support, offers the child up for adoption? Wouldn't that serve as some form of expiation?"

Much of the congregation looked on in puzzled discomfort. What was he getting at?

Lucinda was not one of the puzzled. She looked sidelong at Jackie, who did not return her gaze.

"I am aware," the Reverend continued, "that many members of our little parish have found themselves in this predicament. For some it is not a moral issue. For others, it is particularly troubling. But what it all boils down to is intent and responsibility. By 'intent,' I mean an honorable intention to enter into the holy sacrament of marriage, and by 'responsibility,' I mean responsibility to nurture and educate the child. These two things are key– for it is the welfare of the child that is paramount both for the child's sake and for the future of a Christian society."

He looked out over the congregation, his eyes sweeping over the entire group and briefly focusing on the front row, then on Lucinda, then Jackie.

"For those of you who seek counseling on this issue or simply clarification, I will be available in my office immediately after the service. Now let us turn to page..."

Tony, like Jackie, was one of the puzzled. If Hall was, in fact, Jackie's father, then was this some sort of veiled apology or excuse for neglecting her all these years? And what about Lucinda? Was she the fallen woman who decided to abandon her child and 'pursue a life of promiscuity and debauchery'? Or was it the Reverend Hall himself who was the amoral seeker of pleasure?

At the end of the service, Tony waited in the yard for the Lynwood clan to file out. Edwina simply nodded to him, while Mansfield slapped him on the back and made a jocular comment about Coleman's 'accident proneness,' as he put it. Lucinda seemed in a hurry to leave and barely noticed him. Jackie stood behind Mansfield and waited for him to finish his story about Coleman's numerous hunting mishaps of the past.

When Mansfield had moved on, Jackie addressed Tony:

"Do you think he was talking about you?"

"Me? I thought he was talking about you."

Jackie seemed taken aback. "Why would you think that? He mentioned adoption. I thought–"

"I wasn't adopted–you were."

Jackie at first seemed angry, then perplexed. "I suppose I was, wasn't I ? Then do you think the Reverend Hall knows who my father is?"

"I think he might."

"Jacqueline!" It was Edwina, who had backtracked. "Are you coming?"

"Yes–Mother. In a moment." She turned again to Tony. "Perhaps we should go to him and ask him straight out."

"You go on. I'll ask him."

"But I want to know!"

"Jacqueline!" Edwina called from the carriage.

"Go on. I'll meet you later."

"When?"

"Tomorrow. Come to the bank at ten o'clock."

"Tomorrow, then." She touched his hand lightly and followed Edwina to the landau where the others were waiting.

Tony stood silently in the shade of a tree and waited until the Reverend Hall had spoken to the last parishioner. Then he disappeared into the church.

Tony decided that he would give the Reverend a little time to rest from his labors on the pulpit and perhaps refresh himself with a cup of coffee. So he walked across the street to examine the ruins of the original Sheldon Church.

It was eerily beautiful. The columns and high archways were unusual in that they were made of brick instead of limestone or marble, as was so often the case with the more ambitious examples of church architecture. It was not a large building, but with the topless columns and roofless walls, it exuded a certain majesty and spiritual reaching for the heavens. He thought he might like to be married in this church just as it was.

After twenty minutes or so, he returned to the New Church and found his way to the office. The same woman who gave him the hymnal earlier greeted him and immediately ushered him into the Reverend's inner sanctum.

"I noticed you lingering beneath the shade tree after the others had gone," the Reverend said. "I hope I can be of assistance. Won't you have a seat?"

Tony picked an armchair near the Reverend's desk and sat down. The Reverend sat as well.

"Now–what's on your mind, young fellow?"

Tony slightly resented being referred to as a 'young fellow,' though he was that. After all, he had been called worse. "My name is Tony Jones. Actually, Antonio Jones, Jr."

The Reverend seemed to reach back into his memory. "Jones? Antonio Jones? Oh, yes–your father was–no, it must have been a different Mr. Jones. The one I knew was–"

"A white man," Tony said helpfully.

"Uh, yes. A white man. Major Antonio Jones. He was the head of the

Freedman's Bureau after the war. Ah!" A smile of recognition came across his face. "You are the son of Major Jones and one of the teachers at the Penn School."

"That is correct."

The Reverend leaned back in his chair and gazed at the ceiling. "He was committed to the freedmen's cause–as I was–but unlike me, he married one of the teachers who was a free black from–was it Boston?"

"Um, not exactly."

The Reverend sat up and looked at Tony. "No? Philadelphia, then."

"I'm afraid not. My mother is one hundred percent white. And she's from Georgia. In fact, her name is Georgia."

Hall stared at him for a moment. The smile on his face evaporated. "Georgia Benson? You're...that boy?"

"I'm afraid so."

The Reverend looked very agitated for a moment, then abruptly stood up, went to the open door, and closed it. He returned to his desk and sat down again. "I performed the christening at Lynwood."

"So I've been told."

Hall folded his hands in front of him and twiddled his thumbs. "You were a great surprise to all of us. We thought that you would be the son of Edward Benson, but when you emerged from your mother's womb, it was clear that that was not the case." He let out a barely audible whistle between his teeth. "So Major Jones was the father! And all these years I thought–"

"You thought what?"

"That–I don't know. I have to confess I didn't think about it that much. I had my own problems to think about."

"Such as?"

The Reverend took a hard look at Tony. "Now, Mr. Jones, I'm not here to discuss my own problems. What is it that you wished to speak to me about?"

"If I'm not being too presumptuous, Mr. Hall, I'm here precisely to talk about your problems–because they affect me."

"Is that so?" Hall's voice now took on a threatening tone. "And can you explain to me just how my personal problems–if that's what they are–affect a young man like yourself?"

"I'm in love with Jacqueline LeRoux."

Hall's eyes opened wide. He had stopped twiddling his thumbs and was now toying with a ruler on his desk. He placed it thoughtfully against his lips. “You? In love with Miss LeRoux?”

“That’s right. She was just here, you know.”

“Yes, I know. Along with her mother and her aunt. Did you all come together?”

“No. I came on my own. They were not expecting me.”

“And Mrs. LeRoux approves?”

“Not really.”

“And her Aunt Lucinda?”

“I’m not sure. She’s rather difficult to read.”

Hall again tapped the ruler against his lips. “Yes, she is, isn’t she?” He stared at nothing in particular on the wall for a few moments, then turned back to Tony. “So why have you come to me? I’m afraid I can’t marry you, my boy, as much as I would–”

“I have reason to believe that you are Jacqueline’s father.”

Hall stared at him as if he hadn’t heard correctly. “Do you, now? And what has led you to that conclusion?”

“Hearsay, mostly. But from a very reliable source.”

“And who is that very reliable source, may I ask?”

“My mother. Georgia Jones. Though, legally, I suppose, she is still Georgia Benson.”

“Pshaw!” Hall sputtered as if he had just ingested a mouthful of ashes. “How would she know? She was in confinement when Lucinda and I–” He abruptly cut himself off.

Tony smiled. “Yes? When you and Lucinda were...?”

“You’re very smug, aren’t you, Mr. Jones? Are you here to blackmail me?”

Tony stood. “I’m not a blackmailer, Mr. Hall. I came here for Jackie’s sake, not my own. We don’t need you to marry us.”

“Then who will you get to marry you? Interracial marriages are rather frowned upon in South Carolina, you know, if not downright illegal. The legislature is considering an anti-miscegenation bill in Columbia as we speak.”

“We may have to leave the country. But we would like to have your blessings before we do so.”

“My blessings?” Hall turned to the window that offered a view of the Old Church. “You want my blessings? What about Lucinda’s?”

“We hope to have hers, too.”

Hall sighed and picked up the ruler again. He tapped it against his lips. “Yes...Lucinda’s blessings...I must speak to her–I must...”

“Thank you, sir.” Tony eased his way to the door. “I appreciate your taking time for the interview."

"Hmm?" Hall continued to stare out the window. "Yes of course. My pleasure."

"Goodbye, sir."

"Yes–goodbye."

CHAPTER 45

Jackie arrived at the bank the next morning at precisely ten o'clock and was met at the door by Mr. Ferguson, who complimented her on her appearance and ushered her into Tony's office.

After noting that the bank was unusually busy that morning, Mr. Ferguson gracefully excused himself and closed the door behind him. There was no window to the lobby.

"Sit down, Jackie," Tony said. "I have some news for you."

Jackie sat. "Then the Reverend Hall told you? He told you who my father is?"

"In so many words, yes." Tony sat in a chair next to hers.

"Well? What did he say?"

"It's what he *didn't* say that betrayed him."

"Betrayed him? Tony–what did he say?"

"He said that he performed the christening ceremony at Lynwood when I was born."

Jackie's eyes, which were naturally large, grew larger. "You were born at Lynwood?"

"Yes–it's very complicated. But the point is that you were also born there–several months later."

"Well, of course I always assumed I was born at Lynwood, but how did you–"

"Never mind me. You wanted to know who your father is."

"Of course. That's why I'm here. And he is..."

"None other than the Reverend Hall himself."

Jackie stared blankly at him for several seconds. "The Reverend Hall...you can't be serious."

"I'm very serious. Edwina and Mansfield apparently took him in because he was new to the area and needed a place to live while he was looking for a house. It so happened that my mother was married to your Uncle Edward at the time and–"

"What! Your mother was married to Uncle Edward?"

"Yes. But he died shortly after I was born and my mother left Lynwood to live with my father. The Reverend Hall stayed on."

Jackie shook her head in disbelief. "So my mother–Lucinda–took up with my father–the Reverend Hall–while the latter was enjoying the hospitality of my...of Edwina and Mansfield?"

"That about sums it up."

Jackie continued staring at Tony, more in bemusement than in shock. She was about to ask for more clarification when they both heard a loud explosion and breaking glass.

Tony immediately went to the door and opened it. The lobby was filled with smoke and the plate glass window was shattered. People were lying on the floor, many bleeding. Horses' hooves were heard among shouts of, "No more nigger banks! No more nigger property rights! No more niggers in the state house!"

Mr. Ferguson, holding a bloody handkerchief to his temple, approached him. "Red Shirts!"

"Red Shirts?" Tony said. "In Beaufort?"

"The Constitutional Convention is coming up soon. They want to make sure no blacks go to the polls and vote."

"Take care of that cut, Mr. Ferguson."

"It's just a scratch. There're people hurt much worse than me."

"Help me! Oh, Lawd, I'm dyin'!"

Tony went to help the woman lying on her back, her dress covered with blood. Mr. Ferguson went to help an elderly man whose arm was almost severed by the flying glass. A doctor happened to be in the bank at the time of the blast and was already helping the wounded with makeshift tourniquets torn from their clothing. Mr. Smalls appeared in the front door and rushed to help as well.

Jackie stood in the door of Tony's office for a moment, gazing numbly at the carnage, but then collected herself and rushed to help a pregnant woman who was bleeding from her abdomen.

"Oh, my baby! Help me! My poor baby!"

Another doctor arrived and the sheriff and two deputies followed him.

The chaos soon settled and the screaming diminished into moans and groans. The sheriff and his deputies made a count: twelve people wounded, only three seriously, and no one dead. One of the doctors declared that the pregnant woman would survive, but the fate of the fetus was in doubt.

With the smoke clearing and the shouts dying down, Mr. Smalls approached Tony. "You see what we're up against, Tony," he said. "The Red Shirts have even dared to bring their terror tactics to Beaufort."

"I thought they went out with the Klan," Tony said.

"They're still very much alive as you can see. And the Klan ain't dead, either. I hope we can count on you at the Convention."

Tony surveyed the scene. The lobby looked like a battlefield. The wounded were being helped into ambulances. Jackie was now helping an elderly woman who seemed dazed and confused, though otherwise unhurt.

Tony turned his attention back to Mr. Smalls. "I'll do whatever it takes, Mr. Smalls. Just tell me what you want me to do."

Jackie spent the rest of the morning trying to be as helpful as she could. She rode in one of the ambulances to the hospital and held the hand of the pregnant woman as the doctor examined her wounds. Primus followed in the phaeton.

Tony had his hands full supervising employees and volunteers as they cleared the lobby of glass and debris. A number of depositors, who had not been present at the time of the bombing, now appeared, wanting to withdraw their funds. Tony convinced most of them that their money was safe, that the bombing was intended only to intimidate, not to rob the bank. Reporters from *The Gazette* and *The New South* arrived within a half-hour of the blast, and interviewed nearly everyone who was willing to talk. Tony was their prime person of interest, however, and he spent about an hour explaining that he had no idea who was responsible for the attack, though he suspected white supremacists.

Was he aware that there had been similar attackers in other parts of the state?

Yes, he had heard that there were, but he had not been reading the papers lately.

Did he know that there had been a recent resurgence of incidents like this involving the Red Shirts?

Yes, he had heard that. too.

Did he know that Ravenel Coleman, rumored to be a candidate for governor, was deeply involved in the Red Shirt organization and had in fact, led attacks on black Republicans after President Hayes removed Federal troops from the state in '76?

Ravenel Coleman? A Red Shirt? No, he hadn't heard that.

The reporters scribbled away furiously and, determining that Tony was rather uninformed about South Carolina politics, hurried off to interview others, notably Mr. Smalls.

At the end of the day, Jackie returned to the bank, where workers were already in the process of replacing the plate glass window. She met Tony in the lobby, where he was reassuring a customer of the safety of his money and the security measures to be taken in the future. Having allayed the customer's fears, he ushered Jackie into his office.

Jackie, exhausted from her labor, hardly noticed the blood stains on her dress as she collapsed into the chair she had been sitting in before the bombing. "Who would do this?"

Tony sat down, this time behind his desk. "Somebody like Ravenel Coleman, that's who."

Jackie sat up. "Rav? You think Rav had something to do with this?"

"I don't know. A reporter suggested he might. Said he was a leader of the Red Shirts back in the 70's."

"That was a long time ago, Tony. He was a young man then."

"I don't think he's changed his views about black people over the years. Don't you want to clean up? There's a wash room through that door there."

Jackie looked down at her dress. "There's not much I can do until I get home. Do you really think Rav was behind it?"

"Again, I don't know. The last I heard, he was convalescing in Charleston from the wound I inflicted on his leg."

"Maybe it was simply revenge."

"I doubt it. He would have just shot me down in the street or had me kidnapped and lynched. No, this was aimed at black people in general. Disenfranchisement seems to be the goal."

Jackie leaned back in her chair and closed her eyes.

Tony studied her for a moment or two. Her blond hair, usually neatly pinned back and secured by a barrette, was hanging loosely over her face, which was besmudged with soot. She wore little make-up, but that was also smudged from wiping her brow with her hands. Even in this disheveled state, she was beautiful.

"I'd accompany you back to Lynwood, but I'm afraid that present circumstances make that impossible."

She opened her eyes. "Yes, I'm sure you're right. Oh, Tony! What are we to do?"

"First of all, I think that we'd better postpone any meeting with the

Reverend Hall."

"Oh–I'd almost forgotten."

Tony chuckled. "How could you forget? He's your father."

She cast her eyes down at the carpet. "It doesn't seem like it. I still think of Mansfield as my father."

"Don't forget–Coleman is Mansfield's best friend."

She blinked as if to bring into focus an indistinct image. "Mansfield couldn't have had anything to do with this."

"I didn't say that he did. But he and Coleman are of the same opinions generally. Although I have to admit he's been very gracious towards me."

"His prejudices are general–he treats individuals with kindness and respect."

Tony sighed. "There are thousands of white men who fall into that category. A kind of savage gentility."

Jackie frowned. She wondered if Tony wasn't himself prejudiced against white people. Suddenly, she felt that there was a widening gulf between them. She stood. "I'd better go."

Tony rose from his desk. "I'll see you to your carriage."

"That won't be necessary. I'm sure that you still have a great deal to do." She turned to leave.

"Jackie," he said almost plaintively, "when...when can I see you?"

She paused for a moment. "I don't know. As you said, it's impossible under the present circumstances. Send me a note when things have settled down a bit."

"A note?"

"Yes. We can't pick up a telephone as we could in London or Paris, can we? Goodbye, Tony."

Tony watched her as she approached the door. "Thank you, Jackie."

She stopped and turned around. "For what?"

"For helping...for helping my people."

She thought for a moment. "Aren't they my people, too?"

CHAPTER 46

When Jackie arrived at Lynwood, she noticed that an unfamiliar carriage was parked in the drive.

She thought it might belong to Dr. Fischer and was anxious as she ascended the steps to the front door. Had Edwina or Mansfield fallen ill? Lucinda? Perhaps a servant.

As she entered the foyer, she noted a black bowler on the hall tree that was also unfamiliar. Dr. Fischer always wore a broad-brimmed Stetson to protect him from the sun on his rounds to see his patients.

"Jackie! My Lord! What's happened to you?" It was Edwina, who had just come in from the garden, wearing a sunhat of her own and wielding the familiar trowel. "Do you need a doctor?"

"No, no, I'm fine. There was an...accident at the bank and I had to help the injured."

"My goodness! It must have been a terrible accident!"

"Yes..yes, it was. But I'm all right–I'll just need to clean up."

"I should say so. What kind of accident was it?"

"I'll tell you all about it after I clean up. Who's our visitor?"

"Oh–the Reverend Hall. He seems to have some business with Lucinda. They're in the library. I'll have Hanna prepare your bath. You look a fright!"

Jackie stood stock still for a moment, absorbing this bit of news, which was almost as alarming as the bombing. Then she ascended the stairs to her room.

Hanna heated some water and poured it into the tub as Jackie undressed.

"You're not hurt, Miss Jackie?" Hanna said.

"No, Hanna. I was very lucky."

"I heard you saved Mrs. Woodcock's life."

"Who told you that?"

Hanna smiled. "Word moves fast amongst black folks."

"It certainly does. But I didn't save her life–I just tried to make her comfortable."

"Yes, ma'am. Can I bring you some salts?"

"That won't be necessary. Thank you, Hanna–that will be all."

As Jackie reclined in the tub and gazed out the window at a pair of sparrows that had alighted on the sill, she contemplated the tête-à-tête between Lucinda and the Reverend Hall. What could have brought him to Lynwood? And what were they talking about? Was Tony right about Hall being her biological father? He had no proof, only hearsay and speculation.

While dressing, she wondered what she should say to the Reverend. How should she address him? And if he truly was her father, why did he never acknowledge the fact? Had he been sworn to secrecy by Edwina and Mansfield...and Lucinda?

She descended the stairs wearing a white taffeta dress, the same one she had worn for her debut in Charleston a few years earlier. The occasion seemed to demand it. She was about to meet her father–her real father. True, she had seen him numerous times at church preaching from the pulpit. But she had hardly paid any attention to either his preaching or his complimentary remarks to her and her presumed parents afterwards. Now she saw him in a completely different light.

When she arrived in the parlor, there was no one there. She went to the library and again, no one there. There was an eerie silence in the house. Where had everyone gone?

She went to the kitchen, where Louise was cooking supper. "Have you seen Aunt Lucinda, Louise? And the Reverend Hall?

"Louise had been stirring a large pot with a wooden spoon, and turned around at the sound of Jackie's voice." Miss Lucinda? My, don't you look lovely! You steppin' out this evening, Miss Jackie?"

"No...I thought we had guests. The Reverend Hall, I mean."

"The Reverend? Oh, he gone. You know, he stay the longest time in the library with Miss Lucinda. Hanna took'em some sherry, but they hardly touched it. Seemed deep in thought, Hanna said. Just staring at each other like a couple of hoot owls wondering why they 'lighted in the same tree."

"And Miss Lucinda?"

"She out on the terrace watching the sun go down. This time she take the bottle of sherry with her."

Jackie stared at Louise for a moment, then left the kitchen without a word and headed for the terrace.

She found Lucinda seated at one of the wrought-iron tables on the terrace facing the river. She was sipping sherry from a glass and seemed to be contemplating the play of light on the water and the golden reflections off the hull of the *Southern Pride*.

"Lucinda?"

Lucinda turned around. "How lovely you look, Jackie. Are you going to a ball?"

"No. I thought...I just felt like dressing for supper. It's been a difficult day."

"Yes, it has, hasn't it? Won't you sit down and join me in a glass of sherry? Where's Hanna? She's never here when you need her."

"Oh...she's upstairs. I'll just sit down and we'll chat until–"

"There she is," Lucinda said. "Hanna, bring Miss Jacqueline a glass and while you're at it, some cheese and crackers. The brie. The good brie."

"Yes ma'am," Hanna said, and disappeared back into the house.

Jackie sat down.

"Careful you don't crush those petticoats, dear," Lucinda said.

"No, I won't. Lucinda...

"Yes? Oh, look–ducks! There're swimming up to the stern of the *Pride*. Frederick is tossing them something–bread crumbs, I suspect."

"Lucinda..." Jackie began again, still uncomfortable with this form of address. "What was the Reverend Hall doing here?"

Lucinda continued to watch the ducks. "He was proposing marriage."

"Marriage! To you?"

"To whom else?" Lucinda laughed. "Rather late, isn't it? If he had done it twenty-five years ago, I might have accepted."

"Then you turned him down?"

"I told him I'd think about it."

Now Jackie gazed at the river and watched as Frederick teased the ducks by pretending to toss out a handful of crumbs to one side of the boat then releasing them to the other.

"He's my father, isn't he?"

Lucinda looked at her. "Did you never notice the resemblance?"

"I never thought about it. I could see that he was a handsome man, but I never look at priests in that way. I've always thought of them as being...I don't know–celibate."

Lucinda laughed and swallowed the last ounce of sherry in her glass. Hanna, with her impeccable timing, appeared with a tray containing a glass for Jackie along with the cheese and crackers. She filled each of their glasses.

When she had gone, Lucinda continued. "Phillip is anything but celibate. In fact, I would describe him as something of a rake."

"A rake? How can he be a man of the cloth and a rake, too?"

"He's not the only one, dear." Lucinda suspended her glass in the air. "Shall we drink to the philandering male of the species?"

Jackie reluctantly raised her glass. "Was he so...promiscuous as that?"

Lucinda clinked her glass against Jackie's. "Hard to tell, really. But I understand that he has a few little pickaninnies running around in Sheldon."

"Mother! I mean...Lucinda. What language to use about, about–"

"Your little half-brothers and sisters? Yes, that is rather coarse of me isn't it? But the slur is directed more at Phillip than them. And I suppose most of them are grownup by now, like you."

They watched Frederick feeding the ducks until he was out of bread crumbs and went back to the galley of the *Pride*.

"What will you do?" Jackie said.

"I don't know. I suppose go back to London as I've always intended. And of course my offer still stands: an acting career awaits you there. You'll never make ends meet performing in little theaters here. Even Broadway offers few opportunities for women."

"I don't know that I care so much for an acting career."

"Jackie, dear," Lucinda filled her glass again. "You must never put your fate into the hands of a man. If you marry, all of your property will be his and he can leave you at any moment for a younger woman. Which will happen, you can depend upon it."

"Tony would never be unfaithful."

"Ha! You think not? He's a man, isn't he? It's the hallmark of the species."

"What about Mansfield? He's always been faithful to Edwina–at least as far as I know."

"Mansfield is an exception. And he has no gumption. He's more afraid of Edwina's censure that he is of a raging boar."

"Still–I think Tony's different."

Lucinda seemed to be getting a little tipsy. "They say that black men are more prone to wander than whites. In every sense of the word. What if you should go to Paris with him and he takes up with one of his models? In fact, I've never known an artist who didn't maintain a harem, even the older ones who are half-deaf and nearly blind. No, Jackie you must come with me to London and pursue the brilliant career that awaits you. When you conquer London you will have lords and members of Parliament at your feet and you can pick and choose as you please. And you will not be dependent upon them even should you decide to marry, which I would advise you not to do."

"Never marry? Like you? What will you do, mother, when your beauty fades and you're all alone? Shall we be a pair of old maids doddering at our knitting?" Jackie swallowed a draught of the sherry. "I want to have children. I want to have grandchildren. And I want them at my feet before the fire on cold winter nights as I read stories to them."

Lucinda stared at her for a moment and then turned her gaze again to the river. The sun was setting. "We're not made of the same cloth, you and I, Jackie, in spite of the fact that I'm your mother. The domestic scene you just described has always repelled me. Although I must say I sometimes wonder how I will spend my later years. But that's a long way off, even for me."

The two women remained silent for a time, watching the sun dip below the trees on the other side of the river. The sky was a painter's palette of blue and orange and violet, with red clouds high above.

"It's a lovely sight, isn't it?" Edwina approached with Mansfield a few steps behind her. She was dressed for supper. "May we join you?"

"Hanna," Mansfield said. "Where are you? Oh, there you are. Bring us some mint juleps. Sherry is for after dinner."

"I'll stick with the sherry," Lucinda said. "Bourbon makes me absolutely ill."

Mansfield pulled out a chair for Edwina. "That's because you don't know how to sip it. Good bourbon with a sprig of mint must be savored."

"My sentiments exactly," Edwina said. "Now Lucinda, you must tell us the purpose of the Reverend Hall's visit. He's really a charming man when he isn't spouting some nonsense from the pulpit."

"Jacqueline and I have some news for you, Edwina," Lucinda said, with a wink at Jackie. "But we'd better wait until Hanna arrives with the mint juleps. Too bad the Reverend Hall can't be here to join in the fun."

CHAPTER 47

Tony sat quietly in the carriage as Mr. Smalls, Mr. Miller, and Mr. Whipper engaged in an animated discussion about the Constitutional Convention in Columbia. He was, in fact, a delegate, but a neophyte in the Republican Party. Mr. Miller was an attorney, as was Mr. Whipper, and both had been involved in the party since Reconstruction. Mr. Smalls was the unofficial dean of the delegation.

Tony listened, but only half-heartedly. He was more concerned with Jackie, whom he had not seen since the bombing of the bank. He had sent her the note she had suggested, but she had not responded. A second note, delivered by Scratch, was likewise ignored.

The hired carriage pulled up to the Yemassee Station with about a half hour to spare. The train would arrive from Savannah and take them first to Augusta, where they would change trains and press on to Columbia.

"Quite a crowd," Mr. Smalls said. "Maybe some of them will accompany us and lend their moral support."

Tony stepped down from the carriage and surveyed the crowd. Most were white and well-dressed, as most travelers were when traveling by train. There was almost a festive atmosphere.

All four men grabbed their valises, with the driver unloading the heavier luggage and placing it on a hand cart. They ascended the platform.

It was a sunny day in September, and the ladies all protected their fair complexions with parasols. Many were from Beaufort and instantly recognized Mr. Smalls. He spent the next fifteen minutes shaking hands and trying to rally support for his amendments to the 1868 Constitution that would preserve and extend the voting rights of the Negro. Most were sympathetic and listened with polite attention. Some turned their back on him or simply moved to the edge of the platform to wait for the train.

Tony put his valise down and pulled his watch out of his vest pocket to check the time. He replaced the watch and looked around the platform. There were several bank customers there, both black and white, and he nodded with a smile, but was not inclined to engage in conversation. Mr. Miller and Mr. Whippper were both moving through the crowd, stopping to talk to nearly everyone, while Mr. Smalls needed only to remain in one spot as people came to him.

Tony felt isolated and out of place. He wasn't a politician, nor even a bank president, at least in his own mind. He was an artist, and beginning to feel a great void in his life that was only exacerbated by the void within a void that was the absence of Jackie. Then he saw her.

She stood on the edge of the platform nearest the station master's office, leaning on her parasol.

She seemed not to have seen him, and appeared to be preoccupied with something in the distance.

"Jackie," he said, as he approached her.

She turned abruptly, as if startled by a stranger interrupting her reverie. "Tony."

"I'm on my way to Columbia," he said. "The Convention."

"Yes–I've heard. I think it's marvelous that you finally decided to get involved."

"I feel that it's my responsibility."

"Yes. Of course it is."

Jackie turned away again and gazed out at the trees.

"Where are you headed?"

"Charleston."

"Charleston? By yourself?"

"Yes."

"Why?"

She seemed annoyed for a moment, then abruptly turned towards him. "If you must know, I'm engaged to be married. "

Tony felt as if he had been hit in the chest with a brick. "Married? To whom?"

Jackie bit her lip and turned away again. "To Rav."

"Coleman?" Tony laughed and then checked himself. "I'm sorry–but you can't be serious."

"I'm afraid so. Please don't make it difficult for me, Tony. I ...I care for you very much, but I've come to realize that we can never be more than friends. There're too many obstacles in our path, too many land mines that could explode in our faces–the metaphor is appropriate, I think, considering the bombing of the bank. That–among other things–made me realize that we would always be living in fear and isolation. We would have no friends, no family, even. No one would visit us."

"Is that so important to you? A social life?"

"Yes, of course it is. Oh, it's not just parties and gala balls–it's a sense of community, a sense of belonging."

There was a train whistle in the distance.

"You'll certainly have a busy social life with Coleman."

"Yes. Perhaps more than I care to have. But at least I will have one."

Tony felt that there could be nothing more to say, but still, he couldn't remain mute. "Jackie–you'll never be happy with him."

"And I would be with you?"

"Yes. After the convention I'm turning the bank over to Mr Ferguson. I'll still be a shareholder, along with my mother–who, by the way, will be married to Mr. Cooper in December. I plan to return to Paris."

"Permanently?"

"I don't know. But at least for a few years."

She stared at him intently. "And you want me to go with you?"

"Yes."

"What would I do there?"

"Act. You already know some French."

She shook her head. "No, Tony–it would never work. I would have no chance of a career in a place where I don't have a command of the language. And what would I do all day? Wash your socks and cook your meals and wait for you to come home from your atelier where you spend the day ogling nude women? I would go mad!"

"You will go mad with Coleman."

Jackie's lips tightened.

"Tony!" It was Mr. Smalls waving him to the other side of the platform. "The train's coming. It only stops for five minutes!"

Tony looked at the placard on the locomotive as it pulled into the station. "It's the Port Royal line. I have to go."

Jackie extended her hand. "Goodbye, Tony–I hope the Convention is a success."

"Actually, it's doomed to failure–at least for the black man. But we have to make ourselves heard."

Jackie smiled. "Good luck."

"Tony! Grab your valise and get on this train!"

Tony did as he was commanded by Mr. Smalls and hurried aboard the train.

The Port Royal line ran along the Savannah River to Augusta and offered some lovely views. Tony sat pensively gazing out the window as the others planned out their strategy to deal with the Democrats, who now commanded an overwhelming majority in the House.

"Tony, I'd like you to present the amendment to bar the literacy tests unless they are applied to white and black voters alike."

"Why me?"

"Because you're a Harvard graduate and you'll have more credibility than the rest of us."

"I didn't graduate from Harvard–I dropped out my junior year."

"No matter. Everyone knows you were a student there and you have impeccable elocution. We need to show the white Democrats that we're as intelligent and articulate as they are, even more so in some cases. And you're the 'more so.'"

Tony looked at the document that Mr. Smalls had thrust before him. He read it over. "All right. But I'd like to make a few changes."

Smalls grinned. "Feel free. And don't hesitate to correct my grammar. I never went to school you know."

Tony chuckled. "You've certainly made up for it over the years."

"My daughter's a great teacher."

Tony studied the document and made pencil corrections as the train hurtled towards Augusta. For a time he was absorbed in this task, but there wasn't really much to correct except for Mr. Small's errant spelling, and he went back to staring out the window and thinking of Jackie.

They were met at Augusta by a troop of Red Shirts on horses, who pelted them with tomatoes as they disembarked to change trains for Columbia. These men, mostly in their teens and twenties, carried rifles, but there were no shots fired. They were supported by hecklers on foot who joined in with various missiles, mostly rotten vegetables, along with the usual racial slurs. Mr. Smalls advised restraint under the circumstances, though he carried a pistol with him just in case. He and the others tried to clean up in the station restroom, but were blocked at the door by the station master.

Once they climbed aboard the train to Columbia, a Negro porter led them to a wash room and supplied them with towels.

"One of the more peaceful encounters," Mr. Smalls said with a chuckle. "Did you see the reporters? I'll bet Governor Evans gave orders to lay off the rough stuff–bad for the image of the Democrats–and besides, they know they've got us beat before we even start."

Tony was tempted to say, 'then why start?' But he remembered what he told Jackie about 'being heard.' Yes, Mr. Smalls was right–whatever was said at the Convention would be in all the papers, both North and South.

Still, the futility of their mission–at least in the short run–sapped Tony's enthusiasm for the venture. And added to this was his loss of Jackie to a bigot like Coleman.

As they rolled into the Columbia station, he considered taking his leave of the group, pleading a family emergency, and continuing on to Charleston. But what would he do once he got there? Jackie said she and Coleman were 'engaged.' When would the wedding be? Where? Would she be staying at his house in the meantime? Would he go knocking on Coleman's front door and ask for Miss LeRoux? He would probably be sent around to the servants' entrance....he chuckled at this thought.

"What's so funny?" Mr. Smalls said. The train came to a stop and everyone grabbed their valises.

"The irony of it all, Mr. Smalls," Tony said. "The irony of it."

He stood up, took his valise from the overhead rack, and followed a bemused Mr. Smalls into the aisle.

CHAPTER 48

The Constitutional Convention of 1895 was not a brief affair. It extended into October, then November, and finally ended the first week of December.

Neither Tony nor the other members of the delegation were prepared to stay for the duration. James Wigg and Isaiah Reed, from Beaufort, came and went, as did Robert Anderson, the only black delegate from Georgetown County. All had either businesses or law practices to run. And there were many other items on the agenda aside from the crucial issue of black suffrage.

It was late in November before Tony was allowed to make his speech outlining the parameters of the proposed literacy test, ensuring that both blacks and whites would receive the same test, and that at least one Democrat and one Republican would administer it at each polling station. He sat down to polite applause, but the proposal was voted down.

So he returned to Beaufort.

Mr. Ferguson was barely able to conceal his joy at hearing that Tony was relinquishing his position as president of the bank and that he would nominate him as his successor at the next board meeting.

After his confab with Ferguson, Tony headed for Whitehall to wait for the ferry to St. Helena. Along the way, he picked up a copy of the *New South* and folded it under his arm as he continued to the wharf. Once there he sat down on a hard bench and unfolded the paper. The lead story was about the Convention and the various proposals that the delegates from Beaufort had made before the House. There was much praise for the eloquence of the delegates, but not a single one of their proposals had survived the respective committees they were submitted to. Senator Tillman had even singled out Tony as "a particularly able young Negro."

He turned to an inside page and noticed one article on the lower right-hand corner:

SENATOR COLEMAN'S FIANCÉE
BREAKS OFF ENGAGEMENT

He folded the front page back and read the article:

Senator Ravenel Coleman, rumored to be a candidate for governor next year, met with disappointment yesterday when his fiancée, Miss Jacqueline LeRoux, called off the engagement. The wedding was scheduled to take place this Saturday at St. Philip's Episcopal Church in Charleston. Interviewed by reporters, she said new opportunities had opened' to her and that marriage at this time would make it impossible for her to take advantage of them. Miss LeRoux would not elaborate, but it is well-known that she once had a promising acting career in London. Senator Coleman had no comment.

Tony folded the paper up and waited for the ferry to dock. This was good news or was it? Certainly it was a relief that she had decided not to marry Coleman, but it seemed that she was headed back to London with her auntor rather mother Lucinda.

He brooded over this all the way home, wondering if he should try to contact her again. What was the point? She had expressed her sentiments in no uncertain terms. And she was right. It would be nearly impossible for them to marry in South Carolina, and she had no inclination to be an artist's wife–or concubine–in Paris.

When he and Scratch, who had met him on the St. Helena side, arrived at the house they saw a familiar phaeton in the driveway. The horse looked familiar, too, but Tony thought there must be hundreds of phaetons drawn by roan mares in the area. While Scratch put the gig up, he approached the front door with some trepidation.

He knocked as a herald of his arrival and then opened the door.

"Tony?" It was his mother's voice. "We're in the parlor–you have a visitor."

Tony put his hat on the hall tree in the foyer an entered the parlor.

He blinked several times as if not trusting his eyes. "Jackie? Has something happened at Lynwood?"

She stood from the sofa, where she and Georgia had just finished their tea. "Something's always happening at Lynwood. Although it's less lively now that Lucinda has gone back to London."

"Gone? I thought you were going with her."

"If you'll excuse me," Georgia said, "I've got some lesson plans to tend to. The winter session starts on Monday."

Tony hardly glanced at her as she left the room. He stared at Jackie, who stood stock still with her hands folded in front of her. She was dressed as if embarking on another journey much as she was that day at the Yemassee Station.

"Well," he said, gesturing with his free hand–the other gripped the *New South* tightly. "Sit down."

Jackie sat down again.

Tony sat at the other end of the sofa as if she might have some communicable disease.

"You've seen the paper," she said.

Tony looked absently at the newspaper and put it down on the coffee table. "Yes. I saw the article about your breaking off the engagement to Coleman. It implied that you would be returning to London to resume your acting career."

"Not necessarily. It depends."

"Depends on what?"

"On your feelings."

Tony studied her expression. It was impassive, as if she were ordering fabric for a new dress.

"My feelings? What could my feelings have to do with your decision to resume your career?"

Jackie's expression suddenly changed to one of embarrassment and disappointment. She stood. "I'm sorry. I've made a mistake. I should be going now."

Tony moved to block her way. "Jackie–I didn't mean to be flippant or coy. Sit down."

Jackie hesitated. Tears came to her eyes. She wiped them away and sat down.

"Now tell me what has changed since we last met," Tony said. "You've broken it off with Coleman. I'm delighted that you did. But everything you said at the Yemassee Station–can you have completely changed your mind?"

Jackie stared out of a window. Then she burst into tears and buried her face in her hands. "Oh, Tony–I don't know what to do! I think it *is* impossible for us to marry, but I don't want to lose you!"

Tony put his arm around her shoulder. "And I don't want to lose you, either. But as you say–what can we do? Live here in my mother's house just as she and Papa did? A sort of common-law marriage in which no one–at least no one on St. Helena–questions the legitimacy of it? You're too much the lady, Jackie. More like Edwina than Lucinda, even though you're Lucinda's child."

She placed her head on his shoulder. "You're right Tony. I can't live like a Bohemian. It...it just doesn't seem right to me. But there must be some way...some way."

Tony looked at the family portraits that hung on the wall next to the fireplace. "Isn't it strange that all of my forebears going back at least two generations were white–or at least appeared to be white–and I appear to be black? My mother tells me I'm only one-sixteenth, but that's enough to disqualify me as your husband."

Jackie raised her head and wiped away her tears. "It doesn't disqualify you in my mind. Oh, I've been so foolish! Forgive me, Tony I love you with all my heart! I truly do!"

Tony looked into her eyes and saw both humility and passion, a combination he had not seen in her before. He kissed her on the forehead, then the lips. She threw her arms around him.

"Oops!" Georgia was about to enter the room, but quickly retreated.

Tony laughed. "It's all right, Mama. Jackie and I have patched it up. What's for supper?"

Georgia stepped cautiously back into the room. "I forgot to tell you–I'm having supper at Hi's tonight. I'm sure the two of you would be welcome to come along."

Tony and Jackie looked at each other.

"The two of us?" Tony said. "Are you sure?"

"Of course I'm sure. His dining room seats twenty. It gets boring with just the two of us staring at each other from thirty paces. He often invites someone over at the last minute."

Tony turned to Jackie. "Are Edwina and Mansfield expecting you for supper?"

Jackie smiled. "They set sail yesterday on the *Pride*. Edwina was so mortified that I called off the wedding that she said she couldn't set foot in Beaufort again for a least a month. They're pretending to be on a cruise."

"What about Edwina's fear of sunburn?"

"That was always just an excuse. The real reason she hates boats is that she gets seasick. But she apparently prefers that to the humiliation of having her daughter break off an engagement to the state's most eligible bachelor."

Tony chuckled. "We'd be delighted to join you, Mama."

CHAPTER 49

The days were growing shorter and the torches lining the walk to Cooper's house were already lit. Vivian answered the door and took their coats.

Kena appeared and ushered them into the parlor where Cooper was waiting for them along with five other guests: Mr. Smalls, Mr. Whipper, Mr. Miller and two women who Tony had never seen before. These two women turned out to be the wives of Mr. Whipper and Mr. Miller. Mr. Smalls apologized for the absence of his wife Annie, who he said was ill. Introductions were made.

"Your proposal is still being discussed, Tony," Mr. Smalls said. "Unfortunately, I'm afraid the Democrats are conniving to gut it of its primary purpose: to guarantee that the literacy tests are the same for both blacks and whites."

"And they've introduced a new twist," Mr. Miller said. "A proposal to disenfranchise any male who cannot present documented evidence that he either voted in the election of 1860, or that he or his father served in the Confederate army."

"And of course that excludes all black males," Mr. Whipper said with a contemptuous smile.

"Without," Mr. Miller said, raising his index finger in admonishment, "violating the 15th Amendment."

"Of course," Mr. Smalls said. "But they won't get away with it–at least not entirely. We Republicans have a few tricks up our sleeve as well."

They chuckled knowingly at this comment, though Tony was uneasy.

"But they have all the votes," Tony said. "And they're only six of us."

"Seven, with Mr. Anderson," Mr. Smalls said. "And a number of white Democrats will back my anti-miscegenation amendment."

Tony glanced at Jackie. "Anti-miscegenation? But Mr. Smalls–"

Mr. Smalls laughed and patted Tony on the shoulder. "Don't worry, Tony. It's all part of the strategy. It's so extreme it will be voted down–especially by the white fathers of black children. But we'll extract a concession–a very important concession. I'll tell you about it later."

Kena returned from the kitchen with a tray containing glasses of champagne and began circulating among the guests. Vivian followed with a tray of canapés.

At supper there were the usual toasts, most to the Republican Party and the progress that had been made since the war. There were caveats, of course, but the general tone of the remarks was optimistic.

The last to offer a toast was Hiram Cooper. He tapped his spoon against the edge of his glass and stood. "I have an announcement to make regarding an entirely different–and I hope happier–subject. I have made a proposal of marriage to Georgia and she has accepted."

There was applause all around.

Georgia reddened a bit, but beamed.

"And of course," Cooper said, "you are all invited to the wedding, which will take place at the Brick Church on St. Helena Island, across from the Penn School, where Georgia has taught the freedmen's children for the last twenty-five years."

There was much applause for this choice for the ceremony.

"When?" someone asked.

"Oh–of course. That might be helpful," Cooper said to laughter. "Excuse me–I'm a little nervous. The date is Saturday, December 7th, at eleven o'clock."

After supper the guests retired to the library, where Tony's trompe l'oeil was much praised and marveled at. It was a bitter-sweet evening for Tony, who, though accepting of his mother's impending marriage, was nevertheless distressed that such an event was out of the question for himself and Jackie. She seemed to sense his disappointment and as they sat together on the sofa, patted him on the knee. He smiled at her, but the smile quickly evaporated.

As the party broke up, Georgia whispered to Jackie that she would be welcome to stay overnight on St. Helena since they had taken Georgia's brougham and Jackie's phaeton was still at the house. It was late, and it was a long way to Lynwood.

Jackie accepted. She did not relish the journey back to Lynwood, particularly alone in the dark. Primus had not accompanied her, and the huge house was empty except for the servants. Edwina and Mansfield would not return for several days.

Once at the house, with Georgia scurrying about to prepare the guest room for Jackie, Tony opened another bottle of his father's wine and poured a couple of glasses. Georgia came downstairs briefly and pleaded exhaustion, leaving the two of them alone in the living room.

"Well–what do you think?" Tony said.

"About what? Your mother's marriage to Mr. Cooper? I think he's a charming man, and seems devoted to her. I wish them all the best."

"That's not what I meant. I meant about us."

"Us?" Jackie sat down on the sofa, her cheery countenance having vanished. "I don't know. I suppose we'll have to go to London or Paris or wherever they'll accept us. You heard what Mr. Smalls said about miscegenation. Oh! What an ugly word!"

Tony went to the fireplace and began poking at the charred remains of the fire which had been extinguished while they were gone. He wadded up some old newspapers and threw a couple of logs on top of them. "He said it was part of a 'strategy.' I don't know what he has in mind, but he's a shrewd politician. Maybe it will somehow work."

Jackie took a sip of her wine as she watched Tony light the fire. "I don't know how it could. South Carolina will never accept interracial marriage no matter what laws are passed." She laughed sardonically. "White men fathering countless black children is almost a tradition, but a white woman marrying a black man arouses their homicidal impulses."

Tony, satisfied that the fire was sustainable, returned and sat down beside her. "What do you think our children would look like?"

Jackie smiled as if she could see the children gamboling before the fire. "Some chocolate, some brown, some as fair and blond as me. Who knows? It's idle speculation at this point."

"Is it?"

She sighed. "You know, you're much more the optimist than I. I suppose the difference is in our parents. Mine–or at least the parents I thought were mine–are hidebound by tradition and want nothing to change. Yours thought they could change everything–and very nearly did."

"Nearly did?"

"Yes. Nearly did. Many things are the same, aren't they?"

Tony looked at her for a moment and turned to the fire. He took a sip of the wine. "We could live here–in this house. No one would disturb us."

"And be prisoners on St. Helena Island?"

"My parents never felt they were prisoners."

"No–I guess not."

They sat contemplating the fire for some time.

"Tony?"

"Yes?"

"Never leave me."

He put his arm around her. "Let's see–who has the best record here? You abandoned me on the platform at the Yemassee Station as I recall."

She recoiled for a moment in anger, then nestled her head against his shoulder. "It was a test. I was hoping you would come rescue me in Charleston. But you never showed."

Tony chuckled. "I considered it."

She raised her head. "You did?"

"Yes. But then I realized that that was exactly what Coleman hoped I would do. He would have shot me down and been applauded for it."

She sighed and put her head against his shoulder again. "I suppose it's not easy to be a knight on a white horse when you're a black man."

"Or a damsel in distress locked in the tower of the manor house. Will Edwina and Mansfield ever let me set foot on Lynwood again?"

"Only if you use the servant's entrance."

"Ha, ha."

She raised her head. "Oh, Tony–let's stop this. I don't care what color you are–though I admit to a preference for café-au-lait." She ran the tip of her finger from his cheek bone to his jaw line. "So smooth. Don't ever grow a beard."

"I'm not sure I could if I wanted to."

"Have you ever noticed that our lips are the same color?"

"Really? What color is that?"

"Look." She pursed her lips.

"I'd say...pink."

"Now show me yours."

Tony grinned. "My what?"

She slapped him playfully on the cheek. "Your lips, silly. You have to purse them."

"Okay." He pursed his lips.

"Pink. See, I told you."

"I can't see my own lips."

"Take my word for it. Now close your eyes. I want to see if they *really* match."

CHAPTER 50

Ravenel Coleman did much of his business from the third-floor office of his home overlooking Charleston Harbor. The view was spectacular, and he could keep an eye on the ships that entered and left the harbor, some of which he owned. Occasionally he would ascend the spiral staircase that led to the cupola, where he had a powerful telescope mounted so that he could not only extend his field of vision but could also focus on individual ships and their crews, sometimes even the manifests posted in the wheelhouses. Nothing escaped his attention.

At the moment, however, he was sitting at his ornate Regency desk, hand carved in France, reading a copy of the *Charleston News and Courier*. His personal secretary, a lawyer by trade lured away from one of the city's most prestigious law firms by a handsome salary and the prospect of riding his employer's coattails into the governor's mansion, stood close by.

"Pettigru," Coleman said throwing the paper down onto his desk, "I'm the laughing stock of Charleston. "'Cuckolded Coleman,' 'Ravenel Rabbit,' 'Jilted Julius.'"

"Julius?" Pettigru raised his eyebrows.

"My middle name. Never use it. Hate it. But somehow those blasted reporters got a hold of it."

"Must be on some of the deeds."

"Yes, I suppose that's it. Those reporters are like ferrets–they burrow into everything–libraries, courthouse records, wedding registers–"

Pettigru's eyebrows went up again.

Coleman noticed. "Anyway, we've got to do something."

"What can we do?"

Coleman spun around in his chair and gazed out over the harbor. "I don't know–that's what I pay you to do. Think of something."

"I offered the editor–"

"Bold."

"Yes, James Bold. I offered him a...'stipend,' as you called it. But he refused."

"Yes, yes, I know. It was a bad idea, anyway. The vanity of these newspapermen exceeds their greed. Besides, that kind of thing usually gets out." Coleman picked up the paper again. "Says here that Jackie was seen kissing that Jones fellow at the Yemassee Staion near Beaufort. Kissing a Negro in public! I can't believe it!"

"These reporters sometimes embellish their reports for effect."

"Yes they do. But what if it's true? I guess I was lucky that the girl broke it off."

"I'd say so. It would have doomed your bid for governor next year."

Coleman drummed his fingers on the desk. "Yes, lucky. Still...I love that girl. I can't help it. Such a beauty! And you should see her on the stage–the subtle gestures, the sly looks, the heaving of her bosom when she sighs–every man in the house on the edge of his seat and salivating like a dog after a bitch in heat!"

Pettigru chuckled. "I can introduce you to half a dozen like her at the Theatre Royal. As a matter of fact–"

"No, Pettigru–she's not like the others. She's a lady. Dammit!" Coleman stood up. He absently grabbed his cane, noticed it in his hands, then looked up at the spiral staircase to the cupola. "I can't even climb the stairs anymore to see what's going on in the harbor. That Jones son of a bitch shot me in the leg with of all things–a crossbow!"

"You should have taken care of him then."

Coleman limped around to the front of the desk. "How? I couldn't very well have shot him in cold blood, could I? He was mauled by that boar. Besides, he was a guest of the LeRoux. It would have looked bad. Very bad."

"The boy must have nine lives, like a cat. Driggers didn't have any luck with him either."

"Driggers?"

"The captain of the Red Shirts. Down in Hampton County."

"Oh, yes. Driggers. Botched that bank job, didn't he?"

"He did what you told him to."

Coleman's eyes flashed. "I didn't tell him to do anything. I merely suggested that Jones' bank was making loans to niggers that should have gone to white men. The niggers already own half of the best land in Beaufort County."

"Well, he took the hint. Unfortunately, Jones was in his office at the time–apparently it's built like a bunker and sealed off from the rest of the building."

Coleman sighed, made his way back to his desk again and sat down. He gazed longingly out the window. "What can I do to get the girl back?"

"She seems to be infatuated with this Jones boy. Probably a passing fancy. They could never marry, of course. Perhaps you could just wait it out."

"Wait it out?" Coleman looked at Pettigru dubiously. "I'm not getting any younger, you know. Besides, I'd like to have her at my side at the inauguration."

"Aren't you getting a little ahead of yourself?"

"Dammit Pettigru! What kind of campaign manager are you? You said we'll carry sixty percent of the white vote. And after the Constitutional Convention, there won't be any black vote."

"I'm just being pragmatic. We shouldn't count our chickens–"

"What about the Klan?"

"What?"

"The Klan. I hear they're making a comeback."

"Seems that they are. But their methods are pretty crude."

"Yeah. A bunch of rednecks. Not gentlemen and former officers like the Red Shirts. But they seem to always get their man."

Pettigru at last sat down. "What do you have in mind?"

Coleman gazed out the window again. "I don't know. Do we have any contacts there?"

"Of course. There's Rufus Jenkins down in Jasper County. He's the Grand Cyclops, or Vizier, or whatever he calls himself."

"Why don't you pay him a visit?"

"Me? It wouldn't look good. Everyone knows I work for you. But I could send someone from the firm."

"Then do it."

Pettigru stood. He made an elaborate gesture of bowing deeply and rolling his forearm as if unfolding a carpet. "Your wish is my command."

Coleman looked at him sideways, annoyed. "Get out of here, Pettigru. I'm in no mood for your sarcasm."

Pettigru backed away from Coleman's desk, still bent forward until he reached the door.

CHAPTER 51

Assured by doctors that his wife's condition was improving, Robert Smalls returned to Columbia to present his suffrage plan. He was accompanied this time by Mr. Wigg, Mr. Miller, Mr. Reed, and Mr. Jones.

Smalls' earlier proposal for universal suffrage having been voted down by the white majority, he proposed an amendment to the interracial marriage ban. This would extend the ban to include unions of unmarried couples–with children of such unions to bear the father's name and have the right to inherit from him. The proposal was met with laughter that fairly shook the chamber, and went down to defeat.

A compromise, however, was reached. The Democrats agreed that this ban should extend only to those who had more than one-eighth Negro blood in their veins.

When the final version was passed, Mr. Smalls turned to Tony and smiled. "You're one-sixteenth. Exempt."

Tony, who had been following this process with some consternation, looked skeptical. "I've only been told that I was one-sixteenth. I look nearly as black as you. How can I prove it?"

Smalls chuckled. "It's all in the records of the county courthouse. It was put there by none other than Edward Benson."

"Benson? What did he have to do with it?"

"Benson was tried before a military court right after the war for trying to lynch your father."

"What!"

"Didn't your mother tell you?"

"No. She never said anything about it."

Smalls folded his hands in his lap and turned his attention to the next speaker, Senator Tillman. "No reason that she should, I suppose. Benson presented documented evidence that your father was the son of Cora Rinaldi, your grandmother and a former Benson slave. Lynwood's own records showed that she was one-quarter Negro. Therefore, you're one-sixteenth."

Tony tried to digest this new information. "Why would Benson do that?"

"To impugn the integrity of your father. He passed for white and joined the Union army during the war so he could serve as an officer. In Benson's mind, that made him a liar. And the military tribunal–all Union men–agreed with him. Benson was acquitted."

"But that means–"

"You can marry your sweetheart, Miss LeRoux. Perfectly legal."

Tony slumped down in his seat. He should have been elated, but he still wasn't convinced the path was clear for him and Jackie. "What if–"

"Shh!" Smalls said. "Tillman is about to speak. Let's hear what new charges of moral depravity and incompetence he intends to inflict upon us. We'll need to counter him point by point."

Tillman offered no surprises. He fulminated against the Constitutional Convention of 1868, the 13th, 14th, and 15th Amendments to the U.S Constitution, and the 'corruption and incompetence,' of the South Carolina legislature while under the 'domination' of black Republicans during Reconstruction.

As if enduring all of this abuse were not enough, Senator Tillman then launched an attack on Mr. Smalls, dredging up nearly twenty-year-old charges that he had accepted a bribe while serving in the South Carolina legislature during the 70's. Mr. Smalls was forced to defend himself, as he had done so long ago, pointing out that the evidence was trumped up by Democrats who wished to eject him from the legislature and that he was pardoned by Governor Simpson, a Democrat, after taking his case to the US. Supreme Court.

After a visit to Mr. Smalls' house on Prince Street, where Mrs. Smalls appeared to be heavily sedated, Tony took his leave and went to his mother's house on St. Helena.

He tried to explain to Georgia the intricacies of the miscegenation amendment.

"I suppose it was the best we could get," she said. "But at least it means you and Jackie can get married. We should celebrate! Perhaps we could even have a double wedding."

Tony sat down on the sofa. "I don't think we should rush it. Besides, Edwina and Mansfield still think of Jackie as their daughter–they're not likely to give their consent."

Georgia sat down beside him. "She doesn't need their consent. She's a grown woman. What about Lucinda? She seems to view herself as a progressive person."

"She's returned to England. But I think she would approve."

"Then it's all settled!"

"Not exactly. I can't even be sure that Jackie will go through with it. She broke off an engagement to Coleman–she may with me."

"That was completely different. Her engagement to Mr. Coleman was an act of desperation–she felt she had no alternative due to the uncertainty surrounding these miscegenation laws. Now that that barrier has been removed, she can marry the man she loves–you."

Tony managed a faint smile. "We'll see."

The next day Tony rode Leto out to Lynwood. Primus met him at the foot of the stairs and told him that Jackie was out riding.

"Where?" Tony took the reins and climbed back into the saddle.

"She usually go down to an old slave cabin by the river. The one Pliny used to live at with his family before the war. She say it a peaceful place where she can think."

"Which way?"

Primus pointed towards a well-beaten trail that ran past the stables behind the main house. "Just follow that till you get to a big oak tree between two forks. Take the left one–it go down to the river."

"What about the LeRoux? They here?"

"Naw–they cruising round in the *Pride* somewhere off the coast of Florida, I reckon. They stop here last week and stock up on vittles and fuel. Don't know when they be back."

"Thanks, Primus."

Tony nudged Leto in the ribs with the heel of his boot and was off at a gallop down the trail.

He soon came into a clearing populated with wildflowers and tall grass that ran all the way up to the river's edge. Scheherazade, Jackie's Arabian that Mansfield had purchased for her sixteenth birthday, was grazing among the flowers, untethered. Jackie was sitting on the cabin porch facing the river, reading. She looked up as he emerged from the woods and Leto slowed to a walk.

"Am I disturbing your reverie?" Tony said.

"Yes. But it's all right. Come and join me."

Tony dismounted. "And Leto?"

"She's a bit old for Scheri, but I'm sure they'll get along famously. Just let her go."

Tony dropped the reins. Leto ambled over to Scheherazade and examined her hindquarters, then nudged her muzzle.

"You see," Jackie said. "They're already friends."

Tony smiled and stepped onto the porch. Jackie indicated a rocker and he sat down.

"Who was Pliny?" Tony said.

"Primus' predecessor. He was my Uncle Edward's driver and majordomo."

Tony stared silently at the river for a moment. "Did you know that your Uncle Edward tried to kill my father?"

Jackie put her book down. "I thought it was the other way around. That your father tried to kill him in a duel. But one of Uncle Edward's tenant farmers killed him instead."

"I don't know much about the duel. But Mr. Smalls tells me that Edward tried to lynch my father down in Port Royal sometime before that."

"Lynch him? Why?"

"The usual reason. He was an uppity nigger. Not to mention that my mother preferred him over your uncle."

Jackie looked out over the water. "And that's what the duel was about."

"Yes."

Jackie sighed. "Oh, Tony–our families are so entangled with each other, it's hard to know who did what to whom."

"They're about to become more entangled."

"What do you mean?"

"I just got back from the State House in Columbia. They passed a bill to ban miscegenation. It's now part of the state constitution."

Jackie picked up her book again and found the place where she had left off. "That's not surprising."

"No, it's not. But what is surprising is that the Democrats approved a limit to it."

"What limit?"

"It doesn't apply to anyone who has less than one-eighth Negro blood in their veins."

She stared at him for a moment as if peering deep into his skin to discern the admixture of his blood. "And you are...?"

Tony smiled broadly. "One-sixteenth."

"How do you know? Can you prove it?"

"Mr. Smalls says it's a matter of court record. Thanks to your uncle."

"Oh, Tony! Then we can...we can–"

"We can marry. That is , if you're still interested."

Jackie threw down her book and stood up from the rocker. She clapped her hands together. "Oh, Tony! Of course I'm–is this a formal proposal?"

Tony rose from his rocker, took her hands in his, and went down on one knee. "I guess this is the way it's done, isn't it?" He looked up at her. "Will you Jacqueline Benson LeRoux, marry me?"

"Oh, yes! I do, I do!"

Tony stood and embraced her. His smile, though, turned to a grimace. "You know it's still not going to be easy, don't you? There's Edwina, Mansfield, your mother–"

"Lucinda will approve, I'm sure of it! And Edwina and Mansfield will just have to get used to it."

"And the Reverend Hall?"

Jackie frowned. "He abandoned me at birth. He has no say at all."

"Still–we need to be careful. There're others who'll want to stop us.'

"Others? What others?"

"I don't know exactly. Maybe...maybe Coleman."

"Poo! Rav is a worn-out old man. You should have seen him when I broke the news to him in Charleston. He burst into tears." She looked away at the river. "I almost felt sorry for him, even though I knew all he wanted was to parade me around the state and hang me on his arm like a Christmas ornament. He'll find another aspiring ingénue who'll be delighted to fulfill that role for him."

"I hope you're right."

She turned to face him again. "Oh Tony–I'm so happy!"

They kissed until they were interrupted by Scheri, who had wandered up to the porch and nudged Jackie's arm.

"What's she want?" Tony said.

"She's jealous," Jackie said with a laugh. "Either that or she's tired of eating flowers and wants something more substantial."

"I've got some apples in my saddlebags."

"I could use one, too."

Tony went to Leto, retrieved the apples, and returned to the porch.

Scheri snorted and gobbled the first one down. Tony gave her another with the same result.

They laughed.

"No more for you," Jackie said, bopping her on the nose. "It'll make you fat."

They sat down in their rockers, looked out over the languid waters, and bit into their apples.

CHAPTER 52

On Tuesday, November 5, Mr. Smalls' second wife, Annie, died. Nearly overcome with grief, he did not venture out of his home for several days after the funeral. Tony and the other delegates, along with a host of prominent Beaufortonians, attended.

On the 14th, however, Smalls had sufficiently recovered to return to Columbia to resume the battle for the rights of the black people of South Carolina.

On December 4, Governor Evans announced that all business of the convention had been completed and asked that all delegates sign the final document. Mr. Smalls refused, saying that he could not endorse a constitution that deprived black people of the right to vote and that it was in direct contravention of the 14th and 15th Amendments of the U.S. Constitution. He was excused from doing so and returned to Beaufort.

Two days later, on a Saturday at two p.m., Georgia Rhodes was married to Hiram Cooper at the Brick Church on St. Helena Island. Miss Laura Towne, Georgia's longtime mentor and headmistress of the Penn School attended, as did Mr. Smalls and innumerable former students of both ladies. Tony gave away the bride and Jackie was Maid of Honor. The LeRoux were invited, but did not attend.

The Coopers moved into the mansion on Bay Street in Beaufort and Tony remained at the house on St. Helena, which his mother deeded to him. Jackie returned to Lynwood, where she withstood the icy stares of Edwina and the bemused indifference of Mansfield until her own wedding was to take place at the Old Sheldon Church in the spring.

Jackie reconciled–if that is the proper word–with her father, the Reverend Phillip Hall, who agreed to conduct the ceremony amidst the ruins of the Old Church, at the request of Tony.

"Should we invite him?" Jackie said on one of the rare evenings that she spent with Tony at his house on St. Helena.

"Who?" Tony said. He was reading by the fire, a coffee table book with color plates of the paintings of J.M.W. Turner.

"Rav."

Tony looked up. "Coleman? Are you serious?"

Jackie put down her own book, a novel by George Eliot. "He was always very kind to me. I don't want him to think I hold any ill feelings towards him."

Tony sighed. "Maybe not towards you, but he's no friend of the black man."

"You're not black."

"As far as he's concerned I am. Jackie, you've got to get over this notion that I'm not really a Negro."

"But we know now that you're only one sixteenth."

"That's purely technical. Everybody but you regards me as black. Even my own mother thinks I'm black."

She smiled. "Your mother is color blind. It would make no difference to her if you were green."

"All right–she's a mother. But that's beside the point. Rav is running for governor and one of his campaign promises is to see that the new constitution is enforced."

"Well...if he becomes governor, he will have no choice but to enforce the law."

He glared at her. "Is that what you want?"

"Of course not. I'm just saying that if he wants to become governor he's going to have to say things like that to get elected. What he does once in office is an entirely a different matter."

"Like all politicians eh? Well, suppose he does just exactly what he says he'll do?"

"I doubt that he will."

"Why not?"

"Because, like my father, he has black children."

Tony clapped his book shut and set it aside. "I'm beginning to think I'm about to marry a child. Jackie–Thomas Jefferson had black children and never acknowledged them. He even made them his servants and required that they sleep in the slaves' quarters."

"That was a long time ago. Slavery is gone. My father has sent his oldest son–my half brother–off to college in Pennsylvania."

Tony pressed his forefinger against his temple. "And I suppose Coleman is sending his eldest black son to Harvard where he'll study law and return to South Carolina to overturn the Constitution of '95."

"Oh, Tony–I don't know anything about his black children. I just think it would be the polite thing to do and–who knows? It may soften his prejudice against Negroes a bit."

Tony opened his book again. "Maybe you're right. But I doubt it."

"Then I can invite him?"

"You can invite anyone you like. I've already invited Mr. Smalls. It'll be interesting to get them in the same room together."

Jackie smiled and went back to her book. She felt that this little argument–their first since they became engaged–could be chalked up to the distaff side.

CHAPTER 53

Ravenel Coleman sat at his desk with his elbows on the blotter, holding the engraved invitation close to his face. His eyes weren't what they used to be.

After reading it over for the second time, he put the card down and spun his chair on its axis so that he was facing the harbor.

"How could she do this to me?" he said.

"Spite." Pettigru stood in front of the desk with his hands clasped behind his back. "Pure spite."

Coleman spun his chair back around. "You think so?"

"Of course. Women always get their revenge indirectly, crab-like, so as to inflict pain without fear of retribution."

"But what did I do to her?" Coleman's question was almost plaintive, like a child whose favorite toy had been taken away.

Pettigru shrugged his shoulders. "Who knows? Nothing, everything. But it shows she cares about you."

Coleman turned to the window again. "Maybe I was too harsh with Jones when he shot me in the leg with that crossbow. But I could't help it. It hurt like the dickens."

"Of course it did."

"Or maybe it was some comment I made that I don't even remember making."

"Women take offense at the slightest innuendo."

Coleman contemplated the mysteries of the feminine psyche for a few moments and turned back to his desk. He picked up the invitation and read it for a third time. "Did you ever talk to that fellow down in Jasper County?"

"I did."

"And what did he have to say?"

"Well, after the usual fulminations about niggers taking over the state–apparently he hadn't heard about the convention–he said Beaufort was a hard nut to crack."

"Oh?"

"He said it was the capital of Niggerdom. Furthermore he said that St. Helena Island, where Jones lives, is like a fortress surrounded by water. And all the niggers there are armed."

"But he doesn't spend all his time there."

"No. There's the bank in Beaufort. But he seems to have turned over the day-to-day operations to a fellow named Ferguson. And since the bombing they've stationed armed guards there around the clock"

Coleman sighed. "So this Klan fellow–what's his name?"

"Jenkins."

"So Jenkins is going to give up? Let this upstart nigger marry a white woman?"

"He says Sheldon is a soft target."

"Sheldon?" Coleman looked at the invitation. "Oh, yes–it's out in the country. Fifteen miles from Beaufort. But–"

"And a ferry ride from Port Royal Island. It would take the sheriff's men an hour to respond. And by then it would be too late."

Coleman's eyes widened. "You mean this, this Jenkins fellow plans to attack Jones at the wedding?"

"'Attack' is not the word I would use. 'Abduct' might be a better one."

Coleman rubbed his chin. He had forgotten to shave that morning and there was an agreeable masculine stubble that tickled his fingers. "I wouldn't want Jackie to get hurt."

"Not likely."

"But the Jones fellow. He needs to be taught a lesson."

"My sentiments exactly."

"And then maybe Jackie will come to her senses."

"I expect so. She won't want to be married to a man who's been humiliated in his own community."

"Humiliated? You mean like tarred and feathered?"

Pettigru smiled. "Something like that."

"There can be no possible connection between me and this Jenkins fellow."

"None whatsoever. Jenkins doesn't need any encouragement."

"He's not waiting for a word from me?"

"He just wants to know that the powers that be–especially in the state house–will not stand in his way."

"Stand in his way? Doesn't the man read the newspapers?"

Pettigru chuckled. "No, he doesn't. He's illiterate."

Coleman sighed and turned again to the window. "Well, I'll not stand in *your* way. Do what you have to do."

Pettigru did not respond, but nodded his head and left the room.

Rufus Jenkins spread the map out over the table, using lanterns to hold down the corners. He used his forefinger to point out the itinerary.

"This here," he said, "is Tarboro. That's where we at right now. We take the Tarboro Pike down to Ridgeland, then–"

"What we want to go to Ridgeland for?" said Earl Jenkins, his wife's cousin. "Why don't we just cut over to Coosawatchie?"

Rufus looked askance at Earl. "'Cause the road to Coosawatchie is done washed out, that's why, dumb ass. There's a good road that goes to Ridgeland near the old Devant place. Then we cut up to Coosawhatchie."

Earl shook his head. "Seems out of the way to me. And the Coosawatchie Road will be dried up and hard as your momma's corn muffins by the time we set out."

"I ain't seen you turn down no corn muffins when you et with us Thanksgivin'."

"I hadda be polite, didn't I? And she ain't–"

"Forget the goddammed corn muffins," Horton Matthews said. "How we gonna git to Sheldon from Coosawhatchie?"

"I was just gettin' ready to tell you before dumb ass here interrupted me." Rufus smoothed out the map. "Now–we go to Coosawatchie, only on the good road by the Devant place. Then we turn north and follow the railroad tracks to Pocotaligo."

"Them tracks was tore up by the Yankees," Earl said.

Rufus sighed and shook his head. "You ain't been to Pocotaligo in your whole life. Them rails been straightened out for the last thirty years–before you was born, even. There's a good flat bed alongside–"

"Why don't we just go straight to Sheldon," Burton Langford said, pointing to the town on the map.

"Cause we don't want to cross no river," Rufus said. "Besides we gonna take this nigger up to the Yemassee Station and–"

"The Yemassee Station?" Earl said. "What for? That's as busy as a beehive."

"If you'd just listen instead of talkin,' shit head, you'd learn somethin'."

Earl stared at his cousin for a moment, ire in his eyes. "Ok–so learn me."

"I was just fixin' to." Rufus turned back to the map. "This here is Yemassee–"

"No, it ain't," Earl said. "That there's Pocotaligo."

"All right. So my finger lit on the wrong name. I don't read so good. But I know where things is at."

"We be wearin' our hoods?" Burton said.

"No," said Rufus. "Not till we get to Sheldon. It ain't like the old days when we could strut our stuff in broad daylight and the niggers would scatter and the white folks would cheer us on. We don't want no sheriff's posse headin' us off at the pass."

Horton spat a stream of tobacco juice on the threshing room floor. "Looks like they'll be more at the weddin' than they is of us."

"That's a fact," Rufus said. "But so what? Most of 'em will be women and maybe half of them niggers. You think they'll put up a fight?"

"Maybe. How many we got? Twenty?"

"I figger seventeen–countin' pigeon brain here."

"Where's the others? Tonight, I mean."

"Church meetin,'" Rufus said. "They thinkin' bout joining up with the Coosawatchie Baptist. Attendance fallin' off here in Tarboro."

"Sho' is," Burton said. "Preacher showed up a half hour late last Sunday, pickled to the gills. Talked so much gibberish couldn't make no sense of him. Me and Millie's goin' over to Ridgeland next week."

"It don't matter nohow," Rufus said, folding up the map. "We the Executive Committee. Just pass it on down to your dens."

"Wait a minute," Horton said. "What're we gonna do with this nigger once we get him to the Yemassee Station? Tar and feather him and put him on the train to Charleston?"

Rufus chuckled. "According to Mr. Pettigru, the Yemassee Station is where Mr. Jones come in from New York. We're gonna send him back there, but not covered with no tar and feathers. He's goin' back the way he shoulda come. In a pine box."

"You mean we just gonna shoot him?"

"Naw," Rufus said. "That would be too easy. We got to make an example of him. Remember?" He clenched his fist and raised it abruptly, tilting his head to one side.

Horton grinned. "They got plenty of trees at the Yemassee Station?"

"Better'n that," Rufus said. "They got a signal post. Next train load that come through'll get an eyeful of what happens to niggers who try to marry a white woman."

Horton grinned again and spat on the floor.

"Hey!' Rufus said. "No more spittin' tobacky juice here. The missus got to clean that up. Where you think you are–a barn?"

Horton made a show of looking around. "Look like a barn to me."

"Well, it ain't. It's a threshing shed. Ladies got to work here."

"Sorry. So what do you thresh?"

"Barley, dumbell. Barley. Sell it to distilleries upstate. Some of it goes all the way to Kentucky and Tennessee."

"Why don't they grow they own barley?"

"'Cause they ain't got the soil we got. Don't you know nothin' bout makin' whiskey?"

"I just know about drinkin' it."

They all laughed at this and filed out of the shed, their horses waiting.

CHAPTER 54

Edwina stepped into the octagonal sun room directly from the terrace one fine spring morning and removed her gardening gloves. Hanna promptly arrived with a tray on which lay a letter. Edwina rather absently took the letter and put it down on the table.

"I'll have my tea iced, Hanna," she said. "It's rather warm out. We do have some ice, don't we?"

"Oh, yes, ma'am. Primus just brought a whole block of it in from Beaufort."

"Good. And ask Miss Jacqueline to join me if she's about."

"Yes, ma'am."

After Hanna left, Edwina gazed out through the glass doors at her rose garden. She smiled. Her hard work was paying off. She looked at the letter: postmarked Southampton, England.

She slit the envelope open with a convenient butter knife and began reading:

My Dearest Edwina,

I will be arriving in Savannah on the ninth by private yacht. I cannot tell you the owner at this time, but suffice it to say that he is of high rank and wishes to be as discreet as possible. I was able to entice him to visit Lynwood in part due to his keen interest in quail hunting. I assured him that the Lowcountry has the best in the world and, of course, he always insists upon the best. He has never known anything else. Can we put up in the guest suite that Papa always reserved for visiting dignitaries? I hope you don't find it too shocking that we intend to sleep in the same bedroom, but he will insist upon it–or if denied, storm out and take another house in the vicinity. He's quite a spoiled child in that way. My companion is quite keen on attending the wedding, especially after I told him that it would take place in a ruined church. He loves to poke about in ruins. Give Jackie my love, and assure her that I approve

of the remarkable Mr. Jones.
Your affectionate sister,
Lucinda

Edwina put the letter down and wondered who Lucinda's new beau 'of high rank' might be. An English lord? A duke? More likely of the lesser nobility–a baron, perhaps. She, Edwina, would show this minion of the British aristocracy that there is a Lowcountry aristocracy and that Lynwood is every bit as splendid as any English manor house. Her rose garden should be in full bloom by then.

"Am I intruding?" It was Jackie at the door.

"Oh, of course not. Do sit down Jacqueline. I just received a letter from your–from Lucinda."

Jackie sat down and looked at the letter.

"You may read it," Edwina said.

Jackie read it over. "I wonder who this gentleman of 'high rank' is?"

Edwina sniffed. "You know how Lucinda tends to exaggerate. I suppose he's a secretary to some member of parliament or the like. Or considering your, ah, mother's penchant for clergymen, perhaps to a bishop."

Hanna arrived with two glasses of iced tea.

"Thank you, Hanna," Jackie put the letter down and looked at Edwina. "Can't a person have two mothers?"

Edwina slowly turned her gaze to her. "Two?"

"Yes. I can't help thinking of you both as my mothers. You raised me, after all, and Lucinda, though distant, has always been kind to me and it just so happens that she is my biological mother."

Edwina sighed and took a sip of her tea. "Well, I suppose that's one way of looking at it."

There was an awkward silence.

"What was it you wanted to see me about?" Jackie said.

"I've been thinking about your wedding."

"I don't suppose you could avoid thinking about it."

"No. I've tried, but it simply won't go away. And now that Lucinda's bringing this–this gentleman friend of hers with her, it would be quite awkward for Mansfield and me to stay at home while the nuptials are proceeding elsewhere."

Jackie smiled. "Then you'll come?"

"As much as it pains me, I'm afraid we have no other choice."

Jackie leaned across the table and gave Edwina a kiss on the cheek. "I'm so glad. And it will be a beautiful wedding. You should see how the afternoon sun plays off of the brick columns of the church."

"Yes, I'm told that it's majestic, though I've never been there in the afternoon." Edwina picked up the letter again. "And I must say, Lucinda's right. Your Mr. Jones is a remarkable young man. It's a pity that–" She stopped herself.

"That he's part Negro?"

"Well...I don't mean to harp on it. He is rather light-skinned, actually. And handsome, I must say. But Jacqueline, dear, where will you live? Not on that dreary island inhabited by former slaves, surely. You must have some white people to talk to."

"There're plenty of white people on St. Helena. Mostly teachers at the Penn school, like Tony's mother. But Tony wants to go back to Paris for a while to make another go as an artist. There're certainly plenty of white people there."

"Yes," Edwina put down her glass. "I would like to go back to Paris myself, but I don't know if I can endure another sea voyage. I was morbidly ill for half of our trip to Florida. When will you return?"

"I don't know. It could be years."

"Just as well. Perhaps this whole racial thing will have settled down by then. I have to say, I've never understood why the Negroes should be permanently assigned to an underclass. Mansfield says that people like Tony and Mr. Smalls are exceptions. But I say–how many exceptions do there have to be? I read in the *Columbia Register* recently that the delegates from Beaufort, Negroes all, were among the most eloquent speakers of the Convention. Surely, merit should be the sole consideration for advancement in our society."

Jackie smiled with approval.

Edwina sniffed and finished her tea. "I haven't changed that much. I've always thought the races should be on an equal footing. But the Negroes have a lot of catching up to do. In the meantime–"

"Are we beating that dead horse again?" It was Mansfield, who had just entered the room. He was dressed in riding gear. "Let the chips fall where they may. Where's Hanna? I'd like some of that iced tea. It's hot outside." He plopped his riding cap down on the table and sat down. Hanna apparently heard him and arrived with a pitcher and a glass.

"Hanna," Mansfield said as he watched the tea flow into his glass, "what do you think of Jackie here marrying one of your own kind?"

Hanna looked first at Jackie then at Edwina, then Mansfield. "I think whatever Miss Jackie wants is fine with me."

Mansfield swallowed some tea and put his glass down. "Very diplomatic of you. But what do you really think? That mixing the races is a good thing?"

"Don't put Hanna on the spot, Mansfield," Edwina said. "What do you expect her to say?"

"I expect her to tell me what she thinks. Well, Hanna?"

Hanna glanced at the women again. "I think Miss Jackie will be as happy with Mr. Jones as any man."

Mansfield stared at her for a moment. "All right, Hanna. You may be right. You can go now."

Hanna curtsied and left the room.

"You've been drinking from your flask while out riding, haven't you?" Edwina said.

"So what if I have? I need a good bracer in the morning these days. Lots of things to think about. Who's the letter from?"

Edwina pushed the letter over to him. "See for yourself."

Mansfield pulled a pair of spectacles from his vest pocket and read the letter. "So Lucinda's bringing a new beau with her, eh? Wants to shoot quail. Well, Lucinda's right–we've got the best quail hunting in the world here. Rav's coming down for the wedding, too, and–"

"Rav's not coming," Edwina said. "He sent his regrets yesterday."

"Yesterday? Why didn't you tell me?"

"I did."

"What? Oh, yes–now I remember. I was a little tipsy at supper last night and–"

"He can hardly be expected to attend considering recent events."

Jackie looked down at her empty glass.

Mansfield glared at her. "No, I suppose not. Well, this English fellow will bag Rav's share of the birds, that's all. All the better for him."

"I'm sorry for Rav," Jackie said, still looking into her glass. "And I'm sorry for the embarrassment you both suffered on my account. But I simply couldn't go through with it."

A silence ensued.

"No matter," Mansfield said at last. "You'll marry the man you choose. And I like the boy. It's just unfortunate that–"

"What was it you said about beating a dead horse?" Edwina said.

"Yes," Mansfield said with a sour expression. "It's all settled now. What's for dinner?"

CHAPTER 55

Jackie returned from riding one morning and noted a Victorian carriage parked in the drive. It looked like any other except for a finely embroidered cloth–something like a doily–draped over the doors. On closer inspection, she saw that the fine gold threads against a background of blue and red spelled out someone's initials: HRH.

She put Scheri in the barn, where the groom (a new hire) gave her some water and oats. Then she ascended the steps of the terrace, where she found Edwina, Mansfield, Lucinda, and a portly middle-aged gentleman having tea.

Mansfield, as was his habit when any lady entered his presence, stood. The visiting gentleman did not.

"Come and meet Bertie," Lucinda said. She stood and gave Jackie a hug and a kiss.

"Did you have a pleasant crossing?" Jackie said.

"Pleasant enough," Lucinda said, "although we had some nasty weather and had to put in at Bermuda for a couple of days. Bertie, this is my daughter, Jacqueline."

Bertie nodded and finally stood. He had curiously hooded eyes, as if he were perpetually tired–or perhaps bored–and a pointed, Mephistophelian beard. He leaned on his cane with one hand and extended the other in Jackie's direction.

"Charmed," Bertie said. He kissed her hand and glanced at Lucinda. "Your description hardly does justice to your lovely daughter. A young lady of surpassing beauty!"

Jackie blushed slightly and smiled.

"His Highness will be staying with us for a week," Edwina said proudly.

"His Highness?" Jackie said.

"His Highness, the Prince of Wales," Edwina announced, almost a if she were a herald.

Jackie looked at Bertie, who simply smiled and continued leaning on his cane with both hands. "Oh, pardon me, Your Highness. I didn't know–"

"Just call me Bertie. Lucinda and I are traveling rather incognito, you know."

"Oh, yes," Jackie said, unsure of whether she should curtsey or not. Finally she decided she should, but her curtsey was only a slight dip.

Bertie laughed. "No need for that, my dear. I shan't want our American friends to start alerting the press, you know. That would give the whole game up."

"No, of course not." Jackie, nevertheless, made another involuntary dip. Everyone laughed.

"Jackie, dear," Lucinda said, "perhaps you would like to change out of your riding clothes and join us for a tour of the gardens. Edwina has done such a fabulous job of expanding them and planting new varieties that we–"

"Yes," Bertie said. "I'm quite keen on gardens. Your American ones aren't quite up to our English gardens, of course, but I'd like to see how far you colonists have come along in that regard."

"Bertie," Lucinda said. "We're no longer colonists, you know."

"No, that's true," Bertie said. "And the poorer for it in my opinion. If my great-grandfather hadn't made such a mess of things–"

"Bertie," Lucinda said with a twinkle in her eye. "Incognito, remember?"

"I don't see any newspaper men around, do you?" Bertie said irritably. "If we can't talk about family, what can we talk about?"

"Horticulture and hunting," Lucinda said, not about to be silenced, even by the Prince of Wales.

Bertie smiled. "Right you are, Lucinda. Family talk does get to be a bore, doesn't it? I'd like to see the gun room you were talking about, Mansfield, old boy. I'm keen on seeing your Winchesters, especially."

"We've got some interesting weapons, Your Highness," Mansfield said. "Including a couple of crossbows."

"Crossbows? Oh, they don't interest me at all–we've got dozens of them at the old pile at Windsor. Primitive things, and they can break a man's arm. Why, I remember–"

"Bertie," Lucinda said, "Why don't you save all that for this afternoon? We need to explore the gardens first."

Bertie looked at Lucinda, then at Edwina. "Quite right, Lucinda. Well, I've had enough tea to sink a frigate. Let's get started, shall we?"

Jackie joined the group after changing into her sun dress and found the prince chatting amiably with Calvin, the gardener. He seemed very interested in the methods employed, especially the use of phosphate fertilizer.

"Where do you get this phosphate, Calvin?"

"Right up yonder, Mr. Prince," Calvin said, pointing up river. "My nephew, Jessie, and some of his pals own the mill."

"Do they now?" Bertie said. "And how did they acquire such an enterprise?"

"Oh, they done bought it from Major Jones years ago, after the war."

Bertie looked quizzically at Jackie. "Jones? Isn't that the name of your fiancé?"

"It is," Jackie said.

"Major Jones," Lucinda said, "was Tony's father."

"And he done a heap of good for us black folks," Calvin said. "Helped us buy property and protected us from the Klan."

"The Klan?" Bertie said.

"A white supremacist group," Lucinda said. "Mostly defunct now, but still operating in some parts of the state."

"And what do these Klan fellows do?" Bertie said.

"Set crosses afire," Calvin said. "And ride around at night wid sheets on they heads tryin' to skeer black folks."

"How extraordinary," Bertie said. "Why don't the authorities put a stop to it?"

"'Cause they *is* the authorities," Calvin said.

"Oh, let's not talk about those imbeciles," Edwina said. "Calvin, why don't we show His Highness our African violets in the hot house? They've come out beautifully just in the past week."

All proceeded to the hot house.

After the garden tour, the assembled company retired to the *Pride* for luncheon. As Uli and Sherman scurried about catering to their needs, the prince seemed to take a particular interest in the painting over the mantelpiece in the main salon.

"I say," Bertie said. "That's an unusual picture. Reminds me somewhat of that Frenchman–what's his name, Lucinda?

"I'm not sure of whom you're speaking, Bertie, dear."

"You know–the one who had an exhibit in the Paris recently."

"Oh," Lucinda said. "The Impressionist–Cezanne."

"That's the fellow! All these angles and squares and globs of paint as if he spilled it onto the canvas and decided that it was so charming that there was no need to clean it up. Shocking what these artists get away with these days." The prince looked at Jacqueline, then the painting, then at her again. "I say, is that you, my dear?"

"It is indeed," Jackie said proudly. "You're very perceptive, Your Highness."

The prince looked at the painting again. "I am, aren't I? Though I'm not so sure that a painting should present a riddle to the viewer. I'd rather be struck by the beauty of the sitter first, then concern myself with the technical skills of the artist."

"Who *is* the artist, Jackie?" Lucinda said.

Jackie hesitated for a moment. Then she decided to plunge ahead. "The artist is none other than Mr. Jones."

They all turned to look at the painting again.

"Mr. Jones?" Edwina said. "Jacqueline–do you mean to say that the artist who painted this at the behest of Ravenel was your Tony?"

"Yes. Tony visited me on the *Pride* in Savannah and disguised himself as a French sailor with an artistic bent. Ravenel bought it for me."

"Who is this Ravenel fellow?" Bertie said.

"Our next governor," Mansfield said, a little uneasily.

"Governor, eh? Well, I must say your governor has good taste, even if it is a bit unconventional."

"He depises the painting," Jackie said, almost gleefully.

"What? Well, so much the worse for him." Bertie looked down at his plate, which Sherman had just put before him. "I say–what is this? It looks like turbot."

"Flounder," Edwina said. "Your Grace will find it very similar to turbot–a bit sweeter, perhaps."

"I don't like the way it looks at me," Bertie said. He stuffed a napkin into his collar. "Eyes like a frog's."

They all laughed as Sherman and Uli circulated, filling their glasses with champagne.

CHAPTER 56

Tony had never owned a top hat in his life, much less a swallow-tailed morning suit. But now that his stepfather was a haberdasher, he owned both. He held the hat carefully in his lap as the brougham bumped over the dusty road to the Coosaw ferry. His mother sat to his right and Hiram to her right.

"I heard a rumor yesterday at the Emporium," Georgia said.

"Oh?" Tony said absently, gazing out the window, watching a flock of geese glide effortlessly over the water. "What rumor was that?"

"Lucinda has brought a new beau with her from England."

"Lucinda seems to always have a new beau."

"This one, though, is different. He's rumored to be the Prince of Wales."

Tony's attention finally engaged, he turned to his mother. "The Prince of Wales? Isn't he married?"

"I think so. But he's a notorious womanizer."

"And Lucinda's the womanizee."

"It appears so. But think of it–the Prince of Wales will be attending your wedding."

"What makes you think he'll come?"

"He may not. But then Lucinda will be there, so why shouldn't he?"

Tony turned to the window again. "I'm beginning to wonder if even *I* should be there."

Georgia patted him on the knee. "Just the usual butterflies. You'll be fine once the ceremony begins."

"My knees knocked uncontrollably at both of my weddings," Hiram said. "The second one less so."

Georgia laughed. "Let's hope there won't be a third."

The crossing of the Coosaw was uneventful, and the road to Sheldon likewise. The Old Sheldon ruins were just across the road from the New

Church, where most of the guests parked their carriages.

"There's the LeRoux's landau," Georgia said. "And Mr. Small's gig. I don't see–"

"His Majesty's carriage is right over there," Hiram said. "Beneath the oak tree."

"How do you know?" Georgia said.

"His crest is draped over the door. "'HRH.'"

Georgia peered out the window. "Oh. And that stands for–?"

"His Royal Highness. Curious that he would advertise it, considering his wish to be discreet."

"I hear that his vanity often trumps his discretion," Georgia said.

Hiram chuckled. "We'll see."

Most of the guests were milling about the New Church, waiting for the Reverend Hall to emerge and give them the signal to proceed to the ruins. They were a very diverse group, both black and white, prominent citizens like Mr. Smalls, and servants to the LeRoux and Mr. Cooper. There was polite, muffled applause–due to an abundance of white gloves–as Tony donned his top hat and entered the new church. Jackie was nowhere to be seen.

After a minute or two, Tony emerged with the Reverend Hall at his side and the guests began to fall into line as they proceeded across the road to the old ruins.

For the first time in more than twenty years, Edwina approached Georgia and extended her hand. "How are you, my dear Georgia?"

Georgia, somewhat taken aback at this cordial reception, nevertheless extended her hand as well. "Quite well, Edwina. Where is your niece?"

"Hidden away, dear," Edwina said. "As she should be. She'll appear at the proper time. May I introduce you to Lucinda's very special guest?"

Lucinda stood a few feet away, talking to Mansfield and the prince.

Edwina didn't let go of Georgia's hand, but nearly dragged her over to the small group. "Your Majesty? May I introduce the groom's mother? Georgia, ah, Jones, isn't it?"

"It's now Cooper," Georgia said.

"Oh, yes, of course. Well, then–"

"Let's stick to first names, Edwina," Lucinda said. "Bertie wishes to be discreet, remember?"

The prince gave a slight bow and extended his gloved hand. "Charmed." He kissed Georgia's hand. "Lucinda, you continue to astonish me with all of the beautiful ladies of your acquaintance in these parts. And here I thought America was full of rustics."

The company all laughed.

"We have our share, Bertie," Lucinda said.

Edwina proceeded to make the rest of the introductions and they continued to the old church.

Pews from the new church were set up in the nave and a makeshift altar was erected in the chancel. There was no roof, so the sun shone directly in, though clouds were gathering to the east.

Tama sat at an organ against one of the brick walls.

"What if it rains?" Tony said to the Reverend Hall.

The Reverend nodded to a shadowy structure beneath the trees. "We have a tent. And extra umbrellas for those that don't have them."

It was from this tent that Jackie would appear at the appropriate time.

The guests filed into the church and, guided by ushers, took their seats.

As Tony had been Hiram's best man at his mother's wedding, Hiram was to be Tony's best man. And though the Reverend Hall was Jackie's biological father, as the priest conducting the ceremony he deferred to Mansfield, who, after all, had been Jackie's de facto father for most of her life.

After the Reverend recited a few passages from scripture and delivered a homily pointing out the grave responsibilities of marriage, Tama began to play the classical march announcing the entrance of the bride.

The sound of the organ, however, was nearly drowned out by first, a clap of thunder, and second, the sound of horses' hooves slamming into the earth.

Jackie, resplendent in her white dress with its long train carried by two children (one white and one of indeterminate race), was knocked down by the passing horsemen. These horsemen wore sheets and hoods nearly as white as her own dress.

The first horseman thundered into the church through the wide entry of the nave, while others poured through the tall archways that had once contained stained glass renderings of the Last Supper.

Before Tony could react, he was scooped up by the first horseman and dragged outside. The others, carrying rifles, fired into the air.

"Ain't no nigger gonna marry no white woman!" one of the horsemen yelled, his bay horse prancing on its hind legs, his rifle pointing towards the sky. And in no more time than it took to abduct Tony, the horsemen were gone.

Mr. Smalls, always armed with a pistol and anticipating such an attack, ran through one of the portals and fired several shots at the intruders, but it was too late.

"I say!" the prince exclaimed, standing from his pew. "This is rather like the Old West I've heard so much about. Is it part of the show?"

"No, no, it's not!" Lucinda said. "We've got to do something! They'll kill him!"

"Damned fools," Mansfield said.

"Jacqueline!" Edwina screamed, and ran out through the archway towards the tent, where Jackie had just picked herself up and was brushing away the dirt that had soiled her dress. The two little girls who were holding her train stood stock still in amazement.

Jackie, apparently unhurt, pushed Edwina aside. "Tony! They've got Tony!" She ran into the church and saw the Reverend Hall standing with his Bible, his surplice askew, looking dumbfounded. "You've got to go after them!"

The Reverend looked at her for a moment nonplused, then threw his Bible down on the altar and began stripping off his vestments. "All right! We'll go after them–but where the devil are they headed?"

"I heard one of them say something about Yemassee," Mr. Smalls said. He had just re-entered the church and put his pistol into his belt. "We need a posse! Who'll volunteer?"

Several men raised their hands, some shouting "I will!" and "Let's get after the scoundrels!"

"Oh, jolly good!" exclaimed the prince. "I say–this is exciting."

"Don't Bertie!" Lucinda tugged on his arm. "You'll only get hurt."

"Nonsense!" The prince pulled his arm away. "I've got a pistol in the carriage and I'm a crack shot. We'll show these blighters they can't get away with this sort of hooliganism."

Mr. Smalls ran across the road to his carriage and released the horse from its traces. Then he mounted and urged the others to follow. He galloped off in the direction of Yemassee.

The prince urged several men to leap into his rented Victoria, and Mansfield recruited two or three others to join him in his lighter, faster landau.

In moments they were all off on the Sheldon Road, disappearing into clouds of dust under a darkening sky and the crackling sound of thunder.

CHAPTER 57

Tony grabbed at his collar, which was choking him. His legs dangled beneath the horse's belly and he felt that if the collar gave way, he could be trampled. Suddenly, the Klansman reined in the horse, kicking up dirt and rocks, and they came to a halt. Another horseman pulled up behind them.

"Better hogtie him," the second horseman said. "You cain't carry him all the way to Yemassee like that."

"What do you think I'm stoppin' for, turnip brain? Gimme some of that rope."

Tony's feet hit the ground and he tried to run, but the collar held and the Klansman's grip was like a vise.

"You tie his legs. I'll do the arms. Then we'll throw him across ol' Sadie's rump like a sack of flour."

Three other Klansmen pulled up behind them as they were tying Tony.

"We ain't got time for no fancy knots!" one of them said. "They's a nigger right behind us, with a pop gun."

"Then you just shoot him when he gets in range. We don't want this one to get loose and run off into the woods."

"Hurry up, then."

"Who's runnin' this show, dog breath? You, or–"

But a pistol shot interrupted him. They turned and saw a black man on a horse racing toward them.

The others returned fire with their rifles and then ducked behind a tree. Their pursuer pulled up and did likewise.

"Don't get in no gun battle," the lead horseman said. "It'll give the others time to catch up. Hold him off for a minute or two and then light out after us."

Two of the others fired off more shots as the third helped sling Tony over the back of Sadie. And again they were off.

It was a bumpy ride for Tony. He couldn't roll off the back of the horse because one of the ropes was tied to the cinch strap of the saddle. He wondered why they were taking him to Yemassee. Were they going to tar and feather him and put him on a train? Or would they tie him to the tracks to be cut in two? Maybe they would lynch him, but why did they need to go all the way to Yemassee for that?

While Tony was contemplating his fate, the Klansmen who had taken cover abandoned their position behind the trees, and were now racing to catch up.

He saw two black boys, eight or nine, picking cotton in a field nearby, looking up to see what the commotion was about. Would they be subjected to this same terror twenty years from now?

"Stay still, nigger!" his abductor said, spurring Sadie on. "It's hard enough ridin' flat out in these robes without you squirmin' around back there."

Tony wondered at this fellow who seemed to be the leader. What if he could somehow get loose of the ropes and grab his rifle, which was sticking out of its scabbard? It would have to be before they got to Yemassee. A long shot, but what else could he do? He began picking at the knot that secured his hands behind him.

He heard a train whistle in the distance. They must be getting close to Yemassee. He fumbled at the knot, but it was as tight as if it were welded iron. He wished he hadn't trimmed his nails before the wedding.

They were still far out ahead of the others, though Tony could see that the first three were now joined by nearly a dozen more. There must have been about ten or twelve in all, kicking up clouds of white dust that contrasted with the darkening sky.

Then the inexplicable happened. A bolt of lightening struck a tree some twenty yards ahead of them with a deafening crack and one half of the tree fell across the road. Sadie came to a screeching halt, reared her hind legs, and Tony, his abductor, and the saddle all came loose and crashed to the ground in a tangle of ropes, sheets, cinches and leather. Another crack of thunder and Sadie ran off into the woods.

Tony, always limber, slipped his bound hands under his buttocks and over his ankles. His tormentor was still trying to free himself from the sheet twisted around his head and neck. Tony saw the stock of the rifle sticking out from beneath the saddle and grabbed it with both hands. It was of the repeater type, with a lever action. He worked the lever and ejected a spent cartridge. It was ready to fire.

He aimed the rifle over the heads of the approaching Klansmen and fired. Suddenly, they stopped, hesitated, and turned their horses into the trees. He heard his abductor cursing, turned the barrel of the rifle in his direction, and worked the lever again. An empty cartridge flew aside.

"Put the gun down, boy."

"Sit," Tony said.

"What?"

"I said, sit. And put your hands on top of your head."

The Klansman, now bereft of his hood, stood still for a moment, his eyes searching the woods.

"Your friends aren't going to help you now," Tony said. "They're trapped between me an *my* friends."

The Klansman spat. "No, they ain't. They's only one of you and–"

A fusillade was heard behind them. The Klansman ducked down, crouching, expecting Tony to turn towards the shots, but he didn't.

"I said sit," Tony said.

The man complied.

A snapping of branches and crashing of horses into brush was heard, followed by more shots and shouts of familiar voices.

"Run, you rascals!"

"By Jove–I bagged one of the blighters!"

"Tony!" It was the voice of Mr. Smalls. "Are you all right? Don't let the scoundrel get away!"

Mr. Smalls approached on his horse, his pistol pointed in the air, the barrel still smoking. "Ah! Our old friend, Mr. Jenkins. Who sent you, Jenkins–Senator Tillman?"

"Ain't seen you since Hamburg in '66, Smalls," Rufus Jenkins said. He spat again. "They done kicked you out of the legislature, I hear."

Mr. Smalls laughed. "That they did, Jenkins. You won that one–but we won this one."

The prince rode up in his Victoria, which seemed not to be so slow after all, and his driver pulled on the reins. "I say–is this the blighter that snatched you from the church, Tony, old boy? Looks rather harmless to me."

"Hold your pistol on him, Mr. Windsor," Smalls said, "while I cut that rope around Tony's wrists and ankles."

"Where are the others?" Tony said.

Mr. Smalls pulled out a pen knife and cut the ropes. "Mr. Jenkins' friends? One's got a bullet in his shoulder, thanks to Mr. Windsor here, and the rest have skedaddled. It's a long way back to Jasper County, isn't it, Jenkins? Specially through the swamps."

"We was just havin' some fun," Jenkins said, as Smalls transferred a length of rope to Jenkins' wrist and began tying them together. "Like a bachelors' party, you know. Just a prank." He grinned.

"Well, you and your pal there will have a bachelor's party of your own–in the Beaufort County jail."

Another crack of thunder was heard, followed by a pouring rain.

Mr. Smalls led Jenkins to the prince's Victoria, where his driver put up the hood. The wounded Klansman, Earl, was trundled into Mansfield's landau. Tony joined the prince, sitting in the back and keeping the rifle trained on Jenkins. He and the prince stayed relatively dry, while Jenkins and the driver, sitting up front, were fairly soaked by the time they returned to Sheldon.

The sheriff and his men were waiting for them and took the two Klansmen into custody.

EPILOGUE

On the first of May, a bright and sunny day with cumulous clouds billowing to the east, Tony sat on a deck chair of the *HMY Osborne*, the prince's yacht, as it cleared Tybee Island. He was reading an article in the *Savannah Morning News.*

SC Klansman Released From Beaufort Jail

> Beaufort–*Rufus Jenkins, the reputed 'Grand Giant,' or ruler, of the Jasper County chapter of the Ku Klux Klan, was released from the Beaufort County jail Thursday for time served and paying a fifty dollar fine for disturbing the peace and misdemeanor assault. He was originally charged with kidnapping and attempted murder for which he could have received thirty years imprisonment, but an all-white jury decided...*

"What are you reading?"

Tony looked up to see Jackie standing over him, wearing a navy blue and white striped dress with mutton sleeves, and carrying an open parasol over her shoulder. "The *Morning News.* Take a look if you don't mind being a little sick to your stomach."

She took the paper and sat down in a chair next to his. "I'm not prone to sea sickness, you know." She read the first paragraph of the article, expelled a puff of air with disgust, and handed the paper back to him. "How could they? He and his friends will simply go out and try to murder someone else and they'll probably be successful this time."

Tony opened the paper again and began scanning the other articles. "Oh, I don't know–Mr. Smalls says that Jenkins is one of the last Klansmen in the state and that his 'dens,' as they call the local chapters, are disorganized and losing members. And you have to admit that their attempt to abduct me was rather amateurish."

"Tony! They came that close to killing you." She put her thumb and forefinger a fraction of an inch apart to emphasize her point. "Others may not be so lucky."

"Who's lucky?"

They looked up to see Lucinda, wearing a similar dress to Jackie's, only with red and yellow stripes. Her parasol matched her outfit.

"Jenkins," Tony said. "They let him go."

"What? Let me see." She took the paper from Tony and skimmed over the article. "Well, it's not surprising–they've succeeded in keeping Negroes off the voting rolls, and now the juries. Even Beaufort is no longer safe."

"Well," Tony said, taking the paper, "it still is for some people. Mama and Hiram will be safe–and Mr. Smalls, too, because of his reputation around the state. But the others–Oh, look at this."

"What?" Jackie said, looking over his shoulder.

"Your former fiancé, Mr. Coleman, is engaged again to be married."

"Let me see." Jackie took the paper from him and read aloud:

South Carolina Gubernatorial Candidate Announces
His Marriage to Miss Priscilla Pinckney

Ravenel Coleman, a Democrat running for Governor of South Carolina, announced his marriage to a belle from one of the most influential families in South Carolina. Miss Pinckney, a daughter of Mr. and Mrs. Boifeuillet Pinckney (known as 'Bo' to his friends) is a graduate of Miss Gaillard's lycée of Charleston and has worked for Mr. Coleman's campaign since January. She was also runner-up in last year's Miss Charleston beauty contest, finishing just shy of the top honor by one vote...

She put the paper down in her lap and stared out at Tybee Island as it receded in the wake of the *Osborne*.

Tony looked at her. "Regrets?"

She turned to him and smiled. "None." And gave him a kiss.

"I say!" It was the prince, who had just returned from the wheelhouse, where he liked to captain the vessel until it was out to sea. "More nuptial celebrations? Why not? Ian–a couple of bottles of champagne, if you please. Nothing like it to start our journey across the Great Pond."

Tony, though at heart a Republican in every sense, felt it only proper to stand whenever the prince entered a room–or deck–where he was sitting. "Your Highness is most gracious, as usual. And Jackie and I can't thank you enough for inviting us to accompany you and Lucinda back to Europe."

"Tut, tut, my boy! Think nothing of it. You have the courage of a lion to turn the tables, as you Americans say, on that bounder in the white sheet. What a silly costume! I daresay I could hardly understand a word the fellow said while we were driving back to the church. Is that a native dialect? Reminds me of some of the denizens of the Isle of Wight. Bloody incomprehensible."

They all laughed as Ian, the yacht's steward, returned, along with two waiters and buckets of champagne. Once the party was settled again, and the champagne poured, the prince offered a toast:

"To the success and happiness of the newlyweds!"

"Hear, hear!" Lucinda said, who initiated the clinking of glasses. "And to the success of Tony's artistic career in Paris!"

Another clinking and tipping of glasses.

"Ah!" the prince said. "That's the bloody point of the voyage, isn't it? I'd almost forgotten. That painting of Jacqueline on the LeRoux' little runabout is a harbinger of bigger and better things, what? It's a shame Lucinda and I can't accompany you all the way to Paris, but I can't keep Mummy waiting, you know. She's very demanding and wants me to take on more of the ribbon cutting ceremonies. A bloody bore, but the old girl hasn't the energy she used to, and I'm the next in line, you see. However, I'll certainly provide you with references, which may be useful to you."

Tony thanked the prince for his thoughtfulness, and the waiters poured more champagne.

Jackie, though she found the prince's remarks amusing and charming, was not inclined to join in the festivities. She was suddenly pensive, even apprehensive.

What would she do in Paris? Tony seemed not to be the possessive type, but now that they were married...Lucinda had said that marriage makes men feel they are entitled to treat their wives like property...well...perhaps she could divide her time between London and Paris...no, Tony would never agree to that.

Suddenly she had the urge to leap into the water and swim to shore–escape. Escape to what? She loved Tony and she was convinced that he loved her.

She looked at him, staring into the distance as the shore receded...he was smiling, sipping his champagne...he seemed supremely happy–but was it because they were now married, or that he had once again escaped the South and all of its bigotry and violence?

"Tony..." she said.

"Hmm?"

"What would you say if I went to stay with Lucinda for a while? I mean after we're settled in Paris."

Tony looked askance at her. "A period of adjustment?"

"No, no! I don't mean that. I want to be with you...but I'm afraid I'd be terribly bored in Paris."

Tony laughed. "Bored? In Paris? Impossible!"

"I don't mean with you, dear. Or with the city itself."

Tony now turned to her and put his glass down on the table between them. "You want to pursue your acting career."

"Well...not exactly 'pursue'...just for some...well, artistic stimulation. Surely you can understand that."

Tony picked up his glass again and stared out at the coastline, which was rapidly receding. "I thought we had discussed this."

"Well, we did. But we never decided on a...a solution."

"The solution is...that you may do whatever you wish. I won't stand in the way of your career."

"And if it separates us for months at a time?"

"I can move to London."

She brightened. "You would do that for me?"

"Of course. Besides, there's a lively art scene in London. Mr. Whistler and Mr. Sargent divide their time between the two cities–why can't I?"

She smiled and grasped his hand. He returned her smile and they both gazed out over the swelling waves as their silvery tips eclipsed the treetops of the mainland, which was sinking farther and farther away. And finally there was nothing but water in every direction.

www.ingramcontent.com/pod-product-compliance
Lightning Source LLC
Chambersburg PA
CBHW030626110726
47901CB00002B/340
9780966614541